The King
of Ragtime

Books by Larry Karp

First, Do No Harm

The Music Box Mysteries
The Music Box Murders
Scamming the Birdman
The Midnight Special

The Ragtime Mysteries
The Ragtime Kid
The King of Ragtime
The Ragtime Fool

The King of Ragtime

Larry Karp

Poisoned Pen Press

Poisoned
Pen
Press

Copyright © 2008 by Larry Karp

First Trade Paperback Edition 2010

10 9 8 7 6 5 4 3 2 1

Library of Congress Catalog Card Number: 2008923142

ISBN: 978-1-59058-701-0 Trade Paperback

Poisoned Pen Press
6962 E. First Ave., Ste. 103
Scottsdale, AZ 85251
www.poisonedpenpress.com
info@poisonedpenpress.com

Printed in the United States of America

This one's for

PATRICIA LAMB CONN

Who has enchanted ragtimers
for a half-century
by bringing their legends to life

Gee, Kid, But I Like You.
I'll follow you to Coney any time.

Uneasy lies the head that wears a crown
—King Henry IV, Shakespeare

I want to thank Edward A. Berlin for permitting me to quote from his excellent biography, *King of Ragtime: Scott Joplin and His Era*, Oxford University Press, New York, 1994, pp. 211-212.

Acknowledgments

Many kind people helped me construct the historical framework for *The King of Ragtime*; without their contributions, I doubt I could have written the book. I take full credit, however, for any errors.

Genealogists Mark Forster, Pat Lowery, and Gerry Lowery guided me through the Internet's maze of family histories, census records, and vital statistics, such that I was able to flesh out many of the real-life characters. G. Miki Hayden not only took me on a private walking tour of Harlem, she also tracked down ancient photographs that helped me visualize New York in 1916. Betty Singer made it possible for me to imagine summertime St. Louis, and sent information regarding train travel between St. Louis and New York. Dan (of Spokane) Brown was always available to consult on dress, customs, personalities, music, and behavior of the time. Dale Lorang told me what I needed to know about Catholic theology. Gwillim Law, Frank Ruffino, Mark J. Cuccia, and Robert Crowe answered questions about telephones and their use in 1916. Serita Stevens sent information regarding the state of handgun-related forensics in 1916. Reference staffs at the New York City Library, City Hall Library, and the New York Historical Society dug up important regulations and laws of early-twentieth-century New York.

Patricia Lamb Conn talked to me at length about her father, Joe Lamb, and responded promptly and pleasantly to endless written questions and requests for photographs. Anyone interested in ragtime history will enjoy David Sager's interview of Pat at the Smithsonian; the URL is listed in the bibliography.

A big hug for my love, Myra, finder of typos, mender of loose threads, tolerant hostess to the people I pluck from history or thin air, and bring to live with us for extended periods.

I'm deeply grateful to the many gifted ragtime performers, composers, and historians who patiently answered my many questions, and went out of their way to make me feel welcome in their world. Particular thanks to Ed Berlin, Nan Bostick, Rich Egan, Sue Keller, John Petley, David Reffkin, Jack Rummel, and Washboard Kitty Wilson (who loves mystery novels almost as much as she loves ragtime).

Chapter One

Manhattan, New York City
Monday, August 21, 1916
Mid-day

The short, dark-skinned man standing in front of the Strand
Theatre Building shaded his eyes with a hand, and looked up
past the marquee to the gold letters on the third-story windows.
WATERSON, BERLIN, AND SNYDER, MUSIC PUBLISHERS. That
wife of his, she wouldn't let him out of the apartment till she
wrote out the address for him. He told her he was almost ten
years in New York now, he didn't need any numbers on a piece
of paper to find his way to Broadway and Forty-seventh Street,
but she wrote it down anyway, and pushed it into his pocket.
Women are like that. If they don't have a real baby, they find a
man to treat like one.

Heat rose from the pavement, made the building and the
people look wavy. Made *everything* look wavy. Damn, he didn't
like that. He was nervous enough, just coming down here with
his music, which of course he never would be doing if Martin
hadn't convinced him he should. Question was, could he really
trust Martin? Could he trust *anyone* anymore, after all he'd
been lied to, ignored, pushed aside, even by people every bit as
black as himself, those fancy Negroes with their three names.
Will Marion Cook. J. Rosamund Johnson. James Reese Europe.
None of them would give him the time of day any more. Lester

Walton once had been partial to him, wrote a bunch of nice words in the newspaper about his music, but not since Cook, Johnson and Europe got hold of Walton's ear. Scott Joplin was low-class, him and his ragtime music. Low-class and old hat. An embarrassment to the race.

He pulled a well-used handkerchief from his pocket, mopped water from his forehead, glanced at the sheaf of papers in his left hand. *Was* there anybody he could trust? Well, sure, his wife. Lottie was always square at his side. And Nell—of course. Never mind her father, he could trust Nell with his life. He sighed. And yeah, he really did think Martin was okay. Nice kid, wanted to play piano just like Scott Joplin, came up every week for his lesson. He kept the books at Irving Berlin's, and he got himself some inside information. Berlin was doing musical shows now, not just writing popular songs. "Let him see your music," Martin had said. "What can you lose? I'll go along with you, and I'll make good and goddamn sure he doesn't steal anything off you again."

Joplin had his doubts, but decided to give it a try. With no contacts of his own any more, little money, and less time, he really didn't have all that much to lose, did he? But he was not about to take Martin along with him, no need to do that. Scott Joplin was the King of Ragtime. Go walking into Irving Berlin's office with a baby-sitter? Uh-uh.

Besides, his head had felt pretty good earlier this morning. It wasn't till he got outside and started off downtown that he commenced getting nervous and shaky in his mind. All this heat and humidity, all that noise, gasoline motorcars with their backfires, all the people, pushing, yelling, waving their arms. He tried to will calm, blew out a deep breath, then moved, a little unsteadily, toward the door.

A white couple, old people, passed by; he heard the woman say, "Just look at that—drunk on the street, and in broad daylight." Joplin tried not to react, but in his anger, he caught his foot on the step, stumbled, finally managed to hold his balance. Damn! Lottie had fixed him up right to go downtown, shaved him close, got him into his best dark suit and tie, but as far as that old woman was concerned, Scott Joplin was just another drunk nigger. But what was he supposed to tell her? No, he wasn't drunk, just that his brain didn't work right anymore because he once upon a time lay down in bed with the wrong woman?

He turned to go back home, but pulled himself up short. No, that wouldn't serve. He had to leave Lottie some money. *Had* to. And besides. A man sees he's got no future, he wants to leave something of himself in the world, and what did Scott Joplin have to leave? No children. No paintings, no books, no buildings. Nature had filled his head so full of music there never was a moment's time for anything else, his blessing, his curse. If all his music disappeared along with him, better his mother would have gone to the old woman down the road and gotten something to put up inside her, so next day she'd have passed a mess of blood, and Scott Joplin never would've seen light of day.

He wheeled about, then walked carefully up the steps to the door, pulled it open and went inside, past the elevator, up the staircase. The third floor hallway was stifling. He felt dizzy, afraid he might pass out. Guiding himself with his free hand against the wall, he made his way down the corridor and into the Waterson, Berlin, and Snyder Reception Room.

Nobody there. He looked right, left, right again. A receptionist's desk sat between the take-off points of two hallways; two other passages ran back from the opposite wall. Joplin felt like he was standing at the hub of a wagon wheel. The wheel started to spin, sending the composer staggering toward one of the cheap wooden chairs against the wall opposite the receptionist's desk, He dropped his manuscript to the floor, fell into the chair, lowered his head into his hands.

The wheel slowed, stopped. Joplin raised his head by degrees. Still no one in the room, nobody waiting to show a tune to a buyer, or hoping to bag a tune for a vaudeville act. No receptionist at the desk. The composer picked up his music, stepped cautiously across the room, peered down the corridor to the right of the desk. No luck. He walked a few steps past the desk to check the second corridor. Again, no one in sight...but then he heard a loud, phlegmy cough. He gripped his papers, started walking.

The door to the fourth office on his left sat open. Joplin saw a man sitting at a desk, his back to the door. The composer paused. This nervousness was going to be the death of him. Even when he sat alone at his piano these days, trying to put a tune together, he felt ants crawling up his legs, butterflies sailing around inside his stomach. "I'm Scott Joplin," he muttered. "The King of Ragtime. I don't need to give any apology—least of all not to *him*." He stepped into the room, cleared his throat.

The white man at the desk swiveled to face him. Joplin recognized him instantly. "Good day, Mr. Berlin," the colored man said.

The white man smiled. "Why, Scott Joplin—how are you? I haven't seen you since forever."

Not since 1911, Joplin thought. Not since "Alexander's Ragtime Band." He worked to keep his attention on his business. "Well, I guess that's so. I know I haven't been by since you moved up to here from Thirty-eighth Street—when was that again?"

"1914, two years ago. What brings you down?"

The stale smell of old cigar smoke burned Joplin's eyes. He held out his offering. The pile of papers shook; he was afraid he might drop the whole stack onto the floor. "I've got some music I want to talk to you about."

The white man stood, pushed a hardbacked wooden chair toward his visitor. "Sit down, Scott, huh? Take a load off, catch your breath. You say you want me look at your music?"

Joplin nodded. Lottie had warned him. "Take it slow, Scott, nice and easy. You get to talkin' fast, your tongue gets all tied up in knots, and even I can't follow you. An' if *I* can't, Mr. Berlin sure won't."

"Sorry, Mr. Berlin." Joplin could hear the difference, much better now. Slow and easy. He lowered himself into the seat. "I said I want to talk to you about some new music I've got. Theater music."

He saw the publisher's eyes go glittery as they lit on the pile of paper. Like a buzzard spotting a chunk of meat in the gutter. The colored man's hand moved to cover his manuscript, but he told himself, don't go getting mad now. What's done is done. And Martin'll be right in the office, he can keep watch. He won't let Berlin swipe it.

The publisher extended a white, well-manicured hand. "You gonna let me see it, Scott? Or you just want to keep me guessing?"

Joplin laid his music, slow-motion, on the desk. The white man craned his neck to read; his eyebrows went up. "*If*, huh? A musical drama in two acts."

"That's right."

"Looks pretty long."

"Not too long. Not any longer than *Treemonisha*." The colored man jabbed a finger toward the manuscript. Shaking even worse now. Thinking about *Treemonisha* right there in front of Irving Berlin couldn't help but make him nervous. He fought to go on talking. "Why don't you look at it, Mr. Berlin? See what you think."

Instead, the white man leaned back in his chair and took a moment to study his visitor. "Who did the book?"

"I did. Just like for *Treemonisha*. I do my own work, all of it. Only Scott Joplin can put the right words to Scott Joplin's music."

"Okay. But listen, I got to ask you. How is it you're bringing it here? To me?"

Anger hit the colored man like a wild animal released from a cage to pounce on his chest. For what felt like an hour, he couldn't get out a word. Lottie spoke to him in his mind, gentle but firm. "Scott, now don't you forget, you ain't goin' down to pick no fight with Mr. Berlin. What you want is to get him to take on your music."

The composer struggled to slow his breathing, finally managed to set a firm gaze into the white man's eyes. "You know, after you published 'Alexander,' I swore I'd never have anything

else to do with you. But I'm sick, Mr. Berlin, which you probably know already. I wrote this musical, and I'm working on
my *Symphony Number One*, and before I go, I want to see them
both on their way. My piano pupil, Martin, he works in your
office, he said I ought to let you take a look at it."

The white man scratched at his head. "That's Martin
Niederhoffer? Our bookkeeper?"

"The same. I can never remember that last name, but he's
the one. Why don't you call him in here? Ask him if I'm not
telling you the truth."

The white man's face split into a huge smile; he waved the
idea away. "No need for that, Scott. I believe you. Anyway, it's
half-past twelve. Martin's out to lunch right now."

"He said he was going to keep a good eye on my music for
me. That boy is a fine piano student, Mr. Berlin. And he knows
every note of *If.*"

A lie, and it threw Joplin off track. For the better part of a
year now, he'd kept all his music locked in his piano room, and
when he went in to compose, he even locked the door behind
him. No one was ever going to steal another piece of music from
Scott Joplin, then use it to make his own career. "Alexander's
Ragtime Band!" Those three words never failed to set his mind
into a whirl. He jumped from his chair, arms waving. "Six years
it's been now, I left my opera with you, *Treemonisha*, and you
gave it back, told me you couldn't use it. But you kept a part of
the "Real Slow Drag" tune, and it earned you a fortune. I tell
you, Mr. Berlin, that's not going to happen again. Not ever."

The white man pushed back in his chair to keep clear of the
flailing arms.

"You steal one note out of *If*, just one single note, and I'll
take you to court, you hear?" The furious colored man pounded
a fist on his manuscript, once, twice; a letter opener jumped
off the desk and clattered to the floor. "My play is going to be
a landmark in musical theater—it'll make anything by Cole or
Johnson or Cook seem tawdry and cheap. I want to see it on
stage before…"

He was out of breath, been talking so fast, all out of control. He wondered vaguely whether the white man had understood what he was saying. "Slow down," he heard Lottie croon. "Slow and easy, now, Scott." But words kept pouring out of his mouth, loud, insistent, rude. "Mr. Berlin, I'm telling you, you steal *any* of this, and we won't *need* a court hearing…because I swear I will kill you."

The white man raised a hand. Joplin ducked away, but as he straightened back up, his head whacked against the edge of the open door. He staggered, then settled to his knees. He felt blood pour down his face from his forehead, saw it splatter onto his white shirt, coat and trousers. He had to do something. But what?

He saw the white man jump to his feet, and take a handkerchief from his pocket. "Come on, Scott." The publisher pressed the cloth to the composer's wound, pulled him up, guided him back to his chair. "Scott, take it easy, now, huh? Quit worrying. I ain't gonna steal your music."

As if in a dream, the colored man saw a second white man come at a run into the room. "What the hell's going on here," the newcomer shouted.

Joplin saw the first white man wave the other one quiet. "Scott Joplin's got a new musical drama he wants us to have a look at. He, uh, tripped and hit his head on the door there."

Joplin's eyes followed the publisher's finger, saw the blood splattered on the door, splashed on the floor. The second white man whistled. "Nasty cut."

"He'll be all right." The voice seemed to come from a great distance. "We're going to give your work every consideration, Scott, don't you worry." The colored man saw the white man smile at the newcomer, who replied with a grin.

〈〉〈〉〈〉

The Pennsylvania Railroad, like any rail company those days, was run by pious men who believed the last should be first, so they put the colored cars in their trains in front of the white cars. That way, the colored passengers were privileged to receive the lion's share of soot that blew back from the smoke stack of the steam engine. Even in the third colored car, a fine layer of black dust nearly obscured the curlicue pattern on the thread-bare carpeting. The horsehair stuffing in the seat cushions had long since deteriorated into powder, such that passengers sat on petrified lumps that assaulted their hindquarters with every bump of the train on the tracks. The dingy, worn seat covers were pocked by cigar and cigarette burns; many armrests were gone. The railroad company used the condition of the colored cars as evidence of how reasonable their policy was. Why, if they let those people just sit anywhere, the whole damn train would look like that, and then how many decent people would want to take a train trip?

Halfway back in that third colored car, a man in his mid-thirties, with a thin, stylish mustache and a forehead extending all the way to the crown of his head, sat hunched over lined music paper. He hummed short passages, changed a note here, a chord there. Occasionally, he smiled, or said, "Yeah, that's right."

As he stretched and gave a tug at the starched collar on his brand-new white Arrow shirt, a man who'd been sitting across the aisle got up, stepped over, and started eyeballing his music. The bald man put down his pencil and looked up. Young guy, not even twenty, nice-looking kid except for a three-inch raised scar along his left cheek, and a nose that had been broken and not set back nearly straight. Skin like coffee with a good shot of cream, big brown eyes, ivory-white teeth set just so. Dark hair rippled over the top of his head, parted cleanly in the middle. But the suit of clothes on that boy—where on *earth* did he get those duds? Yellow and black checked jacket over a black vest and a bright pink silk shirt. Black patent leather shoes with pearl buttons. Just a kid puttin' on the style, thinks he looks like the last word, but what he looked like to the older man was a pimp who couldn't keep clear of fists and knives. The boy fiddled absently with his trousers, pulled at his vest, straightened his tie. "You write music, huh?"

St. Lou to New York could be a damn long train ride, the bald man thought, but nasty just wasn't his style. He half-turned in his seat. "Yeah, I write. Play piano, too." He extended a hand. "My name's Eubie—Eubie Blake. Pleased to meet you."

The young man answered with a handshake too energetic by a country mile, then slid past Blake to settle into the inside seat, and turned to face the older man. "I be Dubie. Dubie Harris."

Blake laughed out loud. "Dubie and Eubie? You pullin' my leg?"

The boy shook his head. "No stuff. It's short for DuBois, my gramma was Creole. An' Mr. Blake, I done heard of you. 'Chevy Chase'? 'Baltimore Todolo?' Those ain't no easy pieces. He glanced at Blake's hands. 'Less, maybe, a man got fingers long as yours."

Blake tried not to smile. "You a musician, Dubie? Takin' yourself off to the Big City?"

Dubie grinned extravagantly, opened his eyes wide as nature would allow. "Betcha sweet patootie, Mr. Blake. St. Louie ain't near big enough to hold me. I play clarinet and horn, and of course, pianna." Dubie pointed toward the overhead storage across the aisle. "Got my instruments up there. Going to get me a spot in Mr. Jim Europe's band, learn me all of his tricks, and in a couple a years, gonna have my own band, just see if I don't. I write, too—but I ain't no dummy, gonna let some two-bit publisher in St. Lou or Chi or Kay Cee jew me. I'm gonna take my music straight on over to Tin Pan Alley."

Where every music publisher is a Jew, Blake thought. He couldn't decide whether this kid had moxie to burn, or if he was just plain foolish. "New York can be a tough place, boy. I hope you got yourself somewhere good to stay."

"Oh yeah, you bet. My uncle and auntie got plenty room. They went up to Harlem a few years back, buyed themselves a nice house on West 131st Street, and put in a grocery on the ground floor. They live in the upstairs. I'm gonna stay with them, 'least till I get my own place."

"They'll meet your train?"

"Naw. I tell 'em don't bother. I know how to get myself around a city."

This kid's gonna get some lessons in a hurry, Blake thought. For sure he had a little money in his pocket, a plum ripe for picking. But that's how you learn. Blake hoped the boy was a quick learner. "Been playin' in St. Lou?"

"No, Sedalia. You know Sedalia?"

Blake shook his head. "I grew up in Baltimore, and I've pretty much lived east my whole life. I was just out to St. Lou a couple of days, business, and that's the closest to Sedalia I ever got. I hear it was a damn good music town, say twenty years ago, then all the joints got closed up a little after the eighteens went away. Where ever you been playing in Sedalia?"

Dubie paused. "Well…actually I was at the George R. Smith College, studyin' music." His speech moved up-tempo. "But I played in every place I could, dances and balls, concerts in the park, marching bands—"

"You don't mind me saying, boy, music school and marching bands ain't likely gonna get you too far in Harlem."

Dubie moved in his seat like his pants had suddenly gotten too tight. "Well…"

Whole-story time, Blake thought.

"Sedalia still got some places where a colored man can play, for sure on a Saturday night. They's bars, a couple houses… sometimes they get a professor in from Kay Cee or St. Louie, maybe somebody come up from N'Orleans. And I always listen hard. 'Course the college don't want us doing that stuff, they ever found out, they'd'a expelled me right that minute. But they can't keep watch on everybody, every night, can they?" Dubie's face relaxed into a full smile.

My, my, Blake thought, what fine and gorgeous teeth. Flash them pearls like that, this kid could get trampled to death by women.

"And I tell you the truth, Mr. Blake. Nobody—I mean *nobody*—could get 'em up and hollerin' like me when I start in to blow. Sure, we learned all them dead European composers, but that didn't do me no harm. After classes I'd go take a walk out in the trees where nobody's gonna hear, and I practiced my Schubert and my Mozart, they be my warmup. Then I played that New Orleans music I learned from the professors. Sometimes I played till I seed blood on the reed."

Blake thought Dubie might just jump up, grab his saxophone out of the overhead storage, and start playing, right there in the train car. The kid's eyes widened, shone. "Day I finished school, I say to myself, now it's New York for me, that's the onliest place to be. I blowed for near-on two months, any place they pay money, any music they wanted. And I saved every penny, bought me a good suit and shoes, and a ticket for the train." Dubie pointed at a slip of paper peeking out from his shirt pocket, behind his vest. "See there—that be my ticket to tomorrow. Gonna take me to a chair in Mr. Europe's Society Orchestra."

"Sure enough," Blake said. "You're gonna walk right in and say, 'Mr. Europe, here I am. Make space.'"

Dubie fumbled behind his vest, came out with a limp piece of paper, which he unfolded and passed to Blake, who read silently, James Reese Europe. Superior colored musicians. 67-69 West 131st Street, New York. Telephone 7930 Harlem.

"See? You see now?" Dubie could barely contain himself. "Mr. Europe ain't only got just *one* Society Orchestra, he got a barn full of them. Send one out here, one there, go to all sorts of fancy dances, white, black, whatever. That man need a passel of musicians."

Blake took care not to say anything that might let the cat out about how tight he was with James Reese Europe. Then, there'd have to be an introduction, and Blake had long ago learned the folly of giving a man a reference based on what he tells you he can do.

"My auntie, she be the one tell me about Mr. Europe, and you know who *she* get it from? Mr. Scott Joplin's missus, no other. Joplins live right nearby, and Miz Joplin sometimes buy groceries at my uncle and auntie's. You ever meet Scott Joplin?"

Blake took a deep breath. "Oh, I heard Joplin play a couple times."

Dubie's eyes were like lanterns. "You ever hear him play 'Maple Leaf?' People in Sedalia, they still say hearing Scott Joplin play 'Maple Leaf Rag' was like hearing Gabriel blow his horn on the Judgment Day."

"Some men get to be more in remembrance than they ever was in life," Blake said. "Fact is, there was lots better players than Scott Joplin, but never a composer could touch him. Scott Joplin is the King of Ragtime. He says it himself, and it's truth."

Dubie flashed a look like a six-year-old whose mother had just walked out of the kitchen and left cookies on the table to cool. "But all the newspapers say Mr. Irving Berlin be the King of Ragtime."

The boy burst into hilarious laughter, but stopped on a dime at the sight of Blake's face. "I'll tell you, and I'll tell you true," Blake said. "No one ever lived on this earth, had ragtime in his soul like Scott Joplin. There were plenty of rags before 'Maple Leaf,' but it was 'Maple Leaf' and Scott Joplin, put ragtime on the map."

A thought crossed Blake's mind; he stopped, considered, then decided to come out with it. "All right, here's something for you. If you want to take your tunes to the very top, go see Irving Berlin. I used to play at the Boathouse in Atlantic City, and Mr. Berlin would stop by, Lord, those pointy bright-yellow shoes he always had on." Blake shook his head. "He'd holler, "Play my song for me, Eubie, you know which one. So I'd play 'Alexander's Ragtime Band' for him. That man can't even play piano himself, and his music ain't in any way ragtime, but oh my, how he does know just exactly what people want. Give him a few years, and mark my word, he's gonna be the biggest composer *and* publisher in the whole country, never mind just in New York. You want me to write down his address for you?"

Dubie, open-mouthed, and, for once, silent, nodded.

Blake pulled a blank music sheet from his pile, picked up his pencil, and wrote, in heavy block capitals, WATERSON, BERLIN, AND SNYDER. STRAND THEATRE BUILDING, BROADWAY AND 47TH STREET. Then he gave the paper to Dubie, who smiled, folded it, stuck it into his shirt pocket along with James Reese

Europe's address. The kid's smile grew into a full-faced grin. "I'm sure on my way, now, Mr. Blake. Not very long, an' you gonna be playin' *my* tunes for people."

Eubie Blake smiled. "Good luck, boy."

‹›‹›‹›

Five o' clock. The young couple hurried out of the office, skipped down the stairs, through the door, and out into the swirling, boiling mob on the sidewalk. The girl reached for the boy's arm, then grasped his hand instead. The crowd pressed them together; he felt the softness of her breast against his elbow. His heart leaped, and he stopped walking to admire the treasure at his side. Full lips, neatly painted, flashed him a smile of expectation. Warmth beamed from wide brown eyes. She was beet-cheeked, breathing heavily from the heat of the day, and maybe more. The boy grabbed her by the arms, pulled her to him, and planted a hard kiss on her mouth.

She quickly pulled away. "Martin, not out here on the street, with everybody watching." But she was still smiling.

"Where else, then? We have no place we can go."

"We will."

A fragment of a tune ran through Martin's mind. 'Oh, tell me how long…do I have to wait. Why can't I get you now? Why must I hesitate?' Hesitation Blues was what he had, all right. But the piano tune reminded him of his appointment; he put his hand to the girl's back, started steering her along the sidewalk. "Come on, we don't have much time. I have to be up in Harlem at seven."

Half a block down, they went into Schneider's Deli. The boy inhaled the fragrance of corned beef, pastrami, smoked fish. His stomach growled. He and the girl took a table, ordered. As the waiter walked away, Martin said, "Your old man's not going to let up an inch, is he?"

"He says I'm only seventeen, too young to get married."

"How old is old enough?"

Birdie shrugged. "Who knows? But what difference does it make? If it's not *my* father, it's yours. He won't ever think a stupid little *Litvak* is good enough for his Austrian son."

Martin tried to swallow his anger. His girlfriend was a doll, round and soft in all the right places. But his father was not impressed. "Give her ten years, she'll be so fat you won't be able to *shtup* her with a *putz* three feet long." Nothing Martin could say would make it right with his old man. The Niederhoffers were Austrian Jews, at the top of the Hebrew social heap, and for one to marry an Eastern European peasant was almost as big a shame on the family as marrying a *shiksa*.

"My father can think what he wants," Martin said. "But I'm twenty-four years old, and I'll marry who I want…which is you."

The vinegar-faced waiter slid plates in front of them, then moved off, not a word said. The girl cut a piece of blintz with her fork; Martin lifted the top piece of rye bread off his corned beef sandwich, and spread mustard. "Well, we're not going to wait forever. One of these days, I'll get a car, and we'll go down to Elkton and get married. Then, it won't matter if your father says 'Too young,' or if mine says, 'Not good enough.'" He took a savage bite, as if the sandwich had somehow insulted him.

Birdie's high color faded. "If we do that, your father might never talk to you again."

"Good, " Martin muttered around a mouthful of corned beef. "I've heard more than enough from him for twenty-four years now. What is he, anyway? A lousy fruit peddler. But he's Austrian, so his blood is noble. Well, this is America, not Austria, and I'm going to make my own money. I'm not going to be a bookkeeper forever. I keep my eyes and ears open, and one of these days, I'm going to get myself into music publishing for real, maybe even the theater. *Then* we can get married whenever we want, no matter what anybody says."

Birdie put down her fork. "Martin, dear, you don't have to get so worked up all the time. You know I'll marry you and no one else. And I don't care if you're a bookkeeper. We could live on that."

He patted her hand across the table. "I'm not going make you live in a cold-water flat, one dirty room, our children hungry all the time. My mother says, 'Love is like butter, it goes well with bread,' and I've seen enough to know she's right about that." He shot a glance at his wrist watch. "I've got to go. Mr. Joplin gets sore when his pupils don't come on time."

Birdie's lips parted in a warm smile. "You really like him a lot, don't you."

"I love him," Martin blurted. "And I love his music. I get him to play one of his rags, then I try to do it exactly the same as he does. Come on, walk me to the subway." He threw money on the table.

Birdie stood, walked around the table, and slipped her hand into Martin's. The young man thought his chest might burst with love and pride. He'd get his butter, all right, and bread to go with it. And if his plan worked the way he figured it would, he might just have them both before leaves started to fall.

Chapter Two

Harlem
Monday, August 21
2pm

One look at her husband as he walked in, and Lottie Joplin threw both hands to her brow. "Scott, your head! What on earth done happened to you?"

Joplin slowly raised a hand to touch his forehead, then winced.

"And your shirt. You look like you was in some kind of a fight." Lottie's speech faded, her eyes narrowed. "Did Irving Berlin beat you up and take away your music? Wasn't Martin there, helpin' you?"

Joplin's arms waved wildly. "Damn, woman! He was out to lunch."

Lottie braced herself. "Now, you tell me, Scott, I want to know. Did that jivin' li'l jew-man steal your music?"

"He steals my music, I'm gonna kill him. I told him that. I told him!" Joplin grabbed a vase from the little table next to the door, hurled it at the wall. Pieces of pottery rebounded in all directions. The composer, every muscle tensed, seemed to be looking around the room for his next victim.

Least he don't never go after me, Lottie thought. She calculated the wisdom of leaving her husband alone in the room for a few minutes, then muttered, "Ain't got no choice." She trotted into the hall, up the stairs, grabbed the telephone receiver from its cradle, gave a number to the operator. Then she drummed fingers against the wall until she heard the hello from the other end. "Nell," she cried into the mouthpiece. "Can you please come over right away…yes, it be Scott again. What else?"

〈〉〈〉〈〉

Lottie was quick to answer Nell's knock, pulled the white woman into the house, closed the door quietly. She put a finger to her lips, then led her guest into the living room, where Joplin sprawled on a sofa, feet on the floor, his head twisted grotesquely to rest on a cushion. The room was littered with fragments of ceramic and glass, metal ashtrays, pictures in frames. "He done run outa steam ten, fifteen minutes ago," Lottie whispered. "Guess I really didn't need to call you, sorry."

Nell Stanley gazed at the wreckage. Them blue eyes a hers, Lottie thought. They could freeze you or they could melt you, dependin'. "It's just I got scared, Nell. Thought he might tear the whole house to pieces."

Nell rested a hand on Lottie's shoulder. "I'm glad you called. I'll wait with you, and we'll see how he is when he wakes up."

"But you got things to do—"

Nell waved off her concern. "August's always a slow month anyway, but with all the theaters being closed because of the polio epidemic, I really don't have much to do right now. I could have gone along with Jim on his tour, but I decided to stay home." She smiled. "So here I am."

You decided to stay because you knew how bad Scott was gettin', Lottie thought. The notion brought such a sudden grief into her throat, she let out a sound somewhere between a sob and a honk. "Nell, I'm scared. No two ways about it, one a these days, I'm gonna have to put him away."

Nell pointed toward the kitchen. "Let's have some coffee, and you can tell me what happened."

〈〉〈〉〈〉

Joplin didn't stir till late afternoon. The women glanced at each other, then, as if by signal, got to their feet. Joplin raised his head, grunted, dropped it back to the cushion. Lottie gently swung his legs around as Nell lifted his head. "Oh my." Joplin groaned. "I feel like I've been through a war."

Like a newborn lamb, Lottie thought. Devil gets hold of him, then he sleeps it off, and he be gentle as a baby. She couldn't help feeling a pang under her ribs, the way her husband looked at Nell, and for that matter, the way Nell looked at him. But she knew that was ungenerous. Without Nell's help, she'd have long ago had to put Scott in a hospital, which would've been the end of him. Besides, Nell wouldn't ever do anything out-of-bounds, and it'd been years now since Scott even *could*. She went off to the kitchen and returned with a glass of water, which Joplin took from her and drank down in a couple of gulps. He looked from her to Nell and back. "I'm a fortunate man," he said slowly. "Having two such fine women to look after my well-being."

He sounded so like the Scott Joplin she'd taken up with, she couldn't help but feel hope. Never mind how many times that hope had been dashed when the disease got back in control of his mind.

Nell spoke. "Scott, what happened to you?"

He looked her a question.

She pointed. "Your head. Your shirt."

He touched his forehead, breathed, "Whew," then took hold of his shirt, and stared at Nell like a man trying to make sense out of some abstruse text. He shook his head slowly, back and forth, back and forth.

Lottie took his hand. "Scott, now, you remember. You went downtown to talk to Irving Berlin about your play, but you come back without your music. And your face and shirt—"

Joplin was off the sofa in a bound. Panic ran rampant across his face. "He took my music," a howl, then he made for the door. Nell blocked his path, grabbed his arm, led him toward the kitchen. Lottie followed, arms at the ready in case he pulled away and tried to run off. "Scott, I'm going to help you," Nell said. "Just leave this business to me. You've had nothing to eat all day, so Lottie's going to get you dinner while I go upstairs and make a phone call."

Lottie marveled at the grit that woman could get into her voice. The door to the hall opened, then slammed shut.

When Nell came back, the living room was positively fragrant with the aroma of bacon. Porcelain shards cracked with every step she took. Lottie must have heard; she walked out of the kitchen, and softly asked, "Did you learn something?"

Nell caught sight of Joplin at the kitchen table, doing heavy demolition work on what she guessed was a plate of bacon and eggs. She cupped a hand to her mouth. "What I learned is that no one at Waterson, Berlin, and Snyder would let me talk to the Big Man. Same thing at Irving Berlin, Incorporated. And no one at either place could—or would—tell me anything about Scott and his play."

Lottie sighed. "If that Berlin steals Scott's music again, it'd just kill Scott."

Nell nodded. "I thought about going down there and raising a fuss, but I really don't think I'd get any further than I did on the phone. Another couple of hours, my father will be home from work, and I'll call him." She almost smiled. "I suspect if *he* goes marching into that office, they just might listen."

Lottie put a hand to her mouth. "You think he really would come out? I mean, with all's gone on between him and Scott?"

Nell's smile crept outward from the left corner of her mouth. "He'll come if I have to drag him by his shirt collar all the way from St. Louis." She dropped to her knees, smoothed her skirt. "Go back and sit with Scott. I'll get these pieces picked up before I leave."

<><><>

Pistol in John Stark's right hand, old Colt 44, weighs a ton. Stark stares at his target, a fifteen-year-old colored boy, frozen in a half-crouch, ready to skedaddle if only he could get his muscles to moving. In the boy's eyes, Stark sees a reflection of his own fear and horror. The boy gasps, as if trying to store up air against the time when his lungs will no longer be able to bring it in. Stark hears his own tortured breathing.

From his left, a harsh growl. "Gol' damn your eyes, you rabbit-hearted bugler. *Shoot* him! Else, I'll do it myself."

Stark turns slowly, looks at the lieutenant, then at the colored boy. He puts every ounce of energy at his disposal into lifting the gun. The colored boy lets out a strangled scream.

Out of the corner of his eye, he sees Sarah, standing off to the side, reproach all over her lovely young face. What in the name of anything holy is *she* doing here?

Stark tenses his arm. He pulls the trigger.

Three harsh rings of a buzzer-bell, two long and one short, brought Stark up straight and stiff. A teenaged girl, waist-length braids flying out behind her, dashed past the old man in the rocking chair and across the living room. Stark blinked, shook his head, tried to free himself of the vision. How many times had he lived through that dream; how many more times would he be compelled to endure it? He blew out a mouthful of air, then straightened his spectacles. As the girl reached for the telephone, he smiled. What he wouldn't give to still have that energy.

The girl snatched the receiver from the wall. "Stark family residence, Maplewood, Missouri, Margaret Eleanor speaking." A pause, then, "Aunt Nell! How are you and Uncle Jim?…Oh yes, we're all fine. You want to talk to Daddy?" A moment, then Margaret Eleanor turned to hold the receiver out toward Stark, using both hands. "Grandpa, it's Aunt Nell, from New York. Long *distance*."

Stark nodded. "New York would be long distance, Meggy."

The old man wiped his forehead on his sleeve. Four days in a row, now, over a hundred in the shade. Slowly, he pulled himself to his feet, but once up, he stood soldier-straight, no weakness in his stride as he crossed the living room. He patted the girl's shoulder as he took the receiver from her. "Hello, Nell. What is it that requires a long-distance call?"

A woman shouted from the kitchen, "Margaret Eleanor! Meggy! Come back in here." But the girl seemed not to hear.

She leaned forward from the waist, focused on her grandfather to the exclusion of all else.

"You might take a lesson in manners from your granddaughter," Nell snapped. "She had the courtesy to ask after Jim and me."

Stark closed his eyes, counted to five. "Nell, I am not in need of reprimands or didactic narratives on deportment from my daughter. Long-distance calls are not cheap, and I believe my question covered any possible concern, whether personal or otherwise."

Stark waited through several seconds of silence. Apples don't fall far from their trees, he thought, and once they send out their own roots, they struggle against the shade older plants cast over them. Finally, Nell spoke. "All right, Dad. Jim and I are fine, thank you. But an old friend needs your help. He's in serious trouble."

Stark's daughter-in-law, a properly-stout woman in her forties, with a flushed face and patches of flour in her dark hair, sailed through the doorway from the kitchen. She strode over to Meggy, put a hand on the girl's neck, and began guiding her back toward the kitchen. Meggy pulled away, stamped a foot, ran ahead. Her mother looked at Stark, rolled her eyes. Stark smiled, then spoke into the phone. "If I can help, you know I will. Who's the friend and what's the trouble?"

"It's Scott Joplin. He's—"

"Nell, I haven't talked to Joplin for a great many years, and I don't see why I should start now."

"If you'd be so good as to just listen..."

Stark began to calculate in his head how much money he might be able to send.

"...I need you to come to New York."

"Come to New York? Nell! Did I hear you right?"

"Yes, you heard right. It looks as if Irving Berlin is trying to steal another piece of music from Scott. We can't let that happen."

Stark rubbed at the right side of his forehead, where a water-hammer seemed suddenly to have taken up residence. Nell talked on. "This sounds even worse than what happened with 'Alexander's Ragtime Band.' Scott's written a musical play, and one of his piano students, who just happens to be a bookkeeper at Waterson, Berlin, and Snyder, persuaded him to try to get Berlin to buy it and put it on stage. The bookkeeper was going to go down with Scott to make sure there was no funny business, but Scott took it into his head to go by himself... Dad, he's sicker than you know. The disease has changed his whole personality. He's suspicious, moody, forgets things. He flies into rages over nothing. You remember how careful he was of his appearance? Now, most of the time, he looks like a Bowery drunk. He'll compose for two days and nights running, then he might not get out of bed for a week. And he's lost all his good judgment. As well as I can make the matter out, he went down to see Berlin, and when he came back, there was a gash on his head, blood all over his shirt, and he didn't have the manuscript. He says Berlin 'took his music.' I've tried to look into it, but no one there would listen to me."

Stark took in a breath of air, then blew it out in a puff. His daughter's message came through all too clearly. 'No one there is *going* to listen to me, because businessmen *don't* listen to women. Including my own father, who refused to publish Scott Joplin's two operas, no matter how much pressure I put on him. Who told me that as good as those operas might be, no publisher in his right mind would put a pile of money into an opera by a colored man. Might as well just donate every cent in his business to the county poor farm, then go live there.'

Stark cleared his throat. "Nell, you know as well as I do how badly Joplin and I fell out eight years ago. Even if I come to New York, I don't think he'd listen to a word I'd say."

"That doesn't matter. *I* can talk to Scott, and most of the time he listens. It's Berlin I need you to talk to." Stark heard a cough, or maybe a choked sob, then, when Nell began to talk again, her voice was hushed, uneven. "Dad, I don't think Scott can last a lot longer, and it's not just the syphilis. He spent five years trying to get *Treemonisha* put on stage, and I think all by itself that affected his mind."

Stark closed his eyes. He wanted to take Nell by the shoulders and give her a good shake, then give the same to Scott Joplin. The man had a gift from Nature, a towering genius for composing music the equal and then some of anything Chopin, Lizst, or Brahms ever wrote. But that wasn't good enough. To get himself the respect he thought he deserved, he had to compose operas and symphonies—*serious* music. He'd put years into writing *Treemonisha*, and because no music publisher would touch it, Joplin published it himself. Then he spent more years and every cent he had, trying to mount a stage production. Not surprising his mind might have given out.

"Now Scott's written a musical play called *If.* I can't let him lose it, Dad, certainly not to Irving Berlin, but I need your help. You know Scott, you know your way around the music-publishing business, and you've always been proud of your sense of honor. How many times have I heard you say you've always been equal to all requirements? If you don't at least try to help Scott, you can never say *that* again, not to me, anyway."

Meggy poked her head around the corner from the kitchen. "Dinner's ready," she whispered, mouthing the words theatrically.

Stark held up an index finger, then looked longingly across the room at his rocker. "Nell, I'm seventy-five years old," he said, almost a groan.

For answer, he got a sharp, "Some men are better at seventy than others are at twenty. Isn't that what you told my brothers when they wanted you to retire after Mother died, and let them run the business?"

How many platefuls of his own words was she going to serve him up, and insist he eat every bite? Stark sighed "What about this musical of his? Is it any good?"

"I've got no idea. He kept it under lock and key, wouldn't let anyone see it. But he's convinced it's not only going to establish his reputation for all time, it's also going to bring in money to support Lottie after he's gone. We've all been trying to encourage him. What else could we—"

"Nell, I'm sorry to interrupt, but what on earth possessed Scott to take his music to Berlin? After all that fuss over 'Alexander's Ragtime Band?'"

"I know. But Berlin's bookkeeper convinced Scott to put the past aside, and said he'd keep an eye on the music and Berlin."

"Do you think the bookkeeper's in on some funny business?"

"That, I don't know. Lottie seems to think he's no worse than naive, and just wanted to help Scott. But there's no point in my trying to talk to him—if he *is* involved, he'll go right back to Berlin, and that will only give them more time to cover up. Dad, you've got to come out here. If Berlin steals this music and Scott goes to his grave knowing you sat in your rocking chair in St. Louis and didn't even lift a finger, you won't be able to look in a mirror the rest of your life."

Apples and trees. He had to hand it to her. "All right, Nell. Give me a little while to consider the situation, and I'll get back to you. I promise."

"Today?"

"Don't push me. You know my word is good. I'll call you just as soon as I can. And I'll give your love to Till and Margaret."

He replaced the receiver slowly, as if too vigorous a hang-up might trigger an explosion. Then he shook his head, strolled out of the living room, into the dining room, and took his seat at the dinner table. Through the barrage of silent questions, he said, "Nell sends you all her love."

At the head of the table, his son, Etilmon, cocked his head and studied his father. "That's why she called?"

"No. It's Scott Joplin."

"She still keeps up with Scott, doesn't she?"

"Always has. Now she wants me to get on a train to New York, and help Scott out of some music-publishing pickle."

"Just like that? Get on a train and go to New York?"

Stark thought Margaret looked like a cow shocked with a prod. "I believe I said that was her wish."

"Nell should have more sense than to ask that of a man your age," said Etilmon. "After what Joplin said about you back in oh-eight, you don't owe him a thing. Now, let's say grace. Meggy?"

The girl folded her hands, lowered her eyes. "Though I have all faith, so it could move mountains, and have not charity, I am nothing." The girl looked up, glanced from her father to her grandfather. "Amen."

Stark thought he might split a gut. But later, as he sat over his cup of coffee, a thought came into his mind and sent him bolt upright. Could his granddaughter's impertinence have been directed not at his son, but at him?

He excused himself, jumped to his feet, strode out-of-doors into one of those heady summer evenings that quicken the blood of the young and revive memories in the old. The scent of the little white Autumn Clematis blossoms in the beds in front of the house made his head spin. Evenings like this, back on the farm in Maysville, he'd sit on the front porch and play his guitar, Sarah at his side, accompanying him in that beautiful clear voice, while the children, Etilmon, Will, Eleanor, kept up as best they could. As he remembered the duet Sarah and Nell sang on "Aura Lee," his eyes filled. "Our boys will shine tonight," he murmured, "Our boys will shine…" The farmhouse faded from his mind's eye, and in its place, Stark saw endless files of men in blue uniforms, marching and singing in chorus. "John Brown's body lies a-mold'ring in the grave. John Brown's body lies a-mold'ring in the grave. John Brown's body lies a mold'ring in the grave. But his soul goes marching on."

The old man did an abrupt about-face, hurried back up the concrete walkway to the house and inside, slammed the door shut. He marched to the phone, double-time, barked a number to the operator, then shifted from one foot to the other as he waited. Finally, he heard his daughter's hello. "Nell," he said. "I'll be taking the New Yorker out of Union Station tomorrow, so I'll see you the day after. I hope that will do."

A pause, then he heard a quiet, "I'll meet you at Pennsylvania Station…thank you, Dad."

As Stark walked away from the telephone, a thousand miles away, his daughter slowly replaced the receiver and swallowed hard, trying to keep the tears that filled her eyes from streaming down her face. She did not succeed.

Chapter Three

Bartlett Tabor, office manager for Waterson, Berlin, and Snyder, walked slowly through Reception on his way back from the can. All collars in the office were open, ties askew, sleeves rolled up. Fannie Solomon, the receptionist, flashed him a big smile as he came within range of her desk. "Five days in a row over ninety. Mr. Snyder was smart to take his vacation now, huh?"

Tabor grunted a vague acknowledgment. He didn't give a fiddler's fart for Ted Snyder or the weather; right then, all he could think of were those numbers he'd left for Martin Niederhoffer to check out. He needed those figures, and he wanted them now.

He dodged a *schmegeggi* who was waving sheets of music manuscript at Harvey Jacobs, one of the arrangers. Music publishing, Christ, what a business. The manager hustled out of Reception and down the hallway, past the secretaries' space, past his own office, past Ted Snyder's. In the next room, he saw Henry Waterson, feet up on his desk, pawing through a racing form. Tabor checked his pocket watch, just past one-thirty. He leaned through the doorway. "Henry, what the hell're you still doing here? Those poor ponies're going to think you don't love them any more."

"Ach." Waterson swung around, lowered his feet. His thick lips curled, jaw set, ready to broadcast a piece of his customary derisive humor. "Berlin again. Every time I think we've got things settled, him and that lawyer of his come up with another angle on copyrights or royalties or whatever. We had a meeting today that was supposed to be be done by one o'clock, but it lasted till fifteen minutes ago. Every word outa my mouth or my lawyer's, that shyster Max Josephson jumped on it, turned it all around and fed it right back to me. Son of a bitch jewed me out of God knows how much money. Now, Irvy's back in his hole there, door shut like always, doing God knows what. I can't trust the little bastard an inch out of my sight." Waterson waved the racing paper at Tabor, then worked himself out of his chair and to his feet. "Well, there's still some good horses running. I guess better late than never, huh?"

Tabor thought Waterson was sorer about missing the early races than losing the money to Berlin, but fine, all the better. He clapped a hand on Waterson's shoulder. "Sorry, Henry. We can't win 'em all, can we?"

Both men looked around at the sound of raised voices coming from Reception. Tabor laughed. "Another genius composer, sore that we don't think his crap is gonna sell a million copies."

Waterson snickered, folded his racing form, and walked out.

Tabor marched down the hall, and into Bookkeeping. Birdie, the assistant bookkeeper, went red and looked away; five'd get you ten she and Niederhoffer had been paying attention to the wrong figures before they heard him coming. "Miss Kuminsky!" he snapped.

Birdie jumped to her feet; her pen rolled off her desk onto the floor.

"Go up front and ask Fannie if she's heard from Sam Goodman today."

As the girl flew through the doorway, Tabor strode up to Niederhoffer's desk and turned a humorless smile on the book-keeper. "You got it?"

Without a word, Niederhoffer grabbed a folder, opened it, and handed Tabor several sheets of paper with columns of numbers. Tabor scanned them, chortled, then choked off the sound. "Good work, Niederhoffer—but hear me now, and hear me clear. Not a word of this, not to anyone. That includes your girlfriend."

Niederhoffer bit on his upper lip, then looked back to the ledger he'd been working on, but Tabor interrupted him. "Niederhoffer!"

The bookkeeper looked up.

"Do you understand me?"

Niederhoffer set down his pencil with exaggerated care. "Yes, sir, I understand. I speak pretty good English for a greeny. What's on those papers is none of my business."

Tabor smirked. "Boy, one day that temper is going to get you into some real trouble. Listen—you're going to have to stay after hours tonight to get the monthly sales figures caught up. I'll see that you get overtime." Tabor waved the papers. "I appreciate this."

"Thank you, sir." Niederhoffer's words lacked enthusiasm, but he did feel some considerable satisfaction, and why not? It was no secret in the office that Mr. Waterson had a lot more interest in cards and ponies than in music, and Niederhoffer had just given Tabor solid evidence that Waterson was regularly raking money off the top, probably to pay gambling debts. That should be worth something, somewhere, to someone. He'd keep his ears open.

<><><>

By five o'clock, Scott Joplin's locked room was a pressure cooker. The composer pushed away from the piano, wiped his face with a handkerchief, filled a dirty glass from a pitcher of luke-warm water, took a long swallow. He gazed at the music rack on his piano, ground his teeth. This symphony was harder going than he'd anticipated. He'd learned symphonic music, form and structure, first from Mr. Weiss in Texarkana, then at General Smith's College in Sedalia, but the minute he sat at the piano and tried to write down his *Symphony Number One*, his knowledge seemed to drain out of his head. The notes he put down on paper didn't hang together the way he wanted. He walked to the window, stared into the street, where a bunch of kids had opened a hydrant and were running around, screaming and laughing, under the cascades of water. "The Cascades"…St. Louis World's Fair. That rag came to him so easily, it practically wrote itself. They all did back then, but no more. The composer felt panic grip his heart as he remembered his friend, Louis Chauvin, shortly before he died, when his disease had filled his mind with garbage.

He forced himself back to the piano, played a few notes, but then heard Lottie's voice. "Scott…*Scott*! Come on, now, Scott, open up. He ain't gonna wait forever."

Who's not gonna wait forever? Then he realized he'd only thought it, hadn't said it out loud. "Who's not gonna wait forever, Lottie?"

"Irving Berlin. He's on the phone for you. Now, would you come on out of there and talk to the man."

Joplin was through the doorway in a flash, up the stairs, into the hall. The telephone receiver hung from its cord like a lifeless thing. The composer snatched it up. "Hello, yes. Mr. Berlin?"

"That's right. How you doing, Scott?"

"Fine, just fine. I'm working at my *Symphony Number One*. It's going to be good. Really good."

"Glad to hear that. Look, I'm calling about your musical."

Joplin couldn't talk. His muscles froze; he couldn't draw breath.

"You there, Scott?"

He managed a choked, "Yes."

"All right then, listen. I think it's got some possibilities, I want to talk to you about it. Can you come on down?"

"Now?"

"Yeah, now. Is that a problem?"

"No. No problem at all. I'll be right there."

"Good. See you soon. Just come on in, I'll keep an ear out for you."

Joplin hung up the receiver, dashed back into the apartment. Lottie gave him a curious look. He took hold of her by the shoulders.

"Hey, easy, Scott, you hurtin' me."

He let go, then grasped her again, this time as if she might have been made of glass. "Berlin *likes* it, Lottie. He says he thinks it's got real possibilities, and he wants to talk to me about it."

Lottie's smile was cautious. "Well, that does sound good, all right. When you goin'?"

"Now. He says come on down right now."

"*Now*? You sure that what he say?"

"Lottie, my ears still work all right. He says he wants to see me now."

"It's past five. Don't you think maybe you ought to wait till tomorrow, so Martin'll be there? Or maybe—"

"What am I supposed to do, woman? Tell Irving Berlin I can't come and talk to him without having his bookkeeper there in the room? Now, let me be. Time's wasting."

She sighed, then took him by the arm, motioned him toward the bathroom. "All right, Scott, if that's what you want. But you're *not* going down there looking like a colored beggar off the street. You are going to let me give you a shave, and put a clean court plaster on your forehead, and then you're going to wash up and change into your good suit. Won't take but fifteen minutes, if you don't argue. Come on."

<><><>

Bartlett Tabor stepped lively up from the subway station, and across Seventy-second Street. Not a woman under sixty failed to give him the eye as he went past, but he was used to that. What could he say, the ladies loved him, with his wide shoulders, dark eyes, long lashes and heavy eyebrows. They couldn't seem to keep their fingers out of the dimple in his chin—not that he ever tried to stop them. He glanced at the manila folder in his left hand, and smiled as he thought how well his plan was working out. 'Berlin, Snyder, and Tabor' had a nice ring. As he looked up, still smiling, he caught the eye of a delicious little thing in a pretty white summer dress, then chuckled as he watched her blush. If he weren't otherwise engaged…but he was. The girlies would have to wait.

He crossed West End Avenue and hurried on along Seventy-second to the end of the block. There, he turned left under the awning at the doorway to the Chatsworth Apartments. The doorman, a slightly-built Negro in a red uniform with gold trim, and a little circular hat to match, grinned, bowed, then opened the glass door. "'Afternoon, sir. Goin' up to see Mr. Berlin?"

Tabor nodded.

Less than two minutes later, he was on the fifth floor, knocking at Berlin's door. Practically before his hand was off the brass lion's-head, the door opened and there stood Robert Miras, Berlin's valet, looking down his long, slim nose at Tabor in that infuriating way of his. Too bad the lousy bum-sucker was Berlin's property. Tabor would've loved to give him a good what-for.

"I'm sorry," Miras said through his nose. "Mr. Berlin is not available at the moment."

Tabor narrowed his eyes. "What do you mean, 'he's not available at the moment?' This is the 'moment' he told me to come. I've got to talk to him, it's important." Tabor brandished the folder. "He's not going to like it if he finds out you're the reason I couldn't show him this."

"I'm sure it really is very important, Mr. Tabor. But Mr. Ziegfeld needed to see Mr. Berlin urgently, about *The Century Girl.* You know, the musical he's working—"

"Yes, I know about *The Century Girl.* I'm his office manager."

Miras' face suggested that Tabor might have just said it was a nice day. The valet extended a hand. "I'll be glad to give it to Mr. Berlin as soon as he returns."

Tabor pulled the folder away, started to step inside. "I'll wait."

Miras glided a step to the left, blocking Tabor's path. "He has an interview scheduled for when he gets back, and then he and Mr. Hess are going to dinner and a show. If you wish to leave the material with me, he should be able to look it over later and get back to you in the morning. But if you'd rather make an appointment for tomorrow, I'll be glad to consult his calendar."

Tabor fought an intense desire to punch the supercilious bastard square on the snoot. Miras' faint smile said he knew exactly what Tabor would like to do, and more, knew he never would. Finally, Tabor thrust the folder at Miras, who gathered it up and slipped it under an arm. Tabor jabbed a finger. "Be careful. Make sure you don't drop any of those papers."

Miras pulled himself up to his full height. "Mr. Tabor, I do not occupy my position because I'm in the habit of being careless." Then he shut the door—not gently—in Tabor's face.

As he stormed out of the building, past the doorman, the office manager's mood was 180 degrees from what it had been when he came in. All along Seventy-second Street, people moved aside to let him pass. No admiring looks from women, or anyone else. When he got to Broadway, he stopped short of the subway entrance, and shaded his eyes to look down the street. Three doors down, a bar and grill, praise the Lord. Tabor hustled down the sidewalk and inside, slumped on a stool at the far end of the bar, ordered bourbon and water, knocked it down in one swallow, then ordered another. A man sitting three stools away moved another five seats down.

<>‹›‹›

Martin Niederhoffer pushed back from his ledger, rubbed his eyes, pounded a fist onto the account book. From a chair next to the little desk, Sid Altman reached to steady the glass inkwell that Martin had set into a dance. "Jeez, Martin, take it easy, huh? How's it gonna help if you spill ink on the books and you've got to start all over?"

Martin stood and stretched. He and Sid had been pals all through school, spent as much time in each other's apartments as in their own. Sid was a chunky towhead, so affable that Martin sometimes wanted to slug him. Like right then. "Sidney, have you ever gotten sore at someone? Just once in your life?"

Sid chuckled, gave a mild shrug. "I guess so. But not too sore, or for very long."

The mildness in his friend's large brown eyes was like iodine on a cut on Niederhoffer's finger. "You *like* to let people walk all over you? You like it when your boss screws you around?"

Another shrug. "That's what bosses do, Martin. Dogs pee on fire hydrants. Cows do their business in a pasture. No point losing sleep over it."

Martin shook his head. "*Damn* Mr. Tabor! He's a trash can with legs. I spent most of the day getting him his evidence that Mr. Waterson's raking off profits from the business, so what was my reward? I get to stay late to catch up the monthly sales numbers. Tabor'll give me overtime, big deal. When he comes by to check me out, he'll make sure he doesn't overpay by a nickel."

Altman smiled. "Better than a poke in the eye with a sharp stick."

Martin winced. "I'm talking to a wall. Maybe that'd be fine for you, Sid, but I'm not going to spend *my* life being grateful I didn't get poked in the eye. Give me a few years and see if I'm still sitting here, adding up columns of numbers and saying, 'Thank you, sir,' for every piece of crap Tabor pushes in my face. I'm learning this business from the inside…matter of fact, I got something in the works right now." Martin paused, glanced around. "My piano teacher, Mr. Joplin? Wrote 'Maple Leaf Rag?' Well, he just finished a musical play, and I talked him into letting me help him sell it to Mr. Berlin, 'cause Mr. Berlin's getting into the theater in a big way. He wrote scores for two Broadway shows in the last two years, and right now he's working on one for Florenz Ziegfeld. *And,* he just opened up a new office, his own place, for show-tune music. So, I got to thinking about what Mr. Berlin could do for a Scott Joplin musical, and what a production of a Scott Joplin musical could do for Mr. Berlin's new company."

Sid's usual bland smile went sly. "And there's nothing in it for you, right?"

Martin leaned toward him as if spies might be outside, ears against the wall. "I'll tell you what's in it for me. Part of the deal's got to be that I'm an assistant to the producer, and then I'll put what I learn about the theater together with what I'm learning about publishing, and who knows? Sid, for crying out loud, this is America. You gotta be a go-getter. When people see how sharp you are, then they want you on their team. And then…" Martin poked a finger into his friend's chest. "*Then*, Sid, you get enough money and enough know-how, you get your own team. Niederhoffer Music. That's for me."

Through Martin's little speech, Sid nodded and smiled, smiled and nodded. Then he said, "Well, okay. What's this big musical about?"

"What's any musical about? They sing, they dance, lots of pretty girls wearing not a whole lot of costumes. What do you mean, 'about'?"

"Is it any good?"

Martin paused. "Well, sure it's good. Didn't I tell you, Scott Joplin wrote it? How can it not be good? He's just finishing it up now, and when he's done, we'll make an appointment and go pitch it to Mr. Berlin."

Sid laughed. "In other words, you haven't seen it?"

Martin stomped to the window, stared at the crowds flowing along the sidewalks. Like sheep, he thought. They move this way, then the other, never even think about where they're going and where they're gonna end up. He spun around. "I'll see it soon enough, Sid. And when you're still stacking fruit and vegetables in a grocery, you'll come and visit me in my own office, giving orders to other people. I'll buy you lunch."

Sid just smiled. "And I'll bring you a box of raspberries." He pushed back his sleeve, checked his watch. "After five-thirty already. Birdie went on home?"

Martin grimaced. "Yeah, her old man makes sure of that. She left right before you got here."

"Hey, Martin, I know it's none of my business, but you're really sure about getting married? You're only twenty-four. And she's what, seventeen?"

Martin felt the familiar glow come over his face. Was love at first sight for real? Certainly seemed to be, at least for him. He wasn't much on going to religious services, but one Friday evening last winter, his mother pleaded hard and long, and he finally gave up, agreed to go. And guess what. God rewarded him. After services, outside the synagogue, he caught sight of this marvelous girl, took two seconds to compose himself, then walked over and said hello. Before they were done talking, he'd invited her to go with him the next night to the New Amsterdam Theatre and see *Around the Map*, Klaw and Erlanger's latest. She loved it, hummed "Here Comes Tootsie" all the way home. She was working in a shirtwaist factory, she told him, and hated the job, the boss, the older women, the whole works. Martin couldn't believe his luck. The assistant bookkeeper at Waterson, Berlin, and Snyder had just gotten herself pregnant and quit. So two days later, Birdie was set up in Martin's own office, five days a week. Within three months, never mind their parents' objections, the two had an understanding.

He knew he had a goofy grin all over his face, couldn't help it. "Yeah, Sid, I'm sure. I've never known a girl like her. She's smart, she's pretty, she cooks like an angel. And I can't figure where somebody only seventeen got such great common sense. If I let her get away, I'll hate myself the rest of my life. What I've been telling you about getting my own business, that's not just for me. *She* doesn't deserve to hear for the rest of her life about how my boss said jump and I had to ask him how high and how many times."

Sid laughed easily. "Relax, Martin. Okay, you're in love, it's wonderful—but come on, it's getting late. Go finish your columns before your boss gets back. We don't want to miss the fights, and besides, I'm hungry."

Martin fluttered a long breath through his lips, ran fingers through his red hair, squeezed at his scalp. "Yeah...okay. Just gimme a couple of minutes. I got myself so worked up, I need to take a leak. Be right back."

Sid sat on Martin's stool. "Go pee. I'll check your numbers for you, make sure you didn't get so worked up you added two and two, and got five."

‹›‹›‹›

Martin strolled down the long hallway, past the bosses' offices, through Reception. Days, you couldn't hear yourself think in that place, and now, the quiet seemed unnatural. He dragged his feet all the way to the mens' room, started toward the urinal, but decided he needed a sit-down in a stall. When he finished, he buttoned up, walked to the sink, washed his hands, then bent down and splashed cold water on his face. It felt so good, he kept at it, paid no mind to the water running down inside his shirt. Finally, he wiped his face on his sleeve, took another look down through the opened window at the packed herds, shifting and flowing along the sidewalk. "I'm not gonna be like them," he muttered.

Sid's voice came from within Martin's head. "So what're you gonna do? Stand around in a toilet, and then one day, by some kind of magic, you're gonna be a big shot?"

Martin closed his eyes. "All right. Okay. I'm gonna have those goddamn numbers done in jig time, you just watch." He pushed through the doorway, started back to his office.

‹›‹›‹›

Scott Joplin strode past the Strand Theatre, glanced up at the blank marquee, then remembered the polio epidemic that had closed New York theaters for the summer. Well, that would be over in a few weeks, and maybe after that, some marquee in town was going to read, IF, THE NEW MUSICAL. BY SCOTT JOPLIN. And maybe in just a few minutes, he was going to find out *which* marquee.

He hurried around the corner and into the building, but took the stairs more slowly, one at a time, first the left foot, then the right, all the while sliding his hand along the wooden rail. Careful. A fall wouldn't be his first, but it could be his last, and he didn't want to be found, broken-limbed, broken-necked, at the foot of the stairs, then be carted off to the morgue and dumped into a grave with five other bodies and enough quick-lime to dissolve them all, leaving Lottie to wonder the rest of her life what had happened to him. *If* could bring in money, enough to last that dear woman as long as she lived, and still provide the composer a dignified grave with a headstone. SCOTT JOPLIN, it should say, AMERICAN COMPOSER. And the dates of his birth and death.

On the second-floor landing, he paused to catch his breath. The glass door to an accounting firm faced him; he caught sight of a figure inside, an old stooped colored man. Probably the janitor, grown long in the tooth on his job, his employer kindhearted enough not to sack him. But then Joplin realized, no, that wasn't what he saw. He was looking at his own reflec-tion in the glass. He turned away, hurried up the next flight of stairs faster than wisdom would have recommended, then started down the hall.

All of a sudden, a man barreled past him, put a hand to his shoulder, and ran to the stairs. The shove sent Joplin reeling, nearly knocked him to the floor. Someone ought to teach that fool some manners, the composer thought, but before he could say a word, the man was gone, crashing down the staircase. Joplin sighed, then walked the rest of the way down the hall and through the open doorway into Waterson, Berlin, and Snyder's empty Reception Room.

Like his last visit: no one in sight. No sounds. Was Berlin back in his office? Joplin walked past the reception desk and along the far corridor, past one closed door after another. Near the end of the hall, he saw sunlight streaming through an open doorway to form a rectangle on the floor. Berlin must have left the door open for him; he hurried into the room. But no, it wasn't Berlin's office. It looked like a bookkeeper's little space… and, yeah, there was Martin, his pupil, head-down on his desk. Must be working late, and fell asleep on the job. Or could he be waiting for Joplin? Did he find out Berlin wanted to publish

Scott Joplin's new musical and put it on stage, and now he was going to help his piano teacher?

Joplin trotted into the room. "Martin…hey, there…*Martin*." No answer. Boy must've been up dancing all night, that little girl of his was a real live wire. The composer reached toward the young man's shoulder to shake him awake, then suddenly realized it was not Martin. Martin had red hair; this man was blond. Just another bookkeeper. Oh, Scott Joplin, you fool, you goddamn fool! You thought that boy was different, he was going to help you like he said he would, but he's just like everybody else. Just like Walton, just like Europe and Johnson, Otis Saunders…that pimp Morton, calls himself Jelly Roll…*everybody*. A little sweet talk, a promise that's a lie from the start, that's enough for Scott Joplin, he can go to hell, and nobody would care. The composer grabbed the blond man by the collar of his jacket, pulled him off his seat, and flung him to the floor.

‹›‹›‹›

Martin Niederhoffer, primed to blast through those columns of sales figures in nothing flat, marched through the doorway, then stopped as if he'd walked into a glass wall. For a few seconds, he stood like an ox, gawking at Scott Joplin, a razor in his hand, crouched over Sid Altman, down on the floor next to the desk. Blood all over Joplin, over Sid, over the floor, over *everything*. The open ledger was covered with blood; blood dripped from the top of the desk. Finally, whatever held the bookkeeper in place let go, and he ran toward Joplin, dodging the pooled blood on the floor, taking care to keep Sid between the composer and himself. Quick glance at his friend's doughy, blood-smeared face, oh, Jesus! Throat gaping ear-to-ear, like a second mouth, shirt a blood-soaked rag. Martin looked a question at Joplin, but Joplin didn't seem to pick up. Finally, the bookkeeper pointed from the razor to Sid, then managed a strangled, "Mr. Joplin… What…why?" Sounding to his own ears like he was choking on his words.

"I came in to see Irving Berlin, and I saw…" Joplin jabbed the razor toward Sid. "He was in your chair, there, he looked like he was asleep at his work, and I thought he was you, maybe you were waiting to come in with me to talk to Mr. Berlin. But when I saw he didn't have your red hair, I got sore, and gave him a shove, and that's when I saw…" With a wave of the razor, the composer took in the cut throat and all the blood; Martin quickly ducked away. "…this razor, down there on the floor, and I picked it up. Stupid!" Joplin flung the razor down; it bounced off Sid's chest, onto the floor.

Martin had to strain to make out Joplin's words, flying by at breakneck pace, no space whatever between them. "You didn't…?" The young man could only point at his friend, sprawled like a recently-dispatched cow in an abattoir.

Joplin shook his head violently. "I'd never…Martin, you know me. Do you think I could *ever* do a thing like that?" Without waiting for an answer, he added, "We better call the police."

Which brought Martin around. "You really didn't kill him?"

"As God is my witness."

"All right. I believe you. But if we call the cops, *they'll* never believe you. They'll cart you off, and you'll be as good as convicted."

"But I didn't do it."

Martin tried to think. Wash the blood off Joplin's hands, then tell the cops…*what?* That Martin and Joplin came in together and found Sid's body? Then they'd both be suspected; there was nobody else in the office. Besides, did he really think Joplin could remember all the details of a made-up story, once the cops went to work on him? They'd break him down in nothing flat, and then the two of them would be in the soup for fair. And if they told the cops the truth, that Martin came out of the bathroom and found Joplin and Sid and the razor…wait. What if they got rid of the razor? Toss it in the incinerator, *then* call the cops? Martin sighed. No good. Joplin would forget, say something about a razor, and that would be that. Tell the story any way it didn't happen, Joplin would give it away; tell it the way it did happen, Martin walking in on a colored man, razor in hand, squatting over a dead white man, and Joplin was a dead colored man.

Martin looked from his teacher's bulging eyes to his open mouth, to his trembling fingers. Those fingers had been shaking so much lately, he'd been having trouble getting them onto the right piano keys. No, Martin, thought, he didn't kill Sid. Sid spent all day hauling sacks of vegetables and fruit, tossing them around like they weighed nothing. If Joplin had grabbed Sid, Sid would have made Hamburg steak out of him.

The bookkeeper tugged at the composer's sleeve. "Come on, Mr. Joplin—the cops'll be sure you or me or maybe even both of us did this. We've got to get out of here."

Joplin pulled away. "I've got to see Mr. Berlin, that's why I came here. He called me to come down to talk about my musical."

Martin blinked. How much crazier was this going to get? "Mr. Berlin *called* you?"

"Yes. About *If.* I think he wants to publish it and put it on stage. I've got to find him."

"But how would he know about it? We haven't taken it down to him yet."

Joplin turned away and started toward the door. Martin caught him with both arms, wrestled him against the wall. "Mr. Joplin, listen. Please. Mr. Berlin isn't here."

Joplin writhed and squirmed, but was no match for Martin's strong, healthy arms. "He *called* me, Martin. Let me go now, hear? I've got to see him."

"Damn it, Mr. Joplin, I told you, he is just…not…*here.* Please, Mr. Joplin, trust me. Right now, you and me have got to get someplace else, fast. Then, after we figure out what's going on, we can go talk to Mr. Berlin." Martin paused to catch his breath, glanced at the razor on the floor, beside Sid's hand. He'd read in the papers, police could sometimes use fingerprints to catch killers, and even he could see Scott Joplin's prints, clear as day, in the blood on that razor. Martin snatched it up, wiped it briskly on Sid's shirt sleeve, then folded it and dropped it into his pocket. "Mr. Joplin, take off your shirt, put it on inside-out. That way, the blood won't show so much. Your suit's OK, it just looks like dark stains. Come on, now, hurry up."

<>
<>
<>

Bartlett Tabor walked slowly up Broadway. The clock on the big billboard atop the roof of the Strand Theatre Building read six twenty-five; to the right of the clock, thick red letters stated it was TIME TO LIGHT A CHESTERFIELD. Time to check out Niederhoffer, Tabor thought. He walked into the building and up to the elevator, but then remembered, the operator left at five-thirty. He muttered a curse, and started up the stairs.

A couple of stairs down from the third floor, Martin heard footsteps. He put a hand on Joplin's arm, peered over the railing, saw Tabor, whispered a brief curse of his own, then put a finger to his lips and pulled the composer into the pass-through behind the elevator shaft. Carefully, he edged his head forward to watch the top of the stairwell. When he saw Tabor come up onto the landing, he ducked back to the far side of the space, pulling Joplin with him, then listened hard. Key in a lock…door opening… slamming shut. Martin blew out a sigh, then pulled Joplin from behind the elevator shaft and onto the stairwell. "Let's go!" he half-whispered.

Tabor walked through Reception and down the corridor to the bookkeeper's space. One step inside the doorway, he stopped cold at the sight of a body on the floor, sprawled in a lake of blood. Niederhoffer? Tabor rushed forward. No, not Niederhoffer. Who in hell—

Tabor sprang back from the body, flattened against the wall. The office was stone-quiet. He charged out, through the Reception Room, into the hallway, and leaned over the rail to peer down the stairwell. Footsteps, but all the way down—he'd never catch them. Back he charged through Reception and into his office, yanked the window up, and leaned forward just in time to get a clear view of a red-headed white man hustling a colored man out of the building, onto the sidewalk, and then out of sight past the Strand marquee. "Christ," Tabor muttered. "Niederhoffer—and that looks like Scott Joplin with him. God *damn* that crazy nigger." He banged a fist on the wall, then hurried back to the receptionist's desk and picked up the phone.

‹›‹›‹›

As Martin and Joplin shoved their way through the Broadway crowd toward the Fiftieth Street subway kiosk, a young man lowered himself into a dark-red plush armchair next to a gleaming mahogany grand piano in the living room of his suite in the Chatsworth Apartments on Seventy-second Street, just short of Riverside Drive. Six-thirty, the workday finished for most people, but this young man wasn't most people. He was Irving Berlin, Composer of A Hundred Hits, The Boy Who Revived Ragtime. When Irvy first saw light, twenty-eight years earlier, in Russia, he was Israel Baline. Six years later, the boy came with his family through Ellis Island, then grew up on the teeming streets of New York's lower east side, where he was known as Izzy. No one in the Great Land of Opportunity had a sharper eye for the main chance than Izzy Baline, but what the skinny little guy had in push, he lacked in polish, and so, when the newly-designed-and-labeled Irving Berlin moved uptown, he was determined to leave Izzy behind on Cherry Street. But a little thing like a court document changing his name was not nearly sufficient to convince the tenacious, rough-spoken Izzy he no longer existed. Where Irvy went, Izzy went, and he spoke his mind freely whenever he thought Irvy was in any way falling short.

Berlin eyeballed the magazine reporter, smoothing her skirt on the couch to his right. One of those women, flirting with forty, eats like a bird and smiles to herself when her friends call her Slim. Creamy silk blouse under a perfectly-tailored smart gray suit, blonde hair curling every which way from under the matching gray cloche hat. That sparkler on her left ring finger was a whole year's-worth of royalties from "Alexander's Ragtime Band" and then some. She's gotta be a sharp dame, not enough going on around the house to keep her busy and interested, so she writes articles for magazines. Respectable articles, respectable magazines. Kinda magazines where Irving Berlin's name needs to be.

The composer cleared his throat. "Sorry to be a little late, Mrs. Allred, but I had some pressing business. I'm writing a musical with Victor Herbert for Flo Ziegfeld, and the time's getting to be pretty short." He lowered his jaw just enough to part his lips, then opened his eyes wide and dropped his gaze. He chuckled, just the right bit of self-deprecation.

It worked. It always did with woman-reporters. Mrs. Allred smiled openly. "That's all right, Mr. Berlin. Your butler made me very comfortable. And considering how busy you are, it was good of you to fit me in at all."

"Well, you said your deadline was in the morning." Berlin extended his hands in an extravagant shrug. "So what could we do, huh?" Big smile. Pain in the ass, but it'd be crazy to kiss off a feature piece in *Green Book*.

Mrs. Allred pulled a notebook from her purse, flipped it open, said, "I do appreciate that, and I'll try not to keep you too long. My piece will be titled, 'How The Ragtime King Writes His Songs.'"

"I guess I can help you with that, all right." Berlin gestured at the lustrous grand. People think I just sit down at the piano, hit maybe a couple of keys, half an hour, and boom, there's my next hit song." Quick finger-snap. "But that's not how it goes. A song's kinda like a kid, you know, bashful, but maybe a little bit of a wisenheimer, it stands there sticking out its tongue at me, and it goes, 'Nyah, nyah. Betcha can't catch me.' But I sit at the piano and play and play, because I know the song's there, all right, and if I don't let the kid get my goat, sooner or later, I *am* gonna nail it."

He ratcheted the corners of his lips for the lady. Sweet, endearing little Irving Berlin, just a tiny bit embarrassed.

"I'm sure that must be very frustrating, Mr. Berlin."

"Quick flash of panic. 'I'm sure that must be very frustrating, Mr. Berlin'. Sarcastic? And that smile on her face—was she mocking him? He rushed to speak. "No, it ain't…that is, it *isn't* frustrating, not really. Just part of the game. That's why a good songwriter can't be on any kind of a schedule. I'm *always* writing songs. The tune I was working on last night? It's in my head right now. Even while I'm talking to you."

The woman's smile covered her face. "Would I be presumptuous…that is, would you be willing to play that tune for me?" She pointed. "On your piano. It would be just fascinating."

"Well, sure, why not? Berlin stood, then walked slowly to the piano, stretching his fingers as he went. Draw the woman's eyes to his hands, and maybe she won't notice how he's only five-six. He slid onto the piano bench, looked back at the interviewer. "Remember a little while ago, I told you what I'm working on right now?"

"Yes, of course. Mr. Ziegfeld's new revue. Victor Herbert and you. It's called *The Century Girl*, isn't it?"

Izzy cackled. *"Herbert and you! Not you and Herbert."*

God damn it, she *was* mocking him. Irving Berlin was a songwriter, but Victor Herbert didn't just write songs. He composed serious music, conducted orchestras, played instrumental solos. Next to Victor Herbert, Irving Berlin was a singing waiter with a *shtick*. Berlin willed himself to keep talking. "I'm working on this one particular song," he said, then turned to the piano and tossed the rest of his comments back over his shoulder. "It's for Hazel Dawn, a duet for her to sing with one of the male leads. I'm calling it 'Alice in Wonderland.'"

He began to play a musical theme, a bit hesitantly, then picked up speed. Mrs. Allred leaned forward to peer over his shoulder. Perfume like that, she didn't buy at the Five and Dime. Berlin felt sweat pop out across his forehead; a drop ran down from his armpit. "Mr. Berlin—you *do* play only on the black keys, don't you?"

"Nigger keys." Izzy snickered. Show-biz lingo, everyone said it, even the colored. But Berlin knew better than to say it to a woman-reporter, never mind a society woman-reporter. Instead, he said, "That's right. I compose in F-sharp major. The key of C is for people who study music."

The woman smiled. Going along with the gag? Or patronizing him? Keep talking, just keep talking. "Wait'll you hear this song in the theater. It's going to be one of my best. Most of the lyrics, I've got already." His fingers tapped out the first theme again. "All I need now is to make the music—"

"Fit," said Mrs. Allred, just a little too brightly for Berlin's taste.

"Yeah. That's right."

"And of course you will."

Berlin moved to take back control over the interview. "I know what—I'm gonna get you tickets for opening night. Then, you can let me know if I made it fit right. How's that sound?"

"Why, I'd be delighted," Mrs. Allred crooned. "I'm certain you'll make it fit, and I know I'll simply love the song. Particularly after having been present at its birth."

"At least during the labor," said Berlin, then winced as Izzy slapped his face. *"Schmuck! One thing with the boys or chorus girls at rehearsals. But this is a society woman. You don't talk about stuff like that in front of her."*

"I...I'm sorry," Berlin stammered. "I hope I didn't offend you."

Mrs. Allred looked surprised, then confused, then finally burst into a full-throated laugh. "Oh, Mr. Berlin, no, of course not. You didn't offend me in the least. And even if you did, I wouldn't have valid grounds for complaint, would I? After all, I was your straight man." She glanced down at her pad, pursed her lips, then looked back to the songwriter. "May I ask you just one more question?"

Berlin resisted a fierce urge to look at his watch. He'd sooner sweep floors for an hour than give an interview, but every reader was one more potential sheet music buyer. And of course, once the articles were written, he loved to read them. Shy smile. "Well, yes. Of course. What's the question."

"You've been so very successful, writing popular tunes, and musical theater as well. But you've been saying for a couple of years now that you're going to write a ragtime opera with the story set in the south. 'Syncopation for peoples' hearts as well as for their toes?'. Is that an accurate quote? *Theatre Magazine?*"

Berlin swiped his hands against the sides of his pants legs. "You've been reading about me."

"Oh yes. I always try to know my subjects as well as I can before I interview them. How are you coming along with that opera?"

Berlin thought frantically. This society-broad scribbler knew better than he did what he'd said to other reporters, and the last thing he wanted to do was contradict himself. "An opera...now that *is* a project. But in the meanwhile, a man needs to make a living. I work at the opera when I've got a few minutes here and there. Not saying I wouldn't like to, but I can't just up and take off a year or two to turn out—"

Mrs. Allred smiled. "Donizetti wrote *Don Pasquale* in two weeks."

"Oh sure. Sure he did! But Donizetti was studying music from before he even got outa diapers. When the damn guinea was just a kid, he was playing a violin in front of fancy people. When I was a kid, I was waiting tables at Nigger Mike's, singing dirty songs so they'd throw nickels at me".

Berlin picked up on the alarm in the woman's eyes as she moved a step away from him. He muscled Izzy aside, and said quietly, "I think things were a little bit different for a composer those days."

"Oh, Mr. Berlin." Never mind her well-applied face powder, Mrs. Allred's name described her complexion. "I'm terribly sorry. I didn't mean to offend you. It's just that your songs and shows are so popular and so wonderful, you've got us all curious over your opera. I'm just dying to hear it."

"Well, you will, you can count on it." Delivered through the most ingratiating smile in his repertoire. "Here, let me show you something." He led his guest past the piano to an inbuilt bookshelf, filled with every piece of European literature Robert Miras could find, all in the classiest leather bindings. On the lowest shelf, waist-high, sat two Swiss music boxes. Berlin opened one, a fair-sized rectangular case with an impressive inlay of brass, ebony and enamel on the lid and across the front. He turned the oval-headed key that stuck out from the left side of the box, then pushed a small lever beneath the key. Music began to play. Berlin pointed to the little brass plate inside the opened lid. "See, now, Mrs. Allred, this is 'La Donna Mobile.'" He pronounced the last word, 'Mo-beel.' "By Verdi, from his opera, *Rigoletto*. Nice, huh?"

Mrs. Allred nodded. "Lovely. Just exquisite."

When the music stopped, Berlin said, "Okay, now," and opened the second box, a much smaller one with a decal featuring musical instruments on its lid. The mechanism inside was about one-third the size of the first one, and when Berlin started the music playing, Mrs. Allred fought to keep her feelings off her face. The tone of the first machine had been rich and full, the musical arrangement gorgeously ornamented, but this box spoke in painfully strident tones as it played a pedestrian arrangement of some popular song she'd heard a few years back. The tune finished, but Berlin let the box play on. A few bars into the second melody, Mrs. Allred said, "Oh…why, that's *your* song, Mr. Berlin, isn't it?"

If Berlin had been a cat and Mrs. Allred a canary, it would have been all over right then. "Sure, that's my tune, but so was the first one. That was 'When the Midnight Choo-Choo Leaves for Alabam,' and now you're hearing 'Alexander's Ragtime Band.' See, the other box was made in Eighteen-sixty-something, back when Verdi's music was popular. This one was made just a couple of years ago, so it's got my music on it. You gotta give the people what they want. Back then it was Verdi, now it's Berlin. So, yeah, one of these years, you're definitely going to hear my opera. And I'll tell you something else. If a syncopated opera isn't high-class enough for the Met, I'll take it over to Broadway and call it a musical play in syncopation. And everybody except maybe the Juilliard profs'll love it. I'll be sure and send you comps for that, too. I don't forget."

The woman smiled, closed her pad, slipped it into her purse. She extended a gloved hand. "I'm sure I'll be applauding madly, Mr. Berlin, thank you. And thank you for taking the time to talk with me."

"No trouble. No trouble at all. My pleasure."

As Berlin opened the door to the hall for Mrs. Allred, he saw himself reflected in the reporter's eyes: a sawed-off runt, swarthy, scrawny as a starved cat, all got up in an expensive dark blue summer-worsted suit, sharp lapels, vest to match, perfect tie, spotless neckband starched to the limit. Shoes shined, clean-shaved, not a trace of five-o'clock shadow. Dark, wavy hair pomaded to the nines, cleanly parted on the left. But with his grand piano in his luxury apartment facing Riverside Drive, Mr. Irving Berlin was just a brassy little...what was that French word he knew they called him behind his back? Parvenu, yeah. He could call himself Irving Berlin till he was blue in the face, but to people like Mrs. Allred, he'd still and always be Izzy Baline, a cheeky little kike from down on Cherry Street. A parvenu. She'd probably crucify him in the article.

She didn't, though. Never even thought to do it. As she walked slowly back to her office, she felt the article start to grow in her head; she tried to encourage it. Yes, it *was* like trying to persuade a bashful child to come forward—why, what a marvelous thought. Such a clever man, Irving Berlin, such a talented young songwriter. So sad, though, and strange. Standing in his doorway as he said goodbye, he'd seemed positively forlorn, looking for all the world like the timorous child holding the key to his own song. She'd wanted to put her arms around him and tell him not to worry, he'd get it right, everything would be fine. But she'd hurried away down the hall, heat radiating from her face, feeling as ashamed as if she'd abandoned a lost and frightened little boy.

Chapter Four

*Harlem
Tuesday, August 22
About 7pm*

Lottie heard the pounding at the door from all the way back in the kitchen. Sure trouble, that kind of knock. She sighed, turned off the burner under the cornmeal pancake, hurried through the living room into the hall, opened the door a crack—whereupon her husband and that Martin kid burst through. One look at their faces, and Lottie slammed the door shut and threw the bolt. Oh yes, trouble, all right, big trouble. "Somebody comin' right up after you?"

Joplin and Martin, four wide eyes, two open mouths, two heaving chests, stared at each other. Finally, Martin spoke. "Not for a little while, anyway."

Lottie looked Joplin up and down. Aside from his shirt being on inside-out, and those dark stains on his clothes, he seemed all right, not any more worked up than Martin. She pointed toward the living room. "Come on inside and sit down, the both of you, and tell me what's goin' on".

Martin scratched here, twitched there, as he told a short version of the story. Joplin sat and looked idly around the room. Like he don't even *know* what happened, Lottie thought. Sweet Jesus, where is this all gonna end?

"I figured I'd better get him up here," Martin said. "I didn't know where else to go with him."

Lottie nodded. "No good havin' an anchor around your ankle when you're tryin' to run from the police." She stood. "You just sit there a minute, the two a you. I be right back." She walked out into the hall.

Not three minutes later, she was back. "All right, now." She took Joplin by the elbow, led him into the bedroom. A few minutes later, they were back, Joplin wearing clean clothing, not a trace of blood on him. Lottie motioned the men to the fire escape. "Best nobody sees us goin' out the front door." They all scrambled onto the platform, then Lottie pulled the window shut behind them and led her charges down the ladder to the alley below.

<>‹›‹›

Nell Stanley turned a very hard eye onto the trio as they scampered into her apartment, then ushered them through the little vestibule and into the living room. Joplin and Martin sat on the sofa, while Lottie lowered herself into a straight-backed chair. Nell pointed at an overstuffed armchair. "Wouldn't you be more comfortable there?"

One side of Lottie's mouth curled upward. "Prob'ly so. But sometimes it ain't the best idea for a person to get too comfortable."

Nell nodded. She picked up a wooden tray from the table in front of the sofa, gave each of her guests a glass of iced tea, then settled into the armchair.

Lottie spoke first. "Thanks for lettin' us come by here, Nell. Martin did right, bringin' Scott home, but I knew he couldn't stay there. Anybody wants to go lookin' for him, that's the first stop they gonna make."

"That and *my* family's apartment," said Martin, then squirmed as Nell turned her gaze onto him.

"Tell her, boy," Lottie said. "Tell the lady what-all happened."

Nell leaned forward to take in Martin's every word. When he finished his story, she said, "Well, I'm sure the police *would* have looked on the two of you with a good deal of suspicion. But now, when they catch up with you, they're going to be even more suspicious. Particularly of you, Martin—it was your office and your friend. What were you and…what was his name?"

"Sid. Sid Altman."

"Fine. What were you and Sid doing there after hours, anyway?"

"Putting in overtime."

Nell started to tell the young man this was no time to crack wise, but he wasn't through talking. "I spent most of yesterday going through some numbers for Mr. Tabor, he's the office manager. They proved one of the partners, Mr. Waterson, is skimming profits. It's no secret he plays the horses, so maybe he needs to pay off some losses. But that made me fall behind on this month's sales figures, and Mr. Tabor said I had to get them caught up tonight. Sid usually comes by on his way home from work, and we go the rest of the way together—us and Birdie, my girlfriend, she works at W, B, and S too. But her old man makes a fuss when she's late getting home, so she left on time, and Sid waited for me."

"And you went to the bathroom, came back, and found Mr. Joplin there holding…" Nell looked at the razor Martin had set on the piano bench next to Stark. "I don't see anything unusual there—no initials, no carvings. Just a plain black razor."

"Mine's back home—I can show you. In the bathroom, where it belongs."

The first words out of Joplin. Nell had thought he wasn't paying the least attention, that his mind was off somewhere, trying to put together a line of music. She waved off his concern. "No need, Scott. I wouldn't believe for a minute that you killed that young man."

Martin wondered whether there was anything to the fact that Nell didn't say, 'either of you'.

"Well, of course not, of course I didn't." Joplin spat words like bullets from a machine-gun, punctuating them with jabs of a shaking index finger. "I went down there because Irving Berlin called me. I think he wants to publish *If.* I should have stayed there and found him. I should not have let Martin take me away."

Nell felt pity mixed with annoyance. Joplin, all his life such a reserved, dignified man, was operating at the level of a child, and not a very bright child at that. She felt a fury at the disease that was turning that marvelous brain into mush, then told herself she was being as irrational as Joplin. The situation was as it was, and her job was simply to do what she could to help. As if from a distance away, she heard Martin say, "...never knew Mr. Joplin took his music to Mr. Berlin. We were supposed to go together."

Nell held up a hand, palm out, a patrolman at a conversational corner with heavy traffic on all sides. "All right, Martin, wait with that for now." She turned to Lottie. "We need to get the two of them somewhere safe while we try to figure out what's going on, but neither one of us can keep them. The police will certainly visit you, and they'll probably find out how close I've been to you and Scott, and come here, too. I'm going to call Joe Lamb. I'll bet he'll put them up."

"Hmmmm." Lottie's uncertainty showed all over her face. "Ain't seen Joe in near a year, now. Used to be, there was always a bunch of Scott's friends stoppin' by, Sam Patterson, Bob Slater, Wilbur Sweatman, Will Spiller...so many of them. Joe sometimes came up and played, and he would wow 'em—a white man writin' and playin' real colored rags like he did. But the way Scott locks himself up these days...you think Joe'll be willin' to do that?"

"I'm sure he will. He adores Scott. Every time I see him, he has a new story to tell me about some way Scott has helped him." Tight little smile. "And it won't hurt that Dad published three of Joe's rags last year, one so far this year, and has another one coming up in November."

"But ain't the cops gonna go talk to him, too?"

Nell shook her head. "I don't think so. There's nothing to connect him to Scott. He's just a young white man who leaves Brooklyn to get to his job by nine, then comes home at five o'clock to his wife and baby. He doesn't play in clubs, doesn't even go to them. Yes, he does write ragtime that Dad publishes, but the police aren't going to pick his name off a sheet music cover and go after him."

"Mmmm." Lottie rubbed at her chin, then snickered. "Nell, if they took women in the army, I expect you'd be a general in nothing flat."

On her way to the phone on the little table between the sofa and the armchair, Nell said, "I learned at the feet of the master." Then she thumbed through a small book, held it open with one hand while she took the earpiece off the hook and pressed it to the side of her head. "Yes, operator. Please give me Prospect 4025... Joe, hello, this is Nell Stanley. I've got a little problem and need your help."

〈〉〈〉〈〉

Bartlett Tabor wondered whether these goddamn cops were ever going to leave. His evening was shot. He'd had to call and cancel his date, a real looker, and she'd made it clear enough that she thought he was feeding her a line, and there'd be icicles in hell before she'd ever go out with *him* again. When these flatfeet were done, he'd grab a quick dinner, alone, then go back to his place and hit the sack, alone. Damn!

"Mr. Tabor..."

Tabor blinked himself back. The older man, an olive-skinned fireplug in a dark brown suit, fedora to match, who'd introduced himself as Detective Niccolo Ciccone, stood over him. "Yes?"

"I just want to be sure I have this straight. You were here tonight because...?"

The dick had the face of a beagle in mourning. Tabor looked up at his spare tire and rounded shoulders, then blew a windy sigh. "I've told you—"

"Tell me again." Fatso smirked. "Humor me."

If the son of a bitch wasn't a cop, Tabor thought, I'd humor him, all right. With my knee to his nuts. "Okay, Detective. Niederhoffer, the bookkeeper, was behind in his work, and we needed to get the month's figures straight. So I made the kid stay overtime. At five o'clock, when the office closed for the day, I went up to Mr. Berlin's, on Seventy-second Street, to give him some papers. He wasn't in, so I left them with Miras, his valet. It was still early, so I stopped at Houlihan's, on Broadway, and had a couple of drinks. Then I figured I'd better make sure Niederhoffer had the work done, so I went on back to the office. I got there just about six twenty-five. There was a man on the floor in Bookkeeping, blood all over everything. I didn't see or hear anybody in the office, but when I went over to the window, I saw Niederhoffer going out the door and down the street. I recognized him by that red hair of his. He had a colored man with him, Scott Joplin, we've published some of his music. It looked like Joplin was having some trouble walking, and Niederhoffer was hustling him along. Then I grabbed the phone and called you. That's it."

The detective pursed his lips. "Okay. You don't happen to have this Niederhoffer's address, do you? Or Joplin's?"

"Niederhoffer's, yes, it's out at the front desk. I'll get it for you. Joplin lives someplace up in Harlem."

The young cop in uniform, an angular beanpole Ciccone had introduced as Patrolman Flaherty, took off his cap, releasing a head of thick blond hair that looked to Tabor like it had been cut with a lawnmower. The cop wiped his forehead and laughed. "Great. We can just go out and look for a nigger in Harlem."

The plainclothes detective shot Flaherty a look that got the patrolman's cap back onto his head in a hurry, straightened his spine, and closed his mouth.

Tabor smiled privately, then started to walk to the front desk, but Ciccone called him back. "One other thing. Do Mr. Waterson, Mr. Berlin, or Mr. Snyder know about what happened here?

Tabor shook his head. "Mr. Waterson left a little early today. It's been pretty hot, and he was starting to look thirsty."

Patrolman Flaherty guffawed. Ciccone confined himself to a polite smile.

"And Mr. Berlin's been mostly working at home lately. That's where he does his composing, and he's got a new musical opening in a couple of months. He just comes in now and then to check up on things."

"When's the last time he came in to check on something?"

"Earlier in the afternoon."

"What time did he leave?"

Tabor paused, then shrugged. "I'm not sure. I didn't see him go out."

"And he wasn't at his home a little after five, when you went to see him."

"No. His valet said he was working someplace with Victor Herbert on their musical."

Ciccone scribbled on his notepad. "All right. How about Mr. Snyder."

"He's been away all week, on vacation. Atlantic City."

Ciccone nodded. "Okay. Would you please get me their addresses too."

Tabor walked off, down the hallway. He was back in just a couple of minutes, holding a piece of yellow lined paper to the detective. Ciccone scanned the list. "Niederhoffer…fifteen eighty-two Madison…okay. Waterson…Berlin…Snyder…" He looked up to Tabor. "Who's this other person? 'Birdie Kuminsky?"

"Niederhoffer's girlfriend," said Tabor. "She works here too, assistant bookkeeper. Kid can't keep his eyes or his hands off her. That's probably why he didn't get his work done on time. I figured if you didn't find him at his own place, maybe he'd be at hers."

"Good. Appreciate your help." The detective folded the paper into his breast pocket, then jabbed a hitchhiker's thumb toward the bloody desk, and cracked a wry smile. "Did he get the numbers done before he left?"

Tabor shook his head. "Nope. A lot more blood on the damn page than pen marks."

The detective laughed. Tabor smiled.

"Just one more thing, Mr. Tabor. Do you have any trips coming up soon?"

"No. And I guess if I did, you'd want me to cancel them."

"You're right. I'm asking you to stay in New York for now. Just in case we come up with some other questions."

<>◇<>

Joe Lamb looked like he'd had a hard day. He slouched in his armchair, peering through a wide cowlick at Nell, who perched on the edge of an armchair across a little coffee table from him. When a shake of his head didn't clear his vision, he absently brushed the hair back off his forehead with his fingers.

Nell thought he was fighting to keep his eyes open. "Joe, I'm sorry. I just didn't know what else—"

Lamb pulled himself straighter. "Don't give it another thought. If Mr. Joplin needs help, I'm glad to do whatever I can. Why don't you tell me what this is all about."

Nell looked to the sofa where Martin and Joplin sat side-by-side. Joplin rested his head back against the cushion, looking off into the distance. Nell thought how misleading appearances could be. With his red hair and blue eyes, Martin could easily be taken for an Irish Catholic, and Lamb, with his round, dark eyes and hawk's-bill nose, could be mistaken for a Jew. "All right," Nell said. "There's been a murder, something to do with a piece of music Scott left with Irving Berlin." She crooked a finger at Martin. "Why don't we start at the beginning. Tell Mr. Lamb—and me, for that matter—the whole story. Including how *you* came to be involved."

Lamb shook his head, chuckled. "You can call me Joe."

Martin glanced at Joplin, then looked back to Lamb and Nell. "Well, last Thursday was the beginning. I went up to Mr. Joplin's for my piano lesson, he gives me one every week. I got there a little early, so Mrs. Joplin gave me a piece of pecan pie, and we sat and talked. She told me how she was glad I came to Mr. Joplin for lessons, that he used to be daddy to a whole bunch of young composers and players, but now they all go somewhere else, and play other music. I was just telling her how I didn't think there was any other music that could compare to one of his rags, when bang, the door flies open and he's standing in the room. And the look on his face! I was scared. He started yelling about Lester Walton—"

"Lester Walton!"

Everyone turned to Joplin.

"Lester Walton wrote me up for years, and in a most complimentary fashion. But now he says what I write isn't worth wasting space in the trash can." The composer rose from the sofa, stumbled, regained his footing, and walked across the little hooked rug to stand over Nell. "I'm the King of Ragtime, but they're all against me now, all of them out to deny my name..."

Joplin sounded like a phonograph running low on spring power. Nell sprang out of her chair, took him by the arm, and helped him back to the sofa. He sat, then turned his head and gazed toward the window. Nell heard him start to hum a soft, syncopated melody. She looked to Martin, and with a motion of her head, told him to go on.

Martin shifted to sit a little farther from the composer. "Well, Mrs. Joplin tried calming him down, but he wouldn't have any of it. He told me he couldn't give me a lesson then, I'd have to come back some other time, and that's when I got my idea. I told him I thought maybe I could help him, and why didn't we talk about it. He stopped yelling, and said, 'You are serious?' 'Darn right,' I told him. 'Maybe the Lafayette Theater is the tops in Harlem, but there have been colored revues and musicals on Broadway for more than fifteen years already, and I think that's where you're gonna get the most attention *and* the most money. I work at Waterson, Berlin, and Snyder, and I've met Mr. Ber—'"

Martin paused mid-sentence to look at Joplin; when there was no reaction from the composer, he turned back to face Nell and Lamb. "Well, when I said...that name, Mr. Joplin jumped up on his feet, and leaned all the way across the table, right in my face. 'Boy, have you lost your mind?' he yelled at me. 'Or are you in thick with that thief? Trying to help him steal more of my music to make his fortune and reputation.' 'Please, Mr. Joplin,' I said. 'I want to help *you*. Just listen to me a minute. Mr. Berlin's opened up another office, just for show-tune music, and all the talk at W, B, and S is about how he wants to make it big on Broadway. Think about what a splash he could make with a Scott Joplin musical play. Especially if he thought the Shuberts were interested."

"The Shuberts?" The look on Nell's face sent Martin's Adam's apple into a quick up-and-down. "The Shuberts wouldn't even let Scott into their waiting room. Or you, for that matter."

Martin's voice went up half an octave. "I thought we could just *tell* Mr. Berlin the Shuberts were interested. He'd never check it out. He hates them."

Joe Lamb burst into a full-throated laugh. Nell couldn't decide whether to be amused by the young man's nervy hot air, or wake him up with a good smack on the cheek.

Martin scrambled back to safer conversational ground. "Well, never mind about the Shuberts. Mainly, I thought if I went with Mr. Joplin to see Mr. Berlin, then Mr. Berlin would know he couldn't steal the music. And I'd be right there in the office, watching. I'd pick up on any funny stuff the minute it started to happen."

Joe Lamb cleared his throat. "Does there happen to be anything in this for you?"

"Me? Well, yeah. Besides helping Mr. Joplin, if Mr. Berlin thinks I'm a go-getter, maybe then I'd get to be more than a bookkeeper. What's wrong with that? There's a girl—"

"*Cherchez la femme.*" Now, Nell smiled.

Lamb laughed. "Happens in the best of families. But go on, Martin. What happened when you and Mr. Joplin talked to Berlin?"

Nell rested a hand on Lamb's arm. "That's not the way it went, Joe. Lottie told me Scott took it into his head yesterday to go talk to Berlin by himself."

Lamb pressed his lips together, and nodded.

"Then, today, about five o'clock, Berlin called and asked Scott to come right down and talk about the play."

"That's odd." Lamb scratched his cheek. "To call at the very end of the business day."

Martin broke in. "No, actually it's not odd, not if you know Mr. Berlin. He mostly comes in when nobody's around to bother him, goes right to his office, and locks the door. I usually don't know if he's there or not. I didn't see him all day yesterday, which doesn't mean a lot, but I never saw Mr. Joplin either. If he did come down, wouldn't he have come and gotten me to talk to Mr. Berlin with him?"

"Scott told Lottie you were out to lunch," Nell said.

Martin smacked his open palm against his forehead. "Lunchtime, sure. Mr. Berlin writes his music all night, then he goes to bed and doesn't get up till about noontime. And then he sometimes comes down to the office, while all the help is at lunch."

For a moment, everyone sat silent. Then, Lamb said, "I guess it really doesn't matter whether or not Berlin was in his office at five o'clock today. He could have called Mr. Joplin from somewhere else, his other office, his home, then gone to meet him. He looked at the composer. "Mr. Joplin."

No response.

Nell walked over, leaned into Joplin's face, smiled. "Scott… *Scott.*"

Joplin blinked once, twice.

"Scott, Joe wants to ask you something."

"Well, all right. Let him ask. He doesn't need permission." As if he'd been listening, heard every word.

"Mr. Joplin, I'm trying to figure out what happened this afternoon. Irving Berlin called you—"

"That's right. Irving Berlin called me up on the phone and said to come down, he needed to talk to me about *If*. My musical. But he wasn't there."

Lamb gave the persistent cowlick another finger-combing. "You walked right in to the office? The door was unlocked?"

Martin waved a hand like a third-grader who knows he's got the answer to the teacher's question. "I never thought about that. They always lock the office door after hours. You can get out, but you can't get back in. When I went to the mens' room, I left the door open a crack so I wouldn't be locked out, but when I came back, it was wide open. I didn't think anything about it, but I should have."

As Martin spoke, Joplin studied his face as if the key to an enigma were written across the young man's forehead. "Yes... yes. That's right. I forgot..."

Everyone leaned toward him.

"I forgot all about it till just now. The door *was* open. And while I was coming down the hall on my way to the office, a man ran past me, nearly knocked me over, and then went running on down the hall. Maybe he came out of Waterson, Berlin, and Snyder, and didn't shut the door behind him."

"What did he look like, Scott? That man?" Nell's voice was gentle, a mother talking to a hesitant child.

Joplin shook his head. "He was out and by me before I could even think about it."

"You can't remember anything? Was he old? Young? Big? Small? White? Colored? *Anything?*"

Joplin kept shaking his head. "No... I just didn't notice anything. I was looking in a window..." The image of the colored janitor came back to his mind like a pain somewhere deep inside his brain. "And he caught me on the shoulder and threw me into the wall. He was gone down the stairs before I could get any kind of look at him. But I guess he was pretty big—it felt like I got hit by a horse."

Nell smiled encouragement at Joplin. "All right. What happened next?"

"I went inside, and I saw Martin there... well, I thought it was Martin, asleep on his desk. I wondered if Berlin had talked to him, and he was going to be at our meeting. So I went to wake him up. But then I saw it wasn't Martin—he was a blond man." Joplin paused to let that bitter recollection pass. "And I saw he had his throat cut, there was blood everywhere. I saw a razor on the floor, and I picked it up. Then, Martin came in." Joplin turned suddenly to Lamb. "Joe, you got any music paper?" As if that were a perfectly logical next remark.

"Well, yes, of course. It's in the bench."

"Good. Thank you." Joplin pulled himself to his feet, and walked slowly across the room to the upright piano against the wall. "Got to write down the music I had in my head when Nell broke in there." He lifted the bench lid, pulled out a couple of sheets of lined paper, set them on the piano rack. Then he leaned forward, struck a few keys, scribbled on the paper.

"I thought your play was done, Scott," said Nell.

"It is." Over his shoulder. "Now, I'm working on my *Symphony Number One*. I got to get it finished while I still can." He turned back to his work.

Nell thought Lamb might be about to shed tears, and if he did, she certainly would.

"What about you, Martin?" Lamb's voice was husky. "Where were you when Mr. Joplin came in?"

"Bathroom, like I said. I needed a break."

"You were there how long?"

"Ten, maybe twelve, minutes." The expression on Lamb's face brought an embarrassed little laugh from the young man. "I was goofing off 'cause I was sore about Mr. Tabor making me stay to get those figures ready for morning. I figured he could just pay me a little more overtime."

"But when you saw what had happened, why *didn't* you call the police? They're going to make a lot out of the fact that you both ran away."

Martin glanced at Joplin, now seated on the piano bench, composing in earnest. The young man crab-walked past the coffee table to squat between Nell and Lamb. "When I came in that room, there was Mr. Joplin, standing over Sid's body, holding a bloody razor in his hand, blood all over *him*." A hoarse whisper. "I didn't want to have to explain *that* to the cops." Martin jerked a thumb in Joplin's direction. "I was afraid the cops'd get him upset and if he started yelling, they might've hurt him, maybe even killed him. Besides, Sid was a big guy, strong like an ox. He hauled fruit around the market all day. The way Mr. Joplin shakes, and sometimes stumbles around when he walks? I can't see any way Mr. Joplin could've killed Sid."

Lamb nodded. "So you were the only person still in the office? Except for your friend?"

"Far as I know. Mr. Tabor went out with everybody else at five o'clock. He told me to leave the work on his desk, he was gonna come back some time to check it so he'd know before tomorrow where we stood on the month's numbers. He didn't want to get caught short if Mr. Berlin came by."

"But you just said Berlin doesn't come in till noontime at the earliest," said Nell. "That would have given Tabor all morning."

"Mr. Tabor always checks the numbers before he goes home at night. He says he likes to run a tight ship."

Lamb grunted. "Well, I guess that's really not here or there. You didn't happen to hear anyone coming into the office?"

Martin shook his head. "I wish."

"All right." Lamb paused, tapped a finger several times on the arm of his chair. "Martin, I'm sorry to bring this up, but what about the idea that *you* might have killed your friend—"

"And then I just went to the bathroom and hung around a little?"

"You could have gone to wash off blood."

"I didn't have any on my clothes. Besides, there was that razor."

"What do you shave with?"

"Jesus Christ, what are you saying?" Martin jumped to his feet, fists clenched, eyes sizzling. "Sure, I use a razor, but it's at my place—"

Nell moved between the furious young man and Lamb. "Calm down, Martin. Joe's not accusing you."

"I'm just trying to think about every possibility that will occur to the police," Lamb said. "Martin, your friend Sid wasn't interested in your girlfriend, was he? Or she in him?"

Martin's face flushed to the color of a ripe plum. "Sid wasn't interested in girls…any girls." Then, louder, "And Birdie's only interested in me, she never even looks at any other guys. Come on. You don't really think I did it, do you."

Lamb and Nell said, "No" in unison. Everyone smiled, if the smiles were just a bit tight. Again, Lamb brushed back the cowlick. Except for the sounds from Joplin at the piano, the room was silent.

Finally, Nell said, "It's all right with you, then, Joe? You don't mind having Scott and Martin stay here while we try to sort this out?"

"Not at all. Etty and the baby are off with her sister to the mountains, and they won't be back till next week. There's plenty of room. Even a small house like this one has a lot more space than most apartments in Manhattan. If one of them doesn't mind sleeping on a couch—"

"I don't mind," Martin chirped. "And I really appreciate you helping, Mr. Lamb. I'm sorry I got sore at you."

Lamb smiled. "That's all right." Then, to Nell, "I wish your father were here. When there's a problem, that man is like a bulldog with a bone."

"Careful what you wish for," said Nell. "He's on his way. I called him yesterday, after Scott came back from Berlin's with a big cut on his forehead—"

"I noticed. What happened."

Nell coughed. "He says he walked into a door. In any case, Dad should be here tomorrow. He thinks he just has to deal with Irving Berlin about Scott's music."

"He doesn't know about the murder." Lamb whistled.

Nell smiled through clenched teeth. "He'll find out soon enough."

◇◇◇

John Stark, in his three-piece blue summer-worsted suit, straw hat in his lap, looked out the window of the railroad car, then checked his watch. All windows were wide open but the smell of perspiring humanity filled the crowded car. Can't complain, Stark thought, I'm sure I'm doing my share. He wiped at his face with an already-soggy handkerchief. A lovely girl, dark-haired and slender, carried a light cardboard suitcase down the aisle toward him, and the old man's stomach lurched. She wasn't a great deal older than Meggy, and what was a seventy-five year old man doing, staring like that? The girl reminded him of Sarah, not yet seventeen when he married her, and for the next forty-five years, never mind the wrinkles, the gray hair, or the thirty extra pounds, Stark never stopped seeing her the way she'd looked at sixteen. The girl caught Stark's eye, and smiled, a benediction. Stark smiled back. He and Sarah would've been married fifty-one years now.

The conductor leaned out the window, shouted something Stark couldn't make out. Two boys ran off, away from the car. The woman sitting across the aisle from Stark harrumphed. "Tryin'a hitch a ride," she said. "Serve 'em right if they fell under the wheels and lost a leg or an arm. That'd teach 'em."

The downturned corners of the woman's mouth stood witness to the sincerity of her declaration. She was about Stark's age, stringy gray hair, skinny and mean in a black cotton dress, two shopping bags between her feet. Stark felt weary. He moved away from the woman, into the window seat, and watched the boys disappear into Union Station. When he was their age, he'd done his share of mischief, some of it as dangerous as trying to hitch a ride on a train. Those long, hot summer days seemed to have been created just for the sake of mischief. School closed, planting done, harvesting in the future. Easy enough to get the farmwork done by lunchtime, then off to the bank of the White River to go fishing, or swim. Or sprawl under a tree with a book. And there were the girls, all so pretty in their white summer dresses. Stark and his friends would take them on picnics, or to the fair. The time from late May to late August once had seemed endless, but Stark knew this summer would be gone in the blink of an eye, strawberries ripened and eaten, frost coming on.

The New Yorker started up, pulled out of Union Station, rumbled slowly through East St. Louis, then picked up speed, rolling hellbent for leather through Missouri farmland. Staring through the window into cornfield rows that stretched as far as he could see, Stark saw blue lines of soldiers, marching between the corn-rows, headed south. *John Brown's body lies a-mold'ring in the grave…* Some dreams fade over time, but the older he got, the more that one cursed dream of his came around to torment him. He'd never have had the dream at all if he'd never enlisted in the Indiana Heavy Artillery Volunteers, but then he'd never have gone to New Orleans, never met Sarah, nor a fifteen-year-old colored boy named Isaac who would have been shot dead by the very Union soldiers he'd saved from an ambush. If the price of sleep without nightmares was Sarah, his three children, and the best friend he'd ever had, he'd pay without a second thought.

Thinking of Isaac, just an hour or so earlier, swinging forward on his crutches across the platform toward the train, made Stark smile. "Wisht I could come with you, Mr. Stark." The colored man jabbed an accusing finger at the white plaster cast on his left leg. "But I'd be more hindrance than help." Stark knew better than to argue, just nodded, said good-bye, and shook his friend's hand. But as he turned to board the train, Isaac grabbed him by the arm, then reached around the crutch with his free hand. "Here," a hoarse whisper. "If'n I can't go, I'm gonna send a trusty friend to look after you." Stark stared at the old Civil War pistol, felt his heart go racing out of control. The gun looked clean, freshly oiled. "You take it now." Isaac thrust it into Stark's hand. "I'm hopin' you can bring it back here just the way it is, but if you can't, then I'm gonna be even gladder you took it."

With trembling hands, Stark lowered his suitcase to the ground, snapped the clips open, and laid the pistol inside. Before he could shut the bag, Isaac dropped a knotted red kerchief, which came to rest beside the pistol. "Dog food," the colored man said. Can't take a dog to New York without no food for him."

Stark closed the bag, clapped Isaac's arm, and got on the train.

‹›‹›‹›

Elias Niederhoffer was a stocky man with gray hair like steel wool, and the arms, legs and chest that come from nineteen years of pushing a cart loaded with fruit around the streets of New York. Mr. Niederhoffer enjoyed—as much as he ever enjoyed anything—a reputation on the lower east side as a peddler you didn't try copping a piece of fruit off. Better to give him his nickel for an apple or an orange than to go home with a bloody nose or a blackened eye.

But the two men facing Niederhoffer in the doorway to his apartment were not fruit snatchers, and the peddler was working hard at trying to keep the shakes out of his voice. Back in Austria, police at your door meant you had real problems, and as far as Niederhoffer was concerned, a cop was a cop, same in New York as in Vienna. He extended his hairy forearms, palms up. "Mister Policemen, listen, would you please. I ain't never made no trouble—"

The blond man in the cop suit, standing a bit to the side, snickered. The heavier, darker-complexioned man in the brown suit and fedora hat interrupted. "That's fine, Mr. Niederhoffer. I'm sure you're a model citizen. It's your son, Martin, we're looking for. Is he here?"

Elias looked sideways at his wife, Antoinette, broad-beamed, wide-eyed, mouth gaping. *Wei iss mir*, the peddler thought. They're gonna take us down to the station and beat us with clubs till we're dead. "No, no, sir. Martin ain't here. He didn't come home from work yet."

The dark man made a point of looking at his watch. "It's almost eight o'clock. Doesn't he usually get home by now?" Without waiting for an answer, he added, "Mind if we take a look inside?"

Niederhoffer moved left, his wife right. The two men walked in, then separated to look through the rest of the apartment. By the time they reconnoitered in the living room, Martin's five younger brothers milled around, asking their parents what was going on, and who were these guys? Their mother shushed them, finger to lips, but the interrogation didn't break off until their father raised a hand, and then it stopped on a dime. As the policemen converged on Elias, Antoinette let out a strangled scream. The blond cop snickered again, but the darker, plainclothes cop said, with surprising gentleness, "Don't worry, Mrs. No one's gonna get hurt. I just need to ask a few questions. Mr. Niederhoffer, do you have any idea where your son, Martin, is?"

Niederhoffer shook his head slowly. "He tells us he's a grown man, he comes and he goes as he pleases. I know he takes piano lessons from some *schwartzer* up in Harlem."

"Huh?"

The detective turned to the patrolman. "*Schwartzer*, Charlie, that's Yiddish for nigger." Back to Niederhoffer. "You don't happen to know the name of that *schwartzer*, do you, Mr. Niederhoffer? Or where he lives?"

Niederhoffer shrugged, but the youngest boy, Abe, a hefty sandy-haired fourteen-year-old copy of his mother, stepped up and said, "It's Scott Joplin, sir. He lives up on West 138th. I once went up with Martin to hear his lesson."

The policemen looked at each other. Both smiled. Then the plainclothes detective said, "Thank you, young man." He turned back to Elias, handed him a card. "All right, Mr. Niederhoffer. If you hear from your son, tell him the smartest thing he can do is call me. Detective Ciccone—Nicolo Ciccone. The sooner he does, the better it will be for him."

Mrs. Niederhoffer couldn't hold back longer. "What has Martin done, Officer?"

"We don't know that he's done anything, Ma'am. But a few hours ago, a man was found murdered down at Waterson, Berlin, and Snyder Music, where your son works, and we're hoping he can tell us something about it." He tipped his fedora, then left the apartment, Charlie riding his wake.

For a moment after the policemen left, the Niederhoffers stood silent, then everyone started shouting at once. Elias grabbed Abe by the neck and slapped his cheek, again and again, forehand on the left side, backhand on the right. "Mr. Bigmouth," Elias shouted. "You think the cops're gonna give you a cookie for being a good boy and telling them all about your brother's piano lessons?" He gave Abe a hard shove; the boy stumbled against the side of a stout wooden bookshelf, then fell to his knees. He rubbed his cheek, looked away from his father. In the now-silent room, Niederhoffer glared at his sons. "In Austria, a fourteen-year-old *pisher* knows he only speaks when he's spoken to, 'specially by a policeman. In Austria, what a father says, goes. Not here. Now I got a son who's maybe a murderer. I'm sorry I ever came."

<><><>

Daylight faded. Lottie Joplin turned on her reading lamp, settled into her comfortable chair, swung her aching feet up onto the hassock…and heard a hard knock at the door, followed immediately by a second knock. And then, "Police. Open up or we'll knock the door down."

"No call to be that way," she muttered. She hauled herself out of her chair, walked to the door, and pulled it open. Two cops, a young blond one in a uniform, all red in the face and sweaty, and an older guy, a plainclothes, hook-nosed and round-shouldered, with dark bags under large, brown eyes. Probably an Italianer. The men looked around and past Lottie like they were searching for something or someone inside. The older one flipped a billfold open under Lottie's nose; she had just about long enough to see the shiny star before he flipped it shut and back into his pocket. "I'm Detective Ciccone," he said. "New York City Police. Are you Mrs. Joplin?" Without waiting for an answer, he added, "We're looking for Scott Joplin."

Foolish to get them sore, Lottie thought. "He ain't here," she said, keeping herself in the middle of the doorway.

"Doesn't he usually come home for dinner?"

"Oh yes. He usually do. But he ain't come yet today. He be a composer and a musician, and sometimes he have business in the evening."

The Italian in street clothes allowed himself a faint smile. "You mind if we take a look inside?"

Lottie knew about warrants, but again, no point getting these cops mad at her. One way or another, they'd end up looking around, and the more she made them work to do it, the more she'd pay. She gave silent thanks that right now, only one room upstairs was in use. "Long as you don't tear nothing up," she said. "Onliest thing is, my sister from Virginny's visitin' me, and she's in her room right now, havin' a private talk with a young man, been showin' her some interest. 'Least, you oughta let me go tell 'em you might want to talk to them."

"You just wait right here," the plainclothes said. His partner stepped around Lottie, and walked through the living room, into the kitchen. The detective strode to the open living room window, looked out onto the fire escape, then craned his neck to search above. Then he walked into the bathroom, checked out the bedroom, finally came back to the living room to meet his partner. Both cops shook their heads. "All right, Mammy," the plainclothes said. "Take us up to your sister and her friend."

The blond cop snorted.

Lottie stamped hard as she could, going up the stairs, then turned to the first door on the right and knocked. "Sis...*Sis*. Some policemens're here askin' after Scott, they want to look inside."

"Be right along, Lottie," said a female voice.

That set both of the policemen to snickering. They walked past Lottie, down the hall, opened each door, looked inside. By the time they returned, the door to the first room stood open. A slim, light-skinned colored man and a well-built woman about the man's shade, glared at the intruders. The man's shirttails hung over his trousers; the woman's red dress was higher over her left shoulder than her right, and it didn't take much looking to see she had nothing on beneath the dress. Lottie saw interest in the blond cop's eyes. The Italianer gave the man a long stare. "You wouldn't happen to be Scott Joplin, would you?" he asked.

"I be George Weston," the colored man said, just politely enough to be sure he wouldn't offend the policeman.

"Prove it?"

The colored man reached into his pocket. Lottie saw both policemen tense. The blond cop moved his hand toward the pistol on his right hip. Lottie held her breath. "Slow, there, George," the detective said. "Just you go nice and slow."

The colored man's hand came out of his pocket holding a billfold, from which he pulled a crinkled white card, which he handed it to the detective. "Colored Vaudeville Benevolent Association. George Weston. Member in good standing…hmm." The detective passed the card back to Weston. "You a musician?"

Weston almost smiled. "Yessir. I play horn."

"Okay. Now, Miss…?"

"Stokes," the woman said. "Patty Stokes. Lottie's sister."

The detective nodded. "All right. Sorry to bother you. You can go on back to your private visit."

Lottie wanted to wipe the smirk off his face with the palm of her hand.

Downstairs, the detective asked did she have a picture of Scott Joplin. She pointed at a print on the wall, next to the sofa. "That be me and him."

A quick glance, then the detective told Lottie to be sure to let them know when her husband came in.

"Why you lookin' for him?" she asked.

"Just need to ask him a few questions," said the detective, and then the two of them were gone. Lottie closed the door and collapsed into her chair. Got to tell Nell about this, she thought, but maybe best to wait just a little, make sure those cops ain't right back knocking again.

<><><>

Detective Ciccone took a few seconds to appreciate the sight standing before him. That Niederhoffer kid had good taste in women. Give her thirty years, she'd be just another fat housewife, but right now she was a juicy, ripe peach, begging to be bitten into. Ciccone swallowed, then smiled and said, "We're looking for Martin Niederhoffer, Miss Kuminsky. Do you have any idea where he is?"

The girl shook her head. Dark curls flew back and forth across her smooth cheeks. "No."

Ciccone thought she might be lying. She looked scared silly. The detective nodded to her parents, standing behind her. "It's important," Ciccone said. "Very important. Are you sure you don't know where he could be?"

The girl shook her head. "I don't have any idea. I left the office at five, like always. Martin had to stay to finish up the monthly sales numbers. Then he was going to the fights with his friend, Sid. Why are you looking for him? What's wrong?"

Her father said something into her ear, but Ciccone couldn't catch it. The girl waved him off. "Yes, I'm afraid something is very wrong," the detective said. "Sid was found in your boyfriend's office, dead. Someone cut his throat."

A loud sucking sound came from behind the hand that whipped over the girl's mouth.

"I'm sorry, Miss Kuminsky." Ciccone stopped for a moment, just for effect. A little suspense often worked well for him. "And your boyfriend was seen running out of the building afterward."

The girl rested a hand on the door jamb. Ciccone positioned himself to catch her if she fell. Her father was furious now, eyes bulging, lips nearly colorless. He spoke to her again, this time more urgently, but still, Ciccone couldn't make out the words. The mother looked petrified, one hand to her throat, the other holding her apron in a death grip. Birdie turned her head, said "Papa, I'll talk to you later."

"Miss Kuminsky…"

The girl looked back to Ciccone.

"I'm sorry to have to tell you all this, and I'm sorry to upset you. But I know how close you and Mr. Niederhoffer are, and I figure you'd want to help him any way you can. The best thing you can do is persuade him to come and talk to us, the sooner, the better. The longer he takes, the worse it's going to look for him."

"If you want to find Martin so bad, why are you here, bothering me and scaring my parents?" Birdie snapped. Why don't you go to *his* place? Talk to *his* parents?"

Ciccone fought off a terrible urge to smack her across the face, something he'd have done to his own daughter if she ever dared to talk smart like that to him. "We've done that, Miss Kuminsky," he said without moving his lips. "He's not there. And he's not at his piano teacher's. This is Stop Three, but you need to know, it's not even close to the end of the line, and the train's not going to quit running until we find your boyfriend. Now, I'll ask you again—"

"I have no idea where Martin is," Birdie shouted, and burst into tears. Her mother threw her arms around the girl, and turned a look on Ciccone that he hadn't seen since the time his mother came home too soon from her grocery shopping, and caught him in his bedroom with his girlfriend, who then became his wife a whole lot faster than he'd figured on. He tipped his fedora, walked down the hall, took the steps to the ground floor two at a time, Charlie clumping after him.

Mrs. Kuminsky smoothed Birdie's hair, then said, "Sounds like Martin did something bad."

Birdie pulled away, ran across the living room and disappeared down the hall. A moment later, her parents heard a door slam. They looked at each other. "She better keep away from that Niederhoffer boy," Mr. Kuminsky snapped "He gets her in any kind of trouble, I'll give him a sock in the snoot he'll never forget. She's only seventeen."

Mrs. Kuminsky's smile could have broken hearts. "That's what my father said to me when *I* was seventeen. And how much good did it do?"

<>‹›‹›

Up in Harlem, in their apartment above the grocery store on West 131st Street, Clarence and Ida Barbour, and their nephew, Dubie Harris, sat down to dinner at the kitchen table. Despite a wide-open window, the room was sweltering. Dubie eyeballed the fire escape and wondered whether his aunt and uncle would let him sleep out there. This New York place was hotter and more humid than Missouri, which was saying a bunch. The boy bowed his head while his aunt said grace; when she thanked the Lord for the day's bounty, Dubie's heart leaped. *His* bounty that day made a pot of pork and beans look pretty damn puny. When Aunt Ida finished her prayer, and began to spoon out the meal, Dubie said brightly, "I did mighty good today, my first day in New York."

Clarence half-closed one eye; grooves you could plant crops in spread across his forehead. A corner of his gray mustache twitched. But Ida's moon face radiated joy. "You did, did you? Well, now, come and tell us about it."

"Did James Reese Europe put you in his band?"

Clarence's question was a damper on Dubie's fire. "No, not that. Mr. Europe's out of town right now, but they took my name and told me they'd be callin' me when he gets on back."

Clarence didn't pause, just shoveled in a forkful of beans.

Ida squinched her eyes and bit her lip. "Well, that's something, anyway."

"I gave them the phone number in the booth down in the store—that be okay, ain't it?"

His aunt's smile made an instant comeback. "'Course it is, Dubie. '*Course* it is. How else they gonna find you? You know how happy I'd be, answering a telephone and hearing that."

Clarence laid down his fork. "All right then. Just what *is* this big news you been talkin' about?"

"Oh, well, see, that's what I be tryin' to tell you. Just one day in New York, and already I be gettin' my music published."

Ida clapped her hands. Clarence nodded gravely.

What an old stick-in-the-mud, Dubie thought.

"Just who is it, gonna be publishin' your music?" Clarence asked.

"None other than Waterson, Berlin, and Snyder, best house in town. That's what Mr. Blake tol' me yesterday, on the train. He wrote me down their address. So after I got done at James

Reese Europe's, I went on downtown to Waterson, Berlin, and
Snyder. They put me in a room with some young kid, not any
older'n me, I played him a couple of my tunes, and he said no
thanks, not interested, goodbye. I could tell by the look on his
face, wasn't no way he was gonna buy a piece of music from
some nigger, walk into his office. And that made me pretty
da—" Dubie picked up the frown on his aunt's face. "Pretty
darn' mad. I decided I'm gonna stand up for myself, so I went
out in Reception an' tol' the secretary-lady I not goin' anywhere,
not till I gets to see the boss man, Mr. Irving Berlin hisself. And
you know what? Off she takes herself, and not a minute later, she
be back with Mr. Berlin. He look me up and he look me down,
and then he tell me all right, I a busy man, but come on back
real quick and play me your tunes. So I do that, and you know
what he say? 'Boy, you got yourself a talent. We gonna publish
the two a these, and maybe that be just for starters.' Now, what
you think a that, huh?"

Aunt Ida clasped her hands before her face, like her happiness was almost too much to bear. Uncle Clarence, though, still
frowned. "What kinda contract he give you?"

Dubie tightened his lips. "Well, I ain't got no contract, not
yet. Mr. Berlin said come on back tomorrow, and we get it all
tied up. But I don't see there be any sorta problem. Man love
my music and he want to publish it."

Now, Ida looked as concerned as her husband. Clarence
aimed a finger Dubie's way. "Boy, now don't you be forgettin'
that this's New York you're in. *Or* that you're colored, an' Mr.
Berlin is white. Did you leave that music of yours with him?"

"Well, yeah. Sure I did. How else he gonna publish it?"

Clarence felt like the last rose of summer. Why did every
generation have to learn the same lesson, over and over and over,
no end in sight. The boy needed some sense kicked into him,
but Clarence knew that was not his place. "You just be careful,"
he said. "New York's the toughest place in the world. There's
good people here all right, but there's also a whole lot of bad.

And a colored man's a fool if he goes and trusts a white man he just that minute met."

No point pushing him, Dubie thought. "I do thank you, Uncle Clarence. I hear what you say, and I will take care. Ain't no man, white or colored, gonna take advantage and make a fool outa me."

Clarence picked up his fork, but stopped short of using it on food. Instead, he pointed it at his nephew. "Something else you better keep in your mind. Back some five years ago, Scott Joplin left some music with your Mr. Irving Berlin. After a time, Berlin gave it back, said it wasn't good enough. But right after that, he put out 'Alexander's Ragtime Band,' and then all manner of commotion went and broke loose. Joplin swore Berlin stole that tune, note for note, from his music. It was in the papers and all. Everybody in Harlem was talking about it. You best be on your guard around Irving Berlin." Clarence stabbed his fork into a piece of pork, and filled his mouth.

"Well, I will do just that," Dubie said. "I ain't nobody's fool, never was, never will be." He picked up his fork and started in to work on his pork and beans. Clarence and Ida exchanged looks, said nothing, didn't have to. Nearly forty years of marriage, most couples pick up the knack.

Chapter Five

Brooklyn
Wednesday, August 23
Late morning

Scott Joplin sat at the small upright piano in Joe Lamb's living room, hitting keys and scribbling notes onto the music composition paper Lamb had given him the night before. His *Symphony Number One* would have to do it for him, that and *If.* Maybe one day, somebody might discover *Treemonisha*, and then people would say yes, Scott Joplin really *was* some potatoes, a colored man, wrote a symphony and an opera, think of that. But he had less time to finish his symphony than he had money, which was saying something. Not that he minded about the money—nice to have it, sure, but he'd always figured money was like food. You've got to get enough to satisfy your needs, but go make eating the reason for living, then your stomach grows to where you never can fill it up, and you spend the rest of your life stuffing cheese and oysters down your throat without even tasting them. But time was a whole different story. Seventeen years ago, when he lived in Sedalia, writing and teaching music, helping kids like Arthur Marshall and Scott Hayden write *their* music, getting his penny-a-copy royalties contract from John Stark to publish "Maple Leaf," it seemed like he had all the time in the world. What happened to all that time? If only… *If.* Black fingers glided over white and black piano keys.

Martin Niederhoffer glanced over from the sofa. Strange music. It sounded like something Beethoven or Brahms might have written if they'd just spent an evening in a Harlem club, listening to Luckey Roberts or old One-Leg Willie Joseph. Occasionally there came a short passage Martin recognized as a theme from one or another of Joplin's rags. One such, from "The Entertainer," surprised Martin with an unexpected move into a minor key that tugged so hard at the young man's heart, it brought tears to his eyes. He looked hard at Joplin, but as always, could tell nothing from his teacher's face. If the man had put as much work into playing poker as he had into writing music, he'd be living on the snazziest block of Easy Street.

Martin wiped his face with his forearm. Goddamn house was like a Turkish bath. His shirt was drenched, stuck to his back. He dragged himself into the kitchen, filled a glass of water from the tap, drank it as he stared out the window. "Jim-i-nee," he muttered, "I might just as well be in jail." Finally, he wandered back into the living room, and for a moment stood and stared at Joplin, still playing his Germanic ragtime. Shout 'Fire,' Martin thought, and the man wouldn't even notice.

He had a piece of paper in his pocket with Mrs. Stanley's street address and phone number, and Mr. Lamb's address and phone number at the customs house where he worked. "In case you need help," Mrs. Stanley had said. Some joke. The only thing he needed help with was how to stay awake, sitting around in a boiling-hot little house in Brooklyn, baby-sitting a man who could spend eight hours composing music without saying a word. Meanwhile, no one was checking into Sid's murder. And who was closer to the situation than Martin Niederhoffer? If he could only get this mess cleaned up, he could go back to work, persuade Mr. Berlin to take on Mr. Joplin's music, and then go get a marriage license…hold on. By now, Birdie would have been at work all morning, wouldn't she? Maybe she could tell him something she'd heard or seen that might put him on the right track.

He scrambled to the edge of the sofa, reached over the arm-rest, grabbed up the candlestick telephone from the little end table, put the receiver to his ear, waited for the operator to cut in. And waited. And waited. He tapped his foot, rapid-fire. "Hey, operator...*operator*," he shouted into the mouthpiece,

Joplin turned, looked at him for a second, then went back to his work.

Martin shouted for the operator a second time, a third, a fourth. Then he dropped the earpiece back into the cradle, slammed the telephone back onto the table, and slumped against the armrest. "God damn things never work when you need them." He glanced at his wristwatch. Only one o'clock. Mr. Lamb wouldn't be home until after five—and then what? Eat dinner, sit around, tell his story another time to that Mr. Stark, Nell's father.

"No!" Martin pounded a fist into an open palm. "What do they think, I'm just a stooge? I'm gonna find out about Sid's murder—*and* Mr. Joplin's music."

He jumped from the sofa, running, out of the living room, through the front door, across the porch, down the stairs to the sidewalk. He shaded his eyes, looked both ways, then took off toward the subway kiosk at the far end of the next block, but had to pull up at the corner to let a line of wagons and automobiles go past. He jogged in place, ready to charge at the first opportunity. Not even half an hour, he could be talking to Birdie.

Traffic broke. Martin put a foot down to the street, but froze as he felt a hand close on his arm. He stepped back up onto the curb, ready to swing a fist—and found himself face to face with Scott Joplin. Before Martin could say a word, a short, wiry man with small, mean eyes just visible under the brim of a "straw hat" stuck his jaw toward Martin's chest and piped, "This nigger botherin' you, bub? The little man's fists were balled, his right hand drawn back, ready to fire.

"No," Martin said, and shifted to place himself between Joplin and the pint-sized aggressor. "He's my piano teacher. My *friend*. Beat it."

The man's face showed clearly what he thought of a white man who'd claim a colored man as a teacher, let alone a friend. Martin drew back his own fist. "I said beat it. Get yourself the hell outa here."

The man took long enough to spit, then stomped off across the street.

From Joplin's face, you'd have thought Martin might just have given the man directions to Coney Island, but the composer said, quietly, "Thank you, Martin."

"Well, sure, what else was I gonna say?" He looked Joplin up and down, as if confirming the fact he was really there. "Mr. Joplin, what're you doing here?" Martin jabbed a finger toward Lamb's apartment.

Joplin looked confused. "You said we were going to find out who killed your friend, and what Irving Berlin is up to with my music. I heard you perfectly clearly."

Had he been talking out loud, back there in the apartment? Martin would've sworn he'd only thought those ideas, but Joplin was hardly a mind reader. Too late now, though, to think about that. What he had to do was get Joplin back to the house, fast... uh-oh. "Mr. Joplin? Did the door lock behind you?"

Joplin's expression suggested that Martin might be losing his mind. "Why, yes, of course. I made sure it was locked. This isn't Sedalia. In New York, you lock your door when you go out."

Martin's mind whirled. He couldn't take Joplin back and leave him sitting on the stoop all afternoon. He couldn't even go back and sit with Joplin for four hours, then try to explain to Mr. Lamb and everyone else how they'd managed to get themselves locked out. Especially since Joplin would say they'd started out to find a killer and have a talk with Irving Berlin.

Martin grabbed his teacher's arm. "Sorry, Mr. Joplin, I'm just trying to be extra careful that we locked up, since it's Mr. Lamb's place and he's being good enough to put us up." He jerked his head toward the far side of the street. "It's clear, let's go."

Joplin fell into step beside him.

‹›‹›‹›

Joe Lamb pulled the heavy wooden door open, and walked into the church. He liked to come here during his lunch hour: a few minutes in the cool, dark room seemed to restore him for the afternoon's work ahead, particularly in the heat of summer when people tended to be short-tempered and impatient. In one quick motion he genuflected and blessed himself, then stood and walked into a rear pew, where he knelt, and murmured, "Almighty God, my friend and benefactor, Scott Joplin, is in danger, as is Martin, the young man who so bravely and generously helped him. I ask you to please protect and guide them both out of harm's way. I ask this in your name, with thanksgiving for your guidance."

Again, Lamb blessed himself, then rose from his knees. It occurred to him that some might consider his decision to offer shelter to the fugitives as reason for confession, but he would decide for himself when he'd sinned and when he hadn't. He wondered what Joplin might think about his request for divine intervention. His mentor had little use for churches and even less for preachers, who for nearly twenty years had condemned the wonderful music he wrote as being the devil's own. Well, the prayer couldn't hurt, and in any case, no reason to mention it to Joplin. Lamb practiced his religion; he did not preach it.

‹›‹›‹›

All the way into Manhattan on the subway, neither Martin nor Joplin spoke. Martin tried to dope out an approach; Joplin kept pulling a sheet of music paper out of his pocket, scribbling a few notes, putting it back, pulling it out again. Martin wondered whether he stopped composing when he was in bed at night with his wife.

A block down Broadway from Waterson, Berlin, and Snyder, Martin guided Joplin into a drug store and up to a bank of five telephone booths. He pushed the composer into an empty booth, sat him down. "I just need to make a quick call."

Joplin nodded. "All right."

Martin slid into the next booth, gave the operator Waterson, Berlin, and Snyder's number, put a handkerchief over the mouthpiece, and half-turned so his back faced the door. When Fannie, the receptionist, answered, he said, "Yeah, hello. This is Roger Walker, the bookkeeper up at Irving Berlin, Inc. I need to talk to Martin Niederhoffer."

The young man waited through the pause he knew would come, then heard Fannie say, "Mr. Niederhoffer isn't in today."

"Christ!" Martin counted to three, then went on. "Okay, look. Mr. Berlin wants some numbers, and he wants 'em now. Is Niederhoffer's assistant in, the girl?"

"Birdie Kuminsky? Yes."

"Good. Lemme talk to her."

"Just a minute."

The thump of Martin's heart against his ribs was almost painful. He went through his speech one more time, then when he heard Birdie's "Hello?" he pulled the handkerchief away from the phone and spoke as fast as he could. "Birdie, listen—do *not* say my name. Just say, 'Hello, Mr. Walker,' like you don't know why I'm calling."

Silence.

"Birdie. Say it. Now."

"Hello…Mr. Walker?"

"Beautiful. Now, listen. I've got to talk to you. You know where they keep the monthly sales records, right? Go in there, pretend to pick up last month's numbers, but just grab a handful of blank pages and put them in a file folder. Then come up to Schneider's. I'll meet you there."

"Mr. Walker, please. I'm right in the middle of trying to finish up the numbers that the bookkeeper didn't get to do last night. Mr. Tabor won't let me out to run an errand."

"Yes he will. Listen, Miss Kuminsky, listen careful. You do know where they keep those numbers, right?"

"Yes."

"Okay, then. Do what I said. Get the papers inside a folder, then go in and tell Tabor that Mr. Berlin is up at I-B, Inc, and he wants those figures right now. Tabor's not gonna call to check, and take a chance on catching hell for interrupting Mr. B. I'll meet you at Schneider's. Okay?"

"I'll get right on it, Mr. Walker." Then, the line clicked dead.

Martin grinned. This was some girl. If he didn't marry her fast, someone else would beat his time. But that was not going to happen.

<><><>

Ten minutes later, Birdie walked out of Waterson, Berlin, and Snyder, clutching a manila folder to her chest. Mr. Tabor had looked kind of funny at her, maybe a little mad, but he didn't say no, just that she shouldn't take too long. She cocked a finger in her mind at Martin, and started to tell him what-for, but she didn't get far before she began giggling. Her boyfriend could be aggravating, but he was so enthusiastic all the time, so much fun. Something was always happening around Martin; he *made* things happen. Life with him would never be dull. In spite of the mid-day heat, she shivered when she thought of Martin being the first person she'd see every morning, and the last every night. If he'd asked her to, she'd have emptied the petty cash box and brought him the money. By the time she turned into the doorway at Schneider's Deli, she was running.

She spotted Martin and Joplin all the way in the back, and hurried across the black and white tiled floor to their table. Martin held a chair for her, then called the waiter and ordered vanilla egg creams for himself and Birdie; Joplin ordered sarsaparilla. The waiter, sour-pussed with the knowledge that this was going to be at most a nickel tip, marched away.

Birdie watched him go, then set the folder of papers on the table, and stage-whispered to Martin, "All right, what is going on?" She glanced at Joplin, who looked confused. "And what happened to Sid last night? There have been police around almost all day, and they keep talking about you and Mr. Joplin. Between the policemen and their questions, and the fact that your work from last night has to be done all over because the pages were covered with blood, Mr. Tabor's got the worst heebie-jeebies I've ever seen. You've got to talk fast. If I take too long, he's going to give me real trouble."

Martin checked his watch. "Okay. The problem is, I don't *know* what happened. I was trying to finish up those figures, took off for a few minutes to go to the bathroom, and when I came back, I found Sid with his throat cut. Mr. Joplin was standing there…" Martin paused long enough to decide not to mention the uncomfortable fact that Joplin had been holding a bloody razor. "So I ran, and took him with me."

"You ran? Why didn't you call the police?"

"Because if I did, they'd most likely have said Mr. Joplin did it. I mean, he was standing there in the room with Sid—"

Joplin looked up from where he'd been scrawling musical notes on his napkin. "I did not do it. I came in to talk to Mr. Berlin about my play. The door to that room was open, and I knew it was Martin's office, so I went in and found his friend." The longer Joplin talked, the faster he spoke, and the more his voice rose. Two men at a nearby table turned to look.

Birdie leaned across the table to rest a hand on Joplin's. "Take it easy, Mr. Joplin," she crooned. "We know you didn't do it."

Joplin blinked. Martin saw the muscles in his face relax. "But I've got to talk to Mr. Berlin; he called last night, and I still haven't seen him."

"I just came from the office, and he's not in right now," Birdie said. "Why don't you let Martin try to find out who killed his friend, so no one can ever blame it on you. And then we'll get you another appointment with Mr. Berlin. Okay?" She finished with a warm smile.

Martin couldn't believe it. A line like that, off the top of her head. Butter would melt in her mouth.

The waiter left the drinks, then strode off. Martin watched him all the way to the front of the deli. Then he leaned toward his girlfriend. "Birdie, listen. I don't know what's going on. There was nobody else in that office, but somebody killed Sid while I was out in the bathroom."

Birdie lifted her head from the straw. "How do you know somebody wasn't hiding someplace inside the office?"

Martin blew out a long breath. "I don't, you're right."

"Where are you staying?"

No answer.

Birdie pursed her lips. "Martin, where *are* the two of you staying? I want to know, in case I need to find you."

"Okay. We're at Mr. Joe Lamb's, in Brooklyn. He writes ragtime, and he's a friend of Mr. Joplin's. Come on, now, we don't have much time. Tell me what's been going on at the office. Maybe there's something that'll help me make some sense."

"Martin, you're—"

"Birdie, just tell me. Please."

Sigh. "Okay. When I came in, Mr. Tabor was already there, and old Walter was mopping up the floor in your office. Mr. Waterson hadn't come in yet. A detective was there, and a policeman, the same ones who came to my house last night, looking for you. They took us, one at a time, into your office, and asked us questions about you and Sid. That went on pretty much all morning. After the policemen left, Mr. Tabor called me in and *he* started asking me questions. I told him I didn't know anything about where you were, or anything else. He said he was concerned for you because when he saw you and Mr. Joplin going off down the block, he figured maybe you had walked in after Mr. Joplin killed Sid, so Mr. Joplin kidnaped you, and you might get hurt if we don't find you soon."

"What did he think? Mr. Joplin held a razor to my throat and ran me off down Broadway?"

Birdie tried to stifle a giggle with a hand to her mouth. "That's exactly what I said to him. But he just looked at me, you know the way he does, like I was just the dumbest little cow he'd ever seen. Then he said, 'No, Miss Kuminsky. Of course I didn't think that. But a nig—'" She caught herself. "Mr. Joplin, I'm sorry."

Joplin shook his head. "Never mind. I've heard the word before."

The girl was crimson-faced. "He said a nigger keeps a razor strapped to his leg, a knife in one pocket, and a gun in the other. He thought maybe you were taking Martin away with a gun pointed at him.

Martin pictured Joplin a few days before, raging at Lester Walton, and had to admit to himself, he *could* see Joplin in one of his terrible fits, shooting Walton to death. What he could not picture was Joplin slipping a gun into his pocket in the first place, or strapping a razor to his leg.

Birdie looked at the big clock above the counter, drew in a sharp breath. "I'd better go—there's nothing else I can tell you. After Mr. Tabor was done with me, he gave me that awful pile of bloody papers and told me to recopy them, fast as I could, and not make any mistakes. I've been working all day, and I haven't heard anything else about the murder. Please be careful. And let me know how you are. I'm scared." She squeezed his hand as she pushed the folder of blank pages toward him. A quick smile for Joplin, then she was gone and out the door at a trot, dodging through the foot traffic.

For a moment after she left, neither Martin nor Joplin spoke. Then Joplin said, "She's a lovely girl. When she talks, she puts melodies into my mind."

Martin grinned. "'The Birdie Rag'. You'll have to write it out and dedicate it to her."

Joplin hummed several notes.

Martin sucked the last bit of egg cream through the straw, then muttered, "Damn! I don't even know where to start."

◇◇◇

As he stepped out of the rail car, John Stark looked around the platform, but no sign of Nell. She'd said she'd meet him, and when Nell said something, that something happened. Perhaps she was out at the gate. Stark worked his way ahead, up the stairs, elbow to elbow, until the crowd pushed its way into the main concourse of Pennsylvania Station and suddenly thinned. Like going through a funnel backward.

From the top stair, he spotted Nell, on tiptoes, glancing this way and that. When she finally caught sight of her father, she smiled, if a bit tentatively, then walked up to give him a peck on the cheek. Stark cleared his throat, a sound that never failed to put his daughter on full alert. "I'm glad to see you, my dear. Jim's working, is he?"

"I'll tell you later. Let's get your bags and get out of here."

Stark raised his eyebrows.

At the baggage claim, Nell reached to grab the suitcase away from Stark. He swung it to his other hand. "I'm not incapacitated, Nell. But thank you. Besides." He turned a sly smile her way. "I'd say you have all you can handle with that bag of yours—it's two feet across, if it's an inch."

"It's a foot and a half, Dad. Where else am I supposed to put my music and my stand, never mind all the things you stuff into your pockets? In case you hadn't noticed, women don't have pockets."

So easy to get her goat, ever since she was small. Stark supposed by now it was expected of him, that not to bait her might suggest his affection had lessened. "Just so, my dear. Let's get on our way."

They pushed through the mass of humanity, flowing this way, that way. Whiffs of bad breath, a persistent stink of unwashed bodies, then as they finally pushed their way into the main waiting room, Stark stopped to gawk at the four entry staircases. He raised his eyes up to the gorgeous tiled arches, fifteen stories above his head. Nell chuckled. "You look like a jay, Dad, fresh off the farm. You lived here, remember?"

Stark shook his head. "*You* remember. They didn't open this until after Mother and I left. I've never seen it…magnificent. Wasn't it designed after one of the ancient Roman baths?"

"Caracalla, enlarged twenty percent. Dad, please, enough history lesson. Let's get back to the apartment. We need to talk."

Stark narrowed his eyes. "More trouble than you told me about over the telephone, eh?" He hefted his suitcase and began to walk.

She easily matched his pace. "We've had some new developments, yes."

◇◇◇

Nell led her father into a small room with a four-poster bed, dresser and oak rocker. "Chez Stanley's guest room, Dad. As long as you're here, any stranded musicians will just have to find another place for the night. I hope you'll be comfortable."

Stark looked around, nodded approval. "I'm sure I will be. You've got a very nice place, my dear. West Seventy-second Street, I'm impressed. I could never have aspired to live in this neighborhood."

"Our family never lacked for anything, Dad, not anywhere we lived. Jim just wanted to be in a neighborhood where I wouldn't have to be concerned to go out by myself to buy groceries."

"He's a good man, Nell. I couldn't want a better son-in-law."

He couldn't have missed the cloud that sailed across his daughter's face, but it was gone as fast as it appeared. "He's a good husband."

"At work, is he? Recording session?"

"Yes and no. He's on the road with his Quartette, a short tour through New York State, Pennsylvania and Ohio. One of the music acts in a Keith program fell apart all of a sudden. Their trumpeter had ideas about starting his own orchestra, and ran off with the singer. So Keith asked Jim to plug their hole with the Stanley Quartette."

Stark picked up on the bitter turn in her speech. "In a way, that's a compliment."

No answer.

"But you're their accompanist, and here you are. I hope you didn't refuse to go out of spite."

Her eyes flared; he readied himself for a full frontal assault. But she shook her head, and when she spoke, her voice was soft. "You know me better than that. No, I stayed…oh, Dad, Scott is just in terrible condition. One minute he's his old self, gentle, polite, good-humored, and the next, he's throwing dishes and screaming about the way someone he passed on the street looked at him. Lottie's worn down to her bones, trying to look after him. It was easier to find another pianist for the Quartette than someone who could help Lottie take care of Scott."

Stark banged a fist onto the top of the dresser. "Cruel! Joplin always wanted more than anything to be respected and respectable. To have him dying like this, of such a disease." He shook his head. "I'd have sworn on anything holy he never visited a sporting house, except to play piano to put food on his table."

"Brothels aren't the only places a man can get syphilis, Dad. I won't have you thinking any the less of him."

The Irish in her voice set him on his heels. "I hope you know me better than that. I was commenting on the irony, nothing more. Our Lord in Heaven's got a nasty sense of humor."

Nell began to cry, then walked to the doorway, pulled a handkerchief from her sleeve, dabbed at her eyes. Stark took a step toward her, but stopped, let his hands fall to his sides, and stood, waiting. Finally, Nell said, "It was a good thing I did stay. The situation has gotten considerably worse since I talked to you."

Stark sat on the edge of the bed.

"There's been a murder."

"Scott didn't—"

She shook her head. "I don't think so. But the police do. And the young man with him—"

"'Young man with him…' Nell, where *is* Joplin. Just what's going on here?"

She motioned with her head toward his suitcase. "Why don't you get your bag unpacked, and I'll make some coffee. It's going to take a little while to tell you about it."

Stark began to object, thought better of it. Instead, he swung his suitcase up and onto the bed, flipped the catches, pulled the lid open. Nell's eyes were like dinner plates. "Dad—what on *earth?* You carried that cannon on the train, all the way from St. Louis? What ever were you thinking? This is New York, not the wild west."

Rather than angering him, his daughter's indignation struck him funny, and he began to laugh. "I know where I am. Isaac badly wanted to come along, but he broke his leg squirrel-hunting a couple of weeks ago, and he's got a big, clumsy cast on it. He came to the station with me, and just as I was getting aboard, he handed me the gun and insisted I take it. I was not about to hurt his feelings." Stark opened the top bureau drawer, laid the pistol inside, then the kerchief full of bullets. He pulled a pile of shirts from the valise, and set them in the drawer on top of the weaponry. "There." He smiled at Nell. "Isaac sends his love. For that matter, so do Till, Margaret and Meggy.

Nell flushed. "Sorry, Dad, I should have asked. How are they all?"

Stark shrugged. "Isaac is impatient with his cast, but otherwise well. Till and Margaret, you know. Dear people, both of them, but the same as ever, perhaps more so. And Meggy…" The old man's eyes lit. "There's a girl after my own heart. She's fourteen, and in a few years, she's going to want something more than what she can find in Maplewood."

His daughter gave him the fish eye. "For which, I'm sure, you can take credit."

"As I do with you. I only hope I'll be around long enough to help her when she'll need it."

Nell shuffled in place. "I can't imagine you won't. Why don't you finish unpacking, then come in the kitchen. I'll make us that coffee, and bring you up to date."

‹›‹›‹›

Good thing Martin sat facing the door. He had his hand in his pocket, reaching for a nickel to leave the waiter, when he spotted two bluecoats walk into the deli and up to old Mrs. Schneider behind the cash register. He nudged Joplin's hand. "Mr. Joplin, don't turn around," a rough whisper. "Cops just came in here."

Joplin hunched his shoulders. "So?"

"Maybe they're looking for us. The murder yesterday, remember? We've got to get out of here."

Joplin turned as if by reflex and looked toward the stairs leading down to the men's room.

"No, that won't work. They'll go down there for sure, and we'll be trapped. There's a delivery alley behind this whole block, so there's gotta be a door from the kitchen." He motioned with his eyes to his left, toward the steel swinging doors. "At least, let's hope there is. Come on."

"But when are we going to talk to Berlin about my music?"

"Later. When Birdie tells us we can."

As he spoke, Martin pulled Joplin out of his chair. They slithered across the aisle, and through the swinging doors, into the kitchen. Six pairs of eyes took them in: two cooks behind a stovetop counter, a colored man washing dishes, and three waiters, putting plates of food onto trays. Martin pulled Joplin toward the back of the room, where the outside door sat open, propped with a broom, to vent the broiling heat. One of the cooks, a heavy man in grease-stained whites, moved in front of the runaways, arms folded across his chest, his more-than-ample body blocking the doorway. "Skippin' out on the check, boys?" A snarl.

Martin pointed back toward the restaurant. "I paid the check, but listen—there's a couple gorillas just came in, their boss is holding my marker off some bad horses. They see me, they're gonna start shooting, and neither one of us knows how good their aim is." He stepped toward the door. "Come on, we don't have a whole lot of time."

The cook didn't change expression, but he did move aside. "Aw right, go ahead. I'll shut the door an' tell 'em you was never here."

Martin and Joplin charged into the alley and took off running as the door snapped shut behind them. Martin clutched Joplin's arm, urged him on, taking care he didn't stumble and fall. At Broadway, they turned downtown and melted into the crowd as they worked their way to the Times Square subway station.

Martin dropped the nickel he was going to give the waiter into the slot, pushed Joplin through, then fed the machine a second nickel, charged onto the platform and shoved himself and his teacher onto an uptown local.

As the subway rumbled past Fiftieth Street and through Columbus Circle, Martin snuck a peek at the paper in his pocket. Yes, Mrs. Stanley did live on West Seventy-second, Number 114. He could leave Joplin there. Come to think of it, didn't Mr. Berlin also live on Seventy-second? Sure. Mr. Waterson was always making fun of him behind his back, saying, "I live in d' Cha-a-tswoith, on Sev'ndee-sekkint, right by Riv'sidrive." Which gave Martin an idea. But first, he had to get Mr. Joplin off his hands before his teacher's behavior landed the two of them behind bars.

He readied himself to get off at Seventy-second, but then thought about what Mrs. Stanley would have to say to him for running out of Mr. Lamb's apartment. Besides, Mr. Lamb had given her a spare key, and what would she do but haul him and Mr. Joplin right back there, no questions asked, and there he'd have to stay. He'd better cook up a different stew, and in a hurry. Maybe take Mr. Joplin back to his missus?

They stayed on the train through the stop at Seventy-second, then swayed back and forth with the motion of the car to 135th Street, where Martin herded Joplin out of the car and up the stairs into brilliant sunlight. Five shouting ten-year-olds dodged past the two adults, ran up to a hydrant on the corner, and went to work with a large wrench. Martin laughed, then looked up and down the street, caught sight of a Nedicks sign half a block up St. Nicholas Avenue. He took his teacher's arm, guided him along the sidewalk, into the Nedicks, and up to the bank of telephone booths. He knew the number, had called it many times over the past several months, and as he recited it for the operator, he prayed Lottie would be in.

Three rings, then, "Hello?" A woman's voice.

"Mrs. Joplin?"

"Who this be?"

Probably thought he was the police. "Mrs. Jop…" He faltered. "Mrs. Joplin, this is Martin Niederhoffer."

"Martin, you sound scared. Something the matter? Something happen to Mr. Joplin?"

The boy pushed words through a tight throat. "No, Mr. Joplin's fine. He's here, with me."

"At Mr. Lamb's house, right?"

"Well, no…not exactly. Mrs. Joplin, it's a long story. I had to do something, and I didn't want to leave Mr. Joplin by himself. But I've got more to do now, and I need to get him back to you. I figured I'd better call instead of coming over."

Short silence. Then Martin heard, "Boy, are you tellin' me you walked outa Mr. Lamb's place, took Mr. Joplin with you, and now you're out on the streets someplace?"

"Well, yes…that's kinda it. We're at the Nedicks on St. Nick, half a block up from 135th. That's where I'm calling from."

"Hoo-ey! Well, I guess the best thing I can say is you got at least enough brains in your head, you didn't just come gallivantin' right over here. Cops've been by, and they got one of them all the time out in front of my house. Why you don't you take Mr. Joplin back to Mr. Lamb's?"

"Because we're locked out of there, and Mr. Lamb won't be back for at least another couple of hours. And I *have* got some stuff I need to do. Isn't there some way I can get Mr. Joplin to you? Then you could check with Mrs. Stanley and see if you should take him to her place or back out to Mr. Lamb's. Mr. Lamb gave her a key last night. I'll come by later, when I'm done."

Silence.

"Mrs. Joplin?"

"Hold on to your pants, Martin, I be thinkin'. All right. You know where's the Alamo Club? On 125th?"

"No, I never—"

"Between Seventh and Eighth Avenues."

"I can find it."

"Mr. Joplin'll recognize it. Go through the bar room and on inside the big room. I'll see you there."

"But how are you going to get past the cop?"

"You leave that to me, boy. Just get yourself and Mr. Joplin over to the Alamo, fast as ever your feet can move you."

Martin hung up the phone, feeling like an eight-year-old whose mother had just finished bawling him out and told him he should wait until his father got home. He shuffled out of the booth and looked around. No Joplin.

His first thought was to get himself outside, fast as ever his feet could move him, and not slow down until he was in Chicago. But then he looked toward the rear of the store, and there was his piano teacher, counting out money and giving it to a white-clad soda jerk. Then Joplin walked away from the counter, carefully carrying a waxed-paper cup in each hand. He gave one to Martin, and took a long drink from his own. "I'm real thirsty," he said. "The way we've been running around."

Martin swallowed hard, then took a sip at his drink. "Thanks, Mr. Joplin. Come on, we're going to meet Mrs. Joplin, and she'll get you back home, or someplace."

"Home? But when are we going to see Irving Berlin?" A splash of orange spilled from Joplin's cup onto the tile floor.

"Later," Martin said, and wondered whether Chicago would be far enough away. "Don't worry, I'm going to take care of it. Mrs. Joplin says you know where the Alamo Club is, right?"

"Oh, yes. I've been there." Joplin fell into step beside Martin.

◇◇◇

A few minutes before one o'clock, Robert Miras tiptoed into the study. His boss didn't usually work on his music this early in the day, but the past couple of weeks, it seemed that Berlin's whole schedule had gone topsy-turvy. This revue he was doing with Victor Herbert had made him even more irritable than usual, no small accomplishment. The composer sat side-by-side with Cliff Hess, his musical secretary and arranger, at that special piano with the lever he could move so he could play in whatever key he wanted. They'd been there only half an hour, but the floor around the bench was littered with music paper, much of it crumpled. Miras swallowed hard. "I'm sorry to bother you, sir," he finally managed. "But Mr. Tabor is on the phone for you. He says it's important."

Berlin didn't look around. "Tell him I'm busy, I'll call him later."

"He said you'd say that, sir, and he told me to tell you it really is very important, and it won't take more than a minute.

Berlin banged the keyboard with both hands; the discordant crash filled the room. "Son of a bitch!" He swung around to face Miras. "I *had* that line, I was this close. Ah!"

Hess sat silently, his face a mask.

Berlin leaped off the piano bench and charged past his valet to the telephone with the disabled ringer on the little Sheraton table next to the doorway. "Tabor?" he shouted into the receiver. "God damn it to hell, what is so fucking important, you had to interrupt me?"

Miras' expression didn't change. S.O.P., and like Hess, he had long since become accustomed to it. He turned and walked soundlessly out of the room.

Berlin heard Tabor swallow. "Mr. Berlin, have you had a chance to look over the material I left for you yesterday?"

Christ, Berlin thought. I should have known. "No, I haven't. When I got back last night, there were two cops waiting to talk to me, and they took their goddamn sweet time about it, over an hour. Then it took me another hour to get so I could actually do some work. And I'm working now—or I would be, if people would just leave me the hell alone. When I get some time, I'll look over that stuff of yours, but until then, quit bugging me about it. *I'll* call *you*. Is that clear enough?"

A brief silence, then, "Yes, Mr. Berlin."

"Good. Your minute's up." He slammed down the receiver, started back to the piano, then stopped long enough to snicker, shake his head, and mutter, "Suck-ass toady. Wish I could've seen his face."

<>< >< >

About halfway between Seventh and Eighth on 125th, Joplin pointed at a fleabag Burly-Q house, posters on either side of the theater entryway, showing every detail permissible by law of a Hundred Gorgeous Girls. "There it is. The Alamo Club."

As Martin scanned the entryway, one of the Hundred came up from behind. "You're early, boys—'less you want a private show. I only live down the block."

She was big in every dimension, hair a brilliant red never seen in nature, splashing over her shoulders. But no amount of makeup could compensate for the harsh line of her mouth. Her eyes were blue, with pupils so small, Martin could barely make them out. "I'm sorry...no," he said. "We're looking for the Alamo."

The girl snickered. "Pretty early for that, too, you ask me, but there it is." She pointed toward a narrow wooden door at the far side of the theater. "Go on in there, downstairs."

Joplin executed a polite bow. "Thank you, Miss." Martin grabbed him by the arm, and pulled him away, toward the door.

Inside, the young man led Joplin carefully down a worn wooden staircase, into a cave of a room that reeked of antique cigarette smoke. They walked past the bar, where a colored bartender barely moved as he filled glasses for five men, three colored, two white. Martin heard voices from the big room beyond, a man's and a woman's, and as he and Joplin walked in, he saw the man—a white man—at a piano, gesturing up at a colored woman who stood on a little stage before him. To Martin's surprise, Joplin worked his way quickly through lines of battered wooden tables that filled the room, marched right up to the piano man, and tapped his shoulder. The pianist spun around, took one look at Joplin, and the sunshine Martin thought he'd left outside burst across the man's face. "Well, hey now, look, it's Scott Joplin." The piano player grabbed the composer's hand with both of his own, and gave it a healthy pump. "What you comin' by so early for, Scott, I don't start playin' till

eight." Which seemed to remind him of the woman, standing on
the stage, head cocked, hands on hips. "Hey, honey." The man's
voice was pure gravel. "Go take yourself ten, okay. Then come
on back, and we'll see what we can do with your routine."

The grin on the man's face was infectious. Despite herself,
the woman smiled back, then walked off, down the few stairs,
and out to the bar. Martin also smiled. Only Joplin didn't smile,
but that meant nothing. Martin had never seen a smile on his
teacher's face.

Joplin indicated Martin with a casual wave. "This is Martin
Niederhoffer, Jimmy, my piano student. Martin, Ragtime Jimmy.
He plays ragtime right."

"Pleased to make your acquaintance." Ragtime Jimmy gave
Martin's hand a pump as vigorous as he'd given Joplin's. "So
you're learnin' pianna from the master, huh?"

Jimmy's big, oval face radiated good humor; his eyes sparkled.
Hair hung loose across his forehead. But what caught Martin's
attention beyond all else was the man's nose, long and broad, twice
the size of an average snoot, but neither discolored nor misshapen
by the purple excrescences of a serious elbow-bender. Just an mon-
ster honker, like the man took nose vitamins every morning with
his orange juice. Martin tried not to stare, but Jimmy dismissed
his concern with a casual wave. "It's just how I am. I think maybe
if the good Lord wanted to give me something big, he coulda
picked better. But I ain't got no cherce in the matter."

Martin laughed. The man was a natural comic.

"So what brings you guys out here at four o'clock in the
afternoon? You want to go on tonight or somethin'? Scott, you
don't need no tryout, and if you say the kid's okay, that's good
enough for me. Just come by maybe about ten or eleven—"

Martin saw Lottie sail through the doorway and up to the
trio. She fired a look at Martin that brought sweat out of his
every pore, then looked at the piano player. "Hello, Jimmy.
Thank you for lookin' after my man."

Jimmy looked blank-faced from Lottie to Joplin to Martin.
"Well, Mrs. J, I'm always glad to help, but I ain't sure—"

"I'm sorry, Jimmy, but Scott and me are in a hurry." Lottie pointed at Martin. "He'll tell you about it."

As the Joplins walked away, the woman-singer came back through the doorway, but halfway to the stage, Jimmy motioned her off. "Sorry, honey, I got busier'n I thought. Go on out there an' oil your tonsils for about half an hour more, okay? Tell 'em Jimmy said it's on the house." He gave Martin a light punch to the arm. "Looks like there's a little bit of a story here, hey? You want to tell me? Or do you gotta get your sticks movin' too?

Something about Ragtime Jimmy... Martin couldn't keep a smile off his face. "You want to hear it, sure, I'll tell you."

Jimmy listened quietly to Martin's story, but the instant the young man finished, the piano player exploded. "Well, don't that beat all I ever heard—and you can bet I hear plenty in a place like this. Irving Berlin, huh? Well, I ain't got no trouble rememberin' the fuss Scott made a few years back, tellin' anybody who'd hold still for a minute about how Berlin stole his music and made it into 'Alexander's Ragtime Band.'"

Martin nodded. "I know."

Jimmy rolled right along. "I was a kid then, playin' out at Diamond Tony's in Coney, an' everybody—I mean ev-er-y-body in the music game—was talkin' about it. I didn't know just what to believe, 'cause I didn't know Scott then. But now I do. He comes in every once in a while, an' listens to me play, an' I get to talk to him about this and that and the other. An' one thing I'll tell you—if that man says something, you better take it as the truth from the gospels. I don't think a lie ever came outa his mouth. If he says Berlin stole his music, then Berlin stole it. I can't for the life of me figure what you or anybody else coulda told him that woulda got him to give Irving Berlin more of his music. If you don't mind me sayin', that wasn't a smart thing to do."

Martin thought if he had a sword, he'd fall on it, right then and there, but took heart as he saw Jimmy's face brighten. "Well, but hey, we all of us do something dumb here and there, and at least you was tryin' to help Scott, so I say good for you. Now, we gotta give him *and* you some help. Not to be disparagin' or anything like that, but if you think you can just go off on your own and talk Berlin into gettin' square on that music, you got yourself a whole different think comin'. You got plenty of moxie, but what you ain't got is leverage, know what I mean? If you can hang around a li'l while, I'll go make a phone call and get you some. A whole bunch, in fact."

"That's no trouble." Martin checked his watch. "Mr. Berlin always goes out to a show or a late dinner, then he gets home about 11, 11:30, and starts writing his songs. He once told Mr. Snyder that watching something by Kern or Romberg gets him moving better on his own stuff. He works all night."

Jimmy grinned. "Everybody says he's some kinda owl."

"Right. That's why I figured I'd wait outside his building tonight, and catch him on his way home. Try and make him understand what's going on."

Jimmy laughed. "Which would probably just get you a fist in your kisser, and you'd end up lookin' like me." He got up from the stool, stretched. "Go on, sit down. Let's hear your stuff. Maybe I can get *you* to play behind that li'l songbird later on, while we're waitin' for Footsie Vinny."

Footsie Vinny? Martin thought he'd already bitten off more than he could chew, hadn't even begun to swallow it, and now it looked like he'd taken another huge bite. He sat at the piano, shot both cuffs, and began to play Joplin's "Solace." Seemed about right for the occasion.

<> <> <>

While Nell brought Stark up to date, he sipped at his coffee, didn't say a word. "Now, I think it's time to grab the bull by the horns," she said. I'll take you over to Joe's place, and we can see how Scott reacts to you. And you can hear first-hand what Martin Niederhoffer has to say."

"He's the young man who started all this."

"That's the way it looks."

Stark pulled out his pocket watch, slid it back, said nothing, just stared past Nell as if he found the sight of the kitchen sink fascinating. Nell stifled a sigh. She knew this act; he was preparing to be difficult. "Dad…"

He focused back to her. "Yes, my dear?"

"Don't 'yes, my dear' me. If you think I'm wrong, then just say so, and we'll go from there."

"Well, I wouldn't put it that strongly, but I do think we might be making the situation more complicated than it needs to be. Why don't I just go down and talk turkey to Berlin? Drop in on him, not give him any opportunity to make up stories? Perhaps I can persuade him to return Joplin's music, which is why you asked me to come out in the first place."

"But we've gone far past the first place. There's been a murder, if you'll remember."

"There's nothing wrong with my memory. But we don't know, do we, that the murder has any connection with the theft of the music. Let's deal with the straightforward problem in a straightforward way. If we can recover Joplin's music, then we can turn our full attention to the other concern. All things in good time, my… Nell."

"Oh, Dad." Nell ran her hands through her thick dark hair, just the way Sarah used to do. Stark shivered. "I think you're trying to get out of coming face-to-face with Scott."

"I most certainly am not. I have no reason to be embarrassed on his account. If anyone ought to feel awkward—"

The ring of the telephone interrupted his speech. Nell rolled her eyes, then got up and ran into the living room. Stark poured himself more coffee.

When she came back, he knew instantly there was trouble. She shook her head. "I keep thinking it can't possibly get worse…"

"It can always get worse," Stark said, not in an unkindly way. "And it often does. What's the problem now?"

"That was Lottie. She's got Scott with her. She's bringing him here from Harlem. Apparently, our young man got restless, ran out of Joe's place to go see his girlfriend, and took Scott along. Now, he's left Scott with Lottie and he's off somewhere, doing

The King of Ragtime 101

God knows what. All he'd tell Lottie was that he had some things to do." She paused. "Dad, I'm going to kill him."

Stark worked very hard at not smiling. Even as a little girl, when Nell planted her feet, wild horses couldn't pull her loose. Some of those scenes between his daughter and her mother...

Nell thrust a slip of paper into his hand. "Here's Joe's address. I'm going to take Scott back there as fast as I can, but if he sees you here and goes into one of his states, I'll never get him to Brooklyn on the subway. So go ahead, if you'd like, talk to Berlin, and then come over to Joe's. You can find your way, can't you?"

Stark glanced at the paper. "615 Avenue C, Brooklyn."

"That's in Windsor Terrace, just a few blocks south of Prospect Park. He's got a lovely little house there."

Stark nodded, slipped the paper into his pocket, got to his feet. "I'm sure I'll have no trouble. I lived and worked in this city for five years, and I know my way around." He kissed her cheek, then walked into the living room, took his straw boater off the chair where he'd left it, and went out. Quickly, it seemed to Nell.

She waited a minute, then walked to the telephone table, picked up the city phone directory and thumbed through its pages. Balancing the book in one hand, she lifted the receiver to her ear, and gave the operator a number. When she heard, "Waterson, Berlin, and Snyder, Music Publishers," she said, "This is Geneva Edwards, from *Dramatic Mirror* Magazine. I'd like to make an appointment with Mr. Berlin for a short interview, and I'm working with a close deadline. Would he have just a few minutes tomorrow?"

"I'm not sure Mr. Berlin will be in the office at all tomorrow," said the receptionist. "You might try his home—that's Riverside 5396. I'm sure he'll do all he can to accommodate someone from *Dramatic Mirror*."

Which brought a wry grin to Nell's face. The joke in the music business was that Irving Berlin would stand up his mother if it meant getting an hour with a reporter. Nell thanked the woman and hung up the phone. Yes, her father had once lived and worked in New York City, and he knew his way around, but only in the geographical sense. She had to admit, if only to herself, she found his straight-from-the-shoulder, no-nonsense, my-word-is-my-bond style admirable, and more than a little touching. But to think he could barge in on Irving Berlin, demand the music back, and expect Berlin to hand it over? Nell shook her head. She'd do better, using a little guile and a lot of flattery.

Chapter Six

Stark came up from the subway at Forty-second Street and Broadway, walked downtown to Thirty-eighth, and into Number 112. A few minutes later, he was back outside, scratching his head. Two doors down the block, he saw the Joseph Stern Music Company, started in that direction, hesitated. For several years now, Stern had published Negro ragtime—including some pieces by Scott Joplin—with far more financial success than Stark had ever enjoyed. Finally, he swallowed his pride, walked up to the door and inside, and asked the young receptionist where Waterson, Berlin, and Snyder had gone. The girl told him they'd relocated uptown. "A couple of years ago, actually. Mr. Stern threw a party when they moved. He didn't like Mr. Waterson."

"I didn't like either one of them," Stark said, then thanked the girl and started hoofing back up Broadway. He passed the Palace...Sarah used to love the vaudeville shows there. The huge shield-shaped sign on the ornate facade of the Gaiety told passersby *Turn To The Right* will open shortly. At Broadway and Forty-seventh, the old man stood before the Strand Theatre, and scanned the white block lettering in the windows above the grand marquee. Hendricks and Saloman, Press Agents. Katz and Elliot,

Lawyer and Notary. Charles S. Gellman, Theatrical Bookings. "Ah, there, third floor. Waterson, Berlin, and Snyder."

He shunned the elevator in the lobby, walked up the three flights, and inside. The place was a circus. Young men and an occasional young woman carrying books, note pads, file folders, papers, charged back and forth through a haze of tobacco smoke. Music from pianos in the back corridor fused into painful cacophony. Six songwriters wriggled in chairs at the periphery of the Reception Room, waiting their turn to sit at one of those pianos and play their work. Stark strode across the room to a desk where a darkly-attractive young woman sat as if at the center of a storm, talking on an upright desk-stand intercom, and nodding or winking to the cascade of young runners as they deposited papers onto her desk, or snatched some up. As she finished her conversation, and reached toward another button on the circular base of the intercom, Stark said, "Excuse me, Miss. I'm John Stark, of the Stark Music Company." He took care not to add "of St. Louis." "I need to speak with Mr. Berlin."

The woman barely glanced at him. "I'm sorry," she said. "Mr. Berlin isn't in." Then she swiveled to take a pile of folders from a stout, perspiring young man.

Stark had long preached that persistence is the most important determinant of success. "Would you please tell me where I can find him, then," he said. "It's a matter of some considerable urgency."

The woman swiveled her chair, deposited the folders onto the desk in front of her, and looked up at the old man. "It's extremely important that I talk to Mr. Berlin," Stark said. "Please be so good as to tell me where I can find him."

The woman said, "Just a moment," then pushed back in her chair, got up, and walked quickly away, down the far corridor. She was back in just a couple of minutes, in the company of a stocky middle-aged man, a generation behind Stark, stringy brown hair combed across his balding head. A large diamond stickpin in his tie drew attention to a belly whose every wish clearly was heard as a command. The woman returned to her desk and picked up a piece of paper. Stark knew she'd be listening, didn't care.

The heavy man extended a hand. "Well, John Stark, I'll be damned. How are you, sir?"

Stark took the soft, manicured hand. His own hands had never lost the roughness they'd acquired in his farming years. "I'm well, thank you, Mr. Waterson. Yourself?"

"Just fine, fine." Waterson swept his hand in a wide arc, as if to indicate the reason for his well-being. "And Mrs. Stark—how is she?"

Stark didn't waver. "I'm sorry to say, she is no longer among us. She was ill when we returned to St. Louis six years ago, and she died shortly after."

Waterson's face was that of a man who'd been taking a pleasant stroll, not paying attention to where he was going until he'd stepped smack into a pile of fresh dog turds. "Oh, Mr. Stark, how clumsy of me. I'm terribly sorry—"

Stark put him out of his misery with a slight motion of his hand. "Thank you, Mr. Waterson, but please don't be concerned. I need to speak with you." He motioned toward Waterson's office. "May I?"

Sarah would have been amused at the way her husband had turned Waterson's embarrassment to his advantage. "Why, yes, certainly." the big man said. "Come right on back. What is it? Are you planning to start back up here in New York?"

Stark smiled into his beard, but said nothing as he followed Waterson into his office. The publisher made a ceremony out of closing the door behind them. Stark looked around. A well-worn roll-top desk, couple of nondescript wooden chairs, oak file cabinet, floor-to-ceiling shelves, mostly filled with messy piles of paper. No piano. Waterson was a businessman, not a musician.

The publisher waddled to his desk, sat, then folded his hands across his abdomen, a move that made him look at least twice as big as he looked standing. Stark settled into a chair facing the desk. "No, Mr. Waterson, I'm not considering moving my business back to New York. We're doing very nicely in St. Louis."

Waterson sat forward. "Still publishing those classic rags of yours, eh?"

Stark bristled privately at the condescension, but kept his voice level. "Not *my* classic rags. I might wish they were, and I'll admit I've tried writing them, but none have been good enough to publish. I've got some fine young men, though. Artie Matthews, James Scott, Paul Pratt—"

"But nothing from Joplin any more."

No missing the malice there. Waterson had recovered from his gaffe out in the Reception Room. "No," Stark said. "We've published nothing of his since oh-eight. But I've noticed you haven't put out any work by him for quite some while, either."

"You can't publish what isn't written." Waterson reached for a box of cigars, held it out toward Stark, who declined politely. Waterson hesitated, then took a cigar, flicked a lighter into life, and lit up. White smoke filled the room.

"Joplin hasn't given you any manuscripts, then?" Stark asked. "In all these years?"

Waterson shook his head. "Not a one. Ever since 1911, all he seems able to think about is that opera of his. An opera, can you imagine? He could be turning out hit after hit."

"Like your Mr. Berlin."

Waterson pursed lips, then nodded cautiously.

"Scott wants his music to be respectable," Stark said.

"Respectable?" Waterson spat the question. "What the hell's unrespectable about ragtime?" He turned a waggish grin on Stark. "To read your ads, ragtime is as respectable as music can get."

"I'm glad someone reads my ads."

Both men laughed, Waterson with that unease which sneaks in when the laugher doesn't know where the conversation might be heading.

"But to get down to cases, Mr. Waterson, why I'm here has to do with Scott Joplin and Irving Berlin."

Waterson dropped his cigar into the ash tray, and gave Stark a look that suggested the old man had just spit onto the office floor. "God damn!" Waterson groaned. "You're not going to start up that business about Berlin supposedly stealing "Alexander's Ragtime Band" from Scott, are you? That's a dead issue, it's been five years already. Besides, Irvy doesn't have to steal music from Scott Joplin."

"Because he's got a pickaninny in his closet who writes his songs for him?"

Waterson's jaw fell. He gaped at Stark.

"Don't look so shocked, Mr. Waterson. I'm only repeating your own words, which were in all the papers." Stark paused just long enough for Waterson to get out a syllable of objection, then pressed on. "That was in December of 1911, you'll recall. The same year 'Alexander's Ragtime Band' came out."

Waterson's face was a blotchy map, whether of rage or embarrassment, Stark couldn't tell. He thought probably a bit of both. The stout publisher sniffed. "It was just a joke."

"Perhaps the joke has taken on a life of its own." Stark's tone was conciliatory; if the situation were to get out of hand, it wouldn't do him any good. "Mr. Waterson, I can't prove Berlin stole Joplin's music, so I won't make that claim. But Joplin believes it, which is why I'm concerned. Apparently, he's left another piece of music with Berlin, and I don't want there to be any more trouble. That's why I need to speak to your partner, and I'd be grateful if you could help me arrange that."

Waterson narrowed his eyes, swung his chair around, studied Stark. "Joplin's left music with Berlin, you say? I find that very hard to believe. In fact, I'd say if ever I heard poppycock, I'm hearing it now."

"I understand your confusion, Mr. Waterson. But Joplin's written a musical play, and it seems your bookkeeper, who happens to take piano lessons from Joplin, persuaded him that Irving Berlin would give his work its best chance of being published and produced on stage."

"Our bookkeeper, you say? Young Niederhoffer?"

"Yes."

Waterson leaned across his desk, all seriousness now. "You may not be aware, Mr. Stark, but just last evening, someone was murdered in our office. Matter of fact, that's the reason I'm here now. I originally had…an appointment for this afternoon, but by the time the police were through, it was so late I had to cancel. Anyway, Niederhoffer was seen running away with Joplin, after the body was found."

"Be that as it may," Stark said. "Joplin's music is the reason I need to speak to Berlin, and the murder doesn't change that." He saw Waterson sneak a look at his watch. "I know it's late, and I really don't want to impose upon your time. Would you please take a moment to direct me to Mr. Berlin?"

Waterson looked across the room, dragged his gaze across the expanse of bookshelves, then suddenly grinned, and returned his attention to Stark. "Okay, sure. Probably your best chance of finding him right now is at his flat, Seventy-second at Riverside Drive. The Chatsworth."

Just a couple of blocks over from Nell's place, Stark thought, which reminded him that his daughter and Joplin would be waiting for him at Joe Lamb's. Nell would have a fit when he got there, late as he was going to be. But she'd asked for his help, so she'd just have to wait another hour. He might have something to tell her that would make the wait worthwhile.

Waterson interrupted his thoughts. "Irvy got the place all fixed up for his new wife four years back, but she caught typhoid on their honeymoon, and died a few months later. A shame, shouldn't happen to anybody. Anyway, Irvy works there, 'specially at night. It's private, it's quiet, nobody bothers him. Right now, him and Victor Herbert are writing the music for Ziegfeld's new show, *Century Girl*. Gonna put it on at the Century Theater."

Stark's eyes widened. "Isn't that theater supposed to be cursed? Everything that opens there falls to pieces."

"It is, it is." Waterson sounded more enthusiastic than at any time since Stark had come into his office. "But Flo thinks he can break the curse, so I guess we'll see. One way or the other, it don't matter much to me. Irvy's started up his own firm to handle his theater music, so there's no way W, B, and S is going to see a nickel from that show, no matter what."

Clear to Stark that Waterson wouldn't mind if Irving Berlin's new firm didn't see a nickel either. The old man rose, extended a hand, shook with Waterson. "Thank you, sir," he said. "I'm sorry to have interrupted your day, but I'm grateful for your help."

Waterson smirked. "If I were you, I'd be careful, talking to Irvy right now. He wouldn't admit it to anybody, but he knows that next to Victor Herbert, he's a pipsqueak, soaking wet behind his ears. He wants to score big with Flo, but every time he gets a few notes down, he sees this big shadow laying across the paper."

<>‹›<>

Nell heard them coming down the hall, Scott's angry tenor, Lottie's soprano, first soothing, then pleading, finally warning. Like an opera, Nell thought. Before her guests reached the door, she had it open, and was hustling them inside, ducking under Joplin's wildly flapping arms. "I don't have time for all this," the composer shouted, glaring from one woman to the other. "I need to go home, and get back to work on my symphony."

"Scott, please listen to me." That from Nell.

The five words stopped Joplin cold. Lottie felt a terrible urge to start screaming, herself. She could talk herself blue in the face, and her husband wouldn't bat an eye, but one line from Nell, and he stood there like a pussycat. But shame on me, Lottie thought, I got no right to be anything but grateful. Wasn't for Nell, I'd have had to put him away in a hospital months ago.

"You can't go home right now, Scott." Nell's voice was quiet, her tone, even. If you do, the police will pick you up and you won't get any work done in jail. They're after you for murder, remember? The boy in Martin's office?"

Joplin blinked several times, shook his head like someone trying to shake pieces of memory back into place.

"I'm going to take you back to Joe Lamb's, where you were last night and earlier today. Joe's got a piano and paper. You can write your music there."

Joplin nodded. "I was working there this morning. Then Martin took me out to talk to Irving Berlin about my music, but I don't remember doing that. We went to a deli, met his girl, and talked for a while. Next thing, we were at the Alamo Club, and Lottie came and took me away, and now I'm here. What is this all about?"

Nell glanced at Lottie, who shrugged. "Martin bring that girl with him to his lesson a couple of times. Sweet li'l thing. She be his assistant bookkeeper."

"At Waterson, Berlin, and Snyder? She works there, too?"

Lottie thought Nell looked like a cat about to pounce on a bird. "That what the boy say."

"What's her name?"

Joplin closed his eyes, thought hard.

"Way I recall, it be Birdie," said Lottie. "Pretty sure."

"That's right," said Joplin. "Birdie."

Without a word, Nell walked to the telephone, snatched up the receiver, gave the number to the operator. Joplin and Lottie stared. "Hello, yes. This is Caroline Spooler, with the Visiting Nurse Service." Nell's voice was that of a military commander. "You have an employee named Birdie. I need to speak with her a moment." Nell shifted the receiver to her other ear. "Yes, hello. Birdie? This is Caroline Spooler, Visiting Nurse Service. I need to pay a visit to your family, but I don't want to interfere with your work. Will you all be at home at eight this evening?...Good, I'll see you then. Please tell me your address, so I'll be sure I have it right." She scribbled on a small pad next to the telephone. "Good, thank you, Birdie. I'll—no, no, really, there's nothing for you to worry about. I'll see you at eight. Good-bye."

She hung up the phone, then turned a bent smile on Joplin and Lottie. "I didn't want to take a chance the receptionist might be listening in. Maybe Birdie can shed a little light on this nonsense." She took Joplin by the arm. "Come on, Scott. Let's get back to Joe's so you can go back to work. Lottie, why don't you head on home. The longer you're away, the more chance they might start looking elsewhere for Scott."

"Yeah, but it's just I feels bad about you gettin' yourself all mixed up in this, and it ain't really your problem."

"It is now," Nell said.

‹›‹›‹›

A few minutes before five o'clock, Robert Miras padded into Berlin's study. His boss sat alone at the piano, a sheet of music paper in one hand, striking piano keys with the other. Miras cleared his throat. "Sorry, Mr. Berlin, but there's a Mr. John Stark here from St. Louis, who says it's urgent that he speak to you. I tried to put him off, but he simply won't leave. He says he will not take no for an answer, and will sit in the vestibule until you have a moment to see him."

Berlin surprised Miras by breaking into a wide grin. "Jesus, John Stark, here from St. Lou? He used to be Scott Joplin's publisher. Crazy old guy, he thinks ragtime is music straight from God. Wonder why he's back in New York, and what the hell he wants with me. Urgently, no less."

Miras shrugged. "I suppose there's only one way to find out, sir."

Berlin nodded. "Okay, Robert. Why'n't you show him in."

If Berlin was in any way unhappy to see his visitor, it didn't show. Stark began to introduce himself, but his host interrupted. "Yeah, sure, Mr. Stark, I remember you from the old days. Nice seeing you, again." He shook Stark's hand with enthusiasm.

"I'm sorry to barge in on you like this," Stark said. "I didn't want to interrupt your work—"

"Nah, nah, nah." Berlin shook his head vigorously, silly thought. "It won't hurt me to have a little break, I'm workin' fifteen, sixteen hours a day right now. Gotta get a whole show's-worth of songs for Ziegfeld, and it's all got to be first-class."

Stark nodded sympathy and understanding. "I can imagine how you must feel. After shows like *Watch Your Step* and *Stop! Look! Listen!*, everyone's expecting something very big from you."

Berlin motioned Stark into a forest-green plush chair, then sat on the piano bench. "Yeah, well, I've just plain got to do it," the composer said. "We open in the fall, gonna start rehearsals in just another month or so."

He's strung tighter than his piano, Stark thought. Looks like a man sitting on the edge of a razor blade. The old man leaned back in his chair and turned a favorite-uncle smile on his host. "Oh, Mr. Berlin, I'm sure you'll get it done." Stark pointed at the piano. "Do you have something I could hear?"

A mild backhand wave, then Berlin said, "Nah, Cliff Hess and I still got a lotta work to do before I could let anybody hear any of these tunes. But tell you what. Come back in November, I'll get you a great seat at the Century, you can hear every tune in the show. So, tell me, Mr. Stark. What is it I can do for you?"

Nicely done, Stark thought. Set me up, then a quick sucker punch. "I'm here on Lottie Joplin's behalf," he said. "And I suppose Scott's as well."

"*Son of a bitch!*" Izzy howled, and Berlin's calm vaporized. He spoke quickly. "Look, Mr. Stark—I've been telling people for five years now, and it's getting to be a real pain in the ass. *I* wrote 'Alexander's Ragtime Band,' just like I write all my other songs, and I'm goddamn sick and tired of hearing about little colored boys I've got hiding in my closets—"

Stark raised a hand. "I'm not here to talk about 'Alexander'. I'm here to talk about *If*."

"About if? About if, what? Stark, what the hell *are* you talking about?"

"Here is the situation," Stark said. "Scott Joplin is quite ill. I don't think he can last very much longer. And he's apparently completed a musical play called *If*."

Stark watched Berlin closely, but saw no indication of concern. The young man spread his arms, an elaborate shrug. "So good, good for Scott Joplin. I wish him luck getting it published and produced. I really do."

Stark doubted that. He'd always thought Berlin's solicitude ended at the tip of his own nose. "Joplin was negotiating with Lester Walton to have it put on at the Lafayette," Stark said. "But then he gave the work to you."

"To me? No. Sorry. First I ever heard about this *If* was from you, just a minute ago."

"Joplin says he left the manuscript with you on Monday."

Berlin set himself into a posture of thought. "Listen, Mr. Stark. You just got done telling me about Joplin being 'ill,' right? Well, everybody in this city who's got anything at all to do with music knows that where Joplin is ill is in his head. But nobody says *I'm* ill in *my* head, and *I'm* telling you he didn't leave any manuscript with me. Not on Monday, not any time. And if he ever did ask me to look at something by him, I'd tell him I put my own music—which I write myself—on stage. Nobody else's."

Stark felt his temper rise, tried to hold it back, no luck. "Which you write yourself, eh? Not quite so fast. Remember, I saw Joplin's opera in manuscript, before he had to rewrite those opening measures of the 'Marching Onward' tune because they just happened to be note-for-note the same as your big hit."

"The opening measures!" Berlin's face was scarlet, his features twisted in fury. "A couple of measures in a couple of tunes look the same, so you tell me I stole from Joplin? What about the whole rest of the song—did I steal that from Joplin, too? Maybe a few notes could've stuck in my head, but—"

"If it was good enough to stick in your head, why didn't you publish it?"

Berlin's expression suggested that more than a few of Stark's screws might have come loose. "Why didn't I publish an opera by a colored man? Why the hell didn't *you* publish it?"

"That's not the question. If I both composed and published music, I would take pains never to make a hit tune for myself out of a work entrusted to me for evaluation."

"Jesus, Stark!" Berlin clapped a hand to his forehead, then wheeled around to face the piano. "Here, listen to this!" He began to play, striking the black keys with such force as to suggest the piano had offended him.

Stark gave the performance his full attention. Lot of mistakes, but still… "That sounds familiar."

Berlin stopped playing, then thrust his face forward so it came to within a few inches of Stark's. "Oh, it does, huh?" Shooting a fine spray of saliva into the older man's face with each word. "Well, what it is, it's a little Russian melody I always heard my father sing when I was a kid. Go take yourself a walk around the lower east side, Mr. Stark. You'll hear Russian Jews singing that tune on every street corner. Now…" Berlin turned away to resume his assault on the black keys.

Stark again listened, intent, then said, "That's 'Magnetic Rag.' Joplin published it himself, two years ago."

"Well, what do you know about that!" Berlin waved a fist in front of Stark's nose. "Sounds a lot like my father's song, don't it? You think I oughta sue Joplin? Christ Almighty, Stark! Joplin heard some Russian music on the streets, and he did a little borrowing. If they treated songwriters like bank robbers, every last one of us'd be wearing stripes. So now, if you really don't mind, I need to get back to my work. I ain't got Scott Joplin's manuscript, and I got exactly zero interest in Scott Joplin's manuscript. Been good talking to you, Mr. Stark, but I'm a busy man."

Stark pulled a pen and a small white business card from his pocket, then scribbled numbers and held out the card to Berlin. "My daughter's telephone, I'm staying with her. If you do come up with anything about Joplin's music, I'd appreciate hearing from you."

Berlin took the card, flipped it over and back in his hand, then slid it behind his vest and into his shirt pocket. Without another word, he turned away from Stark, sat on the piano bench, and began to play.

Chapter Seven

Brooklyn
Wednesday, August 23
Early Evening

As Stark walked up to Joe Lamb's door, he heard piano music from inside. Joplin. This was not going to be easy. He set his jaw, knocked.

Nell opened the door. Stark pecked at her cheek, then walked past her, into the living room. Lamb slouched in an easy chair, shirt open at the collar, tie loose. At the far wall, Joplin sat at a piano, playing notes and chords, and every now and again reaching to the rack to write. Stark extended a hand to Lamb. "Good to see you, Joe. How's the family?"

Lamb pulled himself out of the chair to shake Stark's hand. "I'm glad to see *you*, Mr. Stark. I'm sorry Etty and Little Joe are away. I'd have liked for you to meet them."

Nell cleared her throat. "Did you get lost on the subway, Dad?"

Stark glanced at Joplin, still fully engaged with his composition. Then, he turned back to his daughter. "No, I did not get lost, not in the subway or anywhere else. Since I had time, I decided I would speak to Berlin and see what I could learn, so I took the subway down to Waterson, Berlin, and Snyder. They've moved—"

"I could have told you that."

"I talked to Henry Waterson. He remembered me, and gave me Berlin's home address."

"And?"

Stark shook his head. "Berlin swears he hasn't seen Scott in years, and doesn't know a thing about the manuscript."

"Do you believe him?"

"Not for a moment. The man's brass is incredible. But I think it can't hurt that Waterson knows about it now. There's clearly no love lost between him and Berlin."

Stark glanced toward the piano. Joplin played one chord, a second, a third, then raised a shaking hand to write on the music paper. Nell followed her father's eyes, and a good deal of starch seemed to drain out of her. "He's at it night and day," she said to the unasked question. First it was the musical play, now it's *Symphony Number One.*"

Stark sighed. "Perhaps you should tell him he's got a visitor. If he happens to turn and sees me, it will be that much more difficult."

Nell nodded, then walked to the piano. She rested a hand on Joplin's shoulder. "Scott...*Scott.*"

No response.

Nell tightened her grip, shook the composer. He swung around ferociously and jumped to his feet, arms up, fists balled. Stark took a step toward his daughter, but Nell didn't flinch. "Scott, I'm sorry to interrupt you, but you have a visitor."

At the sight of Joplin, face-on, Stark's throat sucked itself dry. He felt as if his shoes had been nailed to the floor. This man couldn't be Scott Joplin. Joplin was always so neat in his dress, meticulous in his personal habits. Hair always cut short, trimmed cleanly above the ears. Every day, a close shave. Crisp collar, tie set just so. White shirt, vest and suit pressed to a fare-thee-well. Eyes that greeted you with self-possessed calm. But this man's eyes were muddy and wild. His hair had not been cut in weeks, nor had he shaved this morning. His collar was wilted, tie open; his suit was wrinkled as though he routinely slept in it. With an odd sensation of disgust, Stark noticed the fly in the specter's pants was unbuttoned. Joplin didn't say a word, just glared at Stark.

"Joplin?" Stark finally managed.

No response.

"Don't you remember me, Joplin? John Stark? From Sedalia and St. Louis?"

At the mention of his own surname, Stark saw the corner of Joplin's mouth twitch; at 'Sedalia', a near-smile. But then Joplin turned to Nell. "What's he doing here? Haven't I got enough trouble already?" The composer chewed at his upper lip, then reached for Nell's hand. "Make him go away—please." A high-pitched wail. "The day he stopped paying me royalties, I told him I was through with him, and I've never talked to him from that time till this. If only he'd published my *Guest of Honor* and *Treemonisha*, I'd have had my symphony done years ago."

Nothing could have prepared Stark for this. The composer's speech was slurred like a drunkard's, hard consonants mushy, words run together, but Scott Joplin had never been a drinker. Even in Sedalia, in those wild days when ragtime was bursting upon American music, and parties went on for entire weekends at a time, Stark had never seen Joplin drink more than one beer at a sitting. A terrible desolation settled into the old man's chest.

"We need his help, Scott." Nell's voice was that of someone trying to talk a man perched on a window ledge out of jumping. "I called him, and he got right on a train to come out and help you get your music back from Irving Berlin. Please be polite to him."

All through Nell's speech, Joplin nodded his head like an automaton. When she finished, he said, "All right," then extended a hand to Stark. "I thank you for your concern," Joplin said as they shook, but before the older man could reply, the composer added, "Is Artie Matthews doing well?"

Stark had begun to adjust to the unpredictable flight of Joplin's mind. "I'm pleased to see you, Joplin, and yes, Matthews is doing just fine. He's arranger for the Booker T. Washington Theater now, working for Tom Turpin, and they've put on some very fine shows." He paused as an idea came into his head. "In fact, Matthews is also doing a good deal of arranging for me, and he's writing some very fine ragtime. Do you know his 'Pastimes'? I brought out 'Number One' a couple years back, and 'Number Two' just this year."

Joplin shook his head. "Haven't seen them. Did you give him royalties?"

In fact, Stark had not. He'd paid Artie Matthews an outright fifty dollars for the latest "Pastimes." "Conditions have become such," he'd told Matthews, "that I can no longer pay royalties to any composer, white or colored, and hope to stay in business. Get your work into print, get yourself a reputation, then you might be able to wangle a royalties deal from one of the big New York outfits." He did give Matthews an additional twenty-seven dollars because the man badly needed a new suit of clothes, but no point mentioning that to Joplin.

"I've never discussed your business with other composers," Stark said, as mildly as he could manage. "So I'm not going to discuss their business with you. I came here to try to help you, Joplin, and I'll do the best I possibly can. But talking to you now has given me an idea for your music. Once we get it back, perhaps I *can* publish it myself, and then talk to Tom Turpin about putting it on at the Booker T. I have to think Turpin would be interested."

"Why would *you* be interested?" Joplin said. "You turned me away with *Guest of Honor* and *Treemonisha*, both."

Stark reminded himself he had to be patient. "As good as any opera might be, if it's written by a colored man, no white producer would touch it, and no colored producer could afford to even try. Not that it's right, but a man needs to pick his fights, and if there's no chance of winning, he'd be foolish to get into the ring. Turpin and Matthews would mount a nice show for you, and if you get some good reviews, who knows? You might just have a New York producer knocking at your door."

"Yeah…yeah…" Joplin seemed to be trying to think the matter through, then exploded in speech. "But I don't want to have it staged at Turpin's. *Or* the Lafayette." He waved his arms ferociously. "Martin Niederhoffer is right. If we can get Irving Berlin to publish and produce my work on Broadway, why, then, everybody will know Scott Joplin's name, everybody in the world. As they should."

The abrupt change in Joplin's speech and manner, and the glint in his eyes took Stark aback. The composer always had wanted respect for himself and his music, but he'd been a modest man, never given to anything remotely resembling such grandiose talk. Was it his disease, or had he been deranged by his years of frustration over trying to get his operas staged? Whichever, Stark grabbed the opening. "That could be, Mr. Joplin, and I'd be the first to wish you well. But aren't you concerned that Berlin might steal your music again?"

"Martin promised me he wouldn't let that happen." Joplin's face clouded. He held up a trembling hand. "I told Berlin that Martin knows all about my play, and he's going to be watching." Joplin shook his head, then cocked it to the left, an odd tic. He gave off a powerful odor of sweat and something more. Stark had smelled it, years before on battlefields throughout the south, the stench of fear. "Mr. Stark, thank you for coming all the way out here on my account. It's just that I don't have much time left to get my music written and staged. You do know what my trouble is?

Stark nodded.

"Well, then." That seemed to settle something in Joplin's mind. "I better get back to writing my symphony."

He took a step toward the piano bench, but Stark called to his back, "I need some information, Joplin. This musical play of yours—what is it? A comedy? A revue? Just what is it we're talking about?"

"That's a little hard to say." Tossed over the shoulder. "I guess a…well, a drama set to music. Some of it might be humorous, but only in an ironic way. I guess you could call it a fantasy, or maybe a dream. So many things can happen to a man at every step along his way, but the one thing that *does* happen determines all of what comes after. That's the 'If,' you see. My play is a man's life in two acts, what did happen and what might have happened. All set to music, but not an opera and not an operetta. A musical drama."

Amazing, Stark thought. Just like that, he's his old self. A musical drama, ironically humorous, a fantasy, or perhaps a dream! There was no end to this man's genius. What might he have accomplished if he'd been white?

Joplin lowered himself onto the piano bench. Nell laid a hand on his shoulder. The composer looked up at her, all gratitude.

"All right," Stark said quietly. I'll see what I can do. He turned to Nell. "I suppose for now, we just need to wait for this Martin fellow to show up."

"*Hope* he shows up," said Nell.

Stark's face was grim, lips like purse strings. "I suppose it wouldn't hurt to have a talk with his girlfriend, and see whether she can fill in any of the gaps. But first we'll have to find her."

Nell tried not to smile, succeeded only partially. "I did find her. And I have an appointment to talk to her, at eight tonight."

Joplin hit a discordant note. Stark opened his mouth, but said nothing.

<>‹›‹›

Nell looked around the small living room. No furniture aside from the four wooden chairs that she, Birdie, and the girl's parents occupied. But clean? You really *could* eat off the floor, Nell thought. On her left, Abe and Eva Kuminsky were giving her as hard a stare as she'd ever gotten from anyone other than her father. To her right, Birdie looked at her as though Nell were a puzzle needing to be solved.

"I'm very sorry to have alarmed you all," Nell said. "No, I'm not from the Visiting Nurse Service. I needed to talk to you, Birdie, and I didn't want the receptionist hearing something I'd rather keep between us—"

"Between you?" Eva gulped down a huge swallow of air. "What's so terrible you got to say, it needs to be between you and Birdie?"

"She done something she shouldn't have?"

Nell thought if Abe's eyes opened any wider, they might fly right out of his head. "No, it's nothing like that. Please let me explain. I want to talk about Martin—"

"Oh, Martin, huh?" Abe crossed his arms over his chest. "I should've known. This is about him killing his friend in his office, right? You're with the police."

Nell waved to dispel that notion as fast and as thoroughly as she could. "No, I'm not with the police. Please, Mr. Kuminsky, listen to me. I'm not with the visiting nurses, the police, or anyone else. I'm a good friend of Scott Joplin, the composer. I want to help him and Martin—"

Abe leaped to his feet. "Look, lady, I don't care who you are. You told Birdie you was with the Visiting Nurses, so her mother spent the last three hours down on her knees, scrubbing and cleaning. You're telling me you want to help some murderers that the cops are after?" He pointed toward the door. "I think you better just leave. I ain't about to let Birdie get in any trouble on account of Martin Niederhoffer. That boy is trouble himself."

Nell returned his flinty glare with interest. She got slowly to her feet, and as she smoothed her skirt, she said, taking care not to look at Birdie, "Martin seems to have some sort of plan for this evening. It might help a great deal if any of you know what it is."

Abe looked ready to go airborne. "Lady, you don't hear so good? The only plan that boy's got that I know about, he wants to marry my daughter, and hell's gonna freeze before *that* happens. Now, get yourself out of here before I call the cops."

Nell calmly extended a hand, which Abe took as if by reflex, then dropped as if he'd grabbed hold of a hot pan. "I'm sorry to have bothered you," Nell said, then nodded to Eva and Birdie, and turned to leave.

Abe wheeled around and stormed away toward the kitchen. Eva stood in place, wringing her hands in front of her apron. Birdie said, "I'll see you to the door, Mrs. Stanley." But as she turned the lock and pulled the door open, she whispered into Nell's face, "I don't know anything about tonight, but meet me tomorrow, Schneider's Deli, twelve-fifteen?"

Nell smiled. "Thank you, Birdie." Then she winked at the girl.

◇◇◇

A little past ten-thirty, on his way up the stairs from the subway at Broadway and Seventy-second, Martin turned a backdoor look on his companion. No way would he ever want to get on this guy's bad side, not for anything. Cap pulled low over dark, piggy eyes, mouth like a bloodless gash, bullet head set directly onto his shoulders, not even a trace of neck. He walked with the rolling gait of a gorilla. "Martin, this here's Footsie Vinny," Ragtime Jimmy had said by way of introduction, after he'd held a brief private consultation with the thug. "When Berlin gets two eyefuls of him, he just might decide he don't need Scott Joplin's music no more." Martin had extended a hand, but Footsie Vinny just nodded and shifted a toothpick from the right to the left side of his mouth. Then, all the way down from Harlem on the subway, the man had spoken only once. "If this mark a yours don't come across, how much you want me to persuade him?" A gutteral growl that had sent the man sitting on the other side of Vinny to a seat at the far end of the car.

Martin shook his head. "I don't want you to actually hurt him. Just scare him so bad he'll *think* you're going to do something. Okay?"

The contempt on Vinny's face set Martin's cheeks glowing. "You want maybe I should get one a them masks like the kids wear for Hallowe'en?"

Martin came this close to saying he thought Vinny's own face would intimidate Berlin more than any Hallowe'en mask, but caught himself just in time. "Just scare him for me," Martin pleaded. "Scare him good."

Vinny coughed, turned his head and hawked a gob onto the floor. Martin fought to keep his face butter-bland. "They don't call me Footsie for nothing," Vinny snarled. "Most guys I work on, they don't say much when all's I do is just talk. But after I kick out their teeth, then all of a sudden they get real chatty."

Martin pictured Irving Berlin down on the ground, his face in a pool of blood, teeth scattered all over the sidewalk. "Yeah, well, I guess that's right, Vinny. Maybe you could do something like twist his arm behind his back, or, say, grab him by his shirt collar and give him a good shake. But don't kick out his teeth. Please."

Vinny laughed out loud. The man at the far end of the subway car bolted out of his seat, through the door and into the next car. Vinny pointed with his head. "Guess maybe I scared *him* a little…well, you're the doc. Jimmy said I should help you, I'll help you. Best I can, anyway, with what you let me do."

<> <> <>

Martin led Vinny into Riverside Park, directly across Seventy-second Street from the Chatsworth Apartments. Just beyond, cars sped past on Riverside Drive. Vinny looked around, seemed to approve of what he saw. "Nice neighborhood your boy lives in."

"He's my boss," Martin said. "One of them, anyway. He makes a bundle writing music."

The words were barely out when Martin regretted them. In the glow of the streetlight above them, Vinny's eyes shone like an animal's. "He does, huh? Makes a bundle? What's his name?"

"Irving Berlin."

Vinny shook his head slowly. "Never heard of him. Sounds like a kike."

To the Irish, Italian, and Polish kids in the neighborhood when Martin was growing up, he was a kike, a mockey, a sheeny bastard. By any name, a dirty Jew. The good side was that he had developed early on into an accomplished street fighter, though not nearly so accomplished he'd even think of showing displeasure at Vinny's slur. "Mr. Berlin's probably the most famous songwriter in America right now."

"If you say so. Myself, I don't go for music much, except maybe for what Ragtime Jimmy plays, and that's because I just like Jimmy. You ain't never gonna meet a decenter guy. I once seen him give a hooker a handful of long green to get herself an operation she needed, and it wasn't even Jimmy's fault she needed

it. I could say he's a sucker, but he ain't. He knows what he's doin',
but he can't just stand around and see somebody hurtin'."

Martin wondered how someone whose specialty was kick-
ing out teeth could admire a man who couldn't say no to a
knocked-up prostitute. But then he saw Berlin, half a block
away, no question who it was. A little man in a snappy straw
boater, moving quickly, head turning first one way, then the
other. All of a sudden, Martin felt glad he'd taken Jimmy's
advice about leverage. Jimmy was right. Berlin would've just
given him a straight-arm and kept walking. He elbowed Vinny.
"That's him."

"Aw right, then. Let's go." Vinny shoved Martin off the bench,
and the two men hustled out of the park and across Seventy-
second, up onto the sidewalk, smack into Berlin's path. The
songwriter stopped on a dime. He seemed about to run, but then
took a closer look at Martin, and relaxed. "You're Niede…"

"Yes, sir. Martin Niederhoffer. Your bookkeeper, at W, B, and
S. I need to talk to you, sir."

"So make an appointment with my secretary. Don't come
up to me on street corners at night." Clearly, he was trying not
to look at Vinny. "Hey, but wait a minute. The cops're looking
for you…"

"That's not exactly what I want to talk about, but—"

Berlin pushed past Martin, took a few fast steps toward the
Chatsworth, but Vinny caught him by the arm. "My friend here
wants a word with you," Vinny growled. "Now, what I think is
we should all of us go across the street and sit down for a minute
on one a them nice comfortable benches. Make it friendly and
quick." He jerked Berlin's arm toward the street.

Berlin swiveled his neck. Vinny jerked his arm again, harder
this time. "You're gettin' bad ideas in your head, Mr. B. Just
open your mouth to do anything but talk to your boy here, and
you'll be visitin' your dentist tomorrow to get yourself a new set
a choppers. Now, let's go."

Berlin turned a look at Martin that made the young man
cringe. He wanted to tell Berlin he was sorry, that he'd just

wanted a quiet word with him to straighten out a problem, but he knew that would be a very bad move. The three men waited for a cab to sail by, then crossed the street and walked into the park. "At least take your hand off me," Berlin snapped to Vinny.

Martin had to give him credit. He didn't think he'd be able to talk that way, in Berlin's place.

Vinny dropped his hand. "Long as you behave yourself. An' if you don't, I'm gonna do a whole lot more'n just grab your arm."

They sat on a bench, Berlin between Martin and Vinny. Berlin adjusted his hat, then turned to face Martin. "So?"

"Mr. Berlin…I'm…" Martin caught the "sorry," swallowed it, then went on. "Scott Joplin is my piano teacher, and he wrote a musical play. He wants to get it published and put on stage, and I thought…" Looking at the face on Berlin, Martin silently cursed himself for a hopeless idiot, but knew he had to go on. "I told him to bring his music down to the office, and I'd introduce him to you, and then maybe you'd be interested in publishing it and putting it on stage…"

His voice ran out of steam as he watched disbelief and fury run wild across Berlin's face. "Are you nuts, Niederhoffer?" the composer shouted. "Are you absolutely crazy? I wouldn't touch a piece of Joplin's music. Not after what he said about me five years ago."

Anger rose into Martin's throat like gall. "Then why did you take it? Mr. Joplin came down to see you on his own, and you told him you wanted to look it over. Then yesterday, you called him to come down and talk about it."

"Called him?" Berlin barked. *I* called *Joplin?* You must be out of your head." The composer glanced at Vinny, then went on speaking, but in considerably softer tones. "Listen, Niederhoffer. I don't even remember the last time I saw Joplin, never mind talked to him, and I've never called him on the phone. I don't know a thing about this musical play of his, and I don't want to. For Christ's sake, I'm the King of Ragtime. You think I'm going to waste five minutes looking at music from a half-dead bozo who once wrote some decent stuff, but now he's an embarrass-ment even to the colored? I got tired a long time ago of hearing from people who think I stole his damn music, and I ain't gonna have a whole lot of patience now with somebody trying to tell me I stole something else from him. You're Number Two in the last six hours." Berlin shifted, spoke to Vinny. "I don't have a clue about what the hell is going on. Yeah, right now I'm scared, I'll admit it. But I can't tell you a thing about Joplin's music, whatever you do to me, and that's the truth."

Martin wondered about that telephone call. If Mr. Berlin had liked Mr. Joplin's music, and wanted to snatch it, he could have decided to get Mr. Joplin and Martin both out of the way. If Martin hadn't gone out to the bathroom when he did…

Vinny rescued the young man from his guilty reverie. All the while Berlin talked, the bruiser had nodded like a mechanical doll with the right side of its mouth painted into a nasty smirk. Now he said, "Lemme ask you something, Mr. Berlin, okay?"

Berlin managed a weak grin. "Guess I don't have much choice, do I?"

"Not if you want to keep the teeth you got. Now, here's the question. "You must be a pretty big guy in music, what with you bein' the King of Ragtime. That right?"

"Well—"

"He does call himself the King of Ragtime." Out of Martin's mouth before it was in his mind. He began to apologize for interrupting the conversation, but Vinny held up a finger, and the young man shut up in a hurry. "So, I guess that's right, hey, Mr. B? You really are the King a Ragtime, huh?"

"Well, yeah, you know. You gotta promote yourself in any business."

"Sure. Sure you do." Vinny's voice was all sympathy. Martin tried not to think of what might be coming. "So I figure like this: The King of Ragtime's gotta have a pretty good idea about what's goin' on in his own kingdom. I'm gonna give you five days to put your mitts on that music by this kid's teacher. Have yourself a good gander at it, decide it's the best thing you've seen in all your life, and get a square contract all ready for the guy to sign. Five days. If you don't have that music in your hand to show Martin here, and a contract to publish it fast, you will be a very sorry person the whole rest of your life...which might not be real long. You can hire all the bodyguards you want, but they ain't gonna be with you every second of every day. Go in to take a crap, they'll find your body stuffed in the can. And a bodyguard can't do nothing about a guy with a gun across the street, maybe behind a window. So please, Mr B, don't go and do nothing dumb. Cops get wind of this, then the talkin's over. And don't think I'm workin' just for this kid here. The both of us represent a person you do not want to mess around with. I'll be back to see you in five days, King Irving, count on it. And I ain't gonna be makin' no appointments with your secretary or nobody else. Just see that you got that music with you, and a contract with your name on it."

Martin gasped as he saw Vinny point a pistol directly at Berlin's chest.

"Do I make my point clear enough for you, Mr. B?"

Berlin nodded.

Vinny smiled without separating his lips, then slid the gun back behind his jacket. Berlin got to his feet, smoothed his trousers, glared at Martin. "Niederhoffer, you're fired. Even if the cops weren't looking for you, you'd still be fired. I run a music business, not a rest home for morons."

Martin watched him turn, then start walking away. But Vinny said, "Hold on there a minute, King. I guess we ain't quite done after all."

The pistol was out again, aimed at Berlin's back. The little man turned slowly. "Now what?"

Vinny gestured with the gun. "Gimme your wallet here."

Berlin hesitated, but when Vinny clicked the hammer, the songwriter dug into his left pocket and came out with a billfold. Vinny took it, passed it to Martin. "Open it up. How much's there?"

Martin counted as quickly as his shaking hands allowed. "Hundred...sixty...four."

"Put it in your pocket. The man just fired you, he's gotta give you severance. Okay, King. *Now* you can go. 'Less you wanna shoot off that big mouth again."

Berlin was out of the park and across the street in a dash. Vinny nudged Martin. "Come on, kid. Let's get outa here before the King sends out some troops."

◇◇◇

Back at the Alamo, the evening's entertainment was in full swing. Ragtime Jimmy, his dented fedora pushed far back on his forehead, banged away at the keyboard while the woman who'd been auditioning earlier belted out a raucous, spirited "Alabama Jubilee." Vinny led the young man up to the piano. Without missing a note, Jimmy looked over his shoulder and asked, "Everything go jake?"

Vinny snorted. "You ever think it wouldn't?"

Jimmy laughed. "I appreciate you helpin' the kid. And Joplin."

Vinny nodded, then started off toward the bar. Martin leaned over to stage-whisper, "Thanks, Jimmy. I bet it works out now." He wiped the back of a hand across his forehead. "I sure wouldn't ever want Vinny coming after *me*."

Jimmy laughed even louder. "Then you better make sure and be a good boy. Don't go messin' with dice and cards, stuff like that. This town's full a guys just as tough as Vinny, and he's tough as they come. It's a darned good thing for his wife he ain't married.

"Hail, hail, the gang's all here, at an Alabama Jubilee." Martin thought the girl might strangle the microphone.

◇◇◇

Past one o'clock. Martin tiptoed up the stairs to Joe Lamb's porch, quiet as a thief, then padded to the door. Any way he considered the situation, he was going to catch Hail Columbia; might as well get it over with. He knocked gently.

Mr. Lamb opened the door, and the look on his face left no doubt in Martin's mind as to what was coming. Against his will, the young man walked into the room. Mr. Joplin, at the piano, played and scribbled. Mrs. Stanley sat on the sofa, beside a man

Martin had never seen. He was old, over seventy for sure, and he looked like a well-to-do businessman. Neatly-groomed gray hair, scanty up on top, mouth tucked behind a bushy salt-and-pepper Van Dyke beard that took off from the edges of a thick mustache. Even in the damp heat of the summer night, he wore a dark vest and a neatly-set dark bow tie. Lines at the sides of his eyes looked to have been cut with a chisel. When he fixed those light-blue eyes on Martin, the young man felt as if his clothes had been stripped from his body, leaving him standing naked before the group.

Then Lamb unloaded on him. "You damn fool—putting Mr. Joplin in danger like that. What in *hell* did you think you were doing?" Without waiting for an answer, he strode off, into the kitchen.

Nell and the old man got to their feet. "Damn and hell in the same sentence?" Nell said. "I've never heard either one from Joe."

"Nor have I. I wouldn't have thought anything could make him that angry."

Nell sighed. "Dad, this is our truant, Martin Niederhoffer. Martin, my father, John Stark, from St. Louis."

"The music publisher? Mr. Joplin's publisher? 'Maple Leaf Rag?'"

Lamb walked back into the room, holding a partially-drunk glass of water. Martin thought he looked calmer, maybe even a little embarrassed.

"I see my reputation has preceded me." Stark extended a hand; Martin grasped it, winced. This old guy had some grip.

"Mr. Joplin's always talking about you." Martin glanced toward the piano. "He says you gave him the biggest break of his life."

"My father's come to help with this mess that seems to be getting worse every minute," Nell said. "I'm sure that he, along with Mr. Lamb and I, would like to know just what you were up to all day and evening."

Martin couldn't speak. Couldn't say a word, just stared into the old man's magnetic eyes. Nell knew what he was going through, but kept her face severe. Finally, the young man stammered, "I'm…I'm sorry, sir, I really am. I didn't mean to take Mr. Joplin with me. I went out on my own, but he saw me go, and came after me. I couldn't get him back inside, because the door was locked behind us."

"In other words, your intention was to leave Mr. Joplin alone here."

Martin held out his hands, palms up, a plea for clemency. "I didn't think…I guess I just *didn't think*. I couldn't take it, sitting around here doing nothing, and I hoped I could get a line on some of the stuff that's been going on."

"Joplin told us you went to a delicatessen and talked to your girlfriend."

"That's right. I got through to her at work by telling Fannie—she's the receptionist—that I was the bookkeeper at Mr. Berlin's uptown office, and Mr. Berlin needed some figures. Then I told Birdie to put papers into a file folder and meet me at Schneider's Deli."

"And what did you learn?"

"Just that the cops think Mr. Joplin and I killed Sid, and they're looking for us. But you know what? Sid was sitting at my desk at work, so I think maybe someone was really trying to kill *me*."

"I might sympathize with them."

Lamb chuckled, but there was no humor in Stark's eyes. "Do you have any idea who might have wanted to kill you?"

Martin bit his lip. "Well, actually, I was wondering…if Mr. Berlin knew I was going to keep an eye on Mr. Joplin's manuscript, maybe he figured he'd call Mr. Joplin to come down there, then he'd kill me, and make it look like Mr. Joplin did it. And then he'd have Mr. Joplin's play free and clear. But if he saw me go to the bathroom, and saw Sid at my desk, he could have decided to kill him, and frame Mr. Joplin *and* me."

Lamb took a sip of water. "Mrs. Stanley told me you'd gotten some figures together that showed Henry Waterson has been embezzling from the company. Could he have found out, and decided to to fix your wagon?"

"I don't think so. Right about three, I went to check and see if he had an invoice I was missing, but he was already gone for the day. He's usually out in the afternoons anyway, at least during horse-racing season."

"You're sure he didn't come back, hide in one room or another, and wait for his chance? He must have a key."

Martin shook his head. "No...well, I guess I can't be sure. But if Mr. Waterson was sore at me on account of the numbers, why would he have killed Sid? Besides, what about Mr. Berlin calling up Mr. Joplin and telling him to come down to talk about his music?"

Stark made a lemon-sucking face, then shook his head. "It seems to keep coming back to Berlin, doesn't it? All right, Martin. Now, suppose you tell us what you've been doing since you left Mr. Joplin with Mrs. Joplin."

Out of the frying pan. Martin told his audience about his and Vinny's encounter with Berlin. When he got to the part about the severance pay, he thought Stark looked fit to explode. "Let me be sure I understand this," the old man said. "You've led Berlin to think that some mysterious and dangerous man has an interest in Scott Joplin's music, and that if Berlin does not publish it promptly, he will at the least have all his teeth knocked out."

Sweat ran from every pore on Martin's body. "I'm afraid so, sir."

Stark blew. "Damn and blast, you young idiot." On his feet, face to face with Martin, who wished he could sink through the floor and vanish. "This has gotten utterly out of hand. First it was a missing musical manuscript, next a murder, and now we're up to our necks in monetary theft and extortion. And who is at the center of this crime wave?"

Brief pause, sufficient answer.

"And for that matter, who had the crackbrained idea in the first place that Irving Berlin might give thirty seconds to the idea of publishing and producing music by Scott Joplin."

Martin couldn't speak, bad enough, but now tears started down his cheeks, and all he could do was drop, mortified, into the nearest chair.

Nell stepped up to Stark. "Dad, calm down." Martin felt a bit of encouragement at the sympathy he read in the brief look she turned on him. "It's two in the morning, we're all tired, and we're going in circles. Let's sleep on it, and get back here tomorrow, dinnertime."

She thought her father was going to launch a debate, but he just swallowed, then muttered, "I suppose that does make sense."

Nell walked to the piano. Joplin played a musical fragment, scratched notes on paper. "Scott…Scott. Time to quit for the day."

He looked up, annoyed, but before he could speak, Nell said, "Joe's got to get some sleep, and you ought to do the same. A little rest, and then you'll both be ready to go to work in the morning." She pulled at his arm. "Come on, now. I'll get you comfortable before I leave."

As they disappeared into the guest room, Stark turned back to Martin. "As for you, young fellow, you will stay here and behave yourself until one of us tells you to do otherwise. You will not leave, not for anything, not for a minute. Do I make myself clear?"

"Yes, sir. I really am sorry. I just wanted to do something for Mr. Joplin"

"I understand, and that is commendable. But we can't all be going off on our own, chasing whims without thinking through the consequences. You and your strong-arm man have made matters considerably more complicated." A smile blasted through the old man's defenses, spread across his face. "Though I do confess, I would have given a fair sum of money to have witnessed that scene. But nonetheless, you will not go off on your own again."

"I won't, sir."

〈〉〈〉〈〉

"God *damn* it." Berlin threw his pencil across the room. "After something like that, how the hell am I supposed to concentrate on writing music?"

Cliff Hess, sitting next to his boss on the piano bench, knew no answer was required or even desired. He gave Berlin a sympathetic nod.

Berlin ran fingers savagely through his hair. "*Damn* Joplin, that soft-headed fool. He must be telling everyone in New York that he gave me his music and I'm trying to make off with it. Sure, the man is sick, but when somebody puts an enforcer on you, you don't feel real charitable. I'm supposed to hand Joplin a contract and print up his music and sell it, very funny. I'm surprised they didn't say they wanted a provision for ten full-time pluggers. Jesus Christ, if Ziegfeld sees what I've got written so far, he'll probably fire me, and I'll be yesterday's news. What in hell am I supposed to do?"

Now, Hess knew an answer was in order. "You don't want to call the police?"

"Cliff, Cliff..."

The sight of his twenty-eight-year-old boss playing the jaded man of the world amused Hess no end, but he kept a solemn expression firmly in place.

"Get on the wrong side of these people, there's only one way you get out, and that's in a body bag. For those guys, it's just business. Let somebody off a hook, it makes it tougher to enforce the next one. And how about that kid who got himself killed in my office? Maybe he got in their way somehow, maybe he wanted a piece of the action, who knows, and Niederhoffer's muscle took care of him. No, Cliff, I'm stuck. I've got to figure some way around this. What I *can't* figure is who's really behind it. Joplin doesn't have the money to hire a hit man."

Hess held up a finger, Eureka. "He might have told them he had money. Maybe he even believes it himself."

Berlin looked far from convinced. "The goon said somebody else is behind all this, somebody I really don't want to get sore at me...Cliff, wait. I bet I know."

Hess waited.

"That old man from St. Louis, Stark. He blows into town and all hell breaks loose. People come out of the woodwork about this musical of Joplin's. Stark's got a bug up his ass when it comes to ragtime. His ads read like something he copied out of the Bible. I can just hear him, preaching to that gorilla how he's on some kind of a holy mission. I told you about the way he talked to me earlier tonight."

Hess nodded, glanced at the clean sheet of music paper on the piano rack. "Yeah…he does sound pretty straight-backed."

"So I guess what I got to do is have a talk with Stark, and find out what it'd take to get him off my back and on his way to St. Lou." Berlin jumped from the piano bench like he'd been goosed, ran out of the room, came back a few minutes later, holding a small white card out to Hess. "He said I should call him if I came up with any information, which was probably his way of telling me what was gonna go down if I didn't come across. You call him for me in the morning, Cliff, okay? Tell him I want to talk to him, maybe about one o'clock…no, wait. I got that woman from *Dramatic Mirror* coming at one, damn it. I'll make it fast with her. Tell Stark to come, say, a quarter till two."

Hess nodded. "Sure."

Izzy's harsh, clipped words broke through into Berlin's consciousness. *"You better be ready to talk turkey to him. Try and sweet-talk a guy like that, he'll eat you for breakfast."*

Berlin's rising tide of hopeful enthusiasm washed away Izzy's rant. "I'll talk to him straight, all right," the composer murmured, then marched across the room, grabbed up his pencil, and ran back to the piano. "Okay, Cliff. Just look over this 'Chicken Walk' with me. I don't know how in hell you're going to make it work, I just know you will. Then you can go get some shut-eye, and I'll put in some more time by myself on 'Alice in Wonderland.'"

Chapter Eight

Manhattan
Thursday, August 24
Morning

John Stark struggles to keep the pistol in his right hand from pulling him over and down to the ground. He stares at the fifteen-year-old colored boy, half-crouched across the clearing. "I ain't gonna tell no one." The boy's voice is strangled, pitched high as a woman's. "Honest. I won't be sayin' nothin'. Please Mr. Yank, don't shoot me."

From Stark's left, a harsh growl. "Gol' damn your eyes, you rabbit-hearted bugler. I'm your commanding officer, and I gave you an order to shoot him. Now, *shoot.*"

Stark turns his gaze toward the voice. "But he saved our whole regiment, sir. We'd have been ambushed, every one of us killed, if he hadn't told us there were rebs hiding behind that knoll."

The solidly-built man in the uniform of a Union Army lieutenant leers at him, dark eyes heavy with contempt, thin lips twisted in scorn. "This is war, Stark. We can't go marching back into Mobile Bay with a colored boy in our ranks. We'd have riots. And you can bet your sorry life there are more of those renegades around. If they get their hands on this kid, they'll give him treatment that even a white man'd have trouble keeping shut through. Now, either *you* shoot him or *I* will, and then you can go before a court-martial for insubordination and refusing an officer's command."

Stark raises the pistol. The colored boy chokes back a scream as the bugler tightens a finger on the trigger. "Sarah," he pleads to the scowling girl beside him. "I've got to do it." Her glower only deepens. Stark closes his eyes a moment, takes aim. Then he pulls the trigger.

The explosion blended with an unearthly shriek to bring Stark up sitting in bed, clutching at his chest, his breath coming in gasps. The bedroom door swung open, banged against the wall. Nell, in her nightgown and flannel bathrobe, hair flying around her face, tore into the room. "Dad, are you all right?"

The image of Sarah. Stark fought to calm himself, nodded. "Yes."

"You had that dream again."

"Again?"

"Yes, again. You've been having it as long as I can remember. What on earth is it about?"

"Nell, for heaven's sake, I had a bad dream, that's all. I'm sorry I woke you. Go back to sleep."

She turned and left the room, slamming the door behind her. Stark took a couple of deep breaths, then looked around. Early daylight. The little round alarm clock on the bedside table read a few minutes before six. The old man worked his legs over the side of the bed, got to his feet and into slippers, then shuffled out of the room and down the hall to the bathroom, where he stood over the toilet and relieved himself in his usual slow, intermittent manner, damn that stupid prostate gland. Then he walked back to the bedroom and lay sleepless until the alarm bell went off at seven-thirty.

◇◇◇

The morning sun through the window bathed Stark and Nell in a golden glow. The old man sat at the table and sipped coffee; his daughter stood at the stove, stirring a pot of gravy. Neither spoke. He knew what was coming, and as they sat down to eat, it came. "Dad, whatever *is* that dream about? That it should bother you so much for all these years?"

Stark shook his head. "Not worth discussing. It's a dream, that's all, just a bit of foolishness."

Nell passed him a plate heaped with sausage, biscuits and gravy. "But to have the same one, over and over, for years—"

"I never said it was the same one."

"But it is. Please don't lie to me."

Stark paused, fork halfway to his mouth. His throat closed; he couldn't possibly swallow food. "Let's talk about the business at hand, why you called me out here. There's no point wasting time talking about a bad dream."

"But—"

Stark slammed down his fork. "Sarah, I've told you. It's not worth discussing."

He didn't hear it until he saw his daughter's face, and replayed his speech in his head. He forced a small laugh. "You've got my mind tied up in a knot, Nell—you so resemble your mother. Your looks, your speech…" He pointed at the plate of food, grabbed for the fork. "And your biscuits and gravy are every bit as good as your mother's…and though I'd never say it publicly, of course, they put Margaret's utterly to shame. I don't imagine there are better biscuits and gravy to be had in New York, or even in Missouri." He shoveled in a mouthful, took a few seconds to chew. "Why, if you were so inclined, you could open a restaurant and have customers in a line all the way down the block."

Nell gritted her teeth. He'd done it again, gotten right around her, and the dream was now a dead issue. Her mother would've put her hands on her hips, set her eyes to glaring at her husband, but at the same time flashed a smile subtly yet unmistakably warm, and told him to cut out the blarney and get down to cases. And that was where Nell knew she came off short. No trouble with the glare, but the amiable smile remained beyond her capacity. "I'm not the least inclined to open a restaurant, Dad, but I'm glad to make them for you when you're here."

They both smiled. Two skilled boxers at the end of a bout, both winner and loser knowing there would be more matches.

They ate in silence until the telephone in the living room rang. Nell pushed away from the table. "Maybe that's Jim." She hurried out, but was back in less than a minute. "For you, Dad, a man named Hess. I've heard of him—he's a sort of musical secretary for Irving Berlin. He says he needs to give you a message from Berlin."

Stark's brows rose. "That ought to be interesting." He walked past Nell into the living room.

When he returned, his face was as puzzled as hers had been. "He says Berlin wants me to come by at a quarter to two this afternoon, to talk about Joplin's music."

Nell seated herself. "Well, that *is* interesting."

"Maybe what I said yesterday had an effect on him after all."

"Maybe." Nell filled her mouth with biscuit to make certain she wouldn't tell him about her one o'clock interview with Berlin. Let her say a word about that appointment, and her father probably would tell her to just leave Berlin to him. And that, she was not going to do.

Stark wiped his napkin over his mouth and beard. "I think I'll go up to Joplin's house, and see what I can learn from Lottie. Would you like to come?"

Nell's conscience went off like the telephone bell, but she said, "I can't." I've got to do some grocery shopping this morning, then I have an appointment to meet Birdie—Martin's girlfriend—for lunch."

Stark nodded. He wanted to ask why she was going to have lunch with Martin's girlfriend, but knew what kind of reaction that question would bring. He'd wait till later, then ask her how her lunch date had gone. "All right, my dear. I'll meet you back at Joe's this afternoon. Can you give me Joplin's address?"

〈〉〈〉〈〉

The motion of the subway threatened to put Birdie to sleep, no great feat. Her parents had subjected her to a longer and far

more heated grilling than the police had. 'If you know where
that boyfriend of yours is, you'd better tell. When the police find
him—and they will, mark my word—they'll get you for trying
to hide him, and off you'll go to jail. You'll spend your best years
there, and by the time they let you go, no decent man will want
you. You'll be an old maid the rest of your life, living in a crummy
little room with a toilet down the hall and a hot plate to cook
your food on. You think that's what we want for you?'

By the time they finally gave up, she was so angry and so anxious for Martin, sleep was impossible. She threw her arms one
way, tossed her legs the other. She must have dozed a dozen times,
only to find herself suddenly wide awake again. She forced down
breakfast, if only to keep her mother quiet, then all the way to
the subway, and as she sat on the train, questions coursed through
her mind. Martin was so loyal, he probably would have hidden
Mr. Joplin away even if he thought his piano teacher did kill Sid.
And now Martin was involved up to his neck. Maybe her parents
were right—the police would catch up with the runaways, Martin
would go to jail for a long time, and they'd never get married.

"What's the matter, dearie? Man trouble, I bet."

Birdie blinked into the round, red face of the passenger in
the seat next to her, a woman trying to deny her fifty years by
means of the most flamboyant bleach job Birdie had ever seen.
The girl wiped at her face. She hadn't realized she was crying.
"I guess so. Kind of, anyway."

"Bah!" With one syllable, Curlylocks dismissed Birdie's
distress. "It ain't worth it, sweetie, take it from me. Most men
are bums, you don't want to take them too serious. The good
thing is, whenever you're in the mood, there's always another one
around the corner, know what I mean?" The woman grinned,
and delivered Birdie a sharp elbow to the ribs. "Always leave 'em
laughin', dearie. That's my philosophy."

Birdie nodded. "Thanks."

The woman's face went soft. "Aw, I know how it is. I was
young once myself." The grin made a comeback. "But I got over
it, and you will too."

The train crawled into the Fiftieth Street station. Birdie nodded to the woman, then practically leaped from her seat into the crowd and out the doorway onto the platform. Stupid old bag! Birdie was never going to get over Martin. *Never.* Not now, not ever.

She pushed her way down Broadway to Forty-seventh, and into the lobby of the Strand Building, then ran past the elevator, to the stairwell. That'd be quicker. She was already five minutes late. Mr. Tabor was going to have a fit.

As her heels clicked onto the second-floor landing, and she started up the third flight of stairs, someone caught her from behind and dragged her in back of the elevator shaft. She tried to scream, but there was a cloth over her mouth and nose, smelled funny, like when they took out her tonsils in the hospital. She aimed a kick backward, but her attacker wrestled her to the concrete floor. She caught sight of a burlap sack next to her head. "Don't you go makin' no noise," a whispered growl. "Just you lay there quiet, elsewise, you gonna get hurt." That awful smell…Birdie's arms felt heavy, eyelids heavier yet. "That be nice," she heard the man croon. "That be the way." His voice faded, and Birdie lay still.

The man counted slowly, just the way he'd been told, then took the rag from Birdie's face. Good thing the girl was late, nobody out in the hall. Otherwise, he was going to have to talk her out into the street, tell her that her boyfriend needed her help. Then he'd have had to shove her into an alley and hit her with the chloroform there. Lot easier this way.

He wiped a sleeve across his forehead, then picked up the burlap bag, dropped the bottle into it, and with no great effort, stuffed the girl into the sack. He hoisted the load to his shoulder, then trotted down the stairs, through the lobby and out onto Broadway. A man loitering in front of the building called out, "Hey, there, Rastus, wha'cha got in the bag? Been sneakin' round the chicken coop?" A couple of people laughed, but the colored man didn't break stride, just kept moving as fast as his feet would go.

◇‹›◇

John Stark walked up to the attractive row house at 133 West 138th, across Seventh Avenue from Strivers Row. He glanced at the skinny cop holding up a streetlight post in front of the building, then marched up the red stone stairs and knocked. A slight woman in a brown summer dress with white polka dots, her hair gathered up under a red bandanna, opened the door. The woman's face said, 'What's this ol' white man want with me?'

Stark removed his boater. "You must be Lottie Joplin—how do you do? I'm John Stark, from St. Louis."

Lottie's suspicion melted away. "Well, for goodness sake, don't just be standin' there, come on in." She practically hauled him through the doorway, then slammed the door behind him. "No reason that cop has to see or hear."

Stark smiled. "No reason at all. In fact, better that he doesn't. I'm sorry for just dropping by like this, but I thought a phone call might frighten you."

Lottie burst into an immense laugh. "Frighten me? Oh, Mr. Stark, it take a whole lot more'n that to frighten me. But I gotta tell you, I am just *so* grateful you would come here and help us out." She pumped his hand as if he were a well from which she expected to draw water.

Stark inclined his head in a polite bow. "I'll be glad to do what I can, Mrs. Joplin—"

"Oh, pshaw, 'Mrs. Joplin.' It's Lottie. I don't want to hear no more 'Mrs. Joplin'."

The woman put Stark in mind of a crow, chattering and sassy, head cocked to the left, constantly hopping about. "But my goodness, what we standin' out here in the hall for? Come on inside. With a grand gesture, she ushered her guest through the spacious receiving hall. To the left, Stark saw a door; to the right, an open passage led into what looked like a living room. Straight ahead, a stairway ran up to the second floor. Stark heard voices, a baritone rumble, a soprano giggle. A moment of concern drifted over Lottie's face. "Got my sister stayin' for a time, she's got her a friend up there. Don't pay them no mind. Come on in the parlor here, make yourself right at home, and I will be back directly with some coffee and a piece a my good cake."

Stark thought to mention the hefty serving of biscuits and gravy he'd recently packed away, but caught himself. He gazed around the parlor, a good-sized room with an old green easy chair and matching hassock, a brown overstuffed wingback chair, a green upholstered love seat, and a long sofa, covered in green and white striped ticking. Every armrest sported a precisely-set white lace antimacassar. Against the far wall stood a writing desk; beneath a window looking out on the street, a little Victrola sat on a square oak table. Not showy, but comfortable. An attractive house in a nice neighborhood. Where was the money coming from? Joplin wouldn't be bringing in much from teaching piano, and the semiannual royalty checks from Stark Music Company, along with whatever might be coming in from other publishers, couldn't possibly account for this standard of living. Besides which, hadn't the man damn near bankrupted himself the past few years, trying to get *Treemonisha* produced and performed?

Lottie interrupted Stark's musings as she sidestepped through the doorway, carrying a huge silver tray with a full coffee service, a sliced coffee cake, and plates. She motioned her guest to the wingback chair, set a plate with a double-slice of cake into his hands, then settled into the easy chair, and leaned forward. "Mr. Stark, I just gotta say again, it is so good of you to come out here now, 'specially after all the ruckus Scott made. I told that man, with all you done for him, if you said you was strapped and couldn't give royalties to no composer, white *or* colored, then he oughta believe you. I never did stop trying to get Scott to patch it up, but…" She held out her hands, palms up, surrender.

"I know," Stark said quietly. "And I was very touched by the kind note you sent after my wife died." His voice went gravelly. "Particularly, considering we'd never met."

"But I felt like I knew you. Nell never does stop talking about you."

Stark smiled. "Well, I'm here, Lottie, and if I can help, I'll be glad of it." He waved his hand. "You've got a lovely home. I'm glad to see Mr. Joplin has been so well looked-after."

Lottie blew out a loud snort. "I'm goin' to tell you, Mr. Stark, it has taken some hard looking-after. Scott is a great composer, a great man. But there ain't one inch of room in his head for nothing but music."

"Never was."

"No. But I got me a good head for business, and Scott'll listen to me, on those things anyways. I made him write me in as managing partner in the Scott Joplin Music Company. I told him, Scott, you write the music, and I'll keep the books, pay the accounts, handle the money."

"Looks as if it's worked well," said Stark.

Lottie nodded. "It's a blessing I thought to do it, the way Scott's sickness has messed up his mind."

A couple walked past the door, laughing. "See you, Lottie" the woman called into the parlor.

Lottie paused long enough to say, "My sister. Not three days up from Virginny, and she's already found her a New York man to court her."

Stark's attention blew to flinders. 'Court her!' Sunday afternoons in the Widow Casey's tiny home in New Orleans, the living room with no more furnishings than a Kelly-green couch behind a rickety wooden table, and a few shabby armchairs. The Widow (as she always called herself) and Sarah's younger sister Theresa and little brother John, always careful to take the chairs, leaving the couch to Sarah, in a modest gingham dress, and her scrubbed, starched suitor, so awkward in his Union uniform. Polite conversation. All present trusted the war would soon be over. The Widow would put on a sly smile, and say, "If you young people think you can do without me for a few minutes, I'll make some tea and get a pile of my molasses cookies together." Walks on warm afternoons, Sarah's hand carefully tucked into the crook of John's arm... Stark's eyes filled, damn! He fought to pull himself together.

Lottie didn't seem to notice. "It was only just a couple weeks ago that I found out what Scott's been workin' on lately. He been writin' a musical play."

Stark nodded. "I've heard. And it doesn't make sense. Joplin always talked as if a musical theater-piece was beneath him. It was always opera, opera, opera."

"Oh, why don't you just go and tell me about that." Lottie rolled her eyes. "Close on to five years, now, it's been *Treemonisha, Treemonisha, Treemonisha.* But then, all of a sudden I don't hear nothing no more about *Treemonisha.* Scott say he workin' on something brand-new, something different. And that was *all* he would tell me. Day and night he locked himself up in that room." Lottie gestured with her head toward the back of the house. "Finally, one day, maybe two weeks ago, out he comes and says it's done, and it's gonna be the savior of us all. 'Make us rich, Lottie. Put my name right up there with Victor Herbert and George M. Cohan and Jerome Kern. Up there *above* them, in fact.'"

Stark frowned. "Joplin's always had a good opinion of his music, but I never heard him try to put himself above another composer."

"Well, to hear him tell it now, he's the greatest composer ever lived," Lottie said. "Next thing, he's gonna work on his *Symphony Number One*, and I should just wait and see, all the big city orchestras gonna fight over who get to play the premiere. And after that, it's gonna be an opera, a new one. Bigger than anything Wagner ever wrote."

Stark shook his head. "He's always admired Wagner—not that Wagner would ever have returned the compliment. But what about this musical play of his? *If?*"

"That's what he call it. *If.*"

"Did he tell you anything about it? Play any of it for you?"

"Just a little. He sat down at the piano, played a little this, little that, and it was lovely. But his music *always* sound lovely."

"And that's all you know?"

"That's it, Mr. Stark. Except I wisht that boy Martin hadn't went and talked Scott into giving his manuscript to Irving Berlin.

For the life of me, I can't figure how Scott agreed to do that. After what happened with 'Alexander's'? That was when I knew he was for sure out of his mind."

Stark ground his teeth as he remembered a visit a few years back from Joplin's friend, Sam Patterson. On his way through St. Louis, Patterson dropped in at Stark Music, and told a dreadful story. When Joplin first heard "Alexander's," he burst into tears and cried "That's *my* tune." Sobbing all the while, he sang a couple of lines from *Treemonisha*: "Marching onward, marching onward. Marching to that lovely tune." Then he sang the beginning measures of "Alexander's Ragtime Band:" "Oh, ma honey, oh, ma honey. Better hurry and let's meander." Note for note, the same. According to Patterson, Joplin had left the score of *Treemonisha* with Berlin, but the publisher told Joplin he couldn't use it. "He couldn't use it with *my* name on it," Joplin howled. And then, Patterson said, before Joplin could publish his opera, he had to change *his own tune.*

"I sure hope Berlin doesn't get away with it this time," Lottie said. "Just because Berlin be white and Scott, black—"

"It's not that," Stark said quietly. "Color doesn't matter on Tin Pan Alley. They steal from each other all day long to make new trash out of old garbage." He drew a deep breath. "I need to find out more about this musical play. Can I have a look inside that room of his?

Lottie shook her head. "Oh, I don't know about that. Just thinkin' about it makes me all cold and sweaty. If Scott ever find out…"

Stark nodded, then set his coffee cup onto the little table next to his chair. "I understand. But it might really help. Let's say there's another copy of *If*—"

"There ain't. Just can't be. It'd take a passel of time to copy it out, and who do you know who ever do that? Why, nobody in their right mind…"

Lottie stopped as if she'd been poleaxed, then got to her feet, and walked from the room. She was back almost instantly, a ring of keys in her left hand. She gestured with her head toward the hall.

Stark stood by degrees. The chair was lumpy, and his sciatica was shooting bursts of electricity down his right leg. But Lottie looked to be even more in pain. Stark put an arm around her shoulders. "Don't worry—we'll get this thing sorted out." Softly, as if reassuring a child after a nightmare. Stark knew about nightmares.

Down the hall, Lottie picked out a key, turned it in the lock, opened the door, then stood aside to let Stark enter first. The shade was down over the only window in the room, and the heavy air smelled like urine and rancid oil. Stark wrinkled his nose, felt embarrassed when Lottie picked up on him. "Scott can go days without washin', an' he keep a bottle in here so he don't have to stop composin' to walk on down the hall."

Stark made a face as sour as the air. "He's a sick man. Let's see what we can find that might help us to help him." He pulled a string; an unshaded bulb on a fixture just inside the door sent light and shadows into play around the room.

The rack on the piano was empty, so they began by looking through a few loose pages of music on the bench. Just exercises for piano students. The scarred wooden bookshelf opposite the piano took some time, but in the end yielded up nothing but sheet music, folios, and several dirty, tattered biographies of famous musicians. Stark noticed notes scribbled into margins, a word here, three there. Passages were underlined: Schubert was said to have slept with his spectacles on, so he would not need to take time in the morning to put them on before resuming his work. Stark shook out each book, peered behind them on the shelves, but found nothing secreted away. "Lottie..."

She looked at him, waited.

"Are the records for the Scott Joplin Publishing Company in here? Or the stock?"

She shook her head vigorously. "I keep all that stuff in the basement, where Scott ain't gonna find it and get any funny notions. You want to see it?"

Stark shook his head. "Not so long as you're the only one who's been into it."

"I makes very sure of that."

"Fine."

Stark walked to the desk under the shaded window, beside the piano. The oak surface was scraped and chipped, with cigarette burns scattered across its surface like blemishes on the face of a teenager. Stark thought the few music sheets there probably represented false starts. As long as he'd known Joplin, the man was forever scribbling tune fragments onto pieces of paper; he said he had to get them down before he forgot them. Some, he'd developed into full-length ragtime compositions, often years after they'd first seen daylight. But there were no extended pieces of music anywhere, certainly nothing resembling the score of a musical drama.

But in the middle drawer of the desk, Stark saw a file folder, creased and ink-smeared, with music papers sticking out, fanlike, from within. He picked it up, tapped the papers back inside, then opened it. At the top of the first page, *Symphony Number One* was printed in block letters, ink smudged in a northwesterly direction from the *One*. *By Scott Joplin*. Stark held the folder out toward Lottie. "Looks like he *is* working on a symphony."

"Hmmm." Her eyes followed the pages as Stark turned them, six in all. "Can you tell if it be any good?"

"Not much to judge by, and in any case, I'd have to hear it. But there's a good deal of ragtime expression." He smiled. "A symphony in syncopation. That's certainly different."

He started to replace the folder, but as he did, he noticed the edge of another sheet of paper at the back of the drawer. He lifted it out, then he and Lottie studied the few lines of cramped script, relieved by flourishes on S's and F's, all overlaid with the squiggles of a tremulous hand. "If is the most important word in the dictionary of a man's life," Joplin had written. "Every day it's If, morning till night, a hundred, a thousand times. If a man gets up out of bed and thinks about all the Ifs, with all their consequences, that will come his way before he gets back into bed that night, he would just stay forever with the covers pulled up tight over his head. But you can't see those Ifs coming. They're upon you before you are ever aware of them. The Ifs that have defined the life of Scott Joplin make up the story Scott Joplin must now tell."

Lottie scratched her head. "That's it?"

Stark pulled the drawer all the way out, but it was empty. He practically dived into the three drawers down the left side of the desk, but all he found were a few pencils, a box of paperclips, and reams of blank music paper. He muttered a soft "Damn and blast," then, still holding the handwritten page, he strode across the room and pulled open the door to the closet. But that space held only a couple of pairs of well-worn shoes, a pair of dark trousers, and a jacket hanging on a rack; all pockets were empty.

As he closed the door, Lottie said, "Mr. Stark, I'm gettin' too nervous 'bout bein' here. There ain't no way Scott's gonna get outa Mr. Lamb's place again, is there?"

"I really don't think so." Stark's words carried more conviction than he felt. "But all right. I think we've been through everything. I'll make sure we leave the desk just the way we left it."

As Lottie shifted and shuffled in the doorway, Stark went back to the desk, rearranged the music sheets on top, then slid the folder with Joplin's First Symphony into the drawer, taking pains to fan out the papers. Then he bent into the drawer, and with his back to Lottie, folded Joplin's summary of *If* and slid it behind his vest, into his shirt pocket.

Out in the hall, as Lottie locked the door and checked the knob, she said, "Well, that wasn't worth nothin', was it?

"Maybe, maybe not. You never know." Stark tried to ignore the voice in his head, telling him how ashamed he ought to feel.

◇◇◇

Nell paced slowly back and forth across the sidewalk in front of Schneider's Deli. For what seemed like the hundredth time, she looked at the window display: sliced salamis, juicy red sirloins of beef, pastramis, glassy-eyed whitefish laid out in neat rows. Twelve-thirty, and she had to be at Berlin's apartment by one. She noticed a man staring at her, a Broadway sharpie, she thought, judging by that red and green sport coat, and the rakish tilt of his hat. He caught her looking, grinned, and walked over. "Hey, good-lookin'". He tipped the Panama. "If who you're waitin' for ain't showin', maybe I could do for you."

"I don't think so," Nell said. "Go away."

"You gonna call a cop?"

She gave him the hardest eye she could manage. "I won't need a cop to take care of the likes of you. Now, beat it."

He laughed, then stepped toward her. People walked past, no one noticing anything out of order. Nell brought her right foot down hard, spiked heel first, onto the top of the man's left foot. He howled, fell into a crouch. Nell turned, walked quickly into the deli, directly into the telephone booth inside the door, and read a number to the operator from a slip of paper in her purse. When she heard, "Waterson, Berlin, and Snyder, Music Publishers," she asked for Birdie Kuminsky.

"I'm sorry," the receptionist said. "Miss Kuminsky did not come in to work today."

Nell thanked the woman, hung up the receiver, shook her head. She checked her watch, twenty minutes to one. If she was lucky, she'd make it to Berlin's by one o'clock. After the interview, she'd have to see what was up with Birdie.

Chapter Nine

Berlin jumped off the piano bench, slammed both palms to his forehead, then glared at his office manager. "God damn it, Tabor! What the hell are you doing, bothering me at my house again? Didn't I tell you *I'd* call *you* about those figures?"

Cliff Hess scrambled off the piano bench. "I'm going to get a glass of water." He walked very quickly out of the study.

"I'm sorry, Mr. Berlin," said Tabor. "But this seems so important, I thought I should, well, keep after you a little. I have solid evidence that Mr. Waterson is regularly raking off profits. Isn't that something that needs your immediate attention?"

Berlin rolled his eyes. One reason he'd opened his own firm was to safeguard his money from Waterson's sticky fingers. Irving Berlin was not about to go down with Henry Waterson's ship, but neither did he want to blow that particular boat out of the water right then. There was already too much distracting his mind from Ziegfeld's show. "I already know about Henry, I have for a while." Berlin spoke softly, but his tone was ominous. He picked up the manila folder from the floor next to the piano bench, thrust it at the manager. "Put these in a blind file and ignore them. When I'm ready, I'll decide what I'm gonna do. Can I make it any plainer than—"

He swung around as Robert Miras materialized at his side. "Sorry to interrupt, Mr. Berlin, but the reporter from the *Dramatic Mirror* has been waiting for fifteen minutes."

"*Great.*" Izzy groaned. "*I can just see the credits.* 'The Century Girl. *Music by Victor Herbert. Useless palaver by Irving Berlin.*'"

"All right, Robert," said Berlin. "Tell him I'll be right with him."

"Her, Mr. Berlin. It's a woman reporter."

"Fine. Him, her, whoever."

As the butler walked out, Berlin worked Tabor toward the open doorway. "Listen, Bart, I don't want to hear another word about Waterson. Go on back to the office and manage it. I need to get rid of that damn reporter so maybe I can write a tune today."

Tabor executed a bow of acquiescence. "I guess I'd better find us another bookkeeper before the numbers get so tangled up that Mr. Waterson can just walk away with the building and everything in it." He executed a brisk turn, then stamped out of the room and down the hall, not even glancing at Robert Miras or the woman reporter, waiting her turn with his boss.

Miras couldn't keep back a smile as he watched Tabor's back disappear around a corner. He straightened his face, then said to the reporter, "Mr. Berlin will see you now, but please do try to keep your visit as brief as possible. He's a terribly busy man."

‹›‹›‹›

Nell gave Berlin a womanly handshake, gentle and brief. "I'm Geneva Edwards," she said, with just the right touch of upper-crust inflection. "*New York Dramatic Mirror.* I know how busy you are, Mr. Berlin, and I promise not to take up too much of your time."

Berlin nodded and smiled politely.

"So I'll come right to the point. There's word going around, maybe a rumor, maybe not. But if it's true, it's a big story, and I'm sure you know how important it would be to my career to publish it. It concerns you and Scott Joplin—"

Izzy's scream drowned out the rest of Nell's sentence. *"God damn Scott Joplin! I just might have to kill the bastard."*

"Can you tell me whether or not it's true?" Nell asked.

"I'm sorry. Whether what's true?"

"What I just said, Mr. Berlin. That you're going to publish and produce a new musical play by Scott Joplin."

She watched closely, but saw only exasperation on Berlin's face. "Listen, Miss Edwards, I'll give it to you straight. I haven't seen Joplin for years, and I don't know a thing about any new musical play by him. That clear enough?"

"But it's common knowledge that you're working on a ragtime opera. You've been quoted in the *Dramatic Mirror,* the *Green Book* and, just recently, in *Theatre Magazine.* Does your present association with Scott Joplin have anything to do with that?"

Nell watched with no little satisfaction as Berlin's whole body tensed, his fists clenched. "There *is* no association with Scott Joplin. How many times have I got to tell you that? I'm the King of Ragtime, Miss Edwards, and I'm going to write my own ragtime opera. I don't need help from any broken-down has-been."

It took all Nell's force of will not to haul off and slap him into next week. Both hands held her little notepad in a death grip.

"That's the story, Miss Edwards, okay? Now, I've got to get back to work."

Nell cleared her throat. "Just one more question, if you wouldn't mind. I happened to be talking to a friend yesterday, someone who writes for the *New York Age.* He said when he ran into Mr. Joplin a couple of days ago, Mr. Joplin was very excited. He told my friend he'd left his play with you, and that you'd just called and made an appointment to talk with him about it. Can you tell me why he might have said that?"

Berlin gawked, jaw slack, eyes wide and staring. His body coiled like a wound spring. *"Jesus Christ Almighty! Everyone in the business knows Joplin's got a heavy dose of the French goods, and his mind's shot all to hell. If I was a doctor running a funny farm, maybe I could tell you what kind of crazy stuff goes through*

*his head. If! But I ain't a doctor, so I can't tell you. Now, would you
please leave a man alone to get his work done?"*

Nell slapped her notebook shut and moved face-to-face with
the raging songwriter. "All right, Mr. Berlin, I've got your quote
down, word for word, thank you."

Berlin writhed. How could he have let Izzy get past him to
talk like that, not just to a reporter, but a lady-reporter? Now,
she had his balls in that notebook of hers; if she ever put into
print what he'd just said, he'd be finished. He muscled Izzy aside,
then turned his best soulful look onto his visitor. "Miss Edwards,
I...I'm terribly sorry," he stammered. "There's no excuse for
talking like that, especially to a lady, and I hope you'll forgive
me. I'm under a whole lot of pressure, not that that makes it
right, but...well, I hope you'll understand. Let me answer your
question the way I should've in the first place. No, I haven't got
the slightest idea why Joplin would've said he got a call from
me, except maybe that's what he wants to happen. Maybe the
whole business about showing me his play is real inside of his
head. But it's not real anyplace else. Now, please, Miss Edwards.
There's absolutely nothing else I can tell you."

If he knew I'm not a reporter, Nell thought, he'd have me thrown
out on my ear, lady or not. "All right, Mr. Berlin." Struggling to
keep contempt out of her voice. "Thank you for your time."

No handshakes on departing.

Robert Miras showed Nell to the door, then walked back to
his boss. Before he was fully into the room, Berlin shouted, "Get
Cliff for me, Robert. I can't afford to waste any more goddamn
time today."

If a messenger's ever going to be killed, Miras thought, it's
going to be me, right now. "I'm sorry, Mr. Berlin, but if you'll
remember, you asked Mr. Hess to invite Mr. Stark by at a quarter
till two. That's only fifteen minutes away."

Berlin sank to the piano bench and flopped his head into his
hands. All right, fifteen minutes. Make a couple of phone calls,
then talk to Stark, get that deal done, and get the hell back to
writing music.

All the way down to the lobby, all the way across Seventy-second Street, all the way to the Kuminskys' apartment, Nell replayed Berlin's outburst in her mind. He hasn't talked to Scott for years, but he did seem to know the name of Scott's musical, didn't he?

◇◇◇

Bartlett Tabor, his face the color of uncooked beef, burst into Reception, straight-armed a man who jumped out of a chair and waved a sheet of music in his face, then charged down the far hallway to Henry Waterson's office. Fannie, the reception-ist, sat stone-still, didn't even say hello. When her boss was in that kind of a mood, the help did all they could to melt into the background.

Waterson's door was closed. Tabor knocked once, then, with-out waiting for a response, slammed the door open and flew in. Waterson swung around in his chair, turned a curious eye onto the office manager. Sammy Varick, one of the young pluggers, perched on the window sill, grinning, but the look on Tabor's face got rid of the grin in a hurry. "Sammy, go sell some tunes," Tabor snapped. "I need to talk to Mr. Waterson."

Varick was out the door before Tabor had finished speak-ing. The manager reached backward to slam the door shut. Waterson raised a hand. "What's up, Bart? Something about that murder?"

Tabor shook his head, and without a word, handed Waterson the manila folder. Waterson opened it, glanced at the first page, then scrambled frantically through the sheets of paper. When he looked back to Tabor, his face had aged twenty years.

"Right, Henry," Tabor said. "I've got it all, every nickel, every penny."

"What are you going to...do?" Waterson's voice was hoarse.

"I could show this stuff to Berlin, couldn't I? But I thought I'd give you first crack."

A bent smile inched across Waterson's lips. "I appreciate that."

"No trouble, Henry. I'm sure you and I can work something out that'll make both of us happy."

Waterson nodded. "I'm sure we can."

◇◇◇

Birdie opened one eye. All she could see was the bed she was lying on and a shiny pine table and chair. No sign of the man who'd chloroformed her. But when she opened her second eye and looked around, there he was, sprawled in an upholstered armchair across the room. A colored man! A lacy curtain fluttered before an open window near his head. Was he asleep? The girl sat up quickly, slid off the bed, started on tiptoes toward the door, but before she'd taken three steps, the man stood between her and the door. "Now, don't go makin' trouble," he growled. "If I gotta, I'll tie you up to the bed there." Then, as if anticipating her thought, he pointed a finger, and added, "And don't be makin' noise either, else I'll shove a gag in your mouth. You be nice, I be nice, too. Okay?"

Birdie didn't answer.

"Hey, I said, 'Okay?' You ain't deef 'n' dumb, are you?"

Birdie shook her head. The man was young, just about her age, but with his bashed nose and that scar across his cheek, he'd clearly done a lot more living than she had. The girl shook hair back off her face. "Why did you bring me here?"

"Don't be askin' questions." He gripped her shoulder, marched her back to the bed, and pushed her down.

Birdie's throat closed, eyes filled. "You're not going to…hurt me, are you?"

For just an instant, she saw his face relax, eyes soften, but his voice was no less gruff. "Not less'n you makes me trouble." He reached into his pocket, pulled out a small pistol, waved it in Birdie's face. The girl screamed, then clapped a hand over her mouth.

"Hey, be quiet, huh?" The man shoved the gun back into his pocket. "I was just wantin' to show you. My boss says I ain't supposed to do nothin' to you, 'less you makes any trouble, and then I gotta do whatever I need to. So, best you don't make no trouble, see?"

"I won't. I promise. But I can't understand why you kidnaped me. My parents don't have any money. There's no way they could pay you a ransom." She began to cry.

"Hey, stop that, huh?" The man's voice turned gentle. "Ain't no call for you to be cryin'…"

She wiped a sleeve across her eyes, looked around the room, then at her captor, who stared at her, puzzled. Finally, she brought herself to say, "Bathroom?"

The man jerked a finger toward the door at the far end of the room. "Right in there. I let you go in by yourself, but you better not do nothing funny, hear?"

"I won't. Thank you."

Birdie edged off the bed, keeping a good distance between the man and herself, and practically ran into the bathroom. She closed the door, paused, then turned the key in the lock. She hadn't gone for hours now, not since she'd left for work. She hoped the man wouldn't hear her, she'd be so embarrassed. Whenever Aunt Ruth came for dinner and went into the bathroom, Birdie and her mother sat and waited for what they knew was coming from her father: "That woman pees like a horse." Then they'd all giggle and snicker until her mother said, "Sha, both of you! She'll hear."

When she'd finished, Birdie opened the bathroom door, and looked around. No sign of the colored man. Then she heard his voice coming from the room beyond. "Yeah, she be fine, just scairt, that's all. No, sir, she didn't say nothin' at all, except for askin' why she be here…she figured you was lookin' for a ransom…You want me to ask her…okay, okay, I ain't gonna say a word, yes, sir. I'll just wait'll I hears from you again.

The girl heard a telephone receiver being replaced, and almost immediately, the colored man appeared in the doorway. He motioned her forward. This be the sitting room. You want to stay in here with me, that be okay."

"Thank you." Birdie did her best to smile. Being in the bedroom with him had been scary. She'd have felt that way if he were any man…well, any man except Martin. And even with

Martin, she guessed she might be just a little nervous, at least the first time.

The sitting room was what she'd have called a living room, larger than the bedroom. She walked to the bar, bottles lined up next to a stainless steel sink. The furniture was good quality, an oak rocker with beautiful decorative turnings, matching chairs, sofa and a fainting couch, all covered with a red, nubby fabric, no stains, no holes. The tan woolen carpet was thick and unspotted. This had to be an apartment, not a hotel, and whoever owned it was pretty well off. A telephone sat on a small table near the door. If the man ever left her alone or went to sleep, she might be able to call home, or the office.

Her back felt sore, legs stiff; she stretched, then settled into one of the upholstered chairs. The colored man stayed on his feet. Birdie thought he looked nervous. He paced the length of the room, peered out around the edge of the curtain on the window, then turned to face Birdie. "Hey, you ain't had nothin' to eat since we been here. You want me to get us some eats?"

Was he just going to leave her there? How stupid could he be? She'd be out and on her way before he ever got to wherever he was going. She worked up another little smile. "Sure...sure, that'd be nice, thank you. I guess I am a little hungry." Though she really wasn't.

The man nodded. "Okay." He walked toward the door. But the girl's fledgling hopes took a barrel-roll and flopped onto the carpet as he picked up the telephone receiver, growled, "Columbus 3487," waited a moment, then said, "Yeah...Fred? We needs us some eats up here in 2A...couple beef sandwiches an' cake be just fine...yeah, but don't you be all day with it... oh, an' don't forget some coffee too...yeah, thanks." He replaced the receiver. "Won't take long, they's only 'cross the street and down a li'l way."

Birdie nodded. "Thank you." A restaurant on this street with a Columbus telephone exchange? They couldn't be far from the office.

The man looked at her as if he was trying to make up his mind about something. Birdie held her breath. Finally, he spoke. "You like to play cards?"

The question seemed so silly, she almost laughed. "Well, yes. Sure."

"What game?"

"Gin?"

Now, his smile was friendly, open. "Gin rummy? I can play that. I had a white-boy friend in N'Orleans, he teached me. You wants a game while we waits for the food?"

"Sure."

The man rushed to pull an end table so it stood in front of Birdie's chair, then ran into the bedroom, came back with the pine chair, and sat opposite the girl. He made a show of whipping a pack of cards from his pocket, flipping the cards into the air, slapping them down onto the table. "You be in for it now," he said. "Li'l girl like you beat me at gin rummy, I guess that be time for me to quit." He shuffled the cards, dealt.

They were on their third hand when there came a loud knock. The man set down his cards, walked over, opened the door partway, and took a large paper bag from the delivery boy. Then he set the bag on the floor, and fumbled in his pocket. Birdie smelled roast beef; her stomach growled. But more important than food—without tipping off Mr. Scarface, was there some way she could get that delivery boy to understand she'd been kidnaped? She pushed back in her chair, but that was as far as she got. The colored man passed money around the edge of the door, and in the same motion, slammed the door and threw the lock. Then he picked up the bag of food, brought it to the table. "Well let's see what-all we got here. Better eat up before it get cold."

"Sure." Birdie tried not to be obvious about looking at the words printed on the bag. Barker's Café, 391 West Forty-ninth Street. So she was on West Forty-ninth, somewhere in the three hundreds, in an even-numbered building, on the second floor, 2A. How could she get the information to Martin? He was staying at Mr. Lamb's, he'd said, in Brooklyn. She scanned the room, but saw no telephone directory.

<><><>

Berlin was just a little too friendly for Stark's taste. The butler had answered his knock, let him in, and brought him directly into the living room, where Berlin sat on the bench before a grand piano, to all intents and purposes lost in music composition. "Mr. Berlin," Miras had announced. "Mr. Stark is here to see you."

Berlin turned; his face lit. "Mr. Stark, thanks for coming by on such short notice like this."

Stark thought he sounded like a novice actor, reading lines off a script. For that matter, the room looked like a stage set. Heavy curtains at every window, each piece of furniture massive. A conventional seascape on one wall, a portrait of a medieval couple on another. Bookshelves filled just so with leather-bound volumes. Behind Berlin, over the fireplace, a pair of British pottery urns flanked a lovely Empire mantel clock. As to the grand piano—Berlin had told every newspaper and magazine reporter in Christendom that he always composed at his special transposing piano, since he could only play in the key of F-sharp. But Stark had just seen him hit white keys. The grand was a prop in this particular play, as it was in the bigger stage production of the Life of Irving Berlin. All right, Stark thought, if he's going to all this trouble to set a scene for me, he must have a good reason. By all means, let's hear it. "Mr. Hess said you wanted to talk to me about Scott Joplin's music. I will always have time for that."

"Well, good, Mr. Stark." The composer clapped his hands together. "Let's get right down to facts. I don't appreciate being buttonholed in the street and threatened with getting my teeth knocked out, or worse."

So that was it. Perhaps Niederhoffer's little game last night was not such a bad thing after all. Stark put on a puzzled face. "I'm sorry you had a problem, Mr. Berlin, but I thought we were going to talk about Scott Joplin's music. I don't see—"

"Mr. Stark, don't try and be cute." Berlin worked to keep any sharp edge off his words. "We're both grown men, we don't need to play kid games. I don't mind telling you, I've got the chance of my life, writing this show with Victor Herbert for Flo Ziegfeld. I'm working every minute to get the music down on paper, and I just don't have time for monkey business. All I need is for some mug to beat me up, and I'll have to throw in the towel."

Stark thought the little man looked barely in control of himself. "Well, I *am* sorry, Mr. Berlin, but I'm also confused. You say a man threatened to knock out your teeth and beat you up? Why? And what does it have to do with me?"

Berlin's prominent Adam's apple rose, then fell. His lips scarcely moved as he said, "He wants me to give Joplin a contract to publish his music."

Stark extended his hands, palms up. "Well, that seems easy enough. Surely you don't need me to tell you how to write up a contract."

"Mr. Stark, would you listen to me, please. I can't publish Joplin's music because I don't *have* Joplin's music. I wouldn't touch Joplin's music with a ten-foot pole, not after the lies he spread all over town about me, five years ago. Now, would you please call off your gorilla?"

Stark kept his face set into an expression of mild puzzlement, eyes slightly squinched, right corner of his mouth twisted. "But Joplin said he gave you the music."

"Are you calling me a liar, Stark?"

Berlin stood over the older man, fists clenched and cocked, eyes popping, sizzling with rage. All pretense at civility was gone; the angry question came through in the harsh gutturals of the immigrant Jews Stark remembered hearing down on the lower east side. But then, suddenly, Berlin pulled himself up straight, adjusted his tie, cleared his throat. "Sorry…I guess I really am a little bit on edge."

Stark marveled at the change; it was as if an entirely different person were speaking.

"Look, Mr. Stark. This has got to be some kind of misunder-standing. How much would it take to get you to call off your goon and leave me be?"

Anger boiled up into Stark's throat, hot and bitter as gall. No more playacting. Up on his feet, shaking his right fist into Berlin's face. "'How much would it take?' Do you really think you can buy me off, then go merrily along your way as if nothing ever happened? You've got another think coming."

"Ah, Mr. Stark, come on, cool off. Look, I don't mean any insult. What's Joplin's music worth, you tell me. I'll give him every cent he hopes to get, then he can go his way and I'll go mine."

"Oh, you'll each go your own way, will you? And in six months, Joplin will walk down Broadway, look up at a marquee, and see *If* by Irving Berlin, the King of Ragtime. No, Mr. Berlin. Joplin wants to see *his* work on stage under *his* name. He wants to receive a royalties check in his mail every six months, and he'll want a percentage of the gate as well."

Stark paused to draw a deep breath. "Now, hear me, sir, and hear me well. You will present a proper contract to publish and produce Joplin's play, and you'll present it within the time con-straints you've been given. If you persist in this tomfoolery of yours, you'll find to your sorrow that my patience is not without limit. Good day, Mr. Berlin."

Stark clapped his hat onto his head, and stormed out of the room, barely nodding to a puzzled Robert Miras. He flung the door open, slammed it behind himself, but once outside, he slowed his pace, and his face relaxed into a broad smile. He wondered whether there might be any demand for seventy-five-year-old novice actors. Pity he'd never given a thought to going on the stage until now. He might have enjoyed it.

◇◇◇

Eva Kuminsky answered the door, bug-eyed, and grabbed Nell by both jacket lapels. "You come to tell me something about my Birdie?" The woman's shriek echoed down the hallway.

Nell gently removed Eva's hands from her jacket, then stepped inside, and pushed the door closed. She leaned into the hysterical woman's face. "Mrs. Kuminsky…Birdie didn't show up for work today. I came by to see whether she's here. Is she?"

Mrs. Kuminsky shook her head, mumbled a few words, the only ones of which Nell could understand were "phone call." She half-pushed, half-coaxed the woman into a chair, then marched off to the kitchen, where she filled a glass with water. Back in the living room, she put the tumbler into Eva's hand. Eva regarded it as if she'd never seen a glass of water before.

"Drink." Nell urged Eva with her hand.

Without taking her red-rimmed eyes off Nell, the woman downed a couple of swallows, then sighed deeply. "You know something about Birdie?"

"Only that she didn't come to work this morning. Do you know where she is?" Nell paused, then added, "I want to help. What can you tell me?"

Mrs. Kuminsky couldn't seem to unlock her tongue, just sat panting like an Airedale after a five-mile run. Nell smiled encouragement. Eva took another swallow of water. "I got a phone call, out in the hall there, not even half an hour ago. A man said he's got my Birdie, and if I want to see her again, I gotta tell Martin Niederhoffer and another man to go to the police and give up."

"Another man?"

Eva nodded. "I forget his name."

"Scott Joplin?"

"Yes. *Yes.* That's the one. You know him? You know Martin, maybe, too? Go tell them please, they should go in to the police. I'm scared—the man who called said if *I* tell the police, then he'll kill my child."

It had been a good while since Nell last had a headache, but now she felt a whopper brewing above her left ear. "Does your husband know about this?"

Eva shook her head. "He works on the trains, engineer. I don't know no name or phone number I could call. I gotta wait till he gets home. I'm afraid he's gonna kill Martin for getting Birdie into this trouble."

Nell started to say it wasn't Martin's fault, but decided that would be a waste of time. She thought about giving Mrs. Kuminsky her own telephone number in case any new developments arose, but what if that hothead husband called instead, or even showed up at her apartment? What if he sent the police? She took Eva Kuminsky's hand, squeezed it. "I'm going to do everything I can to help to get Birdie back safely."

The best the woman could do by way of answer was a distorted little smile.

Nell walked into the hall, down the stairs and outside, then started toward the subway station. But only a half-block along, she stopped. A hefty woman plowed into her from behind; Nell barely managed to stay on her feet. Ignoring the large woman's shouts, she stood a moment as if in a trance, then murmured, "Yes," and walked the rest of the way to the subway. But instead of taking the Number Two train downtown to Brooklyn as she'd originally intended, she pushed her way onto an uptown Number Three, rode to Seventy-second Street, and rushed along the sidewalk to her apartment. A few minutes later, she was at her desk, typing furiously.

‹›‹›‹›

Scott Joplin hit a chord, nodded satisfaction, reached to the music rack to write it down. The symphony was coming along; maybe he really *would* have time to finish it. And if he did, he'd get started on the score for that ballet he'd been thinking about, the one that would make his *Ragtime Dance* look like a practice piece. A symphony, a ballet…the kind of music he wanted to leave behind, music that would stop people saying Scott Joplin only composed music fit to be played in sporting houses.

His fingers wandered back to the piano keys, then he clenched his teeth as his bladder delivered its latest ultimatum. No, Joplin thought, I can hold it. He played a treble sequence, hit a couple of bass chords, wrote more notes on the paper.

Stark pushed himself out of his chair, walked to the window, looked up the street, then down. No sign of Nell. She was going to have lunch with Niederhoffer's girlfriend, what was her name, but it was already past three. What was she up to now? He didn't know whether to worry or be annoyed.

Across the room, on the sofa, Martin turned over a card, placed it in the proper sequence, turned over another card. Solitaire never had been his game, but right then, it was all that was keeping him from going crazy. Time was passing, but nothing was happening. Old Man Stark had gotten nowhere with Berlin, and as for Mrs. Stanley having lunch with Birdie, what was the point? Birdie had told him she hadn't heard anything and didn't know anything. He'd done more yesterday on his own than anyone else was going to do today. At least he'd gotten Berlin nervous...well, Footsie Vinny had, but who'd taken Vinny down there?

He glanced at Stark at the window. He could be up, out the door, and on his way before the old guy could even turn around. He set down the cards, stood, stretched. Quick glance toward the piano. Mr. Joplin looked like nothing but his music was in his head. The young man padded to the door, reached for the knob...and the door flew open, catching him squarely in the face. He let out a howl.

Nell stood in front of him, Stark at his side. "What happened?" Stark asked.

Nell pushed the door shut. "I think Mr. Niederhoffer was in the wrong place at the wrong time."

No sympathy in her voice. She knew. Martin took his hand from his face, glanced at it. No blood. "I heard you out there, and was coming to open the door," he said. "I wanted to do *something* today besides play solitaire."

Stark looked at the manila folder in Nell's hand. "I guess Martin's ears are better than my eyes. I never saw you coming down the street." He made a production of pulling out his pocket watch, then squinted over it, at his daughter. "I'd say you had a long lunch. Was it productive?"

Nell marched past him, dropped the folder onto the telephone table. She pulled the pin from her hat, set the hat on top of the folder. Joplin's apparent attention to his composition didn't waver. "As a matter of fact," Nell said. "I had no lunch. Birdie didn't come."

"What do you mean, she didn't come?" Martin, instantly on the uptake.

"I called the office and asked for her. They said she didn't come in to work today."

"Why not?" Martin's fists tightened. "Where is—"

Nell cut him off. "I couldn't find out right then, because I had an appointment with Irving Berlin."

Above his beard, Stark's face went crimson. "What…when did this happen? I had no idea—"

Nell tried to ignore the hammer, pounding relentlessly at her left temple. "You had no idea because I didn't tell you, and I didn't tell you because I didn't want to have to argue with you about whether or not I was going to do it. I posed as a reporter, and I got some interesting answers to my questions."

"But damn it to hell! What about Birdie?" Martin, not about to let the most important matter be put aside.

"Young man, control your tongue," Stark snapped. "There's a lady here."

"It's all right, Dad." Nell sounded weary. "Anyone in the music business who gets offended at every hell and damn doesn't have time to do anything else. Martin, I don't know what's happened to Birdie. After I finished with Berlin, I stopped at Kuminskys' and spoke to Birdie's mother. She was quite upset. Someone had called her and told her they had Birdie in custody, and that they'd release her if you and Mr. Joplin turn yourselves in."

It took a moment for Martin to process the information; then he barreled over to the piano, and tugged at Joplin's arm. The composer, taken by surprise, nearly toppled off the edge of the bench. Martin pulled him up and toward the door. "Get out of my way," he shouted at Stark and Nell. "I'm not going to let them hurt Birdie."

"You young fool—shut up and sit *down!*"

Martin's expression suggested Stark had slapped his face.

"Turning yourself in now would be the worst thing you could do. Can you really be so foolish as to think whoever's got your girlfriend would simply let her walk out of wherever she is, safe and sound? If we ever had any thought of you and Joplin going to the police, we don't have it any longer. They've forced our hand, and damn it…" He paused just long enough to glance at Nell, who managed not to smile. "We have no choice but to find out ourselves just what in Sam Hill is going on here, and we can't all be running around on our own, each of us trying to outmaneuver the other. If we want to have any hope of getting that girl back safely, we need to work together. Do you *both* understand me?"

Silence for an instant, then Martin exploded into tears. Nell put an arm across his shoulders. Joplin, now ignored, walked back to the piano bench, and picked up where he'd left off when Martin had pulled him away.

"My father's right, Martin," Nell said gently. "Come on, let's go in the kitchen. We need to put together what we know, and decide where to go from here."

Martin wiped at his eyes.

"We'll find her. "Nell's voice was like steel. "The sooner we start, the better."

"No doubt about that," said Stark. "But we do need to be careful. Trying to predict the behavior of a cornered rat can be dangerous business. Tell us about your talk with him, Nell."

<><><>

Stark leaned so far forward in his chair, Nell thought he might fall across the kitchen table. "You say Berlin told you he knew about Joplin's play?"

"Not exactly," Nell said. "He didn't admit it, but I think he slipped and referred to the play by name, *If.* I almost pushed him on it, but thought it might be better to not let him know I'd picked up on him."

Stark nodded. "Good judgment. Did he say anything else?"

Nell made a wry face, glanced toward the living room, then shifted into a whisper. "He said everyone in the business knows Scott's got a dose of the French goods, and is out of his mind. Of course, he lost no time in apologizing, and asking me to understand how much pressure he's under with his new show."

"The man's disgusting. If I were thirty years younger—"

Nell rested a hand on her father's arm. "Dad, enough. He's a crass little man who's terrified that one day he's going to find himself back on the streets of the lower east side. Let's get on. Did *you* find anything useful?"

Stark hesitated. He'd have sooner taken on both his boys at the same time than get down to cases with their little sister. She'd scared off more suitors than Penelope, didn't get married until she was past thirty. The only man he'd ever seen her defer to was Scott Joplin.

Whom he had come here to help, hadn't he? Slowly, he pulled a piece of paper from his pocket, unfolded it, laid it on the table. Nell picked it up and began to read. "I admit to being a bit ashamed of myself," Stark muttered. "I took it from Joplin's desk."

Nell looked up, disbelief all over her face. "Lottie doesn't know?"

Martin scrambled out of his chair to peer at the paper over Nell's shoulder.

"She was scared silly just about our being in there." Stark talked in a hoarse whisper. "I decided not to take a chance she'd say no. Or not let me even copy it."

Nell murmured a soft "Hmmm," then went back to reading. Finally, she looked up. "'The most important word in the dictionary of a man's life…The Ifs that have defined the life of Scott Joplin…' What you think those Ifs might be, Dad?"

"I've been wondering all afternoon. If Scott Joplin had been born white? If reconstruction had been more than a joke? If he could have gotten some real schooling in music composition and performance. If John Stark had published his operas…" His voice faded. "I suppose if I were in his place, it'd be something along those lines."

No one spoke. Nell pushed the paper back across the table; Stark folded it carefully and returned it to his pocket. "In any event, I'm afraid we can't make much of the fact that Berlin knew the name of Joplin's play. I mentioned it yesterday, when I went down and talked to him. I wanted to see how he'd react."

Nell sent her father's eyebrows skyward with a vigorous misuse of the Lord's name.

"I wouldn't be concerned, my dear. Two people, one of them supposedly a reporter, have asked him about that play, so he must have serious doubts by now as to whether he really can get away with stealing it. And…" Stark gestured toward Martin. "Thanks to our young friend and his companion, he must also know he can't try to get out of the situation by destroying the manuscript—not if he wants to keep his teeth. My apologies on that point, Martin. It was obvious this afternoon that Berlin thinks I'm the mysterious person behind the thug who threatened him, and I said nothing to disabuse him of the idea. Your plan might just have been brilliant, after all. Do you think you could get back in touch with this Footsie Vinny person?"

"Probably. I could go up to the Alamo and talk to Ragtime Jimmy."

"Yes, I suppose. I don't like your going out on the street, but I don't see any other way. All right. Nell, you stay with Joplin while Martin and I go uptown and arrange for Vinny to pay another call on Berlin, with Martin and me in his company." He turned to the young man. "But you will keep your mouth severely shut. I want Berlin to think he's up against the boss, and that the boss is angry about a missing girl, and running out of patience in a hurry." Stark pushed away from the table, and started in his stiff-legged trot into the living room.

"Just a minute, Dad."

Stark turned.

"I can't stay here with Scott. I have something else to do now."

Stark walked slowly back to his chair, sat, drummed fingers on the table, blew out a breath.

"I've been thinking about Birdie, too. It's almost four o'clock, and if I move fast enough, I can get to Waterson, Berlin, and Snyder before five. While I was waiting my turn at Berlin's, I overheard Mr. Tabor, the office manager, tell Berlin there's a real problem with the books, what with both Martin and Birdie disappearing, and he needs to hire a new bookkeeper, fast. I'll bet he'd jump at someone with experience at a music publisher's. He'd probably hire me on the spot and put me right to work."

"Nell! You can't do that."

"Why not? Weren't *you* satisfied with my work? When I kept books at Stark Music, you were never a penny off. I've got eyes and ears, and if I'm in that office all day, I might pick up some information about Birdie's whereabouts, and maybe about the murder as well. Don't *you* think they might be tied in with each other?"

Stark frowned. "That could easily put you in harm's way. I won't let you do it."

The silence in the kitchen was like the stillness that precedes a tornado. Martin stopped breathing.

Nell spoke first. "I am forty-four years old, and I'll decide for myself what I will and will not do. If I don't try this, and it comes to a bad end for that girl, do you suppose I'll be able to forgive myself for sitting by because of a half-baked concern for my own skin? That's not the way I was brought up."

Stark studied his shoes. She'd always been like this. There had been episodes in Sedalia where Nell's speech and behavior had sent ladies in for quiet talks with Sarah, but nothing had ever stopped his daughter, or even slowed her down. And blast it, she always managed to couch a proposition in such terms that if he objected, *he'd* be the one to sound unreasonable. No, that was not the way she'd been brought up. He raised his eyes. "Suppose Berlin should see you at the office, and recognizes you from this afternoon?"

"He's not there often, and in any case, I seriously doubt he'd give a bookkeeper a second glance, let alone a first. But I'll make up my hair and face differently. He'll never notice."

"The manager is going to ask you for references. You can't very well walk in and tell him you kept books for your father at Stark Music Company in St. Louis."

"Dad, for heaven's sake. Give me more credit than that. Before I came over here, I stopped home and did a little work." She got up from the table, then marched into the living room, Stark and Martin hurrying after her. "By the time I'm finished with Mr. Tabor, he'll be pleading with me to start work on the spot. Just leave that to me."

But I need to go with Martin up to Harlem."

"Fine. Joe will be back in an hour or so. He can stay with Scott, and you can go then. That will be better, anyway—with the after-work crowds on the sidewalks and in the subway, there's less chance someone will notice Martin." She picked up her hat, adjusted it on her head, set the pin with a thrust that made Stark cringe. Then she grabbed the folder and tucked it under her arm. "I'd better get moving, or I'll be too late."

Martin ran after her. "Mrs. Stanley, I don't know how to thank you. But please be careful."

Nell turned a tight smile on him. "Don't thank me until your girl is back with you. In the meanwhile, mind your manners, and listen to what Mr. Stark tells you. Don't give us anything else to worry about."

Martin looked at Stark, who burst out laughing.

Chapter Ten

Nell stifled a smile as Bartlett Tabor leaned back in his chair, eyes narrowed, forefinger playing at the dimple in his chin. Trying to size her up from across the desk. "Well, I've got to tell you, Miss Stanley—"

"Mrs. Stanley."

Sly smile. "Of course." He pointed at the ring on her left fourth finger. "I must say, this is a new one on me—a person coming in to apply for a position before I've even advertised it."

Nell raised the newspaper from her lap, held it up to him. "The power of the press, sir. Along with what I'm sure was unwelcome publicity, you did get a little free advertising. Having your bookkeeper on the run, gone from one minute to the next, can't be easy for you."

"More difficult than you know. Our assistant bookkeeper didn't come in for work today. It just so happens she's the bookkeeper's girlfriend, so I suppose she took off with him. They're probably on a train, somewhere around Cincinnati by now."

"Well, then." Nell extended a hand, palm up. "Here I am."

Tabor laughed. "The answer to my prayer, even before I've asked it."

"If getting your books in order and keeping them that way is what you were going to pray for, then yes."

Tabor let his chair drift to the upright, then grinned across the desk at Nell. "You're a pretty eager beaver."

"Perhaps just an early bird."

He laughed again. "Whatever, you're plenty quick. Let's see…" He picked up the manila folder Nell had given him when she'd come into the room. "*Mrs.* Eleanor Samuels Stanley… age forty-four…West Seventy-second Street…musician, hmm. What instrument?"

"Piano."

"Why aren't you out looking for performance opportunities?"

"I've had quite enough of that, thank you. I've played professionally, but the truth is, I've never been good enough to get past being an accompanist, and I'm tired of the grind, the bad hours, bad food, difficult traveling."

"You could teach piano."

"Yes, I suppose I could. But I don't have the patience to keep trying, day after day, to get sullen, sulking children to do something their parents have forced upon them, when they'd much rather be playing out-of-doors. That's why I took the bookkeeping courses—"

"At Stephens Secretarial College."

"In Chicago, yes."

"And you worked for five years at Leonard's Department Store."

Which existed only in Nell's imagination. She held her breath.

"Why did you leave?"

"My husband got an irresistible offer to work in New York."

"And you found work at Randall Music. Too bad the family closed the firm when Mr. Randall died."

Nell nodded. "He was a fine old gentleman. He treated his employees very well."

"So you've not worked now for the better part of a year."

"I decided to give the piano another chance, but it just isn't working out. No surprise, really. My husband and I were talking about it the other day, and I told him I thought I'd rather earn my living as a bookkeeper, and enjoy playing piano evenings, at home.

Tabor leaned forward. "Do you need to earn a living? Even with your husband's irresistible job?"

Nell warned herself not to underestimate the man, or get too clever and box herself into a corner. "No, Mr. Tabor, I don't need to. I want to. Would you like to spend your days cleaning a house that's not particularly dirty? Gossiping and making foolish talk over lunch with foolish, idle women? Worrying about whom to invite to dinner to advance your husband's career, then fretting for days before whether it will go well, and days after, whether it did?"

Tabor laughed again. "No, I certainly wouldn't. But does your husband approve of having you work? You can understand, I'd rather not hire someone who'll work a few days, then leave because her husband is complaining his dinner's not on the table on time."

"My husband is pleased to have me do what satisfies me."

She expected another chuckle from Tabor, but it didn't come. "All right," he said. "Your references look to be in order, and you've got very complimentary letters from young Randall and your supervisor at Leonard's."

That's the way I wrote them, Nell thought, and decided to push matters along. "Mr. Tabor, I'd like to work at Waterson, Berlin, and Snyder, and I believe I'm qualified in all respects. In fact, if the firm is ever in need of a fill-in pianist, I'd be right there. If you have doubts, why don't you take me on for a month, on a trial basis?"

Tabor leaned back again, protruded his lower lip, nodded. "You're an interesting woman, Mrs. Stanley. What line of work did you say your husband is in?"

"I didn't. He's chief accountant at a brokerage."

Nell readied herself for a prolonged personal fishing expedition, but Tabor surprised her by suddenly sitting upright and saying, "All right. Would eighteen dollars per week be acceptable, at least to start?"

"I think so…yes."

"Good. As a matter of fact, you may well be more suited to the job than you realize. I need someone with your degree of maturity and confidence. The company is in something of a... well, a delicate position right now. Let's just say there have been some irregularities, and we need to pay the closest attention to every item in every day's figures. Careful scrutiny and discretion will be of the utmost importance."

"I understand. When would you like me to start?"

Tabor studied his pocket watch. "Well, it's after five. Perhaps I can show you your space, and give you a bit of an idea as to what the job will entail. Then you'll be able to start first thing in the morning."

"I'll be glad to stay and learn the job, sir." Now, *she* smiled. "I'm sure my husband won't object if his dinner is a little late."

Tabor laughed. "Touché." He pushed back from his desk and got to his feet. "Let's get started."

<>‹›<>

Stark wondered whether they were on a fool's errand. Nearly three quarters of an hour, sitting on a bench at the southeastern corner of Riverside Park, but no sign of Berlin. Martin looked like a puppet on a string held by a maniac: every couple of minutes, up he'd jump, peer down the block, then flop back onto the bench. Footsie Vinny seemed fully absorbed in paring his fingernails with a vicious-looking knife, but then he folded the blade, jerked his head in Martin's direction, and growled, "Hey, kid."

Martin, halfway to his feet, froze.

"Siddown, would you, and stay down. You want to get people to noticing us, it'd be a hell of a lot easier, you just put up one a them signs with neon lights."

Martin lowered himself slowly back to the bench. "I keep thinking about Birdie," he murmured.

Stark slapped a hand onto the young man's thigh. "I know just how difficult it is to stay patient when you're worried about someone you care for, but that's what you've got to do right now.

You need to wait for the fish to bite. Try to set the hook too soon, you'll lose your fish."

Vinny's face eased into a smile. "Hey, there, Grandpa, you some kinda poet? You talk a damn good game."

"Wait till you see me play," Stark said, then motioned toward a couple of figures crossing West End Avenue, on the opposite side of the street. "Is that our fish? If it is, it looks like he's brought some protection."

They watched as the men came up close. "Don't look like that protection's got much muscle," Vinny whispered. "Aw right, you guys stay here. Be right back with some fish for you to clean."

Vinny scuttled a few yards to crouch behind a hedge at the southernmost tip of the park. Martin started forward; Stark pushed him back onto the bench. "Let him do his work. We don't want to spook them."

Before Berlin and his companion could get within shouting distance of the Chatsworth, Vinny was out from behind the hedge, across the street, and onto the sidewalk, facing the two men. To Stark, it looked for all the world like a man unexpectedly happening upon two friends; if he hadn't been watching for it, he'd never have noticed the way Vinny's right arm was bent at the elbow, the hand extended only slightly, not nearly enough for a handshake. Berlin looked around, but a little wiggle of Vinny's extended hand snapped the composer's head back. The gunman motioned, first with his head, then his hand, and the three men moved slowly, off the sidewalk. They waited as a car came up to the end of Seventy-second, and turned north on Riverside Drive. Then, the little parade proceeded into the park.

Berlin's companion looked frightened, but the composer's face was a study as he caught sight of Stark and Martin on the bench. He started to speak, but got out no more than a syllable before Vinny jammed the barrel of his pistol into the composer's back. "Can it!" Vinny barked. "Mr. B, you will speak when spoken to, and not any other time, kapeesh? And you, Mr..."

"Hess," the man squeaked. "I'm Mr. Berlin's musical secretary. I write down and arrange his music—"

"Well, that's just fine, then." A harsh growl. "I guess you shouldn't have no trouble arrangin' to keep *your* mouth shut tight. Now. We're all gonna get up and walk down the way there, back inside the park. We don't want nobody bustin' up our private business meetin', okay? Let's go."

Vinny directed Berlin and Hess across the grass, toward the border of shrubs and trees that separated the park from Riverside Drive. Stark and Martin followed. Vinny gestured with his gun, then gave Hess a shove in the direction of a bench. "You go and lay down there, have yourself a nice little rest while we talk to your boss. If you gotta take a leak, take it now, in the bushes, 'cause if I see your head come up or your feet go anywhere near the ground, that'll be the last move you ever make. Am I clear?"

Hess, slack-jawed, nodded, then practically ran to the bench, and in one motion, took off his skimmer, set it on the grass, and stretched out on the wooden slats. Vinny turned back to Berlin. "Okay, now, King—that *is* right, ain't it? King Irving of Ragtime? I want to know if you made any progress with our friend's music?"

Berlin's eyes bulged. "Look, I told you already. I don't have the music. I've never *seen* the music. So how am I supp—"

A sharp crack across his cheek from Vinny's left hand shut off whatever else Berlin might have been going to say. "Mr. B, you are getting me upset, and you don't want to do that. Now, I asked you a question that there's two answers for: yes or no. Which one is it?"

Berlin spluttered. Which got him another open palm to the cheek. "Listen good now, Your Highness. I been tryin' to help, you know, shake up your head a little, and maybe you'll remember which word's the answer. But I helped you all I'm gonna. This's the last time I ask you. "Any progress? Yes or no."

Martin hoped he'd never hear anyone talk to him in that tone of voice.

Berlin rubbed his cheek. "No."

Vinny nodded several times. Stark began to worry. He'd told Vinny no damage, just scare the living daylights out of Berlin, but the way Vinny was regarding the little man made Stark hope the thug's enthusiasm for his work didn't carry him away. Vinny blew out a deep breath. "Well, okay, I gotta admit, that is an answer. Not the answer I wanted to hear, and like I said last night, I ain't gonna wait forever for the one I do want."

"You gave me five days." Berlin's voice was like a tightly-drawn string.

"Hey!" Vinny grinned in the direction of Stark and Martin. "You hear? He does listen, don't he? An' besides, he knows how to count. But you know what, King? It ain't a good idea to leave a job till the last minute, and definitely not an important job. 'Cause things can happen, complications, you know? Like the one that happened today. And now, all of a sudden, I ain't feeling so patient like I was. You do know what I'm talkin' about, right?"

"I don't have the faintest goddamn idea," Berlin said.

Against his will, Stark felt admiration for Berlin. The little man kept his eyes level, looked Vinny square in the eye, and there was no pleading in his gaze or in his voice.

"Well, then, I guess I gotta give you a goddamn idea, don't I? What I'm talkin' about is the girl, the one you snatched—"

"I *what*."

The gun waggled. "Mr. B, you got yourself some very bad manners, you know that? It ain't polite to interrupt somebody while they're talkin'. Now, just so everything is above the board, I'm talkin' about this young guy's assistant, who happens to also be his girlfriend. She didn't come in to work today, and then her mother got a phone call, sayin' that she'd get her daughter back when Martin here and Scott Joplin turn themselves in to the cops. So I'm afraid we got us a new situation. I ain't sure we can wait no five days anymore."

For the first time, Berlin seemed befuddled. He looked from Martin to Stark. "Listen, I…I don't know what's going on here. I don't have any idea who this girl is. I don't even know her name."

Vinny nodded toward Martin.

"Birdie Kuminsky," Martin said. "Or Bertha."

Berlin shook his head slowly. "She's the assistant bookkeeper? I don't think I've ever even seen her. I don't schmooze with the help. What can I say to you guys? I don't have Scott Joplin's music, I didn't take the girl. Period. You've got to believe me."

Looking at Vinny, Stark thought of a bull catching sight of a cow in the next field. "We don't *gotta* do nothing," Vinny said. "But what *you* gotta do is get this mess fixed up, and fast. I want a contract for Joplin, and I want the girl back in the same number of pieces she got took away in. Stealin' music, that's one thing—you don't come around, you get to buy yourself a set of new choppers. But snatching a girl…" He pointed toward Stark. "My client there is very upset about that. He says you better know if she turns up hurt, you get a hundred times what she got. And if she turns up dead or she don't turn up at all, I only start with your teeth, and when I'm done, you ain't gonna have any need for new ones, or for nothing else either. Now. Do *you* believe *me?*"

Berlin nodded.

"I don't hear nothing."

"Yes."

"Okay, then." Vinny slipped his pistol back into the holster behind his jacket, but his stance clearly said that trying to take advantage of that move would be foolish. "And just one more thing, Your Highness. I sure hope you understand what goes down if you call in the cops or any kind of muscle. I just made you some promises, and it's bad for me *and* my business if I don't keep my promises. Mr. Stark is my boss on this job, but I got a big boss too, and when one of his employees *or* one of his customers gets hurt or dead, there is hell to pay. For your own sake, I hope you do believe me."

Berlin smiled. Actually smiled. Martin gawked. Stark again felt admiration, if grudging. "Yes, I believe you. I grew up on the lower east side. Worked at Nigger Mike's place."

Vinny nodded. "Good. Glad you know the system." He pushed Berlin toward the bench where Hess lay, every muscle exactly where it had been ten minutes earlier. "Go on then. If your friend there ain't arranged a heart attack for himself, get him up offa the bench and take him home."

◇◇◇

For the first time in Robert Miras' recollection, Berlin didn't go directly to his piano after his evening's entertainment. The valet's eyebrows went up when his employer told him to get a pot of coffee going, and when it was ready, to bring in cups for Mr. Hess and himself. But Miras just said, "Yes, sir," and went off to carry out the order.

Once the valet was out of the room, Berlin and Hess dropped into facing armchairs, and for a few minutes sat and stared at each other. Finally, Hess broke the silence. "I've never been so scared in my life."

Berlin nodded. "Sorry you got involved, Cliff. That's more than I pay you to do."

Hess waved off the apology. "I offered, didn't I? Thought maybe two of us would be safer, some joke. We could have had an army there, and it wouldn't have helped."

Berlin pounded a fist onto the armrest. "God damn, Cliff! That crazy hayseed and my own bookkeeper, pushing me around like that. What the hell am I going to do?"

Hess thought the question might be rhetorical, but decided to take the plunge. "It sounds like they won't be satisfied unless you draw up a contract and put on that play. Considering the alternative…"

Berlin moved up to the edge of his chair. Hess thought he could see the nerves in his boss' face and hands quivering. "How the hell am I supposed to do that when I don't *have* the goddamn play?"

Hess said nothing.

Berlin's face went almost purple. Hess began to worry about apoplexy. "Christ Almighty, Cliff—you think I *do* have it, don't you?"

It's not beyond the realm of possibility, Hess thought, but he was not about to say that. "Mr. Berlin, if you tell me you don't, I'll believe you. Unfortunately, it isn't me you've got to convince."

At that point, Miras glided into the room, carrying a silver tray with a silver coffee pot and two white china cups. He set the tray down on the table next to Berlin, poured the coffee, gave each man a cup, then left the room, more quickly than usual. Berlin and Hess watched him until he vanished around the corner.

"All right," Hess said. "Here's an idea. Tell Stark you did have the manuscript, but you got rid of it." He paused as Berlin choked on his coffee, then raised his eyes to glare across the top of his cup at his secretary. "No, Mr. Berlin, just listen for a minute. Nothing's going to satisfy them short of a deal, so give them a deal. Tell them to have Joplin write up a new manuscript, and to show your good faith, *you* draw up a contract to publish and produce the work when Joplin delivers it to you."

Berlin shook his head. "They'd never go for something like that."

"Why not? If you've agreed in writing to publish and produce that play, they'll go out of their way to make sure you live to do it."

"I still don't like it."

"I didn't really think you would, but have you got a better idea?"

"If I do what you say, then where's it going to stop? Any time Joplin or Stark wants a piece of my hide, I'm going to be looking down the barrel of a gun and hearing about how my teeth are going to be scattered all over Riverside Park."

"Give Joplin a contract for this play, but put in a clause that it's a one-time agreement, no more dealings with either him or Stark."

Berlin sank back into his chair. "I don't know, Cliff…I just don't know." Teeth clenched so firmly, Hess wondered how the words managed to get through. "If I don't get back to writing music soon, I might as well go see if Nigger Mike'll take me back on as a singing waiter…" Berlin's voice trailed off, as if a new idea had intruded into his thoughts. Then he jumped to his feet so suddenly that Hess, without thinking, leaped out of his chair. "Let's go," Berlin said. "We've got work to do. This is make-or-break for me, and I'm not about to flop."

Hess was accustomed to abrupt turnarounds from his boss, but he'd never seen one like this.

"I'll take care of Joplin and Stark tomorrow," Berlin said. "I've got an idea. But I'm not going to waste any more time tonight." He started to walk out of the room.

Hess considered asking whether Berlin had forgotten about that missing girl, but the secretary was already looking at his boss' back. All right, Hess thought, it's your funeral. He'd stay up all night transcribing and arranging. He'd put up with the tantrums that erupted when it became clear that a whole song, a night's work or more, was unsalvageable. But hell would freeze before he'd ever go out again at night with Irving Berlin.

‹›‹›‹›

Berlin worked like a man possessed. Hess had never seen the little composer so focused. Every word out of his mouth had to do with the music; no small talk the whole night long. Not a mention of the incident in Riverside Park. Usually, they knocked off by six, seven at the latest, but this morning, Berlin showed no sign of even slowing down. Hess was so full of coffee, he sloshed when he shifted on the bench. Finally, a few minutes past eight, Berlin stretched, yawned, and said, "Okay, Cliff, any more and I'm going to start doing damage. Let's call it a night."

Amen, Hess thought, and trotted off in the direction of the bathroom. Berlin watched him all the way down the hall, and when he saw the bathroom door close, he pulled Stark's business card from his pocket, grabbed the telephone, and asked the operator to connect him.

‹›‹›‹›

Nell and Stark sat at the breakfast table, she in an unadorned plain, off-white silk blouse and a smart, neatly-fit dark suit, black shoes with sensible heels, her long, dark hair piled up and pinned atop her head. Stark wore a blue and white striped bathrobe, ragged at the ends of the sleeves, and a well-worn pair of slippers. 'Use it up, wear it out, make it do or do without,' Nell thought. His way. Always was, always will be.

Stark speared a chunk of biscuit, raised it, let gravy drip onto the plate, then gobbled the forkful. "Wonderful breakfast again, Nell. You really do need a meal like this to get started for the day."

If you're working on a farm, she thought, but instead said, "You were out late, Dad. I thought you might need a little extra fuel this morning."

He nodded. "It won't hurt you, either, my dear. You have a big day ahead of you." He ran eye tape over her. "And I must say, you've presented yourself very well. You'll have them eating out of your hand, I'm sure."

No, you're not, Nell thought, but said, "I hope so. I'll snoop around, talk to some of the help. Maybe the receptionist and I can go out for lunch. Receptionists know everything that goes on in an office, and I just might get something out of her that the police—"

The telephone bell from the living room cut Nell off. She jumped up and ran to pick it up. "Damn nuisance," Stark muttered. "A man can't even eat a meal anymore without having that blasted thing interrupt him." He jabbed his fork into the biscuit.

Nell called from inside. "Dad, for you."

Stark swallowed, then pushed away from the table and ratcheted his body to full vertical. He shuffled into the living room, where Nell stood, holding a hand over the mouthpiece. "It's Irving Berlin." She held out the telephone.

At this hour? he wondered, then took the instrument. "Hello. John Stark here."

"Mr. Stark, this is Irving Berlin."

"I'm surprised, Mr. Berlin. I thought you spent your mornings sleeping."

"You're right. When we're finished talking, that's exactly what I'm gonna do. But I can't waste any time, can I? What I got to say to you, I want to say now."

"Well, that's fine, Mr. Berlin." Stark winked at Nell. "Should I assume this has to do with our encounter last night."

"Yeah, well, that was an easy one, wasn't it? Listen, Mr. Stark, I want to get this thing taken care of. Let's you and me set up a time, and get together with Scott Joplin. Could we do that?"

"I don't know. My first question is why you want this meeting. If it's to have Mr. Joplin there to sign a contract, I'll certainly say yes. But for any other reason, no. I think we were direct with our requirements last night. A contract, publication, production."

Silence. Stark waited. When Berlin spoke again, he sounded as if he might be strangling. "Look, Sta…Mr. Stark. I know you don't want to hear this, but I don't *have* Joplin's play and I never did. I'm hoping if I can talk to you and him together, maybe we can figure out what's really going on."

"I think what's really going on is that you're trying to weasel out of the situation and keep that play for yourself. But it's not going to work."

Berlin took a moment to swallow. He didn't dare let Izzy go off now. "Mr. Stark…all I'm asking is for you to be just a little reasonable. Joplin says he's sure he gave me his play, and I say I'm sure he didn't. Why can't we all talk about it in the same room?"

"We're not going to do that, Mr. Berlin, and there's an end to it."

Stark heard a gulp. "Look, Mr. Stark—"

"Mr. Berlin—"

"No, listen. Please. If you won't let me talk to Joplin, at least ask him when it was he gave me that music, and where. Then—"

There's no need of that. He gave you his manuscript at your office, Monday, during lunch hour."

"Which office? I got two of them. Did he say which one? And *my* lunch hour is at three or four o'clock. Come on, Mr. Stark. Find out from Joplin which office he saw me at, what day, and what time. Then call me back. Would you at least do that?"

Stark cleared his throat. "All right, Mr. Berlin. I'll talk to Joplin, and get back to you. But don't forget—"

"I know, I got a deadline."

"I was going to say that every hour that passes makes me more concerned for that girl's safety. Whatever you do regarding

Joplin's music will come to nothing if she is not returned safely."

He heard Berlin gulp. "Okay, I'll remember that too. You got my number, right?"

"Oh yes, Mr. Berlin, I've definitely got your number. You can count on that."

The telephone was barely back on the hook when Nell said, "What's he trying to do?"

Stark shook his head. "Squirm out of his dilemma, what else? He wants Joplin to say exactly where and when he gave Berlin his music."

"And then Berlin will deny he was there."

"I'm sure. But there just might be another edge to the sword. If we do pin down the particulars, suppose a third party *can* place Berlin there?" He glanced at the clock on the wall above the stove. "I suppose you'd better be off soon. You don't want to be late your first day. Just be careful. Please."

Nell shot him an evil grin. "Don't worry, Dad. Heaven will protect the working girl."

She started toward the kitchen, but Stark stopped her. "I'll clean up," the old man said. "Go to work."

<> <> <>

Birdie opened her eyes to bright sunlight, surprise. She felt like she'd slept only a couple of hours, but she and the colored man had broken up the card game a little after eleven, then she'd gone straight off to bed. Not that she'd fallen directly asleep. For at least a couple of hours, every little sound had snapped her eyes open to stare through the darkness toward the door, trying to see whether it might be inching open.

She sat up, looked around. No sign of the man. Had he come in at all during the night to check up on her? She didn't think he'd tried anything funny, because wouldn't she have felt it and waked up? But there was that girl in school last year who got in the family way, and swore she'd never been with a man. Once, though, she'd gone walking with a boy in Central Park, and when they stopped to sit for a while under a willow tree, she fell asleep, and thought maybe he'd taken advantage of her. Birdie leaned forward, pulled up her dress, peered underneath. No blood, and her undergarments looked in place. Gingerly, she pressed two fingers against her groin, which told her only that she needed to go to the bathroom.

When she walked out of the bedroom, into the sitting room, there was the colored man, sprawled in an armchair. He grinned. "Thought you was gonna sleep all day."

She smiled. Except for right after she came out of the chloroform, he'd been really nice. While they played cards through the evening, she'd told him about how she and Martin were going to get married as soon as they could, but she'd go on working because they'd need the money. He'd laughed. "Leastwise, till the babies come, right?" She was sure she'd never blushed so hard in her life. "That's why I ain't havin' no truck with women who want to get married," the man had said. "Musicians be a fool to go an' get married, they be on the road so much, an' even when they's home, they be workin' nights. Maybe after I makes a bundle *writin'* music, I can think about gettin' married. An' matter of fact, I be on my way already. Some big publisher's gonna put out two of my tunes."

A huge yawn vaporized Birdie's recollection. She tried to cover her mouth, too late. "Oh, I'm sorry. I couldn't fall asleep last night for the longest time. Getting kidnaped…well, you've been nice to me, but it's still scary."

Which seemed to upset the man. "Oh, now, I don't want for you to get scairt. Hey, listen—my boss, he says ain't nothin' gonna happen to you, otherwise I wouldn't a ever done this for him. He says soon's a couple a bad eggs go down and turn themselves in, then I can open up the door, an' out you goes."

Birdie couldn't imagine that they'd let her walk out the door when she could so easily identify her kidnaper, but decided she'd be foolish to pursue the matter.

"They killed a man, these two guys, then they went on the lam."

Birdie's hands started to shake. Two bad eggs who'd killed a man and gone on the lam? Martin and Mr. Joplin? But what could that have to do with her?

The colored man interrupted her thoughts. "You sick or something?"

"No. I'm all right." Birdie thought frantically. "I guess I'm just hungry, that's all."

The man grinned. "Tell you what. I been pretty hungry myself, but I figured I'd wait till you got yourself up. How about I call down for eats?"

Birdie forced a smile. "That sounds real good."

"Okay, then. But you go on back in the bedroom there, and stay till I comes for you. I don't want the delivery guy seein' you. Go on, now."

Birdie obeyed. He called after her, "I'll get us some orange juice and coffee, an' a good mess a bacon and eggs."

"Okay," Birdie called back. She almost laughed. Here she was, kidnaped and being held in an apartment by a colored man with a big scar on his face, and she was worried about what her mother would say if she knew her daughter was about to eat bacon.

‹›‹›‹›

They sat at a table in the tiny kitchen. Birdie had a little trouble with the first taste, but once it was chewed and swallowed, she decided bacon actually was pretty good. Very good, in fact. She didn't feel any different, and thought if she got another chance, she'd probably eat it again. Her mother didn't have to know everything she did. Besides, she'd soon be married to Martin, and then her mother couldn't tell her not to do anything.

While they ate, the colored man went on about his music, told her how he'd gone to school back in Sedalia, Missouri, the same music school Scott Joplin had attended, and that he guessed those old European composers were okay for their time, but what really got to him was the music coming up out of New Orleans. "I was in St. Louie one night, and I hear this guy, Jelly Roll, he cut everybody in sight—"

Birdie's cheeks went chalky. "With a knife?"

The man started to laugh, but a look at her face stopped him cold. He reached across the table, touched her hand, then pulled his own hand back in a hurry. "Sorry, Miss. No, see, cutting be a kind of contest to find out the best piano player in the joint. They's judges and all, and the winner get a prize, maybe ten or twenty, or in a big one, even a hundred dollars. An' this Jelly Roll man, he made some of the best players in St. Louie look like li'l kids. He play what he call jass, it's a new kinda music from New Orleans. Well, the very minute I heared him, I knew that jass music be the thing for me. When I finished school, I played my horn on the streets, and I hired out for any kinda job that paid money, building, digging, whatever. I saved every penny, some days I didn't eat, and when I got enough together, I come here to New York City. They already be lots a good players in Chicago and Kay Cee, but jass just now be comin' to New York, so I figure I can be the man here. Mr. Jelly Roll, he told me don't just play other peoples' music, you gotta write your own. Besides, they pays you to publish your tunes, and then everybody gonna know your name. You play piano, Miss?"

"Yes. Not really good, though."

"Well, when my music come out, I gonna give you copies. See if I don't."

Birdie's smile came naturally. She looked around. Dust motes drifted lazily in beams of sunlight. This must be what it's going to be like, she thought, sitting over breakfast with Martin, listening to him talk about the big things he's going to do with his life. If she closed her eyes and ignored the southern speech, she could have been listening to Martin. They'd finished eating, but neither one seemed inclined to leave the table. An idea came to Birdie; she paused to think it through, then spoke. "I don't even know your name."

He grinned. What beautiful teeth, Birdie thought.

"Dubie, Dubie Harris," the man said. "You're gonna know it real good some day. What be your name? My boss told me, but I went and forgot."

"Birdie. Short for Bertha."

"Birdie…Birdie…" Dubie seemed to roll it around on his tongue. "That be a nice name, nicer than Bertha. When I gives you my music, I'm gonna sign it for you: 'To Birdie, Best wishes, Dubie Harris.' Then, when you play it, you can think about me."

He's stringing me along, she thought. Maybe he thinks that'll make me behave myself. She got to her feet. "That was a good breakfast, thank you. I'll wash up the dishes."

"Woman's work." Dubie grinned wide, showing off those wonderful teeth. He stood, stretched. "I'll go inside for a bit. Maybe we can play us some more cards later."

"Sure."

She watched him amble into the living room, then set about clearing the table. The strangest thing, how it kept feeling like a rehearsal for married life. She soaped a dishcloth. Someone lived here—who? It couldn't be Dubie's apartment. Probably his boss', whoever that was. First chance she got, if she got a chance, she'd have to snoop around.

As she walked into the living room, she heard a rasping sound, like a piece of machinery not running quite right. Dubie was stretched out on the sofa, mouth open, snoring away. She looked from the sleeping man to the telephone, then back to Dubie, then back again to the phone. She could call home—but no, her mother would be hysterical, no help at all. Martin was at Mr. Lamb's, in Brooklyn, but she didn't know the number. Okay, then, how about the office? Give Fannie the phone number here, and tell her to call the police so they could go to the telephone company and get the address.

She tiptoed to the phone, lifted the receiver, took care not to let the cradle rise too fast and make noise. She needed three tries before the operator heard her whispered request. Her heart pounded at her throat as the telephone at the other end began to ring. Then, Fannie's voice. Waterson, Berlin, and Snyder, Music—"

She shrieked as Dubie tore the phone from her hand and slammed it down onto the cradle. "What you doin'? Who you callin', huh?"

She couldn't speak, just shrank against the wall.

"Damn, girl! Some people, you just cain't be nice to." He grabbed her arm, started dragging her toward the bedroom.

She dug her heels into the carpet. Dubie muttered a curse, then swooped an arm down to catch her behind the knees, picked her up, stomped into the bedroom, slammed her down onto the bed. "Now you don't move, hear? *Hear?*"

Dubie charged out of the room. In less than a minute, he was back, a length of stout rope in each hand. "Oh, don't—" Birdie shouted, but he cut her off. "My boss said tie her up, but that just didn't seem like the thing to do. So I tried being nice, and see what happen? The minute I take my eye offa you, you're on the phone. Good thing I sleeped a lot on park benches, 'cause it don't take the least little noise to wake me. He pushed Birdie roughly onto her side, roped her ankles together, and fastened the other end to the rail at the foot of the bed. Then he tied her hands behind her back. "That hurts," she cried. "Shoulda thought of that before you went and ran off to the phone," the man barked. "Okay, now. You needs to use the toilet, you can call me. Otherwise, you stays right here. An' stop with your crying, 'cause it's your own damn fault." He started to walk away, then looked back at Birdie. "I trusted you," he said. Then he stomped out and into the living room, leaving the girl with the crazy notion that she had, in fact, betrayed him.

Chapter Eleven

By a quarter to nine, Nell was in the Waterson, Berlin, and Snyder Reception Room. She used the next fifteen minutes to get chummy with Fannie Solomon and arrange to go to lunch with her. On the stroke of nine, a gray-haired man with a sensational handlebar mustache came in, and in a thick Italian accent, told Fannie he wanted a tune for a vaudeville sketch involving an organ grinder and a monkey. "Mist' Berlin, he write 'Marie From Sunny Italy,' an' 'Sweet Marie, Make A Rag-A-Time-A-Dance With Me,' yes? So he can make me a good-a song, too. Then, I sing it on-a da stage an' people buy." Fannie directed him to a chair.

The Italian had just settled down when Tabor walked in, along with a heavy, ruddy-faced man, whom he led to the reception desk. "Well, Mrs. Stanley," Tabor said. "You're more than punctual, aren't you?"

"I try to have good work habits, sir," Nell said.

The big man guffawed, and punched Tabor's arm lightly. "Looks like we've got us a go-getter, Bart."

Tabor nodded. "Mrs. Stanley, this is Mr. Henry Waterson, our senior partner. Mr. Waterson, Mrs. Eleanor Stanley, our new bookkeeper.

Nell smiled. "I'm pleased to meet you, sir."

Waterson took a moment to evaluate Nell part by part, starting with her head and working his way down, pausing longer at her bosom than she thought was decorous. In any case, he seemed to approve of what he saw. "I'm glad you came looking for the job, Mrs. Stanley," he said. "I can't deny, we're in a tight spot."

Nell met his gaze. "I expect to have you out of it by the end of the day, sir."

Tabor snickered. Waterson exploded in laughter, which made it clear to Nell he'd drunk his breakfast. "By golly, I *like* your attitude." He slapped his knee. "Tabor, there is after all something to be said for maturity in an employee, isn't there?" He bowed slightly toward Nell. "I hope you'll enjoy working here, Mrs. Stanley."

"I'm sure I will, sir."

Tabor cleared his throat. "All right, Mrs. Stanley. Let me take you back to your place and get you started. You've got a lot to do."

<>‹›‹›

After Nell left for work, Stark dressed slowly. His was a mind that moved relentlessly along a single track, no switching to another line until the first destination had been reached. Why was Berlin being so obstinate? No doubt, the man was under terrific pressure to produce music for the Ziegfeld extravaganza, so why the deuce didn't he just produce a contract to publish *If*, and be done with it? He wouldn't lose much money, if any; men like Berlin never do. Was the man simply too stubborn for common sense—damned if he was going to admit his attempted theft, and give his opponent satisfaction? Stark remembered generals on both sides of his war who showed a positive genius for winning skirmishes that cost them major battles.

Stark checked his watch, a quarter to ten. Berlin had insisted he'd never seen Joplin's manuscript, and wanted Stark to pin down details. All right—perhaps Stark could use those details to pin *Berlin* down. He locked up the apartment, went out, and walked briskly along Seventy-second Street, toward the subway kiosk.

<>‹>‹>

Martin let Stark into Lamb's apartment, then practically jumped into the old man's arms. "Did they find Birdie yet?"

Stark shook his head. "Nell's gone in to work at Waterson, Berlin, and Snyder. Let's see what she comes up with."

Martin shook both fists in the air, a classic pubertal tantrum. "I can't just sit around here, I'm going to go nuts. I need to *do* something."

Stark gave the young man a quick dose of cold-eye. "Son, you listen to me now. You've already done something, and just by good fortune, it's worked out to our advantage. But you may not be so lucky next time. There *are* times to push luck, but when you do, you need to be sure you're gambling with your chips and no one else's. Three lives are at stake here, only one of which is yours."

The old man turned away from Martin, then walked to the piano. "Joplin." Stark shook the composer gently by the shoulder. "Joplin, I need to talk to you."

Joplin turned slowly, blinked his way back to his surroundings, nodded a sort of hello to Stark.

"Do you remember just when it was that you gave your manuscript to Berlin?"

A wave of consternation washed over the composer's face. "Why do you need to know that?"

"To help clear up the matter. I'm trying to go back to when it started, and then move forward from there. Do you remember which day you went down there? And at what time?"

Joplin looked like a man rummaging for a small object in a packed steamer trunk. He chewed at his lower lip. "Few days ago, in the daytime…well, what difference does it make? I gave him my music, just like I gave him *Treemonisha*, and he stole it to make his fortune. After he'd published seven of my rags!" The composer's entire body began to shake. His jaw twitched; he seemed to labor for breath. Then he turned savagely away from Stark to face the piano, struck a chord, made a face, struck another.

Martin tugged at Stark's sleeve. "Mr. Stark, I know. Mrs. Joplin told Mrs. Stanley it was the day before the murder, Monday. While I was out to lunch."

"Which was between?"

"Twelve and one. Like always."

Stark indicated Joplin with a sidewise motion of his head. "Can we really be sure that was when he came by? He might have come during business hours, and Berlin just told him you were out to lunch. Would you necessarily have seen Mr. Joplin from your office? Can we even be sure that he went to that particular office at all? Perhaps he went to Berlin's other office, or his apartment."

No response.

Stark sighed. "I'll give Lottie a call."

<><><>

The instant Stark identified himself, Lottie echoed Martin's first question. "Nell called last night, told me about that li'l girl been kidnaped. They find her yet?"

"No, but we're working at it. The reason I'm calling is to see whether you can tell me just when Scott did go downtown to give the manuscript to Berlin."

"I sure can. It was, lessee, one, two, three, four…four days ago. Monday. He left here right about eleven-thirty, and not two hours later, he was back with that cut on his head and blood all over his shirt. Before he left, I wrote down the address for him, the way all them music places move around. Waterson, Berlin, and Snyder, Strand Building, Broadway and Forty-seventh Street, third floor. Do that help?"

"I think so, yes."

"Scott doin' okay?"

"As well as we could hope. He sits at the piano and works at his symphony."

"I can hear that. Okay, then, Mr. Stark. I thanks you for callin'."

Stark heard her hang up, then, in slow motion, replaced the earpiece into the cradle.

◇◇◇

By the time Nell ran up to the receptionist's desk, the office was quiet. Three minutes after twelve, all the staff was already out to lunch. "I'm sorry to be late," Nell said. "Those books are a terrible mess. I was in the middle of reconciling a couple of columns, and I couldn't stop on the dot of twelve."

Fannie smiled. "Don't worry about it, Dearie, it's only a few minutes. I give you a week, and you'll be just like everybody else. When it's both hands straight up, it's pencils down and out the door." She wrestled her headphone past an impressive beehive of hair, then got to her feet. "Let's go. Got to make up for that lost time."

In the hall, waiting for the elevator, Nell said, "It's nice of you to go to lunch with me."

"Nah, come on, Dearie, it's your first day. *I* shoulda asked *you*. What do you say we go to Schneider's? It ain't cheap, but it ain't too bad either, and the sandwiches are divine."

It's going to be a long hour, Nell thought, as they stepped onto the elevator.

As they ate their divine corned beef, Nell went along with the girl-talk, the let's-get-acquainted banter. She assured Fannie that married life was just fine, assuming, of course, that you find a husband like her own, responsible and easy-going, not a man who tries to run his wife's life as well as his own. They talked about hairdressers and manicurists and doctors. Finally, Nell found her opening, and asked Fannie how she liked working at Waterson, Berlin, and Snyder. "Oh, it's the best," the receptionist said. "Good hours and decent pay, and they treat you good. Mr. Waterson plays the horses a bit too much, if you ask me, but he's nice to all the help. And Mr. Snyder, he's on vacation now, you'll meet him in another week and a half. He's a lot younger, and oh, such a dreamboat. Then, there's Mr. Berlin." Fannie snorted, half-amused, half-derisive. "He's too good to talk to anybody. But at least he don't have hands that go places where they shouldn't, I'll say that for him. Unlike certain other parties I could mention."

The girl licked her lips, obviously enjoying her time on-stage. Nell grinned, and wrapped a girlish twist around her words. "And who might those certain other parties be?"

"Well, I guess you could start with Mr. Bartlett Tabor."

"Mr. Tabor? Nell applied surprise to her face with a trowel. "Why, he seemed all right to me. Maybe a little sarcastic—"

"Oh, Dearie, let me tell you." The way Fannie snaked a hand toward Nell, you'd have thought she was about to drop a delicious chocolate candy onto her new friend's plate. "Mr. Tabor's more than a *little* sarcastic. Wait'll you make your first mistake. You'll know about it for sure."

Well, then, he'd be doing his job, Nell thought, but said, "All right, thank you. I'll watch out. And I'll try not to make any mistakes, at least not big ones."

Across the table, Fannie, a faint smile on her lips, studied Nell. The receptionist twisted a lock of hair in front of her right ear, released it, twisted it again.

"Penny for your thoughts," said Nell.

"Well...I don't know..."

"Now, come on. Don't be a tease." Nell thought if she had to keep up this pretense and tone of voice for much longer, she'd scream.

"Oh, all right. You'll find out soon enough, anyway. Mr. Tabor's not much of a gentleman. The girls say he's got wandering hands, but they don't exactly wander. They know right where they're going."

"If they go where they don't belong on me, they'll never go there again," Nell said. "I promise you that."

"But you'll only make him worse." For the first time, Nell thought Fannie looked embarrassed. "I figure, a little feel here, a goose there, what does it really matter, huh? I can't afford to lose my job. Live and let live, I say. He's a man, right?"

Scott Joplin is a man, Nell thought. And Jim. And my father.

"I just think he oughta show a little more consideration, though." Fannie was launched now, no stopping the flood of information. "It's one thing for a guy to be a little fresh with somebody who knows their way around the block. But he's just terrible with that little Birdie—gives her a pinch or a feel every time he goes past her. She's scared silly of him, and scared even more that her boyfriend might see what he's doing. Martin's got a little bit of a temper, you know? You ask me, that's why she didn't come in to work yesterday or today. I bet she was afraid to be in the office without Martin being there."

"I think she should have come in and spit in Tabor's face if he touched her."

"She's how old, Dearie? Seventeen? Could you do that when *you* were seventeen?"

"I could have done more than that," Nell said. "And I would have."

Fannie shook her head. "Well, I guess you're more nervy than most of the girls. They're all the time wondering what to do if he invites them up to his apartment. That's how he works it, see? Sometimes it's for a 'final interview' for a job. Sometimes it's for a raise."

"Is that really true? Or is it just a rumor?"

Fannie's smile went sly. "Oh, Dearie, it is no rumor. I'm making five dollars a month more because I spent a night at 354 West Forty-ninth, Apartment 2A. Hey, look—maybe it's one thing with you, you got a husband, but for me, what does it hurt, huh? It's the way the world works—like I said, live and let live. You scratch my back, I scratch yours." She started to giggle, all her earlier embarrassment out the window.

Nell willed herself to stay in her chair and keep disgust off her face. The way the world works! But this contemptible woman was the eyes and ears of the office, and the last thing Nell wanted to do was antagonize her. "I guess we'd better be getting back."

Nell pointed toward the big round clock up on the wall behind the counter. "We don't want to be late, do we?"

Fannie's eyes opened all the way. "Oh, my goodness!" She jumped to her feet. "I was having such a nice time talkin' to you."

Nell threw money on the table. "We'll talk more."

◇◇◇

Stark peered into the phone, as if he were trying to see Berlin's face. "You say I have to believe you, Mr. Berlin? Just why should I believe you at all, let alone be compelled to?"

A momentary splutter, then, "Look, Mr. Stark. I was not at W, B, and S at all on Monday, never mind over the lunch hour. I got up at twelve that day, like just about always, had breakfast and a shave, then Cliff Hess came by about one to show me some of the work he did on a couple of my songs. He was here most of the afternoon. Robert can tell you that, and so can Cliff."

Stark blew out a long breath. "Mr. Berlin, I've talked to Joplin and some other people as well, and I have to say, it does sound as though Joplin met with you at Waterson, Berlin, and Snyder four days ago, between twelve and one. Everyone agrees on that."

"Everybody except me. For God's sake, Stark. Whoever it was that told you Joplin was at W, B, and S between twelve and one on Monday—were they there with him?"

Silence.

"I don't hear anything, so I guess the answer is no. Look, I want to get this straightened out as much as you do, maybe more. Why won't you let me talk to Joplin? If you, me and him talk, we just might be able to clear it all up."

"I have to admit, Mr. Berlin, you make a fair point. If it were only myself involved, I'd agree. But I need to think of Joplin's safety as well as Niederhoffer's, and certainly that girl's."

"Give me a break. What do you think, I'm going to have a bunch of cops waiting to nab Joplin on the spot?"

"That is a possibility."

"Stark, listen. You think I'm gonna gamble with my own teeth, and maybe my life?"

Stark wondered whether he should put aside his dislike for the man, and set up a meeting. But time favored him, not Berlin, and besides, he thought he should talk the matter over with Nell and Joe before taking that step. "You make a good case, Mr. Berlin. I need to think it over. I'll get back to you later."

"That's for real?"

"Sir, I do not deal in flummery or taradiddle. I will get back to you."

"When? How soon?"

"Later today, perhaps tomorrow."

‹›‹›‹›

The afternoon heat in the Waterson, Berlin, and Snyder offices was stifling. Men walked slowly, sleeves rolled up, collars open, ties loose. Even the applicants in Reception, usually eager and talky, sat quietly as they waited their turns. Nell labored over the ledger, stopping now and then just long enough to wipe perspiration off her forehead, lest it drip into her eyes or onto the ledger pages, and smear the ink.

By a quarter past four, she had the numbers up to date. Tabor looked at her, astonished, when she presented him with the ledger. He leafed through it, page by page, and when he finished, his face was all admiration. "Well, Mrs. Stanley! I'd thought it would take you at least two days to sort out this mess. You really do deliver the goods, don't you?"

She smiled. "Yes, sir, I do. What would you like me to work on now?"

Tabor shook his head slowly. "I'm concerned about some sales numbers from one of our distributors, but I don't have the files ready yet. I'll get them to you tomorrow morning. Just take the rest of the day off."

I'm not going to learn anything while I'm out, Nell thought, and said, "Is there something I might do for Mr. Waterson?"

Tabor cocked his head, looked at her out of the corners of his eyes. A wicked smile spread over his face. "This time of year, Mr. Waterson has an urgent appointment every afternoon at the race track. I'll see you in the morning." Tabor turned back to his work.

Clearly, the discussion was over, and so was Nell's work day. She said a quiet, "Thank you, sir," and left.

She stopped at her desk, picked up her purse, and walked down the hall toward the waiting room. Fannie looked her a question as she came past the reception desk. "I finished my work," Nell said. "Mr. Tabor said he had nothing else for me to do, and I should take off the rest of the day."

Fannie checked her watch. "It's not even four-thirty. He gave you more than a half-hour off?"

Nell nodded.

Fannie snickered, then motioned Nell to bend down. "*I* say you better watch out," the receptionist whispered. "Next thing you know, you're gonna be up in that apartment of his."

"I'll be careful." Nell waved, and walked out into the corridor.

She rode down to the main floor in an otherwise-empty elevator, stepped out to the sidewalk, and began to wind her way through the Broadway mob. If Tabor tried to get her up to his apartment, she'd give him a good—no, she wouldn't. She'd play hard-to-get, that's what she'd do. Easy enough to string along a wolf, and she was not exactly a little lassie, just out of school… wait a minute. Didn't Fannie say Tabor had an eye for Birdie, and the girl was afraid Martin might catch the manager pinching her, and make a scene that would lose them both their jobs? Well, Martin *was* out of the office now, wasn't he, and it was not past Nell's imagination to see Tabor leading the girl to the apartment after work, then telling her in the morning to do whatever she'd like for the day, and when he came back after work, they'd have a swell dinner and go to the theater. And then, of course, another night in the apartment and a second day off, along with a hint that this might lead to a permanent arrangement.

Nell's gorge rose. A man passing her gave her a queer look and a wide berth. She moved out of the foot traffic to stand against the green marble facade of an office building. What was the address Fannie had mentioned? 354 West Forty-ninth, yes.

Apartment 2A. Nell sidestepped a man locked in place, head back, gawping up at the tops of the buildings. A Reuben, come to the big city for the visit of a lifetime. He'd better pay more attention to the bulge in the back pocket of his trousers.

354 West Forty-ninth was a small brownstone, five floors, probably two apartments to a floor. A nice building, clean-looking, but nothing fancy. She opened the street door, walked in, and up the flight of metal stairs to the second floor.

She stood for a moment in front of 2A. What would she say to Birdie? That the girl should be ashamed for frightening her mother while she enjoyed a little fling with the manager? For that matter, would Birdie even open the door?

One way to find out. Nell knocked, quietly at first, then louder. "Yeah, what is it?" came back at her. A man's voice.

This was a mistake, a wild-goose chase. Fannie was such a dodo; she could have decided to have a little fun pulling Nell's leg. She turned away, started for the stairs, but then heard the door open behind her. "Hey lady, you lookin' for somebody?"

She turned back. The speaker was a young colored man with a nasty scar across his left cheek, wearing a shirt and trousers so bright, they hurt her eyes. Nell forced a bland smile. "I was looking for someone, but I guess I'm in the wrong place."

"Somebody like who?"

"Mr…" She was going to say Tabor, but since the place supposedly was his, she threw out the first name that came to her mind. "Mr. Berlin."

The man looked both suspicious and nervous. "Mr. *Irving* Berlin?"

"Why, yes. The songwriter. You've heard of him, then?"

Mistake. The man's face tightened; he reached into his pocket. "I probably have the wrong address…" Nell's voice failed as the man pulled a pistol from his pocket and pointed it at her. He motioned with the gun: come here.

She backed a step away, toward the stairs, but the man moved two steps out from the doorway. "Woman, get yourself on inside a there, and do it quick. I ain't gonna tell you one more time."

Was he bluffing? Nell decided not to test him. She walked past the man, and inside. He slammed the door, threw the lock.

She looked around. No one else in the room. To her right was a kitchen, to the left, a doorway that she thought probably led into a bedroom. The man still held the gun on her, standing just far enough away that he couldn't miss hitting her if he fired, nor could she hope to grab his arm and wrestle away the gun—which was clearly a forlorn hope anyway, given the man's size. "Okay, now, lady," he said. "What is it you say you come here for?"

"You can put away the gun—"

"That ain't for you to say. What is it you come here for?"

"Well, it's a little embarrassing," Nell said. "This *is* Apartment 2A? 354 West Forty-ninth?"

"What if it is?"

"That's the address Mr. Berlin gave me. I was supposed to meet him here."

"Yeah? That the truth?"

Nell nodded. "Yes."

The man's scowl deepened. He waggled the barrel of his gun toward an armchair. "Sit yourself down and *stay* sittin', hear? Make one move, I gonna tie you in so tight you can't even breathe. Move!"

Nell sat, smoothed her skirt.

The gunman walked across the room, pulled a scrap of paper from his pocket, then picked up the phone receiver and read a number to the operator, a number Nell recognized. Waterson, Berlin, and Snyder's. As the man waited for the receptionist to pick up, he shifted from one foot to the other, all the while muttering under his breath. "Yeah, hello," he finally growled. "I gotta talk to Mr. Berlin, it be real important…no, damn you, I ain't tryin' to sell him no songs. And don't you go tellin' me he ain't there or like that. You don't hook me right up with him, ain't no way you gonna have you a job tomorrow."

The man glanced at Nell; without saying a word, he warned her to stay put. Then he snapped to attention. "Oh yeah, hello. Mr. Berlin, sorry to be botherin' you, but I got me a problem

here. This woman, she knocked on the door and said she supposed to be meetin' Mr. Irving Berlin…what she look like, you
say?" The colored man stared at Nell. "I don't know, nothing
special. Medium-high, kind of old, she got some gray hairs…no,
I didn't get that, you want me to ask? Okay, hold a minute. The
man lowered the receiver. "Woman, what you call yourself?"

"Eleanor Stanley. I work at Waterson, Berlin, and Snyder.
That's how I know Mr. Berlin, for heaven's sake."

"You hear that, Mr. Berlin? What? Hold on again, I'll ask
her." He turned back to Nell. "He says what job you got at his
place. He ain't never heard of you."

"I'm the new bookkeeper. I just started today."

The man returned the phone to his ear. "You hear that?…
Yeah, okay. I won't let her outa the chair she be in. I got my rod
on her, so she ain't goin' noplace. Yeah. 'Bye."

The man hung up the telephone, settled into an armchair
across from Nell, chortled. "Mr. Berlin be right on over, say he
like to make your acquaintance."

"I'll be glad to meet him," Nell said, then told herself she
was foolish to waste irony on this man.

She was right. "I ain't so sure about that," he said.

"Can't you at least put away the gun? It's really getting me
nervous."

The colored man laughed again. "Long as you sit nice in that
chair there and don't do nothing to make *me* nervous, you ain't
got a thing to worry about. It all be up to you."

Nell listened, then pointed toward the bedroom to her left.
"Whoever you've got in there is crying." She had a pretty good
idea who that whoever was.

"What about it? Ain't none a your business." But Nell thought
the man looked distressed, and the longer they sat and the longer
the crying went on, the more uneasy he appeared. Finally, he got
up, waved the pistol in Nell's direction, then walked quickly to
the doorway. "Something the matter?" he asked into the room.
Nell couldn't make out the reply. "Well," the man said. "I truly
be sorry, but I can't attend to you same time I got to be watching

somebody out here. Wait'll my boss comes, then I can loosen up your ties a little." The man stomped back to his chair, his face like a storm cloud, and pointed the gun back at Nell.

"Why can't you make that poor girl comfortable?" Nell asked. "Why do you need to be so cruel?"

The man exploded. "Damn you, woman! Didn't I tell you, it ain't none a your business? Now, shut up your mouth, you're botherin' me."

Nell looked from the gun to the man's face, tried not to linger on the scar. Better just sit quietly and wait to see what would happen when Berlin arrived. If the situation looked bad, she'd tell him her father knew she was here, and that Footsie Vinny was ready to go into action at any time.

Fifteen minutes passed. Nell heard a key in the lock of the door to the hall. The colored man also heard it—he went rigid, then jumped to his feet. The door swung open and a white man burst in, a pistol in his outstretched hand. The colored man's eyes bulged. The white man fired once, twice. A look of wonder came over the colored man's face. The gun dropped from his hand, then he swayed as if doing a grotesque dance, and folded onto the floor.

Nell flew out of her chair. "Mrs. Stanley," the white man called after her. "Are you all right?"

But she was already in the bedroom, taking in the scene. Birdie, tied to a bed, directly beneath an open window. The girl's face was wild with fear. "What happened, what happened?"

"It's all right now." Nell bent to undo the knot in the rope around the girl's wrists, then, as Birdie rubbed her hands together, Nell whispered, "You've never seen me before, understand?"

Birdie nodded.

Nell untied her feet. As the girl swung around to sit on the edge of the bed, she noticed the white man standing in the doorway. Her hand flew to her mouth. "Oh, Mr. Tabor. What are *you* doing here?" She looked back at Nell, all questions.

Nell turned to Tabor. "Do you two know each other?"

Tabor smiled. "This is Birdie Kuminsky, Mrs. Stanley. Miss Kuminsky, Mrs. Eleanor Stanley. Our new bookkeeper."

Birdie clutched at her throat. "But Martin's the bookkeeper... oh no. No, no!" Screaming now.

"What's happened to Martin?" Nell took her hand, squeezed it.

"I've got no idea," Tabor said. "I haven't seen him since he and Joplin ran away from the office after the murder."

"Martin had nothing to do with that murder!"

Tabor coughed. "I don't know whether he did or not, Miss Kuminsky. I only said that was the last time I saw him. And since we were without a bookkeeper *or* an assistant bookkeeper, I thought I'd better hire one." He sucked at his upper lip. "As far as I know, Mrs. Stanley, there are no company books in this apartment that needed your attention. What are you doing here?"

"I was going to stop at the drugstore on my way home," Nell said. And I happened to look up here, and I saw...Miss Kuminsky, is it? I saw her head sticking out the window, and as well as I could tell, she was calling for help."

"Oh, yes. Yes." Birdie practically jumped up and down. "I managed to get myself onto the end of the bed, and I thought if I could get somebody's attention, maybe they'd get me out of here."

Tabor's face beamed with approval. "Smart girl."

Oh boy, Nell thought. Smooth as silk. Young Niederhoffer's going to have his hands full. "So, I came up and knocked at the door, and got more of a reception than I'd figured on."

Tabor shook his head. "Whew. Another five minutes, and both Fannie and I would've been gone for the day. She ran into my office and told me someone was calling for Mr. Berlin, said it was very important, and would not take no for an answer. So I told her to put it through to me. Then, before I could even say my name, he was off and running, told me he had a woman up here who'd come to see Irving Berlin. I couldn't imagine what was going on, but when he said he had a 'rod' on you, I thought I'd better come prepared. Good thing I did." Tabor patted the bulge in his jacket pocket. "That's no little popgun he's got out there."

During the last part of Tabor's speech, Birdie's eyes went wider and wider. When he finished, she charged full tilt into the living room. Nell and Tabor followed. The girl paused as she saw the colored man on the floor, then let out a wail, ran up to the body, fell to her knees, and threw her arms around the dead man's shoulders. "You killed him," she screamed back at Tabor. "What did you have to kill him for?"

Tabor snorted. "He was holding a gun on Mrs. Stanley." Tabor nudged the pistol, on the floor, a few inches from Dubie's outstretched hand. "You think I should have just let him shoot *me?* And her. And maybe you, too, while he was at it?"

"He wouldn't have done that." Birdie sobbed. "He just talked big."

Tabor shook his head. "What the deuce is going on? Who is…*was* this guy? How did you get here?"

Nell reached a hand to Birdie, helped the girl to her feet, and over to the sofa. She rubbed at her wrists, then took a handkerchief from Nell and wiped at her eyes and face. "I don't know. He got hold of me yesterday on my way in to work, pulled me behind the elevator and held a chloroform rag over my face. Next thing I knew, I was here. I was scared, 'cause I didn't know what he was going to do, but then he got really nice." The girl looked at Dubie's body, started to cry again, noiselessly this time. "He called out for food for us, and we sat around, playing cards and talking. He said he was working for a big-time music publisher who was going to put out some of his tunes."

"Did he say who?" Tabor's tone was a jackhammer staccato.

She shook her head. "No."

"That doesn't help a lot."

Enough, Nell thought. "Mr. Tabor, she can't tell you what she doesn't know. We need to call the police, but first, the girl is going to call her mother. The poor woman is worried sick." Nell took Birdie's hand, led her to the phone. "Tell your mother you're all right, and that I'll bring you home as soon as the police let us go."

Birdie acknowledged the directive with a wan smile, then picked up the receiver and gave the number to the operator. She watched silently as Nell palmed a little slip of paper from the telephone table, and walked away. "Mr. Tabor…" Nell said.

"What?"

"I'm just wondering. How is it you have a key to this apartment?"

Tabor looked away, rolled his tongue against his cheek. "Well, all right, Mrs. Stanley, you're a married woman. And working at W, B, and S, you're bound to hear about it sooner or later. I keep this apartment because it's convenient after I've gone to dinner and the theater. He cleared his throat. But I do have friends, and I get requests from them often enough that I keep an extra key. The day before yesterday, one of them asked whether he could borrow the room for a few days. I thought he was going to…well, you know."

"I can imagine easily enough."

"I think we have a problem, Mrs. Stanley."

Birdie hung up the telephone.

"I think we do," Nell said. And I think we'd better inform the police. Now."

Tabor hesitated. "I'd hoped we might come up with a better idea. This will be terrible publicity for the firm."

"I understand that. And if it weren't for that dead man on the floor, I might go along with you. But I don't think any of us should take the risk that one day we might need to explain why we tried to cover over a murder, even one so clearly justified. Now, will you call, or shall I?"

Tabor laughed, and walked toward the phone. "Mrs. Stanley, you make a strong argument."

<>◇<>

Detective Ciccone spent several minutes looking over Dubie Harris' body, then straightened, stretched, groaned. "Floor gets lower every year, Charlie."

Patrolman Flaherty produced a properly appreciative laugh.

Great, Nell thought. We call the police and they send Weber and Fields.

Ciccone looked long and hard at Birdie and Nell, then turned up the intensity as he focused on Tabor. "You seem to be making a habit of coming across dead people. Two homicides inside of a few days, within a few blocks of each other, and the same man calls them both in. Quite a coincidence, wouldn't you say?"

Over Flaherty's snicker, Tabor said, "Listen, Detective Ciccone—"

"That's Sic-cone-E. Like the island, not something you put ice cream in. And I *am* listening, but I'm also thinking. You call in both murders. And Miss Kuminsky there gets a visit from me at home about the first one, and now she's front and center at the second. You better watch it, Miss. You don't want to be the feature attraction at the next event."

Birdie sniffled, began to shiver. Nell wrapped an arm around her. "That's not necessary, Detective. Not with what this girl's been through the past couple of days."

Ciccone treated Nell to a look that should have withered her, but she returned his glare with interest, and in the end it was the detective who looked away. "I'll decide what's necessary," he said, but most of the starch was gone from his voice. "There are two men dead—"

"And one poor girl, kidnaped and frightened out of her wits," Nell barked. "We all want to help you, but one more remark like that, and I'll take Miss Kuminsky out the door and home. You will have to stop me by force."

Ciccone chewed on his lip. "All right, Mrs. Stanley. Miss Kuminsky, I'm sorry I upset you. Please tell me what went on here. Start at the beginning."

When Birdie finished, her account, Nell took over, and finally Tabor. Ciccone took it all in silently, here nodding, there raising his eyebrows at Flaherty. Then he addressed Nell. "Not that I doubt your word, Mrs. Stanley—but are you in the habit of looking two stories up as you walk along the sidewalk?"

"Of course not. But I thought I heard calls for help, and when I looked up to where they seemed to be coming from, I saw Miss Kuminsky, leaning out the window. She looked upset."

"You have good eyesight."

"As a matter of fact, I do. But I'm sure you or anyone else would have come to the same conclusion."

"Hmm." Ciccone smiled. "Miss Kuminsky, if you were tied to the bed, how did you manage to get your head out the window?"

"The foot of the bed is right under the sill. I pushed myself up as far as I could, and then I leaned on the ledge, and called, "Help," but not too loud." She pointed at Dubie's body. "I didn't want him to hear me."

"What did you think would happen when Mrs. Stanley came up? Did you imagine that man with the gun was going to say he was sorry and let you go with her?"

Birdie's lip trembled. "I didn't...I thought maybe a policeman would see me, or maybe someone would call a policeman."

"All right. Mr. Tabor, how is it you happen to have both a gun and a key to this apartment?"

"I keep the gun in my desk. If you want, I can show you my license."

"We'll get to that." Ciccone paused long enough to send a message that the man's attitude annoyed him. "But since you know about gun licenses, I've got to think you also know it's illegal to discharge any firearm in the Borough of Manhattan."

Tabor got the message, didn't like it. "What the hell's the point of licensing a gun if you're not allowed to use it to defend yourself?"

Ciccone shrugged. "I don't write the laws. I just enforce them." He held out his hand. "The gun, please, Mr. Tabor."

Tabor pulled the weapon from his pocket, handed it to Ciccone, who passed it to Flaherty. "Thank you. Now, let's talk about the key."

Tabor coughed and cleared his throat. "The apartment is mine," he said. "I use it to entertain friends, evenings."

Ciccone looked at the body on the floor. "He wouldn't be one of your friends, would he?"

"Certainly not. I'd never set eyes on him until I came into the room today."

"And how was it that you *did* happen to come into the room today," Ciccone asked. "At five o'clock in the afternoon, with a gun in your hand."

Tabor looked at Nell and Birdie, then sighed luxuriantly and turned a wry face onto the detective. "That man called the office and insisted on talking to someone who wasn't there. I'm the office manager, so the receptionist asked me to take the call. Before I could say hello, the man told me there was a problem, he was holding a gun on a woman, and I should come right over. So I figured I'd better be prepared. When I opened the door, he pointed the gun at me. Fortunately, I fired first."

"Who was it the man asked for?" Ciccone's voice went very soft. "On the phone. At your office?"

By now, Tabor was giving a good impression of a man who'd accidentally sat on a nest of fire ants. "Uh…Mr. Berlin, one of the partners."

"Oh. This colored man is in *your* apartment, with a girl he's kidnaped and tied to the bed, while he's holding a gun on a woman. And he calls and asks Mr. Berlin—what? Why would he be asking Mr. Berlin what to do?"

Tabor looked at Nell and Birdie, but there was no help forthcoming. Neither was a good reply written on the wall behind Ciccone and Flaherty. Finally, Tabor looked back to Ciccone. "I loaned Mr. Berlin a key the other day." Nell could hardly hear the words. "Every now and then, he asks about using the apartment. I don't ask him why. He's my boss."

Nell felt Birdie sway against her side; she walked the girl to a chair, sat her down, then marched back to face the detective. "Mr. Ciccone, this girl is at the end of her rope. May I please take her home? If you need to talk more with her, perhaps you could see her there."

Ciccone glanced at Birdie. "Yeah, okay. We've got her address. Just give yours to the patrolman here." As Nell reached for the pencil and pad in Flaherty's hand, Ciccone added, "Just one more question, an easy one. Miss Kuminsky, did you see Mr. Berlin here at any time? Or anyone else, besides the man on the floor?"

Birdie shook her head. "No. No one."

"Okay. Go ahead, then, Mrs. Stanley. Take her home."

Nell glanced at her wrist watch. After six o'clock. Her father would be at Joe Lamb's by now, and at the least he'd be concerned. She took a step toward the telephone, but stopped. That detective was not a fool. All he'd have to do was hear her give the operator a Brooklyn number, right after she'd written down her Manhattan address, and he'd be all over her. Better to just go down to the street and find a phone booth.

<>‹›<>

Martin was up and over to Nell before she got fully inside the room. "Where's Birdie? Is she all right?"

Stark had lowered his newspaper; now he folded it and set it on the coffee table. Lamb came out from the kitchen, a wooden spoon in his hand. Joplin, surprisingly, got up and walked away from the piano, then sat next to Stark on the sofa.

Nell brushed past Martin, pulled off her hat, tossed it onto an end-table next to a lamp, and collapsed into an armchair. Martin followed at her heels. She gave the young man a warm smile. "Yes, she's fine. I suspect she'll sleep very well tonight."

"They didn't hurt her, did they?"

"From what she says, she is no longer kosher, but that's the extent of it."

"Why didn't you bring her here?"

Stark pushed himself up and off the sofa, took Martin by the elbow, pulled him away from Nell. "There are many reasons why she didn't bring the girl. In case you don't recall, you and Joplin are still fugitives from the law, and the fewer people, your girlfriend included, who come traipsing over here, the better. Besides, she'll be able to get some rest now, back in her own home."

Martin wrenched his arm away. "She got kidnaped once, she could get kidnaped again."

Stark saw him glance toward the door. "Martin!"

"Damn it!" The young man stamped a foot. "Mr. Stark, you're old. You don't know what it's like."

It seemed to Nell that everyone in the room, herself included, held their breath. But Stark's face was calm, his voice level. "Old I may be, but my memory is in no way faulty. I remember well when I was twenty-four, and my new wife, sixteen. That was in 1865. I was in the Union Army, stationed in New Orleans, and shortly after the wedding ceremony, my company shipped out to Mobile Bay. Not long after, word came to me that neighbors were threatening my wife's safety, and so I left my unit and made my way back to New Orleans, where I sent my wife, in the company of a young Negro man who posed as her servant, up the Mississippi to my brother's farm. Can you imagine how much I would have given to go with her?"

Nell thought Martin looked like a sailboat suddenly becalmed. "Your leave was only long enough to let you go back to New Orleans?" he asked.

Stark looked at Nell, then pulled himself even straighter. "I was not given leave. I deserted. How I wished I could have gone up the river with my wife, but I knew she was safer on that boat with my friend than she would have been with me. Had I gone with her, and been apprehended as a deserter, she would have been entirely without help. Much against my will, I returned to my unit and served out my time, which passed slowly indeed. So yes, young man, I know very well what it is like. And you have my full sympathy."

Lamb waved the wooden spoon. "I don't know if any of you are hungry—"

"I am, for one," said Nell. "I can fill you in at the table on what's happened."

⟨⟩⟨⟩⟨⟩

"Extraordinary," Stark said when Nell finished her account. "Someone with Berlin's success, going to such lengths to steal Joplin's music and then put him and Martin out of the way."

"Some people can never be satisfied," said Lamb.

"I thought it was odd, though," Nell said. "Everyone in the music business knows Berlin doesn't chase women. I've heard some nasty jokes. But Tabor said Berlin often asked to borrow the apartment."

"He wouldn't be the first man to be hypocritical about his private behavior," said Lamb.

"But why would he need Tabor's apartment?" Martin spoke so softly, Nell had to listen with care to catch all his words. "He has his own place, and no one to stop him entertaining there."

"He'd have to face his staff the next morning," said Stark. "Which would no doubt embarrass him severely. Not to mention what might happen if one of his lady friends were to show up at his home another time, uninvited. It does make sense. Perhaps at this point, we should just sit tight for a day or two. From what you tell me, Nell, I'd say the police are going to make Mr. Berlin shed a great deal of perspiration."

Nell suddenly pushed away from the table, walked into the living room, opened her purse, and came back holding out a slip of paper to her father. He worked a pair of spectacles from a pocket, adjusted them on his nose, then read aloud, "Mr. Irving Berlin. Columbus 8711." He looked up at Nell? "So?"

"This was in the colored man's pocket."

Stark looked over his glasses at his daughter. "I still don't see the importance. He had the phone number handy in case he had to call Berlin. Which he did."

"But it's the Waterson, Berlin, and Snyder number. Where Berlin spends very little time."

Stark shrugged. "Perhaps Berlin didn't want him calling at his home. The receptionist could have relayed messages. It's also possible Berlin didn't even give him the number. He could have decided on his own he'd like to have it handy, and copied it from a card or the telephone directory. In any case, I fail to see—"

"Turn it over, Dad."

Stark flipped the paper. "Hmm. 'Clarence and Ida Barbour. 215 West 131st Street, west of Seventh Avenue.'" Again, he looked over his glasses at Nell. "Who are they, do you suppose?"

"I have no idea, but I'd like to find out."

Stark removed his glasses. "Nell, if this was in that man's pocket, how did it happen to get from there into your purse?"

Lamb coughed.

"In steps. He left it on the telephone table when he called Berlin. Then, after Tabor shot him, when I took Birdie to the phone to call her mother, I palmed it."

"You *palmed* it? Nell! You could find yourself serious trouble, removing evidence like that."

"I'd found serious trouble before I ever called you to come out here. Maybe Clarence and Ida, whoever they are, can give us some information. I'm going to go up there and talk to them, right after dinner." Cagey smile. "I can't very well give the paper to Detective Ciccone now, can I?"

Stark jabbed a finger toward the window. "For heaven's sake, Nell, it's after eight o'clock. You can't go out on the streets by yourself, to a neighborhood you're unfamiliar with." He paused, just long enough to shake his head. "All right. You may consider me your escort."

"You won't object, will you, if I give Lottie a call, and see whether she can slip down the fire escape and go with us? I think it might not hurt to have Mrs. Scott Joplin along. She knows the neighborhood, she knows the people."

"No, of course I won't object, it's a splendid idea. Go ahead, call her, and let's get on our way before it becomes too late to pay a visit."

Chapter Twelve

Cliff Hess had never seen a face on his boss to match this one. Not that he was surprised. He knew right off there was big trouble when those two cops came in to speak privately with Mr. Berlin; then, not half an hour later, Max Josephson, Berlin's lawyer, had rushed into the apartment and straight to the library, where the composer was sitting with the policemen. More than an hour went by before Robert showed the cops to the door, and for a good twenty minutes after that, Berlin stayed closeted with Josephson. When the composer finally stormed into the kitchen and up to the table where Miras and Hess sat over cups of coffee, Hess drew a deep breath. "Everything go all right, Mr. Berlin?"

Robert Miras seemed to remember a job he needed to do. He got up, excused himself, left his cup in the sink, and walked out of the room.

"Christ Almighty!" Berlin's forehead glistened; his cheeks glowed. He threw himself onto a chair, yanked out a handkerchief, mopped viciously. "My God, Cliff, it just gets worse and worse. That girl, the assistant bookkeeper who disappeared yesterday? Some colored guy had her up in Bart Tabor's love nest, and Tabor shot him dead. If it wasn't for Max, those detectives'd be booking me in downtown right now. Max convinced them their evidence wasn't completely airtight, and if they wanted to talk to me some more, they knew where they could find me. He told them if they put me away, I wouldn't be able to finish writing this show, and if they were wrong, they'd be lucky to ever even be walking a beat again." Berlin swiped the handkerchief across his face again.

Hess struggled to make sense of what he'd just heard. He wondered whether the pressure of the upcoming show and the threats from that bumpkin, Stark, were loosening his boss' hinges. "That's awful, Mr. Berlin," he said. "But how can they hold you responsible for what goes on in your manager's playpen?"

"Wait, I'll tell you. The girl said the colored guy told her he had a deal with a 'big music publisher' to publish his tunes." Berlin held up a hand to forestall the objection he saw coming from Hess. "I know, I know. There are a lot of big music publishers in New York. But that doesn't matter. Just before five this afternoon, the colored guy called the office, told the receptionist she'd be out of a job if he didn't get through to me, so she clued in Tabor, then connected him. According to Tabor, the guy said, 'Hello, Mr. Berlin, I got a problem here, a woman came knocking on the door and said she was supposed to meet you—'"

"*You?*"

"Yeah. Me. The woman told the colored guy she was supposed to meet me there, so he pulled a gun and sat her down to wait while he called me to find out what to do. Tabor told him to sit tight, then ran on over like Wild Bill Hickok and blasted the son of a bitch to pieces."

Hess fumbled for the right words. "Mr. Berlin...that's just unbelievable. What did you say to the police?"

"What did I say? What the hell *could* I say? I told them I didn't know a thing about any of this. And then they asked me wasn't it true that I borrow Tabor's key every now and then when I want to do a little 'entertaining.'"

Hess felt his face get warm. Berlin picked right up. "God damn it, Cliff. You don't think I do that, do you?"

"Of course not, Mr. Berlin."

"Well, that's what I told them, so they asked me why would Mr. Tabor say I did. I said that was a good question and I didn't know the answer. Then they told me to watch my wise mouth, and I'd better not set one foot out of Manhattan, or they'd be offering me their hospitality, which is how they put it. Soon as they left, Max and I called Tabor's place, but he wasn't there. But him and me are gonna have a good talk. I'll catch him tomorrow at the office. And oh yeah, while I'm there, I'll also have a chat with the new bookkeeper."

Again, Hess started to wonder about Berlin's stability. The man was on the hook for a murder charge, he had a show to write, and he was going to have a chat with the new bookkeeper? "Why?"

"Because, goddamn it, she's the one who came up to the apartment and said she was supposed to meet me," Berlin shouted. "The new bookkeeper. The one Tabor hired just yesterday."

<><><>

Twilight was fading as Stark and Nell came up from the subway at 135th Street and St. Nicholas Avenue. Lottie waved from behind the railing, then trotted over and embraced Nell. "Did you have any trouble?" Nell asked. "Getting away?"

Lottie shook her head. "Truth, I didn't even see no cops *or* delivery trucks out there today, but that don't really ease my mind. Maybe they's watchin' from some place I can't see 'em. When I goes out to the grocery, I steps bold as brass, but when I comes to see you, I still think best I goes down the fire escape in back."

They walked most of a block eastward on West 131st, past kids playing a noisy game of stickball in the street. There were small gatherings on concrete stoops, women in summer dresses, fanning themselves, men mostly in undershirts and dirty work pants, many of them holding bottles of beer. People leaned out open windows to carry on conversations between buildings. The air was heavy with cigarette smoke.

"Here it be," Lottie said, pointing. "Number 215."

Stark looked down three reddish stone steps to a grocery. From somewhere to his left came the sound of lively syncopated music, a horn and a drum. "I'm sorry, we closed," came a pleasant female voice from the stoop, five steps up from the sidewalk.

Stark's eyes followed the voice. A light-skinned Negro woman, jet hair piled high on her head, skin the color of coffee with a good deal of cream, smiled down at him. Next to her sat a round man, head clean-shaved, whose bread basket stretched his T-shirt to a remarkable extent. A pencil-thin moustache decorated his pear of a face. Two mounds of flesh, filling the entire top step."

"But if you in need of something, I can open up and get it for you."

The woman spoke in the lilting cadence of the light-skinned New Orleans Creoles, each word subtly tinged with French. It fell like music on Stark's ears. The old man thought of what he had to tell her, and felt a pull in the pit of his stomach. He firmed his jaw, drew himself to full height. "That's kind of you, but we don't need groceries right now. We're looking for Clarence and Ida Barbour. Would they be you?"

The large man and woman looked at each other. Lottie stepped forward. "We don't mean you no harm," she said quietly.

As the woman half-rose to peer at the new speaker, her face relaxed into a smile. "Is that Lottie? Lottie Joplin?"

"None other. I didn't know you knew me."

Now, the man spoke. "Everybody here know Scott Joplin and his Mrs. You come in sometimes and buy groceries."

I haven't seen you for some good while now," the woman said. "Or Mr. Joplin." Her face went serious. "I hope he's…"

"He's as good as he's ever gonna be, thank you. Fact, he's been real busy lately. Workin' on a musical play for the stage, and a symphony."

"A symphony, you say," the man said. "Like for an orchestra?"

"Right."

The man hauled himself to standing, and waddled down to the steps. Stark was surprised at how short he was, a real five-by-five. The man acknowledged Nell with a perfunctory bow, then looked from Stark to Lottie, as if trying to decide which one to address. Finally, he said, "I be Clarence, that be my wife, Ida. What can we do for you?"

He can't figure out, Stark thought, what a colored woman from his neighborhood is doing, walking up to his house at eight-thirty in the evening, in the company of a white man and woman. "Mr. Barbour, Mrs. Barbour," Stark said. "My name is John Stark. I'm Mr. Joplin's publisher, and his friend. This is my daughter, Nell, also Mr. Joplin's friend. Mrs. Joplin asked us to do her a favor, and we need some help from you."

"God's truth," Lottie chirped.

Stark looked around. "I don't mean to be rude, but might we go inside to talk?"

"Well, sure," said the man. "I guess it must be pretty important."

"Yes," said Stark. "It is."

<><><>

Stark looked around the Barbours' living room, smiled at the way the furniture fit with the inhabitants. Every chair, the sofa, and a love seat were overstuffed. Given the ten-foot ceilings, the floor lamps at the front and rear of the room didn't spread much light. Grotesquely-shaped shadows fell in every direction. Ida brought out a tall glass of lemonade for each person in the room, and set a glass bowl full of pretzels on a circular table next to the sofa. Then, she smoothed her hair, and sat beside her husband. He reached for her hand, and the two, apparently having concluded that Stark was the spokesman, looked at him.

He was glad Nell had thought to bring Lottie. "Let's begin with the fact that a man was killed the other day in a music-publishing office downtown."

The Barbours exchanged a look that accelerated Stark's speech. "The circumstances made it appear that Mr. Joplin might have been responsible, but none of us believe that. We think it's possible someone tried to make it look that way, and we want to find out what really did happen."

"Mr. Stark…" Ida, her singsong tone now tight and forced. "That publisher—he wouldn't happen to be Irving Berlin, would he?"

"Yes," Stark said, gently as he could. "He would. Why do you ask?"

Clarence's face tightened into a mask. "Mr. Stark, please tell us why you be here."

Stark nodded. "Fair enough. After the murder, a young woman from the office, the intended of a man who also works there, was kidnaped. Someone called the girl's mother to tell her that if Mr. Joplin gave himself up to the police, her daughter would be released. But the plan went sour, and the kidnaper was shot dead."

Ida let out a cry. Clarence's face was stone.

Stark moved along even more quickly. "The kidnaper had a piece of paper in his pocket with your names and your address on it."

"And you're gonna tell me he was a colored boy." Ida's voice was a deathly monotone. "With a great big scar on his cheek."

"Yes," Nell said. "I'm sorry."

Stark sat silent as Ida broke into crying. Clarence put both arms around her, whispered into her ear. Then he gave his wife a handkerchief. She dabbed at her eyes, then returned it. "I beg your pardon," she said.

"Not at all." Stark spoke gently. "Was he your son?"

"If'n he was my son, Mr. Stark, he woulda had a bringing-up so he never woulda done such a thing like this." The venom in Clarence's voice was appalling.

"He was our nephew, my sister's son," Ida said. "Name was Dubie Harris. He grew up in Missoura, didn't have no daddy, and from all my sister say, he was a wild boy. That scar, he got from a fight in a craps game, he was only fourteen years old. But he was good with music, that was the one thing he would do. He played horn, and he wrote down tunes. He come to New York to stay with us while he found a way to make him a living."

Clarence sat forward. "You people ain't some kind of police, are you?"

Before Stark could answer, Lottie broke in. "No indeed. Mr. Stark and Mrs. Stanley there been the best friends Scott ever did have. They been tryin' to find out who really did kill that man in Irving Berlin's office, so the cops'll leave Scott be. Please, won't you see if you can't help them."

Stark said, "Before your nephew got killed, he made a telephone call to Irving Berlin. You mentioned Berlin a minute ago. Do you know whether he was having any dealings with your nephew?"

Ida sobbed into Clarence's handkerchief. Stark took a swallow of lemonade. Lottie and Nell waited quietly. Clarence rested a hand on his wife's shoulder, then began to speak. "Dubie got in just a couple days ago," he said. "All set to make New York his very own. Somebody he met on the train, some musician, told him Irving Berlin's was the place to have his music published, so next day, right after lunch, off he went, first up to get himself into James Reese Europe's band, then down to Irving Berlin's. He told us at supper that night, he played his tunes for some young kid who said they wasn't any good, but Dubie made a mighty fuss out in the waiting room, wouldn't leave till the receptionist went on back and got Irving Berlin out there. Dubie played his music for Mr. Berlin, and Mr. Berlin said he was gonna publish it. I told Dubie he better watch out, else his tunes was gonna end up like 'Alexander's Ragtime Band.' Didn't I tell him that, Ida?"

Ida, bit her upper lip, nodded.

"But that boy wasn't the least little bit concerned. He said nobody was gonna take advantage of Dubie Harris. These young colored, they think everything got set right in 1863, but not bein' a slave any more is only the first part to bein' free." He paused, scanned the faces of his visitors. "I mean no offense."

"None taken," said Stark.

Ida picked up the conversation. "We got worried when Dubie didn't come on home last night and all day yesterday. Clarence figured he found himself a woman. But now you're tellin' us he went and kidnaped a girl for Mr. Berlin? Why would he do that?"

"We think Berlin is trying to steal another piece of Joplin's music," said Stark. "He may have made a deal to publish Dubie's tunes if Dubie would kidnap the girl. Then Berlin could squeeze her boyfriend to turn Joplin in to the police, and he'd have Joplin's music free and clear."

Ida said, "How're we supposed to get Dubie's body now?"

"What I'd like you to do," said Stark, speaking very slowly. "Is go down to the nearest police station and report him missing. I suspect they'll get back to you soon enough. And if you wouldn't mind, please don't say anything about our visit. We've got Scott Joplin in a safe place, but we don't want the police to track him through us. Once they've got him in custody, that will be as far as their interest will go, and Berlin will get off."

Lottie stepped forward. "If you needs to get ahold of any of us, I can give you my number."

Clarence extended a hand to Stark. "I appreciate you coming here and talking to us like you did." He looked around the group. "All of you."

Ida said nothing. Stark thought she looked on pins and needles. Something more than grief... She caught him studying her, and that seemed to release her tongue. "The day Dubie come back after he been down to Mr. Berlin's," she began, her voice a hollow drone. "It was pretty late, after six. Clarence was still in the store, and I was up here, makin' supper. I heard Dubie come in, but he went straight to his room, and when he come out and say hello to me, he had on a different shirt from when he left in the morning. So after we's done eatin', when Clarence and him went to sit outside on the stoop and smoke, I went in to the laundry, and there was the shirt, all wet like it was rinched out, but I saw plain, right on the front, what was left from a bloodstain."

"And you never said one word to me." Clarence was furious.

Ida shook her head. "I figured if I hadn't gone and snooped, I never woulda known in the first place, so I decided I wasn't gonna say boo...oh, Clarence! I was *scared*. And all the time Dubie didn't come home, I kept on thinking about that blood on his shirt, and that made me even scareder. But I thought maybe these people need to know."

"I'm glad you told us," Stark said. "Do you remember what day that was?"

Ida raised a hand, counted back on her fingers. "One, two, three...three days ago. On Tuesday."

"His first whole day in New York," Clarence rumbled. "He was gonna set the town on fire."

⟨⟩⟨⟩⟨⟩

Lottie led Nell and Stark along St. Nicholas Avenue, into a drug store and up to the soda fountain, where they ordered phosphates. The soda jerk, a dark-skinned hunchback, made a snappy production out of mixing the drinks, then set them in front of his customers, smiled, tipped his white paper hat, and retreated to the far end of the counter.

Stark took a long pull at his drink. "I'd say we got more than we'd bargained for. What with the blood on the boy's shirt, it does sound as if the deal with Berlin involved murder as well as kidnaping. 'Help me get rid of Joplin, whatever it takes, and I'll publish your music.' But then you became a monkey wrench, Nell, going up to that apartment."

"I'm about to become an even bigger monkey wrench," Nell said. Birdie told me Dubie bragged to her about the scene he made in the office, and the way the receptionist got Berlin to sort it out. If Fannie could say she was sure it happened on the afternoon of the murder, wouldn't that nail everything down?"

"I'd think so," Stark said. "Perhaps you could talk to her tomorrow."

"I'll talk to her tonight," said Nell. "I'll bet the soda jerk's got a City Directory...Dad, what are you shaking your head for now?"

From the far end of the counter, the soda jerk called, "You wantin' something else?"

"Thank you, no." Nell gave him a big smile, then in much lower tones, said, "The sooner we get the information, the better. I'm going to go tonight. If you insist, you can come with me."

"I think neither of us should go tonight," said Stark. Sometimes, sooner is not better. If we go barging into the woman's home at this hour, she's going to wonder why, and she may be less forthcoming than if you casually mention over lunch tomorrow that you heard something about a ruckus in Reception a few days ago. Then it's no more than a bit of gossip."

"Your daddy be right," said Lottie. "Go runnin' off with your legs movin' faster'n your head, you likely just gonna upset the applecart. Go on home now, get some sleep."

Nell couldn't fight off a smile. "All right. I know when I'm licked."

‹›‹›‹›

When Nell walked up to the Waterson, Berlin, and Snyder office at eight forty-five next morning, the door was locked. She peered through the glass, saw no movement inside. Damn! Fannie was supposed to be in by eight-thirty to open up and have every-thing ready for business by nine. Nell cursed the woman and her flightiness, looked back down the corridor, then sighed and resigned herself to waiting.

During the fifteen minutes she stood and paced, she was joined by secretaries, salesmen, pluggers, shipping clerks, fifteen or twenty in all. Then she heard the elevator door open. Voices, coming closer—Waterson and Tabor. She couldn't make out the conversation. The two men drew up to the door through the small crowd. "Mrs. Stanley," Tabor said. "What's going on here?"

"We're waiting for someone to open the door."

"Fannie's not here?"

"Apparently not."

Tabor pulled a ring of keys from his pocket, searched for the right one, opened the door, then stood aside as the employees ran in and scattered to their posts. Nell walked in alongside Tabor and Waterson. They stood in the Reception Room, looked all around. "Fannie," the office manager boomed, but got no answer beyond an echo of the receptionist's name. He picked up a small wooden box from the desk, flipped the lid, thumbed through file cards. "Ah, here." He held up a card. "I'll call her—maybe her alarm didn't go off. I guess I'll have to put up a CLOSED sign until she gets here."

"Judas Priest!" Waterson roared. "Where can that woman be? The way things are going, we're not going to have any employees at all."

"You'll have a bookkeeper," said Nell. "I'll get to work now. Good morning." She started down the hall to her office.

◇◇◇

By nine-thirty, Nell had her annoyance under reasonable control, and was working over the pile of sales lists Tabor had left for her. She had one ear open, listening for Fannie's voice from Reception, but what came through, all of a sudden, was a man's voice, angry, and from the sound of it, right across the hall. "Tabor, we're going to settle this right now."

No mistaking the reedy, high-pitched, hard-driving tone, the classic lower east side inflections. If Berlin saw her, the game would be over. Nell jumped from her chair to run and hide in the ladies' room, but took only a couple of steps. Do that, and she wouldn't hear anything. She grabbed the previous day's receipts from her desk, carried them to the utility table next to the doorway, pretended to arrange them. If Berlin came out of Tabor's office, she'd go back to her desk and face the other way.

"God damn it, Tabor, I want to know why you told those cops I borrowed the key to your apartment, and I want a straight answer… No, I ain't going to close the door. Stop whispering like a thief at me. This is *my* company, and I don't give a good goddamn who hears what I've got to say to you. Now, I asked you a question."

"All right, Mr. Berlin. What was I supposed to tell them?" Tabor's words were harder to make out than Berlin's; he wasn't shouting. "They'd have found out anyway, and then I'd be in a real pickle."

"Found out *anyway*? Tabor, you're a four-flushing, lying son of a bitch! I've never borrowed the key to your filthy little love nest, and you know it."

"Listen, Mr. Berlin. You can't talk to me like that. I—"

"I'll talk to you the way you deserve being talked to. Now, I want a straight answer. Why did you lie to those cops about me borrowing your key?"

A pause. Nell strained to hear. Finally, Tabor's voice burst through, louder now, as angry as Berlin's. "Fine, Mr. Berlin. You want a straight answer? Here it is. I told the cops you borrowed my key because you did. I told them that you've borrowed it before because you have. I've never asked you why because it was none of my business, but it's not my job to take a fall for you...hey, Mr. Berlin, back off. You lay a hand on me, I'll wipe up the floor with you. Don't think I can't."

"Bastard!" Nell heard the sound of glass or porcelain smashing. "You're fired. You've got two hours to clean out your desk. If you're anywhere in this office by lunchtime, *I'll* call the cops to move you out. Got it?"

Another pause, then Tabor's voice. "Get out of my way...no, you just stay here. I'll be right back."

Nell heard him stamp down the hall and out of earshot. A few minutes later, she heard Waterson's voice. "Jesus Christ, what the hell's going to happen next?" Tabor said something Nell couldn't make out. Then Waterson spoke again. "All right, okay, Bart. Don't worry, I'll set him straight."

A moment later, Berlin shouted, "Henry, you stay outa this. It's between him and me."

"Irvy, goddamn it, get hold of yourself. What the hell do you mean, it's between you and him. He's the office manager and I'm the senior partner—"

"I don't care if you're God Almighty. He's not gonna tell the cops lies about me and hold onto his job—"

"What are you talking about, he told the cops lies about you?"

"That apartment where the colored guy was holding the girl? Our bookkeeper-assistant? He told the cops he lent me the key the day before."

Waterson laughed. "So what the hell's the problem? Bart didn't say you had the girl kidnaped. The night before it happened, you had yourself a nice *shtup*, all private, who the hell would care about that? Listen, why don't you just get your girl to talk to the cops, you know, off the record, and then that takes care of that. God knows how the *schvartzer* got in there. Maybe you didn't lock up when you left. That's the cops' problem."

"Henry!" A shriek. "I have never borrowed that key. I've never seen the inside of that apartment. I don't take girls to love nests. Never!"

"Oh, Irvy, come on. Why do you always have to go around pretending all you got between your legs is air? Now, listen to me. Our bookkeeper's missing—thank God we at least got that Mrs. What's-her-name to fill in. But the assistant's off for we don't know how long, maybe forever, and today, the receptionist didn't come in. So let's fire the business manager, terrific idea, 'cause he told the cops that the great Irving Berlin likes girls the same as any man. Hey, I tell you what. Let's just close up the office. Shut it down. File for bankruptcy, get it over with. Jesus Christ, Irvy, Bart is all that's holding us together right now. I've got to tell you, you ain't been yourself lately, and right now, you look like hell. Go on, go back to your place and get yourself some sleep, then sit down and write your tunes for the show. Leave the office to me for now, okay?"

"God damn it, no, it's *not* okay. I'm a partner—"

"All right, Irvy, enough. What with all you got going right now, I thought I'd show you a little consideration. But you don't want to be reasonable. Fine! Either you butt out of this, or *I'm* gonna call *my* lawyer. You can call Josephson if you want, and then you know what's gonna happen? You and me get to spend the next two weeks in courts, which, by the way, do not meet in the nighttime. You want to do that, or you want to get your show done? You ain't gonna be able to do both."

A short silence, then Berlin spoke. "Okay, Henry, you got me for now." Nell had to strain to make out the words, so thick with fury had become Berlin's speech. "But you ain't even seen the beginning of this, never mind the end."

Nell walked quickly back to her desk, picked up a pencil, leaned over the sales lists and sheltered her face with a hand. A moment later, there was a terrific slam of a door. She breathed a long sigh, then went back to work.

"I trust you're coming along all right with those lists, Mrs. Stanley."

She looked up. Tabor was smiling, but his cheeks were a jigsaw puzzle of red splotches and white patches. "Yes, sir," she said. "I haven't been at it long, but there clearly are some discrepancies. I should have a reckoning for you by lunchtime."

"Excellent. Well, I'm certainly glad you decided to come by and apply for this job. We might just make your situation permanent. With a little raise in pay, of course."

Nell remembered Fannie's warning about what sort of job performance usually led to a raise. "Thank you, sir," she said. "I'm glad you're satisfied with my work. But I lost a good half-hour this morning, standing in the hall when I could have been in my office, on the job. Perhaps you'd be willing to give me a key, so if Fannie is late again, or we have a temporary, I can let myself in and start working."

Tabor fingered his chin, then nodded. "I'd be foolish to say no to that offer, wouldn't I?" His smile widened into a grin. "You're always a step ahead of me, Mrs. Stanley. I called Fannie's place and got the super to check her room. She wasn't there, so I've called in a temp. One of the secretaries will cover Reception till she gets here."

Nell wanted to scream.

Tabor pulled the key ring from his pocket, separated one and handed it to Nell. "Just don't come in too early—they lock the outside door from midnight till seven in the morning."

Nell opened her purse and slipped the key into a change pocket. "My enthusiasm does have bounds, sir."

Tabor gave her the quick once-over. "I suppose you heard some of our discussion from across the hall."

"I did hear voices—yours, Mr. Waterson's and someone else's I didn't recognize. You were all talking quite loudly, but I have no idea about what. I was concentrating on my work."

"Hmm. You're pretty discreet, aren't you?"

"I'll take that as a compliment, sir."

Tabor laughed, then walked out.

<>‹>‹>

Nell gave the group her update over dinner. When she finished, Stark gestured with his fork. "Perhaps we should have gone to see the receptionist last night. I've got to feel concerned for her."

Joplin pushed back from the table, and without a word, walked away. Less than a minute later, piano music floated into the kitchen.

"I heard Waterson say Berlin looked terrible," said Nell. "Maybe he was up all last night doing more than writing music. With Fannie out of the way, he'd feel a lot safer taking on Tabor over the apartment key. I wish we could let the police know."

"We can't," said Joe Lamb. "One question would lead to another, and before they were finished, they'd be here, and Martin and Mr. Joplin would be off to jail. Probably the rest of us right along with them."

Stark said, "Can we find out where Berlin was last night?"

Nell tapped fingers on the table. "I don't know how. His valet's not going to tell us, and neither will that musical secretary of his. And he certainly won't. But I didn't tell you—I talked an office key out of Tabor, supposedly so I can get in to work early. Dad, why don't we go in tonight and look around? Suppose we can find Scott's music tucked away somewhere in Berlin's office?"

Stark's jaw dropped, then he started to chuckle. "My dear, your resourcefulness is a wonder."

"I need to go with you."

Everyone looked at Martin.

"You've got to let me—I know all of Mr. Berlin's files, all the places he might hide a manuscript. If I don't go, you can't be sure you searched everywhere. And it'll be night, so who's gonna spot me in an empty office building?"

"How about on the subway?" said Stark.

Lamb got up from the table, walked out of the kitchen, came back holding a flat camel's-hair cap. "Put this on and pull the brim down over your forehead."

Stark was impressed. "He looks like a different man. All right, I guess having him there might be worth the risk. But let's wait until it's fully dark."

‹›‹›‹›

No one in bustling, after-theater Times Square looked twice at the two well-dressed gentlemen and the classy lady who strode up and through the Forty-seventh Street entrance of the Strand Theatre Building. They took the stairs to the third floor, Nell opened the office door, and they went inside. The stale odor of the day's smoked cigarettes and cigars made the air in the Reception Room oppressive. Nell switched on the light; Stark frowned. "Do you think that's a good idea? Someone might see the light on, and wonder who's here?"

"Who's going to wonder?" Nell asked.

"A night watchman?"

She shrugged. "I don't know if there is one. Besides, how are we going to find anything in the dark?"

"You've got a point. Perhaps we should have brought a flash-light, but we didn't. All right, let's get started. Where's Berlin's office?"

Martin pointed to the hallway past the reception desk. "That's the business side—the partners' offices, Mr. Tabor's, some of the secretaries', mine…" The young man's voice faded on the last word, but he recovered quickly, and led the search party down the corridor.

The austerity of Berlin's office surprised Stark. Just a chair and desk, four file cabinets, and a second chair at the side of the desk. Above the desk, three photographs. "Looks like a monk's cell," he said.

"Yeah." Martin agreed. "One thing about Mr. Berlin, you can't say he tries to put on the dog."

"You haven't seen his apartment." Stark scanned the room. "Well, let's get cracking. I suppose we'd better go through the file cabinets, folder by folder."

Martin walked to the far end of the room, and opened a door. "He's got files in this closet, too."

Nell and Stark peered inside. Their shoulders sagged. "Martin, it looks as though you're earning your keep," Stark said. "Why don't you go through these. Nell, you start on the file cabinets out in the office. I'll go through the desk, then join you."

Nearly an hour into the project, with the desk and about half the files gone through, a noise from outside the room froze the three searchers. Then, the sound of a door closing, and a man's voice. "Anybody in here?"

"Damn!" Nell whispered. "Guess there *is* a night watchman. He's probably checking the floors before he locks up. Tabor told me they lock the outside door at midnight."

"Martin, get back in the closet and shut the door." Stark's whisper was like boots on pebbles. "Nell, come with me."

She followed her father to the Reception Room. An elderly colored man blinked at them as if his eyes were sending some sort of visual Morse code. He was shorter than Nell, with a droop to the right side of his mouth, and he held his left arm bent at the elbow, up against his chest. He took a few steps toward the white couple, swinging his left leg in a wide arc. "Who you be?" the watchman piped. "What you be doin' here?"

Give the man a lot of credit, Stark thought. He could be on a street corner with a cup and a handful of pencils. Still, he had to be gotten around, and the faster, the better. "I'm Henry Waterson," Stark said, and pointed at the reverse-lettering on the door. "And this is Mrs. Waterson." He paused just long enough to enjoy the savage blush on Nell's cheeks. "We were at the theater and I stopped in to pick up some materials I need for a meeting with my lawyer Monday morning. We'll be out shortly."

"The left side of the watchman's face curled into a tentative grin. "Well, Mr. Waterson, sir, I be real sorry. While I was walkin' the halls, I seed the lights on, and I figure, well, now, I better just look into that. But you take long as you need, and I won't be botherin' you no more. The door'll still open for you from the inside, but if I ain't around when you go, please make good and sure it latches tight shut behind you. Somebody come and find it open, then I loses my job."

"Thank you," Stark said. "I'll be very careful of that. And I'm glad to know our night watchman is so thorough. There's no telling who might have been in here." He pulled a small roll of bills from his pocket, plucked a fiver, and gave it to the man.

The watchman worked the bill between his thumb and index finger. "Why, thank you, sir, thank you. Ain't often somebody shows they 'preciation, except maybe around Christmas time. I'll be gettin' on, then." He tipped his cap, turned around, then limped back out to the corridor.

"Conscience bothering you a little, Mr. Waterson?" Nell's face was a study.

Stark coughed. "Maybe just a bit. But we didn't have a lot of choice, did we? Come on, let's finish this job and get out of here."

Another half-hour, they'd searched everywhere. Martin had even pulled the cabinets away from the wall, but there was only dust behind them. Stark sighed. "Is there anywhere else in this place he might be hiding that music?"

Martin narrowed his eyes. "Let's see…the opposite hall-way is Sales, Publicity, and Illustration. Across from that is Catalog Storage and Shipping, then the last hall is the Band and Orchestra Department, the pluggers, and piano rooms. I don't think—"

"No, I don't either," said Stark. Berlin wouldn't have left that music where anyone else might've had even a small chance of finding it. He's probably got it at his apartment, locked inside a nice sturdy safe. Damn and blast!"

"What are we going to do now?" The despair in Martin's voice earned the young man a soft pat on the shoulder from Nell.

Stark didn't hear him. He was staring at the three pictures on the wall above the desk. On the left was a cartoon dated October 19, 1913, a caricature of Berlin grinding a street organ as John Bull and Uncle Sam danced; the drawing was titled "The Whole World Moves to Berlin's Music." In the center photo, Berlin stood, dapper and jaunty in white slacks, dark blazer and straw skimmer, next to a young woman in a white summer dress and broad-brimmed hat. Probably his late wife. The photo on the right was of three men sitting at a table, Berlin flanked by Waterson and Ted Snyder. Stark extended his hand, drew it back, then reached again, and snatched the picture off the wall.

"Dad, what are you doing?"

"I'll tell you. Mr. Berlin wanted a face-to-face meeting with Joplin, and I'm going to give it to him. We'll show this picture to Joplin in Joe Lamb's presence, and ask him which man he gave his music to. Then I'll call Berlin, and we'll have our meeting, him and all of us who saw Joplin pick him out." He pointed at Berlin's image in the photo. "At the very least, I suspect that should get us back the music."

Nell looked dubious. "What's going to stop him from just walking out on us when he sees he's trapped?"

Stark raised an eyebrow. "A man who'll kick out his teeth if he tries."

◇◇◇

As Joe Lamb opened the door for Nell, Stark and Martin, he stared at the photograph in Stark's hand, but Stark just smiled, and asked, "All well here?"

Lamb nodded. "A couple of hours ago, Mr. Joplin started to get frustrated. He said he couldn't figure out how to write down what he was playing—"

"Joe!" Joplin shouted. "Come on back here, I've got the next phrase ready. Hurry up before I lose my hold on it."

"Be right there, Mr. Joplin." Lamb turned his back on the composer, lowered his voice. "He was shouting and banging on the piano, so I went over and told him I'd transcribe for him. That's what I've been doing the last hour or so." Lamb started back toward the piano.

Stark hurried after him, Nell and Martin a step behind. "Joplin," Stark called. "I need to talk to you."

Joplin waved him off. "No time now. Later. Joe here's writing down for me."

"It'll only take—" but that was as far as Stark got. Joplin flew into a passion. "Mr. Stark, now, please, go away. I'm writing my symphony, and I'm not going to be interrupted for any of your chit-chat. Go '*way*." The composer raised a fist.

Nell stepped forward and grasped Joplin by the wrist. Joplin stared, eyes wide. His jaw moved, but no words came out. "Scott, I'm sorry we've got to interrupt you, but this is very important." Nell's voice was warmed honey. "Just listen to my father, then Joe will help you finish up what you're working on, and after that, we can all go to bed. Dad?" She motioned Stark forward.

Stark held up the picture. "Which one of these men did you give your music to?"

Again, Joplin flared. "Mr. Stark, what is the matter with you? How many times do I have to tell you, I gave the music to Irving Berlin, put it right in his hand. Now, let me be. I don't have time to play games."

He twisted away, but Nell pulled him around to face her. "Scott, we know you gave it to Irving Berlin, but if you can pick him out from this picture, that will help us get him to give it back." She motioned with her eyes toward her father.

Stark came forward with the photograph. As Joplin reached for it, Stark hesitated, but then gave it to the composer. Joplin held the picture up to the light. His hands trembled fiercely as he leaned forward to stare at the three men in the picture. "There," he said, all contempt, and aimed a finger. "There he is, right there, Irving Berlin. All right, now? Are you satisfied?"

Not a sound in the room. Lamb, Martin, Nell and Stark looked at each other. Then, Nell said, "Scott, please take another look, a good hard one. You're sure that's Irving Berlin?"

Disgust all over his face, Joplin turned his eyes back to the picture, opened them wide, mocking close scrutiny. He jabbed his finger hard, four times. "Yes, I'm sure. This is Irving Berlin, the man I gave my music to. I've known him for years."

Nell pushed Joplin down onto the piano bench. "Scott, now please. Listen to me. That man is not Irving Ber -"

Joplin bulled to his feet, every muscle in his body contracted. "Nell, don't you go fooling with me, not you. I know Irving Berlin when I see him. His company, it was called Seminary Music back then, they published seven of my rags. I gave him 'Pineapple Rag.' 'Sugar Cane Rag.' 'Paragon Rag.' 'Wall Street Rag.' 'Country Club Rag.' 'Euphonic Rag.' 'Solace.'"

As the composer launched into his recitation, Stark felt something in his mind click into place. He'd heard Joplin make the same indictment just the morning before—why in tarnation hadn't he picked up on it? "Joplin, hold on for a minute. Seminary published those tunes before Berlin was in the firm. They all came out in oh-eight and oh-nine, isn't that right? There were only two partners then, Waterson and Snyder. It wasn't till 1911 that you left *Treemonisha* with Berlin."

Feeling Joplin's arm twist under her hand, Nell tightened her grip, but he pulled away, grabbed the picture, and stared. A scream tore from his throat. "Henry Waterson! I'm going to kill him." He thrashed away from Nell and stumbled toward the door. Lamb stepped in front of him; Stark and Martin came up on either side. "Let me go," Joplin cried. "Let me *go*." Tears coursed down Nell's cheeks as the composer threw a fit worthy of a two-year-old who'd just been told he could not have candy. "I'm going to kill that Henry Waterson, I swear I will. Telling me he was Irving Berlin so he could steal my music!"

The three men half-pushed, half-dragged Joplin to the sofa; Nell sat beside him. "Scott, listen," she crooned. "If you kill him, you'll never get your music back. Now, please, calm yourself down. We're going to get it for you, I promise."

Chapter Thirteen

Manhattan
Sunday, August 27
Very Early Morning

Stark thought Nell looked at least as wrung out as the washrag she squeezed over the sink. "Good job," he said quietly. "I don't think anyone else could have gotten that man under control."

From behind them, in the living room, they could hear Joplin's rhythmic snoring. "I had my doubts," Nell said. "How long was I there, wiping his head and talking to him?"

"Easily half an hour."

She dropped the cloth into the sink, then the two of them walked slowly back into the living room. Lamb and Martin looked up from their chairs, two faces you'd see after a tornado had come out of nowhere and ripped a town to shreds. Stark and Nell dropped into chairs. A quick glance at Joplin, sprawled under a blanket on the sofa, then Nell said, "That throws it all into a cocked hat, doesn't it?"

Stark snorted. "To say the least. Do you suppose Waterson did get wind that Martin was gathering evidence on his embezzling? If so, when the Harris boy started a commotion in Reception, Waterson might have seen it as a godsend. He'd been Irving Berlin to Joplin, so why couldn't he be Irving Berlin to Dubie Harris? 'Do a little job with a razor for me, and I'll publish your tunes.' They set a time, then Waterson lured Joplin down to be caught with the body. Two birds with one stone for Mr. Waterson—but Dubie had never seen Martin, so he killed the wrong man. Then, Martin came back from the bathroom, and we know the rest."

"I'm not sure we do," Lamb said. "Because if that's the way it happened, we'd have to suppose Waterson is also behind the kidnaping. And if he is, why would Tabor tell the police he'd loaned his apartment key to Berlin?"

"Good question," said Nell. "But there *is* something between Tabor and Waterson. When Berlin and Tabor had their squabble this morning, Tabor ran out to get Waterson, and Waterson took his side, right down the line. What's the connection?"

Martin raised a finger, started to speak, but then shook his head and lowered his hand. Lamb and Stark looked at each other. Lamb shrugged. Finally, Stark said, "Well, in any case, it's clear Joplin did not leave his work with Berlin. I suppose we...*I* need to get in touch with him. I owe him an apology."

"I wouldn't do that yet, Dad. If you say anything to Berlin before we've figured out what really happened and what we should do about it, he'll go after Waterson like a banty rooster. And if you think we've got a mess now, imagine what would happen then. Martin and Scott might have to move in here permanently."

An uneasy smile flickered around Lamb's mouth. "I don't suppose the three of you happened to look around in Waterson's office, did you?"

Stark's and Nell's sheepish faces were answer enough. Stark coughed, then got to his feet. "I'll go back down there, and do just that."

Nell stood, but her father motioned her back into her chair. "I'm sorry, Nell, I really am, but I think you need to stay here. What if Joplin wakes up the way he was before, and doesn't see you?"

She shook her head. "After one of those episodes, he sleeps for hours, then wakes up perfectly calm. Maybe a little confused, but that's all."

Stark pulled out his pocket watch, grunted. "Almost two o'clock. The outside door is going to be locked, so I'll have to talk my way past that watchman who thinks I'm Waterson. It'll be easier if I'm alone. I'll tell him I didn't realize till I got home that I didn't get all the papers I needed." Wry grin. "That five dollars I gave him looks more like a good investment every minute. Besides, my dear, you ought to get some sleep before you need to leave for work. I'll take you home, then go back downtown to the office."

"Dad, tomorrow is Sunday."

Stark looked stunned. "I'd completely lost track."

Lamb was already on his feet. "I'll get a taxi and see Nell back to her place. That will save you going back and forth, and it's no trouble for me. I can go to late mass tomorrow." Lamb offered a hand to Nell, who allowed herself to be pulled up out of her chair.

"Very well." Stark extended a hand. "Nell, if you please, I'll take that office key."

Nell picked up her pocketbook from the end table, opened it, took out the key and dropped it into her father's hand. He picked up the photo of the Waterson, Berlin, and Snyder principals, and without another word was out the door, Lamb and Nell right behind him.

◇◇◇

Stark peered through the glass door into the little lobby of the Strand office building, and there was the watchman, asleep in his chair, feet up on his desk. Stark rapped at the door. The watchman stiffened, raised his head, then shaded his eyes and peered toward the door. Stark motioned him over. The man got up, stretched, limped to the door; as he focused on Stark, a broad smile came over his face. Stark pointed at the lock, mouthed, "Open up."

The watchman pushed the metal bar, then opened the door far enough for Stark to squeeze through. "Mr. Waterson," the little man said. "Don't you b'lieve in sleepin' of nights?"

Stark laughed, and clapped him on the arm. "When I can…
Why, I don't even know your name. I'm embarrassed."

"Naw, don't be. I just be the night watchman, no reason you'd
know my name. But it be Jasper, Jasper Billings."

Stark took the man's hand and squeezed. "Well, pleased to
meet you, Mr. Billings, and I regret having to disturb *your* sleep.
Unfortunately, I've got a fair bit of work that's got to be done
by Monday morning, and I didn't take all the papers I need."
He lowered his voice, spoke confidentially. "My wife was tired,
and…well, you know how it goes."

Billings cackled. "Oh, I sure 'nough do. I been married forty-
nine years, and my wife is the best sort of woman. But when she
get tired of bein' where she don't want to be, I knows about it, clear
as the beard on your face. Well, you go right along, Mr. Waterson,
I don't want to be holdin' you away from your work."

"And I don't want to be holding you away from your sleep."
Stark and Billings enjoyed a man-to-man laugh. Then Stark
pulled a bill from his pocket and held it out to Billings. "My
apology for disturbing you."

Billings scrutinized the money. "Oh, now, Mr. Waterson.
You already give me one fiver tonight."

"And now I've given you a second one. Buy your wife a nice
little present, why don't you?"

The watchman grinned, then tucked the five-dollar bill into
his shirt pocket. "I just might buy my wife a little present at
that, Mr. Waterson. I just might. Thank you so much. You are
too kind."

Stark smiled. Not really, he thought.

◇◇◇

He let himself into the Waterson, Berlin, and Snyder offices,
walked to Berlin's room, re-hung the photograph over the composer's desk. Then he went to Waterson's office, saw the bank of
floor-to-ceiling shelves facing him, and instantly felt exhausted.
There had to be hundreds of manuscripts there, hours of work.
Unruly piles of paper covered the big oak desk, the top of the

oak file cabinet, and a good deal of the floor. Stark shook his head. Think, man! Waterson was a fool, but he wasn't stupid; he wouldn't have left Joplin's music out in the open. Check the desk and the file cabinet.

He started with the drawers on the left side of the desk. No luck. Nor on the right, until he got to the bottom drawer, where he found a sheaf of papers held together by a metal clip. At the center of the top page, in large, flowery print, was the word, *IF*; beneath, in smaller, but no less ornate letters, was written, A Musical Play In Two Acts, by Scott Joplin. Stark riffled the pages; words and musical notes flew past his eyes. He marveled at his good fortune. He could be back at Lamb's with his find inside half an hour, wake up Joplin and give him the good news.

Perhaps there was time to patch things up with the composer. Seventeen years earlier, the two of them had done a mighty deed in Sedalia: "Maple Leaf Rag" had changed the face of American music, and in the process, redirected Stark's life. At the age of fifty-eight, he'd found what he'd been looking for all the years he'd been on earth, and from that day forward, he'd campaigned ferociously for the music and the men who composed it. Talented men, but none who could rightly be bracketed with Scott Joplin. Joplin was a gift from Nature to humanity, and Stark should have taken account of that. Damn it, Nell had been right all along. He should have published both of Joplin's operas, *Guest of Honor* back in '03, and *Treemonisha*, eight years later, and then made every effort toward getting the operas performed. But instead, he'd behaved like any mundane businessman, worrying over the finances of his company to the point of driving Joplin away by insisting he could no longer pay royalties. Had Stark heeded his daughter's advice, how different Joplin's current situation might be, not to mention his own. Stark Music Company, that small specialized midwestern music publisher, might now be at the forefront of development of a whole new form of classical music, a living demonstration of what could happen when a Caucasian and a Negro join forces in good faith. Through his timidity and caution, Stark had managed to throw away the opportunity of a lifetime. Make that two lifetimes.

But he still lived, and so did Joplin. How much longer for either, no way to tell, but all the more reason to act now. He'd talk to Nell, and between them, they'd persuade Joplin to let Stark Music publish *If.* Then they'd get the composer to see the wisdom of having Tom Turpin put on the show in St. Louis. And that would be only a start. How long could it be before Lester Walton was clamoring to have it on his stage at the Lafayette? Then, those money-grubbing Shuberts would see the dollars flowing in Harlem, and put on the show in a Broadway theater. If Joplin didn't live to see it all, at least he could die like Moses on Nebo, knowing he'd been successful. Stark would need to take a loan to get the plan moving, but he owed Joplin that and more.

The old man took a step toward the door, but then set the manuscript onto Waterson's desk, and lowered himself into the chair. He couldn't wait till he got back to Brooklyn to get at least a little sense of what he'd found. He removed the clip, slipped the title page to the back of the stack, began to read.

Not halfway down the first page, he felt blood drain from his face, but pressed on. By the second page, his hand shook so badly he could barely read the words. Partway down the fifth page, he stopped, quickly rearranged the pages in order, reattached the clip, then sat still, staring, seeing nothing. Only when he noticed water dripping onto the top page did he realize he was weeping. A moment before, he'd felt young again, a vigorous man of forty, ready to run uproariously through a world of opposition, smash down walls, leave no adversary standing. Now, he felt older than eternity.

He forced himself to his feet, shuffled out to the waiting room, took a moment to pull himself together. Then he picked up the telephone, gave Nell's number to the operator, and scuffed the soles of his shoes against the floor until he heard his daughter at the other end. "Hello? Dad?"

"Yes, hello, Nell. Were you asleep?"

"Of course not. I'm waiting to hear how you made out."

"Well, I've got Joplin's music, and…before we say anything to him or anyone else, we'll have to lay a little groundwork. I'm sorry to keep you awake…but it's…"

"Dad, is something the matter? You sound awful."

Heavy sigh. "I'm afraid we've got ourselves quite a little dilemma, my dear. I'll see you at your apartment as soon as I can get there. Good-bye."

He walked down the stairs to the ground floor, waved to a smiling Jasper Billings, and walked out. He made a move toward hailing a taxi, but shook his head no, executed a sharp left turn, and marched up Broadway, toward Seventy-second Street.

⟨⟩⟨⟩⟨⟩

Nell's face was drawn; her eyelids drooped. Stark's heart skipped a beat. "Nell, I'm sorry—"

"Where *were* you, Dad? I was worried, the way you sounded on the phone."

"I walked."

It took her a moment to process that, then she laughed out loud. "You walked all the way up here from Forty-seventh Street?"

"I'm sorry I worried you, Nell. But the walk did me good."

"Oh. Well, all right, then. Now that you're here, are you going to tell me just what it is that has you so upset?"

Stark opened his mouth to tell her to not be impudent, but instead, he held up the manuscript as if it were an article of holy writ. "Let's go into the kitchen," he said. "We'll look at it together."

"But haven't you already—"

"Only the first few pages. Act One. 'What Did Happen.' Act Two is 'What Might Have Happened—If.'"

She nodded. "This isn't going to be pleasant, is it?"

"No, I'm afraid it's not."

⟨⟩⟨⟩⟨⟩

They'd read no further than Stark had on his own when Nell looked at him with such hurt in her eyes, the old man flinched.

"Oh, Dad, this is awful. 'John Stark told Scott Joplin, now you write more rags, more of those fine classic rags, and have patience with both the world and me. Perhaps we'll go with your music to France, where the color of a man's skin does not seem to matter. And in time, people will come around, first over there, then over here, because what is thought fine on the Continent is always thought fine here. People everywhere will say, why this is first-class music, twenty-four carat through and through. They'll play it at concerts, for people of refinement and taste, who will swear it is the equal of anything by Beethoven and Schubert and Brahms. And then, these people of refinement and taste will say, why does this gifted and brilliant composer of classic ragtime music not write an opera? And *that* will be the time for you to write your opera, Joplin, and I will publish it, and...' Dad, this is a tune? A musical-show tune?"

"I have to believe that was Joplin's intent."

"Where's the music?"

"In the back. He's got the dialogue and song lyrics first, then the music."

She flipped pages, then studied the first sheet of music manuscript. "But this looks...I need to play it."

Stark stopped her with a hand on her arm. "Let's read some more first."

"All right." She sat back down.

As they read, first one, then the other, groaned. "Dad, Dad...'Scott Joplin should stand on a street corner, his cap on the ground at his feet, a basket of apples in his hand, and a sign across his chest, BLIND MAN. The poor fellow can not see what a success he is. He has done precisely what he set out to do, made raucous barrelhouse ragtime over into a true art form. Can he not hear? Is he deaf, as well as blind? In the barrelhouses, they make sport of his classic ragtime. Play it fast! Add notes! Bang away, hard as you can, with the left hand! Take away the measured beauty that soothes the soul, replace it with a savage appeal to the base animal spirit. But poor Joplin can not see what a compliment this is. He turns out better and better work, ever more polished and more complex, putting those barrel-house players to greater shame with every piece he writes. But he doesn't notice, the poor seller of apples, blind and deaf on a street corner in New York.'"

"Like a parody of opera lyrics," Stark muttered. "Look, here's a duet—Scott Joplin and Joe Hayden? *Joe* Hayden? Is he that far gone? He must mean *Scott* Hayden."

"No. Remember, Joe was Scott Hayden's brother. He died young, and it was his widow, Belle, who Scott Joplin married." Nell grabbed the top few pages, began to read aloud.

"'Joe: Joplin, you was a fool. A fool, to marry Belle. How many years you saw her go stompin' out the room when my brother and you start to play? You knew she don't care for music, but you went and married her anyway.'

'Scott: I thought she would like *my* music.'

'Joe: Because your music was special? Different from every-body else's?'

'Scott: She was a good woman, Joe. A good woman was what I wanted. What I needed.'

'Joe: A good woman? Well, I guess she was what they call a good woman. Had good manners, talked fit for a white woman high in society. But such a cold heart. The way she used to talk! Did you not feel a chill when you put your arms around her?'

'Scott: I thought—'

'Joe: That you was gonna melt the ice in her heart, just the same like I thought. You thought you was better'n me, more spe-cial some way, just like your music. You found out different.'

'Scott: Now, Joe it was not anything personal.'

'Joe—What you say? You go in bed with my wife, and then you tell me it ain't nothing personal?'

'Scott: She was not your wife then, Joe. You were dead. Dead men don't have a wife.'

'Joe: (laughs). Ha-ha-ha. With that woman, neither do a live man. And when that live man find out she no more be his wife than mine, he go and be the biggest fool ever. He decide if she have a baby, then maybe things be different. What ever was you thinkin'? Didn't you have no eyes? She already *had* a baby—my son. And she care so much for him, she leave him with his grandma and grandpa to go and live with you in Miss Hawkins' boarding house. But you think *your* baby gonna be different. *Your* baby gonna be special. Fool!'

'Scott: My poor baby. If she had only lived—'

'Joe: (laughs again). That baby never *was* gonna live. Not with the wedding present I give Belle.'

'Scott: So it *was* you after all. I did wonder. The doctors told me that sickness had to come through the mother—'

'Joe: Oh, yes. That puny baby, that was Joe Hayden's present to his wife for her second wedding. Just to show no hard feelings. Nothing personal.'

'Scott: Joe, you should be ashamed. You should be damned to hell for such evil work. She was a good woman. A decent woman.'

'Joe: And ain't that the real reason why you married her? Tell me, now, ain't I right? Belle could put on airs with the best of them, act more respectable than the Queen of England. And that's what you wanted, Scott. A respectable wife. So respectable that white people would look at her with her fine talk and her elegant manners, and then they'd hear your music and say, well now, oh my goodness gracious, what respectable music this colored man do write. Why, his music be so respectable, I can't tell no way that he be a coal-black nigger.'

'Scott: Joe, I won't have you talk like that.'

'Joe: Then I be on my way, and shame on *you*, Scott Joplin. Here and I give my wife a nice wedding present to share with her new husband *and* their baby, just to show there's no hard feelings, nothing personal, and then he talk so bad to me. What's the matter, Scott? Ain't you enjoyin' my gift? Ha-ha-ha-ha-ha.'

'(As Joe laughs, Scott puts his hands over his ears and staggers off stage. Act One, curtain).'"

Nell laid the pages on the table as though they might have been made of thin, fine china. She looked at her father; he looked at her. Neither spoke. At last, Stark turned back the top page of Act Two. Nell leaned forward, started to read. "'Scott Joplin: Mr. Stark, I need to speak to you regarding a matter of the greatest importance.'"

Stark tightened his grip on the edge of the table.

"'John Stark (sitting back in his armchair, looks at Joplin over the top of his newspaper, then lowers the paper and removes his spectacles). A matter of the greatest importance, you say? Well, whatever it is, you've got my full attention. Say on.'

'Joplin (sits opposite Stark, shifts one way, then the other, in the chair): I'm very pleased with the way our business association has progressed. "Maple Leaf Rag" will be available to the public in just a few days, and your publishing company is an actuality. I foresee a fine future.'

'Stark (laughs): Mr. Joplin, I've never heard you so hesitant in your speech, so careful of each word you say. Are you trying to ask whether there's a place for you in the firm? What position might you be considering?'

'Joplin: Thank you, sir, but that is not what I'm trying to ask. I'm no businessman, as well you know. I am a composer of music, and I hope to write many fine works that you and your company will publish. (deep breath). You're about to relocate in St. Louis. I would like to do the same.'

'Stark: Well, for heaven's sake, man, is that all? Why, nothing would delight me more. I see trouble coming in Sedalia. No doubt, the reformers will close down the Main Street establishments, and that will drive music and musicians from the city. By all means, Mr. Joplin, come along with us to St. Louis. I have no doubt we'll enjoy a close and rewarding relationship—or better, a close and rewarding friendship. I can't understand why you appear so reticent.'

'Joplin: (pulls handkerchief from pocket, wipes forehead). Mr. Stark, I can't tell you how much I appreciate what you say. But that is only part of what I wish to speak with you about. Mr. Stark…'

'Stark (leans forward in chair). For the love of God, Mr. Joplin, out with it. Speak your mind. You need have no concerns.'

'Joplin (blurts): Mr. Stark, I wish to marry your daughter. Nell and I have come to regard each other with the most tender affection, and I believe I can provide for her and make her happy.'

'(The two men sit, silent. Joplin appears to be having the greatest trouble keeping himself in his chair). Finally, Stark speaks: Well, Mr. Joplin, I now appreciate your hesitancy, though I can't say I'm completely surprised. I've watched you and my daughter at the piano, and I've listened endlessly to her demands that I publish *The Ragtime Dance*. I assume you've discussed this with Nell before coming to me. What does she have to say?'

'Joplin: Of course she and I have spoken. She says she wishes it as much as I do.'

'Stark: Mr. Joplin, my daughter is a mature woman, nearly thirty years old. I would not in any way presume to object to any course of action she might set for herself. You have no obstacle in me, and you may be sure this will have no effect on our business relationship.'

'Joplin (leaning forward, urgently): But we wish for more than that. We hope for your blessing. Without that, we could not enjoy complete happiness.'

'Stark: My dear fellow. I'm afraid you'll find complete happiness a chimera, but in any event, you do have my blessing. Anything other than that, and I should be a sham, a pious hypocrite. You both know the difficulties you'll encounter.'

'Joplin: Only too well, sir. But I'd say not to marry on that account would speak poorly for both Nell and me.'

'Stark: You will find me your ally in any situation that may arise. (stands). I think I'd best have a word with Mrs. Stark. (He leaves the room).'

'(Joplin wrings his hands, takes out the handkerchief, wipes his face again. As Mrs. Stark enters the room, accompanied by her husband and Nell, he practically leaps to his feet. Mrs. Joplin's face radiates light. She takes Joplin's right hand between the two of hers). Why, Mr. Joplin, I thought you would never ask. I'm so happy for you both. And for us all.'"

Nell's voice cracked. She got up, walked to the window, and with her back to the room, leaned on the ledge. Against his will, Stark read on to the end. "'One musical success after the last. We publish *The Ragtime Dance*, then *The Guest of Honor*, then *Treemonisha*, all to great acclamation, both for the composer and his pianist-wife, who played every piano part' '…triumphant European tour with his darling Nell and the two beautiful chocolate-colored children, both gifted musicians' '…dying in the fullness of his years, never knowing a moment of sadness or frustration.'"

Stark turned over the last page. Slowly, he released his grip on the edge of the table; bursts of exquisite pain shot up his arm. He got to his feet, walked slowly toward his daughter.

She turned a calcimined face to him. "How did he ever…"

Stark's cheeks warmed as he found himself wondering whether the composer had worked altogether from imagination. He groped for the right words, as tongue-tied in reality as Joplin had been in fantasy. "Can you begin to imagine how painful the man's life has been?" he muttered.

Nell wiped at her eyes with her sleeve. "I don't need to imagine it. I've seen it at first hand for seventeen years now."

Stark's hands stuttered forward. He clutched Nell's shoulders, embraced her, but could not speak. At last, Nell pulled back, wiped her eyes again. "Dad, what would you have said if Scott really *had* asked your permission to marry me?"

Stark shook his head, a boxer trying to get to his feet at the count of nine. "Precisely what he wrote, including the part about hypocrisy. It's difficult to believe. Did he ever—"

"Speak to me about it? No. If he had, and was afraid to talk to you, *I* would have."

"I have no doubt of that. What surprises me is that *you* never spoke to *him*."

Nell's self-control melted. She lowered herself into a chair, covered her face, and wept without restraint. Stark rested a hand on her shoulder. "I'm sorry, Nell. I shouldn't have said that."

She looked up. "Can you imagine how many times I've said exactly that to myself?" she wailed. "I have a good marriage, no complaints. But I'll never know what a marriage like yours and Mother's felt like." Nell pulled her handkerchief from below her shirtwaist, did a quick cleanup of her face, then picked up the manuscript. "I've got to hear some of the music. I can't imagine what it'll sound like."

"Unfortunately, I can," said Stark.

Nell sighed. "I suppose unfortunately, so can I."

‹›‹›‹›

After only a few minutes, Stark said to Nell, "That's enough, my dear. I don't think I want to hear any more. It's gibberish. Musical nonsense."

"Not altogether. Some of it is quite lovely." She flipped a couple of pages, played a short passage. Stark nodded. "Yes, but there's no—"

"Connection between the short pieces. It's as if he couldn't remember what he'd just written, or thought he'd written something else."

"Which would be in line with the way he remembered Waterson as Berlin. His memory must be scrambled."

"How in the world are we going to tell him he's too far gone to write any more music?" Nell tapped a fingernail against a piano key, click, click. Then she turned abruptly, and marched toward the kitchen. Stark hurried after her. "Nell?"

She snatched a glass from the shelf above the sink, filled it, took a long swallow, and plopped into a chair. Stark sat beside her.

Nell pursed, then relaxed, her lips. "Dad, there's something… while I was waiting for you, I kept thinking about Henry Waterson." She ticked off points on her fingers. "Scott identified him as the man he thought was Berlin. You found Scott's play in his desk. He's not a musician, so he wouldn't have known how bad the music is. I'll bet he was going to wait for Scott to die, then publish under a pseudonym, but when Tabor cut off his gambling money, his patience also ran out, and he decided to hurry the process along. But the killer got the wrong man, Martin got Scott away—"

"So Waterson borrowed the key to Tabor's apartment, supposedly for a few days of hanky-panky," said Stark. "And if the kidnaping had worked, Martin and Scott would have turned themselves in, Waterson would have given Tabor back his key, and that would have been that."

"But I sent it all topsy-turvy by finding Birdie—and here's the connection. When Tabor came flying into the apartment and shot Dubie, he must have realized what Waterson was up to, and seen both a problem and an opportunity. If Waterson went to jail for kidnaping and murder, Tabor's evidence would be useless. On the other hand, if he played his cards right, he could have the junior partner up on a murder charge, and the senior partner in his hip pocket. So he decided on the spot to tell the police he'd loaned the key to Berlin. Then he made a deal with Waterson, and that's why Waterson took Tabor's side the next morning in the office. They'd probably set the whole thing up the night before."

Stark nodded. "That's brilliant, Nell. Waterson's full of bluster, but I don't know how much nerve he has. I'll pay the man a visit in the morning, and—"

"Waterson's barely in the office weekdays. I don't think you'll find him there on a Sunday."

"Blast! I keep forgetting."

Like a steamroller that can't understand it has to stop when the engine is turned off, Nell thought. She pointed toward the window. "Look, it's light already. I'm exhausted, and I can't imagine you're not. Let's get some sleep. We have all day tomorrow to decide what to do, and make sure we've got it just right." Weary smile. "Might as well take advantage of the Lord's Day."

Chapter Fourteen

Manhattan
Monday, August 28
Morning

Morning came early at the Stanley apartment, Stark's screams piercing the dawn's marginal light a little after six. Nell was into her father's room before she herself was fully awake. "Dad, wake up, wake *up.*" She took him by the shoulders, but he thrashed in her grip, screamed louder, then at last, blinked his eyes open. "Nell…?"

She thought he looked puzzled at seeing her. "You were having that dream again. Dad, what *is* that dream about?"

Stark looked away. "We're not going to waste time discussing a bit of moonshine in the brain." He made a point of peering at the alarm clock on his bedside table. "It's a quarter to six. We need to be up in less than an hour. We'd both be wise to spend that time in sleep, not talking about a silly dream."

"It's so silly, it's been waking both of us for almost half a century."

Stark lowered his head and stretched his legs full length. "Go back to bed, Nell. I'll see you at six-thirty." He closed his eyes. A moment later, the door to his bedroom slammed with such force as to shower plaster from the ceiling onto his head. For the next forty-five minutes, he lay there, examining and re-examining every angle of the plan they'd put together the day before.

◇◇◇

At a quarter to eight, Nell and Stark walked into Reception. Nell locked the door, then led her father down the hall to Waterson's office. The old man quickly opened and closed each drawer in the desk; that done, he followed Nell into Tabor's office, and made straight for the manager's desk. He pulled the center drawer open, rummaged toward the back, came out with a small revolver with a patterned black plastic handle, and held it up to the light. "Hopkins-Allen thirty-two." He pointed at the encircled H&A trademark at the upper edge of the handgrip. "Is this the gun he killed the Harris boy with?"

Nell shook her head. "I never got a good look at it. But Detective Ciccone took it away from him."

"So either he got it back or he got another gun." Stark snapped the weapon open, shook out four lead slugs, slipped them into his jacket pocket. Then he pulled the drawer all the way out, picked up a small cardboard box, emptied it into his pocket. Finally, he replaced the little revolver into the drawer. "It won't be much help to him now. Let's go back out to Reception and wait for our friend."

<>‹›‹›

At precisely eight, Irving Berlin unlocked the door and hurried into Reception. For a moment, he stood in the middle of the room, then growled at Stark, "Where's Joplin?"

Stark raised an eyebrow. "Joplin is not here."

"What do you mean, he's not here? You called me last night and said—"

"That I was going to give you your meeting, but I did not say it would be with Joplin. You assumed that. We're going to meet with Waterson and Tabor. I'm no longer certain you stole Joplin's music or had the girl kidnaped, but I'll need your help to prove that, and to trap the guilty party."

Berlin stared at Nell. He cocked his head, aimed a finger in her direction. "Hey, wait a minute, I've seen you before. You're that reporter, came to my place—"

Nell smiled. "I've also been your bookkeeper for the last few days." She nodded in Stark's direction. "This is my father. And Scott Joplin is my friend."

Berlin's laugh rang flat. "You got a lot of talents, don't you, Miss Stark?"

Stark cleared his throat. "Let me explain the situation."

"First, maybe you ought to explain how you managed to get yourselves into this office. And why you don't just go to the cops, if you think you know what's what."

"The first," said Stark, "is a trade secret, and will so remain. Be assured I did nothing you would be displeased to know. As to talking to the police, I need to be certain of Joplin's and young Niederhoffer's safety until the matter is resolved."

Berlin narrowed his eyes. "So, I'm just supposed to trust you now. How do I know you aren't setting me up?"

"You don't. You can either trust me, or put your faith in Mr. Waterson and Mr. Tabor, and then wait for your dental appointment this evening." He pulled out his watch. "It's nearly a quarter after eight, Mr. Berlin. Your receptionist will be here at eight-thirty. If Waterson or Tabor walks in before we're ready, our plan will be out the window. You need to make a choice."

Berlin glanced at Nell, who smiled with tight lips. "All right," the composer muttered. "But why didn't you come and talk to me last night?"

"Because I was concerned you might go off on your own, half-cocked." Stark stood. "Let's go back to your office and prepare ourselves."

‹›‹›‹›

When Henry Waterson strolled through the door a few minutes before nine o'clock, he smiled at Nell, sitting at the Reception Desk, a pile of ledger pages in front of her. "Doing double-duty, Mrs. Stanley? Fannie's still out?"

"I'm afraid so, sir."

"Where's the temporary?"

"Off running an errand for Mr. Berlin. He asked me to watch the front while she was gone.

The man's demeanor changed on a dime. "Judas Priest! As short-handed as we are, Berlin sends her off on some errand? And what in the name of anything holy is he doing here at this hour?"

"I'm sorry, Mr. Waterson, I don't know. He's back in his office, but he said he doesn't want to be disturbed."

"Oh, he doesn't!" Waterson scowled, then, without another word, stomped off toward his office. Nell went back to her ledgers.

By five past the hour, the cacophony of several pianos being played at once filled the office. Nell realized she'd been check-ing her watch a couple of times a minute. But then, the door swung open and Tabor strode in. He asked the same questions Waterson had, and got the same answers.

Nell watched him disappear around the corner, then jogged across the room and taped a handwritten sign to the door: TEMPORARILY CLOSED DUE TO EMERGENCY. WILL RE-OPEN AT 11AM. Then, she hurried down the business corridor, past Tabor's office, past Waterson's, and knocked lightly at Berlin's door. It opened immediately. She answered the questions on her father's face and Berlin's with a nod, then walked back to Waterson's office.

The senior partner looked up, a cigar in his left hand, a clip-per in his right. "I'm sorry to bother you, sir," Nell said. "But Mr. Berlin wants to talk to you and Mr. Tabor, in Mr. Tabor's office. He says it's extremely important."

Waterson snapped off the cigar tip with a vicious thrust of his thumb, rammed the cigar into his mouth, then spoke around it. "He expects me to jump when he calls, does he?"

"I don't know, sir. He asked me to give you the message, and now I've done that." She turned to leave.

Waterson dropped the unlit cigar onto his desk, muttered something Nell couldn't hear, and worked himself to his feet. She stood aside to let him pass, then followed him down the hall toward Tabor's office. But before he got there, the door to

Berlin's office opened, and the composer and Stark strode into the hall. Waterson gawked, then blurted, "Irvy, what the hell is going on here?" He pointed at Stark. "What's *he* doing here?"

"I invited him," Berlin snapped. "Go on, go inside." The little man practically shoved Waterson into Tabor's office. Nell, then Stark, followed.

Tabor looked up at the parade. His eyes moved from Berlin to Waterson to Nell to Stark. At the sight of her father's face, Nell clutched at his arm. "Dad, what's the matter?"

The old man was ghastly white, eyes bulging, lips drawn and twisted, as if he were in terrible pain. She'd seen that same face just a few hours before, when she'd awakened him from his nightmare. Was he having a heart attack? She eased him into a chair at the side of the desk, then sat beside him, all the while silently rebuking herself. The man was seventy-five, and for the better part of a week, she'd let him go running around the city like a colt, getting his dander up at Berlin or Waterson.

Berlin broke into Nell's brown study. "Henry, Bart, we need to talk a little."

Tabor leaned back in his chair. Waterson spluttered, pointed toward Stark. "I've got nothing to say to him. And what is *she* doing in here?"

"You'll find out," said Berlin. "Sit down. You can talk to us, or you can talk to the police. You'll do a lot better dealing with us."

Nell saw lines deepen around Waterson's eyes and at the corners of his mouth. "Irvy, you're the last guy I'd think would be calling the cops right now. What are you going to do—confess about how you got Bart to lend you the key to his apartment, then made a deal with the *schwartzer* to publish his music if he'd kidnap the girl and—"

"Henry, just shut up and let them talk." Tabor could have been reprimanding a child whose babbling had become irritating.

Waterson slowly lowered himself into a chair. Berlin sat next to him.

Stark cleared his throat. "Mr. Waterson, we found Scott Joplin's musical play in your desk." Not his usual booming tone, but the thin, reedy voice of an old man. "Furthermore, Joplin picked you out of a group photograph as the man who represented himself as Irving Berlin, and took his music. You went on to misrepresent yourself as Berlin to Dubie Harris, and told him you'd publish his tunes if he'd kill Martin Niederhoffer for you. You wanted to frame Joplin for that murder, by phoning him and telling him to come down to the office at just the right time. Then you could have done whatever you liked with his music, no need to wait for him to die before you could publish it. But the murder went wrong, so you—not Mr. Berlin—borrowed the key to Mr. Tabor's apartment—"

Waterson bellowed like a bull being turned into a steer. "I don't have to listen to this. I'm calling my lawyer."

"You're going to need him," said Stark. "And not just about the murder and kidnaping. There's also the little matter of the money you've been skimming to play the horses."

Nell thought Waterson looked like a balloon just punctured by a pin. The big man turned a glower on her. "I suppose I have you to thank for that, Mrs. Stanley."

"You can thank your friend, Mr. Tabor," Nell said. "And Martin Niederhoffer, who put the figures together for him."

"That by itself must have been bad enough for you," Stark said. "But then, Mr. Tabor happened to stumble onto your little kidnaping game, and realized you needed his apartment for something more than a few nights of philandering. I imagine that drove up the price of his silence considerably."

Waterson's cheeks went the color of beets; every muscle in his body tensed. Stark shifted ever so slightly in his chair, ready to block the big man if he made a move toward the door. But instead, he turned to Tabor and bawled. "Damn it, Bart, you told me—"

Tabor pulled himself halfway to standing, leaned forward over his desk, aimed a finger at Waterson. "Henry, shut your stupid mouth. They're talking pie-in-the-sky, trying to get Berlin out of a mess, and the only way he can get off the hook and put you on is if you help him." Tabor leaned across the desk to address

Berlin. "I loaned *you* the key. I didn't ask why. It was none of my business. When that colored boy called in and asked for you, it was just lucky Fannie got scared enough to put me on."

"You gave *me* the key, huh?" Berlin's face was a mask of fury. "When was that?"

Tabor shrugged lightly. "Couple of days before the phone call. You said you had a pretty heavy thing coming up, more than you could handle in just one night."

Stark reached an arm to keep Berlin from leaping across the desk to slug Tabor, who looked as if he'd welcome the attack. "Mr. Berlin was at home at the time of the murder. After he finished his meeting with Mr. Josephson and Mr. Waterson, he stopped here at the office for about an hour, then went back to his apartment. His valet will swear he was there by three. He spent the afternoon with Mr. Hess, working on tunes for his show, then the two of them went out to dinner and the theater, and were back to work by midnight."

Tabor made a go-away motion. "So? Maybe he made his deal with the colored boy the day before, maybe three days before, who knows? And who the hell cares what Hess said? That toad-eater would swear to any lie Berlin wants him to." He reached for the telephone on his desk. "I've had enough of this. Let's see what you have to say to the cops."

"That would be foolish of you."

Stark's tone and the look on his face arrested Tabor's hand, but the man recovered quickly, and grabbed the receiver.

"We've talked to Dubie Harris' aunt and uncle," Stark said. "And we know the boy came to this office in the afternoon on the day of the murder, and not before. He'd only gotten into New York the previous evening."

Tabor looked uncertain. He glanced into the telephone, said, "Never mind, operator," and hung up. Then he aimed a fierce scowl at Stark. "Old man, you are beginning to irritate me."

"I've only just begun. Mr. Snyder has been on vacation, and Mr. Berlin's time is accounted for. You and Mr. Waterson are the only two people who could have been called in to talk to young

Harris when he refused to leave until Irving Berlin himself had heard his music. Isn't that right, Mr. Waterson?"

Waterson harrumphed. "I have no idea. How many times do I have to tell you, I wasn't in the office that afternoon. I was at the racetrack."

"So you've said. But perhaps you lost enough money in the early races, decided it wasn't your day, and came back to the office. And then, when Dubie made a fuss in Reception, you saw your opportunity."

Waterson jabbed a shaking finger toward Stark, began to blubber. "But…but—"

"But Niederhoffer messed up your plan by going to the bathroom at the wrong time, and since Dubie Harris didn't know Niederhoffer by sight, he killed the wrong man. Then, Niederhoffer came back from the bathroom, found Joplin crouched over the body, and the two of them ran off. So you got Dubie to do you another little favor. You'd frame Niederhoffer along with Joplin, and throw in Berlin for good measure. And in a few days, you'd be free of Berlin, free to publish Joplin's music, and free of Tabor's hold on you. Who could he show his numbers to then?"

While Stark talked, Waterson's face darkened; his thick lips were near-purple. Now, he flew from his chair like a man shot from a cannon. "No!" he shouted. "I had nothing to do with any of that. I was late getting out to the track because of my meeting with Irvy and Josephson, but I was there by two-thirty, and I stayed there till the end of the races. Then I stopped for a couple of drinks on my way home. I didn't get in till after nine."

"Well, perhaps the bartender will remember you, and the exact times you came in and left," Stark said. "If not, I'd say you've got a real problem on your hands."

Waterson turned to face Tabor, who was smiling coolly at him from behind the desk. "Relax, Henry," Tabor said. "I loaned my key to Berlin. The cops aren't going to believe that pathetic alibi of his."

"I think they might," said Stark. Sly glance at Waterson. "Especially when the receptionist tells the police who it was she called in to deal with Dubie Harris."

Tabor snickered. "Fannie's been missing since last Saturday." Stark nodded to Nell.

"Fannie and I went out to lunch Friday," Nell said. "She had a good time telling me stories about what goes on in this office, including how unpleasant some of the clients can be. Like the young colored man a few days before who wouldn't leave or even stop shouting until he'd shown his tunes to Irving Berlin." She turned a nasty smile on Waterson. "And since Mr. Berlin wasn't in right then, Fannie had to get someone else to quiet—"

Waterson pumped both fists toward Tabor. "Damn it Bart—it was *you*." Waterson looked back to Stark. "He said with Irvy out of the way, he'd tear up his evidence if I'd persuade Snyder to make him a partner. Then he and I could outvote Snyder on any issue that came up, and—"

Tabor leaned across the desk. "Henry, you pathetic sob sister. You make me sick."

"*I* make *you* sick? Double-damn you, Bart! You were going to let Berlin take the fall, and use me to push Snyder out. And then you'd get rid of me too, right? And publish Joplin's play yourself." The big man clutched Stark's arm. "When Joplin came in with the music and thought I was Berlin, he got himself worked up, and started yelling at me. Then he stumbled around and banged his head on the edge of the office door. Bart heard the noise and came in to see what was going on, so afterward, I told him the whole story and showed him the manuscript." Waterson charged around the desk, waved a fist in Tabor's face. "You miserable son of a Dutchman. You told me why didn't I just hide the music away until Joplin was dead, then I'd have no problems. But you were playing me for a fool right from the beginning."

Tabor regarded the furious man from the corners of his eyes, then in a flash, he had his desk drawer open and a pistol in his hand. He took aim at Waterson's chest. "Stupid kraut—I played you for the fool you are. Turn around." He pushed the barrel into Waterson's ample belly.

Waterson turned slowly. Tabor urged him with the gun. "Move." Waterson walked around the corner of the desk, into open space.

Tabor looked at Nell, Stark and Berlin. "Back away," he snarled. "Up out of those chairs and against the wall, quick."

The three targets looked at each other, then started to laugh.

"You're going to be laughing out of the other side of your faces," Tabor growled.

"I don't think so," said Stark. "Your gun's as much a bluff as your words."

Tabor shoved the weapon into Waterson's back, pulled the trigger. Loud click. He tried again, same result. Stark, Nell and Berlin jumped to their feet, but the office manager shoved Waterson into Stark, who fell back against Nell and Berlin; all four went down like bowling pins. Stark grabbed at Tabor as he rushed by, but the move was awkward, and it was no problem for Tabor to whip his gun roughly against the old man's shoulder, slamming him back to the floor. Then, Tabor burst through the clearing and out of the room.

Waterson lay, clutching his elbow. Berlin and Stark both reached to help Nell to her feet. "I can get up by myself," she shouted. "Go catch Tabor."

They ran through the open doorway, out of Tabor's office, into the hall, to the top of the stairwell, just in time to look down and see Tabor charge through the lobby and out of the building. Stark started down the stairs, but Berlin caught his sleeve. "Forget it," the composer snarled. "By the time we get down there, he'll be blocks away, and no idea in what direction."

Stark blew out two lungs full of disgust, then stepped up to the landing, and walked back with Berlin into the office.

<><><>

Tabor's escape kept the mood that evening at Joe Lamb's to one of relief, rather than exhilaration. Nell tried to put on a better face. "We've done what we set out to do," she said. "Scott's got his music back, he and Martin are in the clear, and Birdie is back safely." She aimed a look of wry amusement at the young couple on the sofa, practically sitting in each other's lap. "And I suspect Detective Ciccone is going to pull out all the stops to bring Tabor in. He's sore as a boil, the way Tabor lied to him."

"Was he angry at you…at us?" Lamb asked.

"Perhaps a little," said Stark. "He said we should have called him in as soon as we knew what was going on, but I told him we were not going to take any chance we might lead him to Joplin and Martin. He doesn't even know about you, Joe. All I said was that Joplin and Martin had been hiding in Brooklyn, and at this point, why would he look into that? Once he finds Tabor, he can take all the credit. None of us, I'm sure, will be inclined to comment or enlarge upon whatever he wants to tell his superiors or the newspapers."

Lamb nodded, then turned to Nell. "That was clever, getting Waterson to think the receptionist had implicated him."

"Dad and I felt sure Waterson and Tabor were in it together, but we didn't know just how. We wanted to drive a wedge between them, and from what I'd seen and heard in the office, I thought Waterson would be more likely than Tabor to come apart at the seams, so we concentrated on him. We didn't feel obliged to be entirely truthful."

Stark laughed. "Berlin was quite impressed. You should have seen his face."

"It was nice of Mr. Berlin," Martin said. "Coming over here with you after he was up all night and all day, to tell Birdie and me we've still got jobs, and on top of that, give us a raise. Now, we can put money away every week, and it won't be long till we have enough to get married."

"Congratulations to you both." Stark's tone was dry, but his eyes gleamed with mischief. "Though I do hope you'll remember what else Mr. Berlin told you."

Birdie giggled. Martin snickered. "'Just keep the books straight, kid. Leave the music decisions to me.'"

Everyone laughed at the young man's imitation of Berlin's voice.

Stark stifled a yawn; Nell caught the virus. "It's been a long week with not much sleep," Stark said. He reached into his pocket, pulled out a small roll of bills. "Martin, perhaps you and your intended might be willing to go up to Harlem, take Mr. Joplin home, and stop at the Alamo to tell Jimmy how this business has sorted out." He put the money into Martin's hand. "And while you're there, settle up with our friend, the tooth-kicker."

"Vinny," Martin said. "Footsie Vinny."

"Yes, of course. I have no personal experience, but from all I hear, it's best not to leave open accounts with professionals in this field."

Martin laughed. "You were pretty sharp, Mr. Stark. Getting Mr. Berlin to throw in the money for Vinny."

Stark smiled into his beard. "It wasn't all that difficult. I'm sure he saw the humor in the situation."

Martin stood, extended a hand to Birdie, but before the girl was off the sofa, Nell said, "I think I'd better have a few words with Scott before you take him."

A fit of coughing worked its way through the small group. "Yes," Stark said. "I suppose somebody should."

"Not 'somebody'." The edge on Nell's words silenced the room. She walked across the room, toward the piano.

◇◇◇

Joplin played a short passage on the piano, then reached his pencil to the music rack and began to write, but as he felt a hand on his shoulder, the music flew out of his head. *Damn!* He wheeled around, a string of angry words in his mouth, but when he saw who had interrupted him, the vexation melted. "Nell…why, what's the matter?"

Oh, Lord, could she carry it off? She felt a pair of piercing blue eyes on her back, and in her mind, heard, 'I've made my share of mistakes and then some, but in the end I do believe

I've always been equal to all requirements.' She swallowed hard. "Scott I need…I *want* to talk to you."

"Well, of course. What is it?"

She pointed toward the bedroom. "It's private. Let's go in there."

As she followed him into the room, she turned to close the door behind her, and caught a glimpse of her father's face, a sight she knew she wouldn't forget for the rest of her life. Tears spurted from her eyes. No, not now. She wiped at them with her sleeve.

Joplin looked curiously at her. "Nell, whatever is troubling you?"

At least he was in something resembling his right mind. "I'm all right," she said. "I just haven't gotten much sleep for a while."

"But everything's fine now. You found the man who was responsible for killing that boy, and you found my music. Now, I can try to get it published somewhere else. I'll have to shake a leg, though. I don't have much time."

Words stuck in Nell's throat. Fresh tears rolled down her cheeks.

Joplin gave himself a silent reprimand. Women get upset so easy, a man's got to watch what he says and how he says it. "Nell, I'm sorry, I truly am. But I know I don't have long. Every day, it seems like there's a little less in my head. I don't know where it's all going off to."

Her cue. Take it, or she might never be able to say what needed to be said. She rested a hand on his chest. "Scott, that's what I'm trying to tell you, and I'm not doing a good job of it. You know I'd never lie to you, or do anything that was not in your best interest. Please believe me—you're more ill than you realize. I can hear it in your music."

A red curtain fell across Joplin's line of vision. He thought the top of his head might blow off. But he had to hear Nell out. If it was anybody else, said that… "What do you mean?" The tremor in his voice disgusted him.

But it encouraged Nell to go on. Maybe she could get past his lunatic grandiosity and sense of persecution. She spoke slowly, calmly. "I've read the whole score of *If,* and it just doesn't hold together." She raised a hand to stop the objection she saw coming. "You know the way you've been forgetting things? I think that's the problem with your music. When you finish a passage and go on, the next line sounds as if you've already forgotten the first one. All those short passages are beautiful, but they don't add up to anything. Do you understand?"

Joplin's face twisted into a grotesque mask. "Understand? Under*stand?* How can you *dare* talk that way about my music? Lying bitch!"

The words slashed through Nell's skull, echoed in her mind. She forced herself to hold Joplin's gaze. After what felt like an hour, the composer began to speak, but in such soft tones, Nell had to strain to hear. "Nell, Nell, I am so sorry, talking to you like that. I hope you can find it in your heart to forgive me."

She put her arms around him, held him close, whispered, "There's nothing to forgive, Scott. That was your disease talking. Not you."

Joplin pulled back, just a bit. "I know you'd never tell me anything that wasn't truth. But could my music be fixed? Could *you* fix it for me."

The hope in his eyes girdled Nell's chest, squeezed the air from her lungs. Why not say, 'I'll try?' Two little words. For as long as necessary, say yes, she was working on it, doing her best to fix it. But the idea nauseated her.

She shook her head. "If I thought there was the tiniest chance, Scott, I'd spend the rest of my life working on it, and every minute would be a joy. But your music is like a long line of the sweetest words picked out of a dictionary and then strung together. It's got no meaning, and there's no way I or anyone else could arrange those words to say what you want them to."

He closed his eyes, bowed his head; his shoulders slumped. His body swayed forward, then back. Nell thought he looked like a dead man standing. If she couldn't bring herself to send him home to die in false hope, neither could she let him go utterly stripped of comfort and dignity. She took him by the arms, shook him gently. "I've told you about the music, but we haven't said anything about the lyrics."

His eyes opened. She felt firmness return to his muscles.

"Scott, those lyrics could never be spoken in front of an audience, not in this world. But it doesn't matter. They're the most beautiful Valentine I've ever received. I'll always treasure them." She kissed his cheek.

He flung his arms around her and held on as if for life support. "Nell, what would you have said…if…"

She pulled back far enough to look him directly in the eyes. "What do you think I'd have said."

"I don't know. If I did—"

"I'd have said yes. If you'd asked, I'd have married you in an instant."

"Even with all the troubles we'd have had?"

"Would they have been worse than the ones we *have* had? The ones we're still having?"

Joplin hesitated, then said, "Did anyone else see those lyrics?"

"Only my father. He's the one who found the manuscript in Waterson's desk. But no one else has seen them, or will."

"What did he say? Please tell me."

Nell's eyes shone. "He'd have said to you exactly what you wrote. If you think he wouldn't have, you never did get to really know him."

"But that would have ruined him—letting his daughter marry a colored man. I never thought…oh, Nell." Joplin's face was a landscape of desolation. "I don't know how I could have been so stupid. So afraid."

Nell swallowed. "My father told me he was surprised that *I* had never proposed to *you*. And don't think I didn't consider it. But I wasn't brave enough to take the chance I might offend you, or frighten you off and maybe never see you again. You were afraid of a no from my father, I was afraid of a no from you, so here we are. But I'll be with you now for as long as we've got."

"I only pray you won't get angry, and go away," Joplin murmured. "The way I get sometimes."

She embraced him again, rocked him like a baby. "I'll only get angry at your disease, Scott. Never at you."

"Thank you, Nell. That makes me happy, and I haven't felt happy for a long while now."

Nell patted his arm. "I guess we ought to go out. We don't want to give them any funny ideas, do we?"

"We would not want to do that." Joplin extended an elbow. Nell slid her hand inside, and walked with him to the door, then into the living room.

A cluster of questioning eyes greeted them. Stark looked from Joplin's reddened eyes to Nell's, then fixed on his daughter's hand nestled in the crook of the composer's elbow. "I see everything is settled," he said.

"Not quite." Joplin released Nell's hand, and walked over to Stark who stood to face him. "I want to thank you for what you've done for my music," Joplin said. "Without what you did, I'd still be in Sedalia, teaching piano and playing at dances."

Considering what's happened over the past seventeen years, that might not be so bad, Stark thought. But he said, "I wish I had done more. And I'm sorry for some of the things I've said and written about you in recent years. I was angry, and it was wrong of me to let that anger determine my words and actions." He extended a hand; Joplin gripped it.

Stark felt the tremors in the composer's fingers. "Well, it's been a long day." The old man's voice was husky. "Joe, I think we're finally out of your hair. Martin, why don't you and Birdie take Mr. Joplin home and settle that business at the Alamo."

"Yes," Joplin said. "I'm very tired. I think it's time for me to go home."

◇◇◇

Stark and Nell walked slowly westward along West Seventy-second. The evening air was warm, but its only perfume was an unsavory bouquet of horse droppings and exhaust from internal-combustion engines. Summer evenings in St. Louis, you could smell the flowers on vines draped over stone walls in the residential areas; in Maplewood, the air was often so heavy with scent, a man could get drunk by taking a few deep breaths. The old man shook his head. "Nell, I think this will be my last trip to New York."

She looked at him curiously. "Dad—you're not sick?"

"No, my dear, don't worry yourself on that score. But I'm seventy-five, and...oh, damn and blast, Nell. It's painful to say, but Berlin and Waterson were right about me. I just don't belong here. I couldn't compete with Tin Pan Alley, not with the music I was trying to sell. You don't see Mr. Tiffany walking around town behind a pushcart, but unfortunately, there's not the call for fine music that there is for fine jewelry. If only I'd stayed in St. Louis, I could have published so many fine rags from those young composers who went to Kansas City instead."

"Another if. You tried New York, and it didn't work out. There's no shame in that."

"'It didn't work out?' No, my dear, that won't do. Put plainly and simply, I failed. And the shame is, if I'd stayed in St. Louis and courted those youngsters, I might have been able to afford to publish Joplin's operas and ballets. His life would have been very different. He doesn't belong out here, either."

"No," said Nell. "He doesn't. But that's not the point. Before Scott ever came to New York, there was a moment that could have made his life very different, but both he and I lacked nerve, and we missed our opportunity. Your failure, if you insist it really was failure, is small potatoes next to Scott's and mine."

Stark groped for words to lighten his daughter's burden, but before he could frame a reply, Nell let out a little shriek. Stark looked around, and in the gathering darkness, saw Bartlett Tabor move quickly to Nell's side. "Just keep walking." Tabor's voice was level, more frightening than if he'd shouted an order. "We're three good friends, taking an evening stroll. I've got bullets in the gun now, and if either one of you makes a wrong move or says a wrong thing, you're both dead. Nice of you to leave your address in the employee file, Mrs. Stanley. I thought you were smarter than that."

"You'd have checked it in the city directory anyway."

Tabor laughed. "You're right. I did." He pressed the barrel of the gun against Nell's shoulder. "Keep walking."

They walked on in silence. Stark thought Tabor was going to herd them up to Nell's apartment and shoot them there, but two buildings before they got to Nell's, the manager growled, "All right, quick now—into the alley, all the way to the back. No funny stuff."

Stark glanced around, saw no one on the sidewalk within a half-block. The four people directly across the street would never notice them duck into the alley. And even if they did notice, they wouldn't think anything of it. Not in New York.

"Come on, Mrs. Stanley, move." Urgency now in Tabor's voice. "You first, then your old man. I'll be right behind him."

The space was wide enough for three people to stand abreast, but they went single-file. Stark could see no way to catch Tabor off guard. Brick walls on both sides, no windows. Tabor delivered a nasty kick to the back of Stark's knee; the old man buckled, but kept his balance. "Watch where you're going, Grandpa." Tabor sneered. "You don't want to take a fall here, all this broken glass. You could get cut pretty bad."

They drew up to a high wooden fence that divided the alley, separating Seventy-second Street from Seventy-third. Tabor motioned Nell against the boards, then turned his attention to Stark. "Bet you thought I was long gone, didn't you, Gramps?"

"No," Stark said. "Scum stays in the bathtub until you wipe it out. I didn't imagine I'd see you quite this soon, but I knew it was just a matter of where and when."

Tabor laughed. "I *will* be gone shortly, but I wouldn't have thought of going off without saying good-bye to the two of you. I have better manners than that. In fact, I'll show you right now how good my manners are. Ladies before gentlemen."

Keeping Stark in view, Tabor pointed the gun at Nell, but before he could pull the trigger, Stark lunged, sending his straw hat flying. Tabor reacted with a knee to his attacker's abdomen, then flipped the pistol in his hand and brought the butt down hard onto the crown of Stark's head. The old man crumpled; darkness swallowed him.

"I ordered you to shoot that colored boy at Mobile Bay." The voice, strange, hollow, seemed to come from a great distance. "But you shot me instead and ran off with the nigger. You thought that was the end of me, but how very wrong you were. Crows and buzzards fed off my rotting flesh, then flew off in all directions, and wherever they came back down, they left part of me. I fertilized locoweed, skunk cabbage, dog fennel, jimson weed, nettles—every foul plant you can name—and everyone who breathed the air for miles around, I infected. The joke's on you, Stark. I've been here long before you ever saw light, and I'll still be around long after you've gone back to darkness. I've been itching to give you what you so richly deserve, and now I'm going to do it."

The blast of a gunshot roared through the alley. "That's it," Stark thought. "I'm dead. The end."

Chapter Fifteen

Manhattan
Tuesday, August 29
Early morning

He was falling, falling, falling, as if the descent had begun at the moment of his birth and would continue through all time. Suddenly he slowed, floated for a moment, then turned heels over head and plunged downward at a rate as exhilarating as it was alarming. The earth rose to meet him; he thought he'd be dashed to pieces, but instead he landed gently in the long, soft grass of a meadow. He knew the place—the open stretch behind Mr. and Mrs. Kohlmeier's little house in Gosport, just a short walk from his brother Etilmon's farm.

A woman stood beside him. Sarah. All Stark's life, he'd pooh-poohed the notion of an afterlife as just so much poppycock, but if this wasn't heaven, what was it? The woman leaned over him. "Dad, you're awake."

Stark blinked several times, then said, foolishly, "Nell?"

She clutched his hand. "Yes, who else?"

"Of course. I was…confused." He looked past her, tried to sit, then groaned, grabbed at the top of his head, and sank back into the pillow. Moving only his eyes, he saw he was in some sort of large room with beds set around the perimeter, most of them occupied, one with a white folding screen set around it. "Where am I?"

"Bellevue Hospital. They brought you here after—"

"Jordan shot me? Did they operate?" He felt at his abdomen. No pain, no wound, surgical or otherwise."

Nell looked puzzled. "'Jordan?' Nobody shot you, Dad. Tabor hit you over the head with the butt of his gun. He *was* going to shoot you then, but I shot him first."

"*You* shot *him*? With what? Where did you get a gun?"

"From the dresser drawer in your room at my apartment. Isaac's gun, remember? The one he gave you in St. Louis."

"But how on earth did you...oh. All those hours you used to spend in Isaac's back yard, shooting at tin cans."

Nell couldn't begin to keep the smile off her face. "Isaac always said I was a better shot than either of my brothers. And after I'd seen Tabor shoot Dubie Harris before he could say a word, I decided I was going to be ready this morning in case either Tabor or Waterson tried to pull anything like that on us. Good thing Tabor found us before we got back to the apartment and I'd put the gun back in the drawer. But, Dad—who's 'Jordan'?"

Stark weakly waved off the question. "I imagine I must be a little mixed up. What time is it, Nell? How long was I out?"

"Almost five hours—it's a little past one in the morning. But you're trying to change the subject, and I'm not going to let you. I want to know why you thought someone named Jordan had shot you."

"I...it was just a bit of temporary confusion, my dear. Considering I'd just been hit over the head—"

"Damn it!" Nell looked around, but no one was near enough to notice her slip in etiquette. She lowered her voice considerably. "Your face this morning, in the office, when you saw Tabor for the first time—you looked exactly like you did when I woke you up from your dream. Now, Dad, you are going to tell me about that dream...*and* about Jordan."

Stark sighed, deeply but quietly. "You heard what he said after he hit me?"

"Said?" She looked puzzled. "After you fell, he turned the gun around in his hand, and stood and stared at you for fifteen or twenty seconds, licking his lips like an animal. It was as if he'd forgotten I was even there. That gave me plenty of time to open the catch on my pocketbook, slide out the gun, and shoot him."

"Well, I'm glad your work compels you to carry that gigantic handbag. But Nell—you didn't hear *anything*? Really?"

She shook her head. "Not a word."

"I can't believe it," Stark murmured.

Nell sat, silent. Waited.

"You know the story." Spoken so softly, Nell had to lean forward to hear. "Mobile Bay, 1865. Isaac was fifteen years old. He tipped off our regiment that a bunch of rebs were waiting for us behind a knoll, so we were able to turn the tables on them. But then, my lieutenant said we couldn't march back into Mobile with Isaac in our company. Word would get around about what he'd done, and we'd have riots."

"Yes, of course I know the story," Nell said. "He ordered you to take Isaac into the woods and shoot him. But you fired a shot into the air, then both of you ran off, and traveled at night all the way back to New Orleans. You sent Isaac and Mother up the Mississippi to Gosport, then went back to your regiment and told them you'd been surprised in the woods by rebels who took you prisoner and killed Isaac, but you finally managed to escape and get back to the unit. My brothers and I have known that story all our lives, chapter and verse."

"Well, there's one chapter you don't know," said Stark. "That lieutenant's name was Preston Jordan. And Tabor was his spitting image."

Nell began to wonder whether she'd been wrong to pry at this particular door. "Dad, it's been over half a century. Your lieutenant would be at least your age now. Maybe Tabor looked a little like the way you remember the lieu—"

"Damn and blast, Nell. You asked, and I'm telling you. Tabor was the very image of Jordan, his build, his face, that cleft in his chin."

Hot and stuffy as it was on that hospital ward, Nell's hands went icy.

"And Jordan didn't send me out with Isaac. He took the two of us into the woods. Not every Union soldier was enthusiastic about emancipation, and it rankled Jordan that he owed his life and the lives of his soldiers to a fifteen-year-old Negro boy. Neither did he have much use for me, a little bugler, a coward who hid behind a horn. He thought it was a good joke to take me out, give me his pistol, and order me to shoot Isaac. I refused, of course. Finally, he told me I was a lily-liver, and if I didn't shoot Isaac, he would. When he reached for the gun in my hand, I shot *him*." And I've been dreaming that scene ever since, fifty-one years now. Jordan insults me, orders me to shoot, I refuse, he goes for the gun, I point it at him, and the blast wakes me up."

"And you never told anyone? Not even Mother."

Stark nodded." Only Isaac and I have ever known the truth."

"Why on earth didn't you tell Mother?"

"Oh, Nell, for heaven's sake. She was all of sixteen, and we were just married. What sort of man would she think I was, shooting down an officer in cold blood?"

"You underestimated her. She knew."

"Nonsense. How could she possibly have known? And how do you know she did?"

"Because she told me. She said after all you'd told her about your Lieutenant Jordan, she was not so silly that she'd believe for a minute he just gave you a gun and sent you out on your own to shoot Isaac, and didn't go along to see it for himself. She was furious."

"At me? For not telling her?"

"No, at the lieutenant. You know what she once said to me? 'Ordering your father to shoot Isaac down like a dog, after he'd saved all their lives? If *I'd* been there with a gun, I'd have shot that man myself, and been glad of the opportunity.'"

Nell disregarded her father's ox-like stare. "Those were her exact words. Now, tell me—what was it you heard Tabor say before I shot him?"

"With Jordan's gun."

"With...Jordan's gun."

Stark repeated Tabor's speech. Nell shook her head. "I didn't hear a word of that, and I was standing right there."

Behind his beard, Stark frowned. He drummed the bed-sheets with his fingertips.

Nell got to her feet just a bit more abruptly than she'd intended. "I'll let the nurse know you're awake," she said. "Then, if you really are feeling all right, I think I'll go home for the night."

"By all means, my dear. You're looking a bit drawn. Sleep late tomorrow, why don't you? I'll be fine."

She kissed his cheek, got to her feet, started to walk away, but then turned around, and came back to the bedside. "I forgot to tell you. While you were still unconscious, Detective Ciccone came by, and I told him what happened. He'll be back in the morning to get a statement from you."

Stark coughed. "Was he concerned about your having the gun?"

"Officially, yes. He told me he was glad I happened to have it along, but thought I ought to stop playing cops and robbers, and let the police do their work. I'll have to face a magistrate for carrying and firing a concealed gun without a license, but he doesn't think there will be any problem."

Stark watched Nell walk across the room toward the nurse's desk. His head hurt like the very devil, and he felt giddy, but that dazed, whirling lightness of mind seemed to mitigate his pain. He felt like a man whose lease on life had been rewritten on more favorable terms.

◇◇◇

Visiting hours didn't begin until three the next afternoon. Stark, sitting up in bed against a couple of pillows, stopped reading his newspaper, and watched the thin stream of visitors coming in through the doorway. No Nell. He was surprised, but thought probably she'd slept late, then had errands to run. He went back to his paper.

By half past the hour, though, he began to worry. This was not at all like her. It was nearly a quarter after four before she came hurrying into the ward and up to his bed. He reached for her hand. "Are you all right?"

She pulled the little wooden bedside chair around, sat, took a deep breath, blew it out. "Yes, I'm fine. I called in to the hospital, but couldn't get anyone to take a message to you. How are you feeling?"

"Much better, thank you. My head is fine now, so long as I don't touch the spot where Tabor crowned me. What on earth have you been up to all this time?"

She set her handbag onto the little bedside table. "Detective Ciccone came by to bring me up to date, and everything considered, he was quite nice. He told me my hearing is scheduled for Thursday afternoon, and not to worry, the shooting will be declared self-defense and I'll get off with a lecture about carrying unlicensed guns. But we shouldn't count on getting Isaac's pistol back." She paused, then went on. "He also told me they'd found Fannie…the receptionist. Just about the time Tabor found us, in fact. She was up against a piling under one of the Hudson River shipping piers. The bullets in her body were the same kind as they found in the gun Tabor was holding on us."

Stark's face darkened; his thick brows bristled.

"They also found two music manuscripts, tucked away between Tabor's desk blotter and the pad. Both had Dubie Harris' name on them."

Stark grunted. "Perhaps Waterson will want to publish them."

"Oh yes, Waterson. He swore he had nothing to do with the murder and kidnaping. Supposedly, Tabor told him Berlin had borrowed the apartment key, and that the price of Tabor's silence about the embezzling would be Berlin's position in the company, once Berlin was arrested and convicted. He also insisted he'd taken Scott's music in good faith, to consider it for publishing, and that he'd tried to tell Scott he was not Berlin. Ciccone didn't believe him, but decided it wasn't worth pursuing."

"I agree. At this point, it doesn't matter." Stark coughed into a handkerchief. "Mr. Ciccone was here before I'd had my breakfast. He asked a few questions, I gave him answers, and he was gone. He must have spent a lot longer talking to you."

"About half an hour." Nell fidgeted with the straps of her handbag. "I made him some coffee, then after he left, I went up to Harlem and talked to Dubie's aunt and uncle. I thought they ought to know how it all came out. Not that it made them feel much better."

"I'd forgotten—that was good of you, Nell." Stark reached to the bedside table for a glass of water, took a drink. "The doctor came by a little while ago, checked me over, and said I'm doing fine. He thinks it's just a concussion, no real damage, and he'll probably let me go tomorrow."

Nell's face brightened. "Dad, that's wonderful. My hearing's the day after tomorrow…and I'll admit, I feel much better, knowing you'll be there. Then I want to go back to St. Louis with you. It's been a while since I've been home, and to tell the truth, I wouldn't mind a little time to catch my breath."

On the verge of telling her he did not need a nursemaid, Stark caught himself. "Yes, of course. But what about Lottie? Who's going to help her with Joplin, if there's a problem?"

"It's all settled. While I'm away, Martin will stay in a room at Lottie's, and Joe will be available if things get out of hand. I'll be back in less than a week."

Stark smiled. "You've got it all figured out, don't you? I shouldn't be surprised."

‹›‹›‹›

As the *St. Louisan* pulled out of Pennsylvania Station, Stark stared relentlessly out the window. *He's closing the book,* Nell thought, and sat in silence until the train had cleared the Hudson River and started to roll across New Jersey. At that point, Stark turned to her and said, "Nell, not a word to the family. Nothing about my dream or my injury."

She managed a crooked smile. "Don't worry, Dad. As far as anyone else is concerned, it took a little while, but in the end you recovered the music from Berlin, as only you could have done."

Stark's eyes were sad. "And nothing about any murders."

"We're co-conspirators. But what are you going to tell Isaac about his gun?"

"Exactly what happened. He deserves to know that his concern saved our lives. I'll get him another pistol to replace his loss. Truth be told, my dear, I'm glad to see the last of that particular gun."

"Not to mention Irving Berlin."

Stark chuckled, then sighed. "I can't help but feel sorry for Berlin."

"I find that difficult to believe."

"No, really. He thinks the castle he's worked so hard to construct will stand forever, but everything on Tin Pan Alley is built on sand. One day, the public will tire of him and turn to someone else. And there he'll be, on his bogus throne, screaming at the top of his lungs that he's the King of Ragtime, but his court will be empty, no one to hear. He'd never admit it, but he's going to worry his whole life long about that dustup with Joplin over 'Alexander's Ragtime Band.' 'Uneasy lies the head that wears a crown,' my dear—particularly when that crown was ill-gotten."

Nell grinned. "'The saddest of all kings, crowned and again discrowned.' She fiddled with a button on the front of her dress. "I have a confession to make."

"I'm hardly a priest."

"Dad, listen to me. While you were in the hospital, the day I went up to Harlem—that wasn't just to see Mr. and Mrs. Barbour. I also gave Lottie some money."

Stark shrugged lightly. "I'm sure that was generous of you, but I don't see—"

"It wasn't generosity, Dad. Not mine, anyway. I sold Scott's music to Irving Berlin."

"You did *what?*"

"Dad please—don't make a scene, not here. Just listen. Right about noon, while Detective Ciccone was still at my place, Berlin called and asked me to bring Scott's music to his apartment. I couldn't imagine what he had in mind. When I got there, Mr. Hess played some of it, then Berlin said it was unpublishable, but he wanted to buy it anyway. He said he could use a lot of those short passages to help him get started on tunes, and offered five hundred dollars. I asked him how much that would work out to for every new 'Alexander's Ragtime Band,' which got him up to seven hundred. And by the time I was through telling him he owed Scott more than that, I had a thousand dollars in cash, and he had a promise that no one but you would ever hear about the deal. Then I went up to Harlem, gave Lottie the money, and told her not to ask questions."

Stark sat back in his seat, rested his head on the cushion, closed his eyes. Berlin! The man couldn't even wait till the bodies were cold, had to call about the music the instant he was out of bed for the day. What kind of person does that? And then the answer came to Stark, and calmed him. Somebody got murdered? Fine, fine. Let's get the blood cleaned up, so I can finish the tune I'm writing, and then start another one. As far as Irving Berlin was concerned, anyone or anything that got in the way of putting music on paper was a distraction and a nuisance. The man was a music-writing machine.

Like Scott Joplin.

Stark turned his head, looked at his daughter. "I'd have sent the scoundrel packing, never mind that would have meant depriving Lottie of a good deal of money. Of course I failed in New York. Had I made you a partner when I was in business here, and given you rein, we would have succeeded famously."

Nell chewed at her upper lip. "You know, Dad, I can't tell whether you're complimenting me or not."

The smile in Stark's eyes spread across his face. "That, my dear, is something you must decide for yourself."

Nell's eyes filled. She took a copy of *Etude* Magazine from her bag, opened it, then pretended to read as she ran an idea back and forth through her mind. Set up a branch of Stark Music in New York? The firm had begun in Sedalia, in 1899, as John Stark and Son. This time, do it right. John Stark and Daughter.

Stark turned back toward the window, watched New York City fly into his past. Good-bye, Irving Berlin. Good riddance, Henry Waterson. Bartlett Tabor, Lieutenant Jordan—till we meet again. I'll be watching for you.

The haunting melody of Joplin's "Solace" began to play in his mind. Damn, *he* could have published that one, and so many others. If only he'd listened to Nell…but there's an idea. What might she think about opening a branch of the firm in New York? She'd have all of Tin Pan Alley eating out of her hand.

Nell lowered her magazine. Stark looked around, met her gaze.

No, they thought. We'd kill each other.

Afterward, neither of them could say who laughed first.

The Last Word

Seattle, Washington
October 22, 2007
Morning

1911 was a red-letter year for Irving Berlin. As sales of "Alexander's Ragtime Band" soared, its composer was welcomed into New York's prestigious Friars Club, got to parade up Broadway in a top hat, performed in a one-week celebrity-vehicle show at the Victoria Theatre, bought a house in the Bronx for his mother, relocated to an apartment suite two blocks north of Central Park, and became a partner in a large music-publishing firm. He also decided that "the name Irving Berlin on a musical composition tends to increase the sale thereof," and so, filed a petition to make his new moniker his legal name, thereby protecting his "exceedingly valuable" piece of intellectual property from poachers.

But not everyone was enchanted with the young rising star and his song about the Negro bandleader. When Scott Joplin heard it, he reportedly burst into tears and cried, "That's my tune."

Some thirty-five years later, members of the Stark family told interviewers Joplin had left some music with Irving Berlin, who returned it, saying he couldn't use it. Lottie Joplin was both more and less specific: "After Scott had finished writing his opera, and while he was showing it around, hoping to get it published, someone stole the theme and made it into a popular song. The number was quite a hit, too, but that didn't do Scott any good. To get his opera copyrighted, he had to re-write it." Joplin's friend Sam Patterson stated that Irving Berlin had stolen two of Joplin's pieces, "Mayflower Rag" (a composition not known to exist) and the "Marching Onward" portion of "A Real Slow Drag" from *Treemonisha*. And W.A. Corey, a columnist for *American Musician*, wrote in his column for November 11, 1911: "Scott Joplin is anxious to meet Irving Berlin. Scott is hot about something."

Tin Pan Alley's grapevine buzzed with rumors about the authorship of "Alexander's Ragtime Band." Word was, the young composer had paid a Black man a paltry sum for his breakthrough hit, and perhaps for other tunes as well. Berlin denied it, demanding that his accusers name the wronged man and bring him forward. If they did, Berlin said, and if the man could write another hit like "Alexander," Berlin would pay him twenty thousand dollars. So far as I know, Berlin never had to pay up.

What can we make of this tangle of accusations and innuendoes? Ragtime historian Ed Berlin compared passages from "Alexander's Ragtime Band" and "Marching Onward," and concluded "the resemblance is not close enough to charge Irving Berlin with plagiarism. Yet...the recognizable melodic linkage... does explain Joplin's *perception* of a theft. And the resemblance between the two pieces may originally have been closer, for Lottie had said Joplin rewrote his theme after hearing the melody used by someone else...But neither can the evidence of a misappropriation be dismissed...It seems unlikely that the greatest of all Tin Pan Alley empires could have been built upon a succession of misappropriations...But could Berlin have pirated a theme once, early in his career? Did he take from Scott Joplin, the first King of Ragtime, a jewel for his own coronation?"

Case dismissed, lack of evidence. But the file likely will never be closed.

<>< ><>

There are people who don't read fiction because "that's just made-up stuff. It never happened. It's not true." But truth has a broader compass than reality. A truth may come into clearer focus when viewed through a fictional lens.

Several biographies of Irving Berlin include a specific account of a champagne party thrown by Henry Waterson in December, 1911, to celebrate Berlin's becoming a partner in the firm (and, incidentally, to get the company a bit of publicity). In a room full of reporters, Waterson, having drunk more of the evening's beverage of choice than perhaps he should have, announced that Broadway wise guys were saying "Alexander" was only the tip of an iceberg—that most or all of Berlin's hits were written by a "colored picka-ninny" man Berlin kept hidden away. Supposedly, the remark so offended the composer that he determined then and there to leave Waterson, Berlin, and Snyder when he could, and start up his own music publishing company.

When I mentioned that story to a prominent ragtime scholar, he advised me to take a careful look at my source material. When I did, I saw that one biographer had presented the incident without reference, and all the others had cited his account. A request to the first author for a primary source brought the reply, "It's just a story, probably a myth." And I could find no report of the incident in a newspaper or magazine of the time.

In my afterword to *The Ragtime Kid*, I explained that my goal had been to use history as a framework for a fictional attempt to illuminate and comprehend the motives of the people involved. Consequently, I'd done my best both to get background information straight and complete, and not contradict or alter established history.

I took the same approach in writing *The King of Ragtime*, and so, my initial reaction on learning that the champagne party probably never took place was to remove all references to the event from my novel. But in the end, I decided to leave the material in. Though I could not verify the anecdote, it was true to my story—consistent both with the envy and resentment engendered in Tin Pan Alley by Berlin's prodigious early success, and with written accounts of Henry Waterson's character.

‹›‹›‹›

On September 7, 1916, a reporter for the *New York American* wrote that Scott Joplin had written a musical play called *If,* and was working on his *Symphony Number One.* No manuscript of either work has ever come to light, but Joplin did leave a large stock of unpublished work that disappeared, largely due to careless and/or improper actions by people to whom he'd entrusted the material. By the summer of 1916, Joplin's health was in serious decline; historical references contain many comments as to his physical limitations and peculiar behavior. I don't think we'll ever know whether the symphony and the musical play existed beyond the disturbed mind of the composer.

‹›‹›‹›

The falling-out between Joplin and John Stark has been variably reported as having occurred in 1908 and 1909, and it resulted in a permanent rupture of the relationship between the men. For several years, Stark fulminated against his former associate both in speech and on paper; curiously, Joplin seems to have maintained at least a public silence on the matter. Angry as Stark was, would he have gotten on a train in 1916 and come to New York to help Joplin through serious trouble? I think he might have, particularly if the trouble involved allegations of improprieties by a prominent Tin Pan Alley publisher. One can read a good deal of pity along with the anger in Stark's declamations against Joplin, but the old publisher had nothing but contempt and disgust for Tin Pan Alley, its music, and its composers. When Joplin died, Stark wrote a moving obituary, which began, "Scott Joplin is dead. A homeless itinerant, he left his mark on American music." And later that year, Stark put aside his vow to never publish another piece by Joplin, and brought out *Reflection Rag,* a tune that had been lying for years in the company files.

‹›‹›‹›

The clinical presentation of syphilis is extremely variable, both in range and severity of signs and symptoms. Belle and Scott

Joplin's baby, who lived only a few months, was said to be weak and sickly from birth. One cause of this "failure to thrive" is congenital syphilis, transmitted to the fetus from an infected mother. Though some historians have assumed that Belle contracted the infection from Scott, it's entirely possible that the reverse was true—that another partner infected Belle, who passed the disease along to both her husband and their baby.

<>‹›<>

According to her contemporaries, Nell Stark was an excellent ragtime pianist. She was a major stockholder in Stark Music Company, vetted tunes submitted for publication, and championed Scott Joplin's work. For some three years, John Stark refused to publish *The Ragtime Dance*, but in 1902, his daughter finally persuaded him to the contrary. As far as I'm aware, no historical or biographical document mentions a romantic attachment between Nell and Joplin.

<>‹›<>

The Century Girl opened November 11, 1916. The audience and the reviewers were enthusiastic, but not for Irving Berlin's music. The Ziegfeld show was a visual extravaganza; the sets, costumes and lovely girls utterly overshadowed both the book and the music. None of Berlin's tunes became hits. The show ran for 200 performances.

<>‹›<>

In 1916, Jim and Nell Stanley really did live at 114 West Seventy-second Street, just four blocks from Irving Berlin's suite at the Chatsworth. I doubt they socialized.

<>‹›<>

Irving Berlin never wrote a ragtime opera.

<>‹›<>

What became of the people in this story?

Scott Joplin's mental and physical decline progressed. He suffered increasing depression, and even burned some of his manuscripts. From October, 1916 to January, 1917, he told reporters he intended to go to Chicago to visit his sister, but never did. Near the end of January, Lottie was compelled to take him to Bellevue Hospital, from where he was sent to a psychiatric ward in Manhattan State Hospital. He died there on April 1, 1917, the same day Victor released the first recorded jazz tune, "Livery Stable Blues," by the Original Dixieland Jazz Band. Some music historians cite this event as signifying the death of ragtime.

John Stark lived the rest of his life with his son Etilmon and Etilmon's family in the St. Louis suburb of Maplewood, and remained active in the family publishing business until shortly before his death on November 20, 1927. He never wavered in his belief that ragtime music was *the* classical American music form, and his last act on behalf of both ragtime and his company was to secure Lottie Joplin's re-assignment to Stark Music Company of rights to "Maple Leaf Rag," after she had renewed the copyright.

Little is known about Eleanor Stark's subsequent life. She continued to live in New York City with her singer-husband, James Stanley, and probably accompanied the quartets in which he sang. Nell survived her father by less than a year and a half; she died of an unspecified illness on April 7, 1929. She had no children.

After Berlin's departure from the firm in 1919, Henry Waterson and Ted Snyder continued in business as Waterson, Berlin, and Snyder. In the early 'twenties, they published some major hits, but in 1927, Snyder decided to go to Hollywood, and sold his interest in the firm to Waterson. Two years later, Waterson's gambling had bankrupted the company. In 1931, Mills Music bought the Waterson, Berlin, and Snyder catalog, and the firm was history. What happened to Waterson after that, I have no idea.

After a short stint as arranger for the J. Fred Help Company, Joseph Lamb decided not to pursue a career in music. A modest, quiet man, he felt ill at ease in the hustling, pushy world of music publishing, nor did he care for the long night hours. For Lamb, ragtime was a passion to be pursued solely for its spiritual rewards. He didn't socialize with musicians, and Scott Joplin was the only ragtime composer of his era he ever met. He continued to work at L. F. Dommerich's customs house until his retirement in 1957. After jazz supplanted ragtime, Lamb stopped writing down his tunes, but continued to play piano at home. His wife Henrietta (Etty) died in 1920, leaving him with five-year-old Joe Jr. He remarried two years later, and fathered four more children, one of whom, Patricia, a frequent attendee at ragtime festivals, carries her father's legacy forward through her delightful recollections of his life. After Rudi Blesh and Harriet Janis tracked Lamb down in the late 'forties, he received a great deal of attention from ragtime revivalists, and began to transfer to paper many of the rags he'd been carrying around in his head for thirty years or more. In 1959, he performed publicly for the first time, at a ragtime festival in Toronto. He died of a heart attack in 1960.

Martin Niederhoffer and Birdie Kuminsky married on December 14, 1916. I don't know whether Birdie remained at work after her marriage, but Martin's draft card, filled out on June 5, 1917, stated he was still at the old firm, still a book-keeper. The 1920 U. S. Census shows the couple living in the Bronx, with sons Arthur, 2-2/12, and Robert, 7/12. (Arthur Niederhoffer became a well-regarded educator and author; he was professor of sociology at John Jay College of Criminal Justice). In 1942, Martin and Birdie were living in Brooklyn, Birdie working at a department store on Fulton Street, and Martin being "self-employed." One reference suggests he was in real-estate. Both lived long lives, and died in Florida, Martin in 1979, at age 87, Birdie in 1992, at age 92.

Lottie Stokes' union with Scott Joplin probably was common-law; no one has been able to find a record of marriage for the couple. Lottie was devoted to Joplin, and while he lived, did all she could both to further his work and keep the wolf from their door, no small task on either account. After Joplin's death, Lottie continued to receive royalties on his work from Stark and other publishers. Her boarding house in Harlem became a major gathering place for Black musicians; the boarders and visitors included Jelly Roll Morton, Willie the Lion Smith, Wilbur Sweatman, and Eubie Blake. Willie the Lion told an interviewer that Lottie once took him down to the cellar to show him a vast accumulation of Joplin manuscripts, all of which subsequently disappeared. Lottie's later years must have brought her considerable satisfaction. Many ragtime revivalists sought her out for interviews, and Brun Campbell, the old Ragtime Kid, then living in California, recorded "Maple Leaf Rag" and other Joplin tunes, and sent Lottie the proceeds from sales. She died in 1953.

I can find no account of a real-life meeting between Ragtime Jimmy and Scott Joplin. Jimmy worked at the Alamo Club in Harlem until 1921, taking care to stay on the good side of characters like Footsie Vinny. The big-nosed piano player loved ragtime, but read the winds of change: in 1917, he formed his own New Orleans Jazz Band. Just a couple of years later, he got together with two young men named Lou Clayton and Eddie Jackson, and his fortunes soared. As good a musician as Jimmy was, he was even better at comedy, and humor gradually replaced melody as his performance mainstay. In the tough entertainment world, no one ever seemed to have an unkind word for Jimmy. He continued to make people smile and laugh almost to the day he died, January 29, 1980, at the age of 86. Good night, Mrs. Calabash, wherever you are.

Eubie Blake benefitted enormously from the ragtime revival, and his gain was ours. He lived to the age of 100 years and five days (though his birth date has been disputed), and his life story is a fabulous read. From the early 1900s, he was a prominent member of the east coast ragtime school, penning compositions such as *Charleston Rag* that became instant classics. In 1921, he joined with Noble Sissle to write *Shuffle Along*, a Black musical that took Broadway by storm, and the two friends enjoyed continued success through the decade. By the forties, Eubie had pretty much dropped from view, but doing nothing just wasn't his style. He enrolled at New York University, and in 1950, received a degree in music. In the 'sixties, he captured the attention of the new generation of ragtime players, and until his death in 1983, Eubie Blake probably was the best-known and most influential composer and performer of ragtime. He appeared at countless festivals and concerts all over the world, cut recordings, and received honor after honor.

Finally, what to say in a short summary of the life of Irving Berlin? Thanks to a stunning gift for musical composition, work habits that would have felled a horse, and a flair for self-promotion, the little man from Cherry Street produced an unparalleled body of popular songs and show tunes. He's been called America's Most Beloved Composer, but I think the real object of all that affection was not the songwriter himself, but his music. Berlin possessed a genius for reading the public mood, then writing tunes that crystallized and expressed societal senti-ments. He gave people what they wanted. But his biographies are saddening. As successful as he was, he seems never to have been satisfied. No amount of adulation was too much; any expression of admiration for another composer's work was too much. Came the 1960s, and a generation appeared that the old composer could not read. The Peace-and-Love Kids disdained his music as corny and old-fashioned, and at the Washington premiere of his last show, *Mr. President*, he suffered the indignity of seeing Jack Kennedy arrive late and leave early. By the late 'sixties, Berlin was eighty, and resented it mightily. For the final two decades of his life, insecurity and paranoia ruled his behavior. He became increasingly reclusive and hostile, often meeting requests of any sort with abusive outbursts. Regarding financial matters, he could be unreasonable, even miserly. Since the public would no longer value his music, he would offer them nothing in its place, and spent his last years as a geriatric Achilles, sulking in his tent. Unlike Achilles, he never relented. It would be difficult not to admire Berlin, equally difficult to love him.

⟨ ⟩ ⟨ ⟩ ⟨ ⟩

Bartlett Tabor, Robert Miras, Fannie Solomon, Dubie Harris, Detective Ciccone, Patrolman Flaherty, Jasper Billings, Isaac

Stark, and Clarence and Ida Barbour were products of my imagination. They bear no resemblance to any person in my real world.

⟨⟩⟨⟩⟨⟩

So, who really was The King of Ragtime?

We know what Scott Joplin thought; we know what Irving Berlin thought. Both men are on the record.

What do I think?

Musicologists and historians are sharply divided as to whether ragtime songs should in fact be acknowledged as ragtime. Most definitions of the form mention syncopation as an important feature, and while almost all vocal ragtime composed and performed between 1890 and 1910 featured syncopation, the music of Irving Berlin contained very little. Thus, some authorities hold that Berlin never wrote ragtime at all. "Alexander's Ragtime Band" has often been called a song about ragtime, not a song in ragtime. Eubie Blake said, "Funny thing about ['Alexander's Ragtime Band'], there's no ragtime *in* it. No syncopation at all! Still it's a great tune, and it sure was what the public wanted."

I think Eubie was on the mark. Who ever was better than Irving Berlin at giving the public what it wanted? As long as people wanted ragtime, Berlin would give them ragtime—or at least what he called ragtime. Perhaps "Tin Pan Alley Ragtime" had its origin in a marketing ploy. Insist long enough and hard enough that a magpie is a nightingale, and you'll likely convince a lot of people. You might even convince yourself. And if I shake my head and say, "Gee, that just doesn't sound like a nightingale," you'll reply, "It's a new breed of nightingale, better than the original. Get with it. 'Everybody's Doing It Now.'"

In a contest to select the King of Tin Pan Alley or Broadway, Irving Berlin probably would get my vote. But the great tunesmith's outrageous assertion that "…such songs of mine as 'Alexander's Ragtime Band,' 'That Mysterious Rag,' 'Ragtime Violin,' 'I Want To Be In Dixie,' and 'Take A Little Tip From Father' virtually started the ragtime mania in America" rings like a cracked bell. By itself, that should disqualify him from any competition for the ragtime throne.

What of Scott Joplin's claim? After all, it was "Maple Leaf Rag" that truly 'started the ragtime mania in America,' and at the same time set the standard for a new form of musical art. Joplin was a major, if not *the* major, influence for a whole generation of musicians, one of whom was Joseph Lamb. He was generous in his teaching and support of young composers. He constantly pushed musical frontiers, composing ragtime of increasing complexity, and sought to extend his idiom into operatic and symphonic music.

But Joplin is not a unanimous choice as the greatest ragtime composer. Pianist Ron Weatherburn (among others) selected Joe Lamb, stating that Joplin's rags are "as good as anything ever written, but not in the same class as Lamb's greatest." Weatherburn went on to explain that Joplin's rags are more "simple," and that Lamb's work is more impressive as classical piano music. Trebor Tichenor did not rank the two composers as to degree of greatness, but remarked that Lamb's music is "…unlike Joplin's incredibly beautiful melodies, of intensely rustic folkishness that only he could create…By [Lamb's] later work he advanced and extended the entire idiom of classic ragtime as far as it would go."

John Stark published the first ragtime blockbuster, then spent his last twenty-eight years publishing and promoting classic ragtime and the composers who wrote it. Had Stark stayed in his music store in Sedalia in 1899, it's possible "Maple Leaf Rag" might have never been published, Scott Joplin might have remained in obscurity all his life, and ragtime music might have been no more than a passing fad. By continuing to force ragtime into the public view until the time of his death, Stark kept the form at least marginally visible until it caught the attention of the revivalists in the 1940s. If titles really are to be conferred, Stark would seem a strong candidate for Defender of the Crown, or perhaps High Priest.

Tom Turpin? Turpin's "Harlem Rag," from 1898, was the first published ragtime tune by a Negro. His Rosebud Café was for many years the center of Black music in St. Louis, and Turpin provided important support to ragtime composers and musicians, Scott Joplin included.

Ben Harney? In 1897, the Kentuckian composer and entertainer claimed to be the originator of ragtime.

Mike Bernard, who won ragtime-playing contests in New York (most of which included only White contestants), and was designated "Rag Time King of the Whole World?"

The incomparable Eubie Blake?

No.

Ragtime is a joyously anarchic territory, only partially explored, and with ever-shifting borders. It's populated by a divided but enthusiastic company of women and men who compose the music, play it, listen to it, study it, research it, write about it, love it. Those among them who've grabbed for a glittering crown have found themselves in the end to be holding only a handful of ashes. *Ars longa, vita brevis.*

In the Land of Ragtime there is no king.

That's not a statement of fact. It's just what I think.

What do *you* think?

Ragtime Resources

RADIO SHOW:

"The Rag Time Machine," David Reffkin, Host. KUSF-FM, San Francisco, Monday, 9-10 pm. Streaming at www.live365.com/stations/kusf

WEBSITES:

Edward A. Berlin's Website of Ragtime and Scholarship. www.edwardaberlin.com/index.htm

Jack Rummel's Ragtime Music Reviews. www.ragtimers.org/reviews/

"Perfessor" Bill Edwards' Ragtime MIDI, Sheet Music, Nostalgia and Ragtime Resource. www.perfessorbill.com/

The Mississippi Rag. www.mississippirag.com/

Cylinder Preservation and Digitization Project. www.cylinders.library.ucsb.edu/

Parlor Songs MIDI Collection. www.parlorsongs.com/

The Ragtime Ephemeralist. http://home.earthlink.net/~ephemeralist/index.html

West Coast Ragtime Society. www.westcoastragtime.com/

Scott Joplin International Ragtime Foundation. www.scottjoplin.org/

Selected Bibliography

RAGTIME HISTORY

Berlin, Edward A. *King of Ragtime*. Oxford University Press, New York, 1994.

Berlin, Edward A. *Ragtime, A Musical and Cultural History*. University of California Press, Berkeley, 1980.

Berlin, Edward A. *Reflections and Research on Ragtime*. ISAM Monographs: Number 24, Institute for Studies in American Music, Brooklyn NY, 1987.

Berlin, Edward A. "A Biography of Scott Joplin." Electronic publication, written for the exclusive use of the Scott Joplin International Foundation, 1998.

Berlin, Edward A. "On Ragtime: A Different Perspective on Tin Pan Alley." *CBMR Digest*, Spring 1991, pp. 5-6.

Berlin, Edward A. "On Ragtime: Ragtime and the Church." *CBMR Digest*, Fall 1991, pp. 6-7.

Berlin, Edward A. "On Ragtime: Scott Joplin, the Educator." *CBMR Digest*, Spring 1990, pp. 3-4.

Berlin, Edward A. "Scott Joplin's Treemonisha Years." *American Music*, Fall 1991, pp. 260-276.

Blesh, Rudi and Janis, Harriet. *They All Played Ragtime*. Grove Press, New York, 1959 (originally published by Knopf, 1950).

Cassidy, Russell E. "Joseph F. Lamb: A Biography." *Newsletter of the Ragtime Society of Canada*, Summer 1966, pp. 29-42.

Conn, Patricia Lamb. "Patricia Lamb Conn in an interview with David Sager." Library of Congress, 2006. http://lcweb2.loc.gov/diglib/ihas/loc.natlib.ihas.200035773/full.html

Conn, Patricia Lamb. Personal correspondence.

Curtis, Susan. *Dancing to a Black Man's Tune.* University of Missouri Press, Columbia MO, 1994.

Gammond, Peter. *Scott Joplin and the Ragtime Era.* St. Martin's Press, New York, 1976.

Haskins, James. *Scott Joplin.* Doubleday, New York, 1978.

Hasse, John Edward, ed. *Ragtime, Its History, Composers, and Music.* Schirmer Books, New York, 1985.

Jasen, David A. and Jones, Gene. *That American Rag.* Schirmer Books, New York, 2000.

Jasen, David A. and Tichenor, Trebor Jay. *Rags and Ragtime.* Dover Publications Inc, New York, 1978.

Lamb, Joseph, with Mike Montgomery. "Joseph Lamb: A Study in Classic Ragtime." *Smithsonian Folkways Archival.* Folkways Records FG 3562, 1960/2007.

Montgomery, Mike. "Joseph F. Lamb—A Ragtime Paradox. *The Second Line*, March-April 1961, pp. 17-18.

Rose, Al. *Eubie Blake.* Schirmer Books, New York, 1978.

Schafer, William J. and Riedel, Johannes. *The Art of Ragtime.* Louisiana State University Press, Baton Rouge, 1973.

Scotti, Joseph. "Joe Lamb: A Study of Ragtime's Paradox." PhD diss, University of Cincinnati, 1977.

Waldo, Terry. *This is Ragtime.* Da Capo Press, New York, 1991.

Wolf, Rennold. "The Boy Who Revived Ragtime. *The Green Book Magazine*, August 1913, pp. 201-209.

IRVING BERLIN

Bergreen, Laurence. *As Thousands Cheer: The Life of Irving Berlin.* Viking Penguin, New York, 1990.

Friedland, Michael. *Irving Berlin.* Stein and Day, New York, 1974.

Furia, Philip. *Irving Berlin: A Life in Song.* Schirmer Books, New York, 1998.

Hamm, Charles. *Irving Berlin: Songs from the Melting Pot: The Formative Years, 1907-1914.* Oxford University Press, New York, 1997

Whitcomb, Ian. *Irving Berlin and Ragtime America.* Century Hutchinson Ltd., London, 1987.

TIN PAN ALLEY

Goldberg, Isaac. *Tin Pan Alley: A Chronicle of the American Popular Music Racket.* The John Day Company, New York, 1930.

Jasen, David A. *Tin Pan Alley: An Encyclopedia of the Golden Age of American Song.* Routledge, New York, 2003.

Witmark, Isidore and Goldberg, Isaac. *From Ragtime to Swingtime.* Lee Furman, Inc., 1939.

AMERICAN BLACK MUSIC

Brooks, Tim. *Lost Sounds: Blacks and the Birth of the Recording Industry 1890-1919.* University of Illinois Press, Urbana and Chicago IL, 2004.

Riis, Thomas L. *Just Before Jazz. Black Musical Theater in New York, 1890-1915.* Smithsonian Institution Press, Washington and London, 1989.

Shaw, Arnold. *Black Popular Music in America.* Schirmer Books, New York, 1986.

Southern, Eileen. *The Music of Black Americans.* Norton and Company, New York, 1983.

NEW YORK CITY, 1916

Adams, Michael Henry. *Harlem, Lost and Found.* Monacelli Press, New York, 2002.

Burns, Ric and Sanders, James. *An Illustrated History of New York.* Alfred A. Knopf, New York, 1999.

Diamonstein, Barbaralee. *The Landmarks of New York II.* Harry N. Abrams, New York, 1993.

Jackson, Kenneth L. *The Encyclopedia of New York City.* Yale University Press, New Haven and London, 1995.

Oppel, Frank, comp. *Tales of Gaslight New York.* Castle Books, Edison NJ, 2000.

Phillips, David Graham. "The Delusion of the Race Track." *The Cosmopolitan,* January 1905, pp.289-300.

Simmons, Peter. *Gotham Comes of Age.* Pomegranate Communications, San Francisco, 1999.

MISCELLANEOUS

Anonymous. "Lester A. Walton Biography." New York Public Library Digital Collection, undated.

Beeson, Paul B. and McDermott, Walsh. *Textbook of Medicine.* W. B. Saunders, Philadelphia, 1975.

Dooner, Kate E. *Telephones, Antique to Modern.* Schiffer Publishing Ltd., Atglen PA, 2005.

Fowler, Gene. *Schnozzola.* Viking Press, New York, 1951.

Walsh, Jim. "History of the Peerless Quartet." Hobbies Magazine, December 1969, pp. 127-130.

Yater, Wallace Mason. *The Fundamentals of Internal Medicine.* Appleton-Century, New York, 1941.

To receive a free catalog of Poisoned Pen Press titles, please contact us in one of the following ways:

Phone: 1-800-421-3976
Facsimile: 1-480-949-1707
Email: info@poisonedpenpress.com
Website: www.poisonedpenpress.com

Poisoned Pen Press
6962 E. First Ave. Ste. 103
Scottsdale, AZ 85251

LaVergne, TN USA
16 March 2010

176196LV00003B/1/P